SAVING
ERIDU

RAVEK HUNTER

info@WorldsOfAtlantis.com

Thank you for the support of the author's rights.

First Edition, March 2018

Copyright © 2018 Ravek Hunter Literary LLC

All rights reserved.

ISBN:

      978-1-948782-03-6 (paperback)

      978-1-948782-00-5 (ebook)

www.WorldsOfAtlantis.com

For Mrs. Wife,
who gave me two incredible boys
that I hope will be proud to read their father's work one day.

Fantasy Novels by Ravek Hunter

Red Wizard of Atlantis
The Fallen
Saving Eridu
The Imaziyen Druid
Shadows of Lyonesse
Beasts of Courth
Ys (Coming 2022)

If you enjoy reading books by this author, please remember to leave a review at your favorite bookseller!

To learn more about the backstory, mythology, and character development in these stories or to view world maps visit us at:

https://www.WorldsOfAtlantis.com!

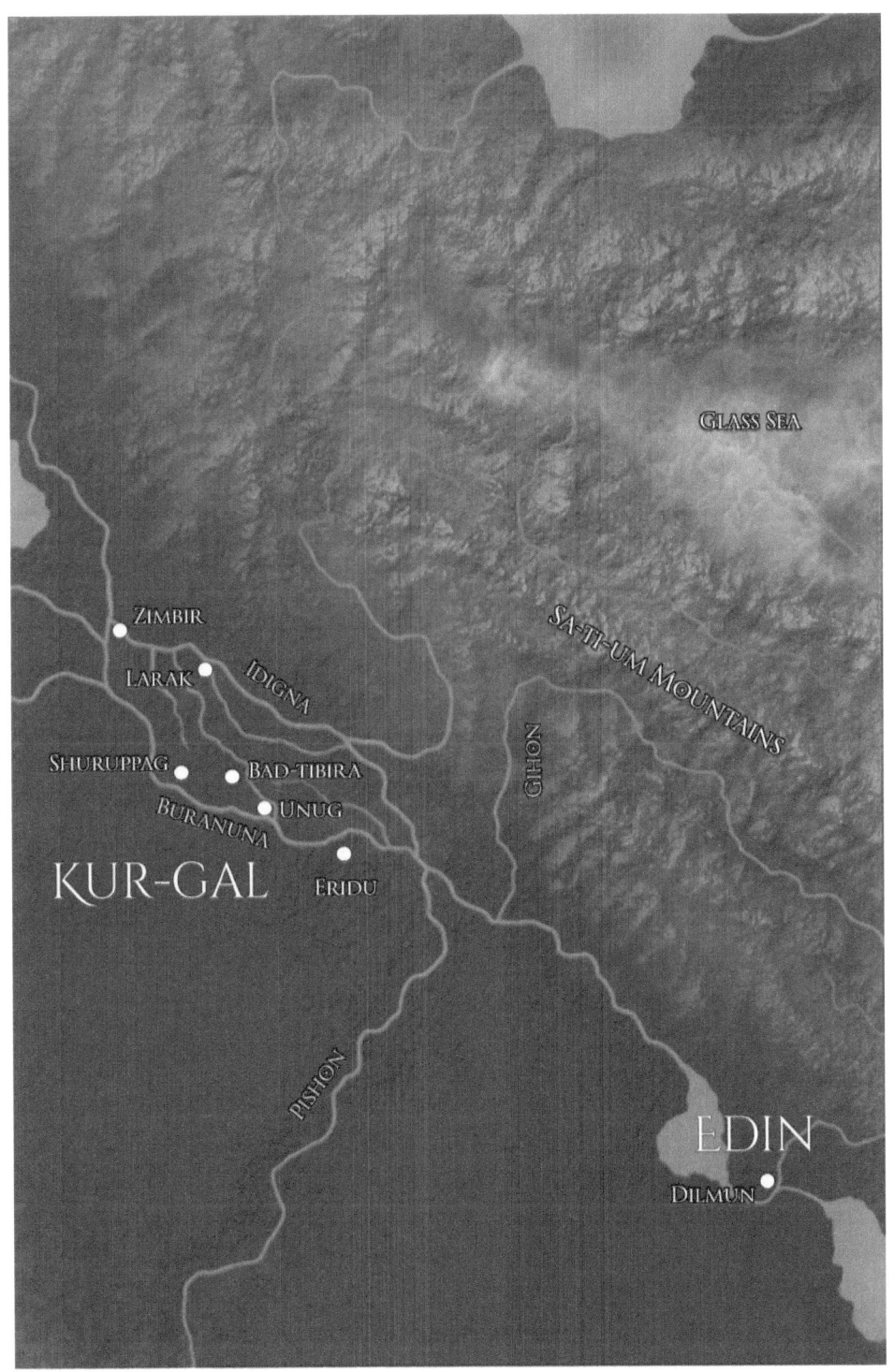

<u>Children of Atlas</u>

It was from the stars they came, out of the vast darkness of the Primeval Cosmos, plunging from the sky in a great wingless beast consumed by smoke and fire. It fell with a thunderous crash upon the earth plowing a long black rift across the open plain before it came to rest in a final shudder of sparks and lightning. The smoking shell of the massive creature lay shattered, yet from its broken maw came hundreds of odd-looking figures that crawled through the acrid haze and stumbled disoriented onto the lush green grass of a new world.

The Sylvan watched the arrival of the newcomers from the quiet repose of the forest. They scrutinized these strange bi-pedal aliens with blue-tinted skin and elongated heads and large almond-shaped eyes that had come uninvited to their tranquil isle, until now isolate and protected from intrusion by the vast expanse of the Primal Sea. They observed how the slender forms worked as a collective to remove the shiny scales of their battered host piece by piece to make shelters, how they buried their dead, how they mourned their passing.

When that was done, they brought red glowing crystals that shown bright even in daylight from the metallic frame of the silver beast's remains. The crystals they handled with great care and reverence, depositing them in caverns deep in the earth near an inlet on the coast. It was there too, that they began to build with stones.

These were a people with no hope of return or rescue, determined to survive and resolute in their struggle to make a place for themselves. A permanent place that would bring irrevocable change the Isle. To the land, to nature, to a way of life that had existed since time began.

Still the Sylvan watched.

The prophesies spoke of events such as these that would herald the beginning of the Fourth Age, the Age of the Golden Aspen, the Age when the winds from the north would bring an icy chill even in the summertime. And end the elves isolation from the rest of the world forever.

In time the Sylvan learned that the unusual blue-tinted people called themselves the followers of Atlas, the one who had risen among them and offered up hope for a new future. They would name the spine of the island in his honor and build a shining city on the sea that would become known as Atlantis.

And they thrived.

Recorded in the Fourth Age of the Golden Aspen
by Watcher CrellianRafkarSil of Avalon

Kur-gal

Enki, the king of the Abzu,
Overpowering in his majesty,
Speaks up with authority:
"My father, the king of the universe,
Brought me into existence in the universe,
My ancestor, the king of all the lands,
Gathered together all the Me's, placed the Me's in my hand.
From the Ekur, the house of Enlil,
I brought craftsmanship to my Abzu of Eridu.
I am the fecund seed, engendered by the great wild ox,
I am the firstborn son of An,
I am the 'great storm' who goes forth out of the 'great below,'
I am the Lord of the Land,
I am the Gugal of the chieftains, I am the father of all the lands,
I am the 'big brother' of the gods, I am he who brings full prosperity,
I am the record keeper of heaven and earth,
I am the car and the mind of all the lands,
I am he who directs justice with the king An on An's dais,
I am he who decrees the fates with Enlil in the 'mountain of wisdom,'
He placed in my hand the decreeing of the fates of the 'place where the sun
rises,'
I am he to whom Nintu pays due homage,
I am he who has been called a good name by Ninhursag,
I am the leader of the Anunnaki,
I am he who has been born as the first son of the holy An."
After the Lord had uttered (his) exaltedness,
After the great Prince had himself pronounced his praise,
The Anunnaki came before him in prayer and supplication:
"Lord who directs craftsmanship,
Who makes decisions, the glorified; Enki praise!"

Translation by Samuel Noah Kramer,
The Sumerians: Their History, Culture, and Character
(Chicago: University of Chicago Press, 1963).

Table of Contents

Chapter 1

The Inn

꘎꘎꘎ ꘎꘎꘎

Ten thousand years before the ancient civilization of Sumer rose to prominence in Mesopotamia, there were the Sag-gig-ga, or "Black-headed People" and they called their land Kur-gal. I traveled among their people for a time, learned their ways, and found myself impressed by their absolute devotion to gods who did not care a wit about them.

Wodanaz, the Wanderer

Namzu couldn't decide which was worse—the sight of death or the smell of it. Both assaulted his senses equally with disgust as he stared at the disfigured bodies lying on the floor from the doorway of the inn's second-story room. He gripped the magical light globe that he carried more tightly, angling the illumination over the gruesome scene before him, scrutinizing every stark detail. There was blood spatter everywhere—the floors, the walls, even the ceiling. But the worst of it radiated from the remains in sticky crimson pools near where he stood.

Taking a tentative step forward, he held his long wraparound skirt above his thin ankles, careful not step in any of the mess. The sight of butchery on this scale in his city sickened him, especially since it had become so common of late. Namzu was the High Priest of the Judicial Order in the city-state of Eridu, and he was not at all pleased to be at this inn again.

"What have you determined so far?" he asked Sabum, the judicial priest first on the scene to investigate the murders.

"They were a man and a woman from the territory of Larak, visiting Eridu for the Creation of Man ritual," Sabum replied shortly in his grave, resonating voice while carefully navigating his way through the room.

Larak, Namzu mused to himself, a city-state far to the north of Eridu. The priest-ruler of Eridu, whom everyone addressed as the En, could draw the faithful from the farthest reaches of the vast country they called Kur-gal, and the people would come in droves. It was considered a spiritual pilgrimage to attend the Creation of Man ritual, dedicated to the creation god,

Enki, at least once in one's lifetime.

"Looks like they were hacked to death in the night by a hatchet or knife." Sabum was kneeling close over one of the bodies, inspecting every detail of the deep cut marks on the victim's flesh. "Perhaps both."

Sabum, in contrast to Namzu, was a thickly muscled man, a little shorter, and moved with the grace of a cat. His head was clean-shaven, with no beard and a perpetually sullen expression that never seemed to change even when he was happy. Namzu had not known Sabum to be often happy.

Namzu's gaze took in the rest of the room. Aside from the carnage of the bodies and the blood-saturated woven mats they lay upon, there was only a mud-brick table built into the wall with a bowl of water for washing and the couple's ostrich-skin travel bags. Nothing was unpacked. It appeared as if they had been murdered on their first night in the city. *What luck,* he thought sarcastically.

"Eridu is swelling with citizens from all across Kur-gal for the ritual, and every inn will be bursting at the seams." Namzu absently plotted a course through the room, frequently pausing to survey the slaughter from a different angle, his sandals sticking on unavoidable crimson droplets. "The opportunity to claim more victims over the next twelve days might be limitless for the killer. If we only knew what was driving this rage . . ." His thought trailed off while he stroked his long, well-kept beard.

"We don't even know if he, or they, is from the city," Sabum cautioned. "For all we know, the murderer could be here for the ritual just like the multitudes of others. Maybe when the ceremonies are over, the problem will go away."

Namzu shrugged. "That may be true, but how many more will die in the meantime? Besides, the killer could just as well be from Eridu and targeting citizens from out of town." Namzu took a linen cloth from inside the leather satchel that hung across his chest and held it over his nose and mouth. "Do they still have valuables on them like the others?"

Sabum delicately moved aside the layers of blood-soaked flax of one of the victims and located a money purse. It was tied closed, and he shifted it just enough to cause the metal bits inside to clink together dully. "It appears so."

"These are not murders that have been motivated by robbery, and like this couple, none of the other victims have had more than average means." Namzu glanced at the opposite wall. "Besides, those marks left behind hint at something far more portentous." He wished the symbols could speak. Tell him what happened. Tell him who was responsible for these horrible deaths.

Namzu stared hard over Sabum at the wall behind him where the cryptic symbols were scrawled in the victims' own blood. Thin trails of crimson ran almost to the floor from the thick lines that formed the diagrams. The blood was fresh when applied but was now nearly dry.

"Whoever did this was experienced at killing. The most puzzling part are these writings on the wall. They may explain why the victims were struck with such fury so many times after the initial killing blows, if I could just decipher them . . ." Namzu hated puzzles, especially ones that he couldn't begin to unravel. There was nothing in his rather extensive experience to draw upon that could help him understand what he was seeing.

Sabum ran a hand over his scalp. "Maybe they were put there just to distract from the true purpose of the murders."

"Or maybe they reflect the true *nature* of the murders." Namzu considered the symbols with as much concern as the bodies below them.

"The *true* nature?" Sabum sounded uncertain.

"Madness."

Sabum just grunted and continued to inspect the scene.

"You are right about one thing, my friend," Namzu spoke absently. "They are certainly a distraction."

Namzu had a sense of unease about the symbols, and the one who put them there, that he couldn't explain. He could shut down the inn, but would that stop the killer or killers if they were intent on continuing their grim spectacle? At least for now, the crimes appeared to be isolated to this inn, and few people in the city knew of their occurrence except through rumors. If he closed the inn and the murders started taking place in the back alleys and streets of Eridu, with disfigured corpses and strange scrawling in blood for the full display of the public—it could cause a panic. That was the last thing he needed with the Creation of Man ritual commencing over the next twelve days.

"What is the En planning this year to honor Enki?" Sabum's casual question seemed out of place as he studied the mutilated bodies. Namzu marveled at the man's excellent ability to compartmentalize his thoughts and emotions. In many ways, he was the perfect inspector.

"Something entertaining, I'm sure. The story is the same every year, yet En Ipqu-aya manages to come up with a new way to tell it that makes the telling sensational. How else could he draw the thousands he does for so many years, now?"

Sabum nodded silently and continued his work, moving his own light globe around the room for a better look at all the grisly details. The pools and spatter of blood on the floors and walls caused the small, windowless

11

chamber to glitter crimson from the sticky reflections cast by the light globes they carried. The bodies and the mats beneath them were so sodden with blood that it was nearly impossible to recognize the features of the victims. Then there were the unusual symbols drawn on the walls, which amplified the unnatural quality of the putrid display. Namzu suppressed a shudder.

Contemplating the horrific scene, Namzu considered that perhaps that was precisely what it was—a display showcasing the terrifying and lurid nature of the violence that had occurred here as with the others. He studied the scene more carefully from just inside the entrance of the room. "Based on the positions of the bodies and lack of any blood trails, it appears they died quickly and in their sleep."

"Maybe," Sabum replied tentatively. "There is a strange blood pattern near the base of the wall with the symbols that I can't explain yet, just like the others."

Without the benefit of ventilation, the stench was nearly overwhelming. Namzu had to stop himself from gagging in front of Sabum more than once, even with the linen he pressed tightly against his nose. It was an unforgettable malodor that would linger in his nostrils long after he was away from it. He wondered how Sabum could endure the fetor while standing in the middle of it all. Nothing seemed to bother Sabum.

Namzu considered the murderer's motive to distract his mind from the foul odor. The heightened level of frenzied anger invested in these murders implied a crime of passion. But why would a presumably random couple visiting from another city incite this degree of fury? Unless it wasn't random. Or it was deliberately random. He would also have to weigh the possibility that the rage had not been uncontrolled after all. If it had been the ritual of a new death cult in Eridu, then the killings and the symbols might be connected through some evil rite or sacrifice. He would keep that to himself for the time being.

This was far from the usual homicide—if there was such a thing in Eridu. Namzu had only seen violence of this magnitude many years ago in the city-state of Shurrupak, where he had started his career as an initiate priest of the Judicial Order. Even still, there was a significant difference, as the murders in Shurrupak were the result of insurrection and the lawless chaos that inevitably came with it, as opposed to what he was faced with presently—a presumed madman with a thirst for slaughter? Now he was the High Priest of the Judicial Order in the greatest city in Kur-gal, where there never had been a murder of this brutality . . . until recently.

Namzu was proud of his success in Eridu over the past few decades. No other city-state was so highly regarded as the safest in Kur-gal, with harsh laws against crime and a strong garrison of city guards that kept constant vigilance to ensure their citizens slept soundly at night. He conceded the rare occasion that a body would turn up in the Buranuna River, dragged into the water by a crocodile, or a lone hunter mauled by a pack of wolves near the Sa-ti-um Mountains to the east. In each of those cases, the kill was far cleaner than what had occurred here and was caused by animals following their natural instincts. Namzu was sure an animal was to blame here as well, but one of a far different sort.

"These two make nine so far in this inn alone, you know." Sabum was holding one of the victim's bloodstained hands under the light to study it closer. "I don't think I would recommend staying here."

This one has a dry sense of humor. Namzu almost laughed out loud. He was right, though. There had been seven other murders of the same sort, and each time the victims were guests at this inn. And the innkeeper was hardly helpful. He was an odd fellow and a bit confused about the details— harmless enough, so far as Namzu knew, but that did not qualify him as innocent. If Namzu learned anything in the turbulent city of Shurrupak, it was that no one was ever as innocent as they claimed.

Then he had a clever thought and turned to Sabum, nearly slipping in a patch of partially dried blood. "Send a man for an Anunnaki Wise-One at the Tower of Tongues," Namzu ordered his second. "If anyone can identify the writing, they can."

Sabum nodded and left the room to pass along the order to one of several guards standing farther down the hall, keeping unwanted curiosity seekers away, before returning to assist Namzu a few moments later. Together, they spent the next hour inspecting the chamber, taking notes of every detail while Namzu drew copies of the symbols on a clay tablet. It was puzzling, thought Namzu, how consistent each scene and circumstance was for seemingly random murders. And senseless. There were never any witnesses, nothing valuable was ever taken, the victims were slaughtered with blades, and there were always strange symbols left behind on the walls. The symbols themselves varied from one victim to the next, and sometimes they repeated, but without understanding what they meant, Namzu was at a loss as to how they fit. That left him with only the innkeeper and his inn as the last common elements of the murders.

Namzu spoke partially to himself as much as to Sabum from the doorway. "I think we should talk more with this innkeeper. It's strange that all the murders have taken place under his roof, yet he never knows anything about them. We will have to put him to more rigorous questioning to clarify his memory. All he's told us is that there have been no unusual visitors or guests staying at the same time as all the murders and there are no new staff in the kitchen." He pulled at his long braided beard distractedly. "Every time one of our inspectors has spoken with him, they report the innkeeper's unusual lack of concern for the victims or the fact that they have died horribly in his establishment. Something is not right with him."

Acting on a gut feeling, Namzu called to the pair of guards standing watch outside the room to detain the innkeeper until he and Sabum had a chance to question him further. The guards left with purpose down the stairs and toward the kitchen.

Minutes passed while he continued to examine the room for anything they had missed. Then there was a violent commotion downstairs, followed by the screams of men in pain that echoed through the halls of the once-quiet inn. Namzu rushed down the stairs toward the kitchen with Sabum only a step behind, following the noise of breaking pottery and the skid of tables.

The two guards sent to detain the innkeeper were on the floor, blood pooling around their twitching bodies just inside the kitchen. Their screams had drawn the attention of other guards stationed nearby in the common room, and now four of them were cautiously closing in on the cornered innkeeper.

The innkeeper, thick-limbed and tall for a native of Kur-gal, was in a blind rage. He screamed words at the guards in a tongue that didn't sound human and expertly spun his blades, lashing out at the approaching guards. By the time Namzu and Sabum were close enough to do anything, another guard was on the floor, twitching from a swift, slicing blow to his throat.

Namzu had seen enough. He waved his arms in a deliberate pattern and wove a spell of paralysis that rendered the blades silent. Then the remaining guards rushed in and beat the man until he was no longer conscious. They had watched three of their comrades die in the space of just a few seconds and were eager to exact retribution on the deadly butcher. Namzu didn't care if the man lived or died, only that the savagery was over and the culprit was incapable of causing violence again, especially if this was the man who had been responsible for all the murders at the inn.

"Is he alive?" Namzu asked one of the guards kneeling over the bloodied body of the innkeeper.

"I cannot feel his breath, First Usgadi," the guard replied, using Namzu's formal title. Usgadi was the name of the sect of priests responsible for investigating crimes and passing judgment in the determination of innocence or guilt, and Namzu was their leader, or first among them. The guard proceeded to check the innkeeper's clothing for anything unusual. "I believe he is dead or close enough to it."

Sabum stood beside the still-kneeling guard and brought his club to bear against the innkeeper's skull, sending the guard reeling backward with a cry of surprise.

For his part, the innkeeper did not stir, but a new trickle of blood ran down the side of his head. Namzu shrugged it off as just another injury added to the many welts and bruises inflicted already. "He seems dead enough to me," Sabum remarked, wiping his club on the innkeeper's clothing.

"Take him to the Hall of Kurnugia," Namzu ordered the guard, and then he turned to Sabum. "Inform the Sanga of what has happened and suggest mania or insanity as the cause."

The Sanga was second only to the En in Eridu, and he would most certainly want to visit the body of the innkeeper in the Hall of Kurnugia, where bodies were purified after death, to ensure no more trouble would come from it. In Namzu's experience, it was possible the innkeeper might be a continued threat if he had been driven to madness by disease or sickness that was infectious. The Sanga would work that out.

A short time later, Namzu's attention was drawn beyond the broken door leading to the kitchen and watched as a tall, thin man entered the inn with the guard that Sabum had sent to the Tower of Tongues. Those who were seated in the dining room—mostly guards and other Usgadi—nearly leaped to their feet and bowed to him in respect. He was an Anunnaki, and more than that, he was a revered Wise-One.

Wearing long, layered robes in shades of yellow that flowed gracefully behind him as he walked, the Anunnaki towered head and shoulders above the Eridu guard that accompanied him. He did not move quickly, yet because of his height, he covered a lot of ground, forcing the guard to nearly jog to keep up. Even the tallest men in Kur-gal didn't grow to the height of the Anunnaki's shoulders. A heavy gold medallion bounced lightly on his chest as he approached. It was carved with symbols of ocean waves and dangled from a thick glass-like chain that hung from his neck. Almost all the Anunnaki Namzu had ever seen wore one just like it. But the most notable aspect to Namzu's visual scrutiny laid in the Anunnaki's physical features—large, dark almond eyes complimented the refined facial features of an elongated skull covered by long hair that was more yellow than it was blond and pale blue-tinted skin that covered the whole of his body. He was directed to the kitchen, where Namzu waited, fascinated as much as any of them by the unusual creature.

After dismissing the guards with him, Namzu bowed respectfully to the Anunnaki. "Thank you for honoring my summons, Wise-One. My name is Namzu, High Priest of the Judicial Order and humble servant of Enki."

"I am Ferulianreg of the Yellow Hall. Please call me Ferulian. I believe your proper title is First Usgadi in your tongue, yes?"

"It is, just as we speak of you as the Abgal." It was a sincere sign of respect that the Anunnaki recognized his position, and Namzu would not forget it.

Ferulian leaned close to Namzu and spoke softly, "If what your guardsman spoke about is true, then I would like to see these symbols on the wall. Please take me to them."

"Of course, Abgal Ferulian. Please follow me." Namzu led the Anunnaki upstairs to where the bodies still lay. He was irritated that the guard had such a loose tongue with the Abgal; rumors would be flying all over Eridu before the day was out. He made a mental note to have the guard beaten for his carelessness. Tales of murder could be dangerous, more so when the killer was still on the loose, and his own men should know better.

Even before they reached the room, Namzu was compelled to hold the linen over his nose again. The stench had grown even worse, but the Wise-One didn't seem to notice. Instead, he gazed beyond Namzu from the hallway and into the room. His eyes were affixed to the strange symbols written on the walls.

"Why do they do this?" the Anunnaki spoke aloud.

"I do not understand, Abgal," Namzu replied humbly.

The Anunnaki tore his eyes from the room and focused on Namzu. "This is a terrible thing to happen in Eridu. I will help you as best I can with the answers you seek."

"Thank you, Abgal. It is my hope that you may apply your wisdom to helping me understand the significance of those symbols. I feel certain they have meaning, but as to what, I fall short with an explanation."

In all his years as First Usgadi, this was the first time Namzu had requested an Anunnaki to assist in an investigation. He hadn't even been sure the Anunnaki would come. Of course, he knew well of their kind from the Ziggurat, the Tower of Tongues, and the occasional sightings around Eridu, but only the Sanga and the En had regular contact with any of them. Namzu had to admit that he was intimidated by the unusual man before him.

"How many died in this room?" Ferulian asked as if the bodies on the floor were not answer enough.

"Two," Namzu replied while he watched the Abgal study the bloody contents of the room. "A man and a woman visiting from Larak in the north."

"Were there more that died in this fashion before them?" the Abgal asked.

"Yes, there were seven others in this same inn," Namzu confirmed.

Ferulian studied the symbols on the wall again. "Were there similar writings on the walls in their rooms?"

"Yes, Abgal, some of them are the same, and others are different. I

16

have the sketches on these tablets here." Namzu fetched the sketches of the symbols on the clay tablets he had stored in his side pack and handed them to the Abgal.

The Anunnaki looked them over briefly before returning them to Namzu. "Do you have an idea who might have caused these deaths?"

Namzu related the night's events regarding the innkeeper and his resistance to being questioned further. "I believe he was the sole person involved in these murders. To what end, I still do not know. I can only speculate that he had a sickness of some sort. Except for those symbols, the crime would be a simple matter of reasoning."

The Anunnaki looked Namzu intently in the eye. "Where is the body of this man now?"

Namzu desperately wanted to tear his gaze away from the Anunnaki's but forced himself to hold fast. "He is in the Hall of Kurnugia by now. We have sent a report to the Sanga, who will most certainly wish to visit the remains himself to ensure there is no pestilence the citizens of Eridu need be concerned of." He felt sweat forming on his brow and briefly wondered why.

"There is no pestilence, but there is a great danger if this man yet lives," the Abgal warned. "Please let me know immediately if this is not the case."

As the Anunnaki turned to leave, Namzu quickly asked, "Will you enlighten me regarding the symbols left on the walls?"

Frowning deeply, Abgal Ferulian's penetrating gaze studied Namzu carefully before he spoke, "Knowledge of this sort may be dangerous to your kind. Are you sure you wish to know?"

"I do," Namzu replied firmly. He had to know.

Taking Namzu by the elbow, the Abgal moved back to the doorway where they could get a clear view of the symbols on the opposite wall.

"The first symbol represents the phrase *Caosga tooat cnila pambt*— 'This land bleeds unto me.'"

Namzu felt a chill run up his spine at the strange, guttural language the Anunnaki spoke while he wrote the translation in cuneiform next to the matching symbol he had drawn on his clay tablet. It sounded the same as the way the innkeeper spoke before he died.

"The second symbol represents the phrase *Unal Sag-gig-ga noasmi cnoqod*—'These people, let them become servants.'"

"Sag-gig-ga?" Namzu repeated. "It specifically says *Sag-gig-ga?*"

"It does." Ferulian was watching him closely, as if he half expected

17

Namzu to figure it all out right them.

"*Sag-gig-ga* is our native word for a citizen of Kur-gal, free or slave." Namzu was perplexed. "So then the message specifically references *our* people."

"Yes."

"I see." The revelation felt deeply meaningful to Namzu, but he couldn't say why. "Please continue, Abgal."

"The third symbol represents A cnoqod biab ozien de bogpa—'The servants are mine to rule.'

"And then the fourth: Zin kures—'I am here.'"

Without another word, the Abgal abruptly turned from the doorway and walked toward the stairway.

"Abgal Ferulian!" Namzu called after him. "What language is that you spoke?"

"The vernacular of gods and Demons," Ferulian replied over his shoulder without slowing his pace, and he disappeared down the stairs before Namzu could say another word.

Gods and Demons?

That implied they shared a common language. More importantly, what madman would know such a thing to write it on the wall of an inn? None of it made sense.

Namzu remained to stare at the symbols for a long while before he, too, made his way out of the inn. The fetid smell from the room lingered in his nostrils for a time after he departed, but the images he would carry in his mind forever.

If Namzu couldn't decide before, he knew now, the sight of death was the worst. But none of that mattered now. The memory of those final symbols and the chilling words the Anunnaki left him with dominated his thoughts, and he wondered what they could mean for the future of Eridu.

Zir kures—I am here.

Chapter 2

Ritual of Man

𒀀𒈬𒀭𒅗𒌇𒉺

Ashmadu had just taken his place on a step below the narrow archway that separated the monumental stairway from the landing on the first tier of Eridu's Ziggurat. The massive structure was oriented true north with two narrower stairways that approached the tier from the east and west. Each of the stairs overlooked a broad terrace that filled the space between them. It was on that terrace where dozens of priests from the temple stood wearing their white ceremonial long wraparound kilts and matching top covers. They spoke quietly among themselves while they waited for the ritual to begin. Above him, a single wide stairway steeply ascended past the second tier and onto the third and final tier high above. There stood the mud-brick temple known as the E-Abzu, where Enki, god of creation, the waters, farming, crafts, wisdom, and magic was believed to live. Most notable was the large quartz in the shape of a four-sided pyramid that levitated an arm's length above the E-Abzu, rotating slowly, and radiating its crimson luminescence over the city and beyond.

Ashmadu didn't understand how it worked, but he knew that the purpose of the quartz was to harness the power of the Orichalcum Crystals from deep inside the Ziggurat and project it far across the land in every direction. He noted with trepidation that it was glowing brighter than usual against the dark night sky this evening, and he hoped it was a sign of good fortune.

The expansive open plaza in front of the Ziggurat was crowded with the devoted worshippers of Enki. They were gathered there on the first day of spring to witness the En Ipqu-aya open the first night of the Creation of Man ritual, which was dedicated to Enki in his role as the creator and protector of mankind and as the patron deity of the great city of Eridu.

This was not Ashmadu's first time attending the ritual. In fact, he had participated in this same ritual year after year for decades. To his satisfaction, the show contrived by the En in reverence to Enki was somehow better and more dramatic every year.

In that broad plaza below the Ziggurat, he could see the thousands of flames produced by lanterns, torches, and light globes, each held by a faithful follower. And hundreds more were arriving, as evidenced by the long trails of lights snaking from far outside the walls of Eridu. He knew the En would wait for the majority of the devotees to fill the plaza to capacity before he began. He loved to please his audience.

Over the many years that he had been attending this ritual and others like it, Ashmadu had never really enjoyed the vista from the heights of the E-Abzu. The Ziggurat of Eridu was among the largest in Kur-gal, considering the importance of the deity it represented, and its height was rivaled only by the Tower of Tongues, located not far away in the city's northeastern edge of the temple district. From where he sat he could see the lights glowing from numerous balconies in the tower; shapes moved and eclipsed those lights from time to time. That was where the Anunnaki resided.

Perhaps Ashmadu's distaste for his current elevation stemmed from the surrounding leagues of irrigated fields visible from where he sat during the day. His mother had toiled as a slave in those fields when he was a child before he was sent to the temple, and his father was a cruel man that abused them for his entertainment. The mere thought of those days sent a shiver through him despite the passage of more than half a century. He was relieved that night had fallen, and everything beyond the lights on the walls of Eridu was covered in blackness.

More than a hundred chanting priests, each holding a torch to light their ascent, had begun to line the long stairway below. Ashmadu was still tired from the exhaustive trial of climbing those very stairs, and he was relieved to rest and enjoy the cool summer breeze that fluttered the red-dyed flax banners with the woven symbol of Enki above him. Below each banner, a wide brazier burned brightly and reflected the illumination off the gold effigy of Enki for all to see. This was where he would stay until the end of the ceremony, and then he would join the En inside the E-Abzu. It would be another long ascent up a steep stairway, but at least he would be well rested by then.

The thousands in the crowd below were remarkably quiet. Only the soft shuffling of feet and the low murmur of voices could be heard from where Ashmadu sat as more of Enki's followers arrived in the plaza. He couldn't help but share in the feeling of excitement as the adherents swayed side to side in perfect unison with the priests' chanting. The anticipation in the air was palpable, and Ashmadu expected that the first two nights of the ritual would be the most spectacular if history served as a good judge.

It was turning into a chilly night, and now that he had cooled off, Ashmadu was glad to have worn his Tugsagadu, a long, heavy wool cloak, over his ankle-length wraparound skirt. His ears and shaved head were cold, but he could endure the discomfort for a while. Ashmadu sat there only because his master, En Ipqu-aya, wanted him close by. If it had been up to him, he would have been among the crowds below. It was likely warmer surrounded by the closely packed bodies massed so tightly there was little room to move. Instead, he was here on the first tier of the Ziggurat in case the En needed him.

Suddenly the crowd, so silent and sedate a moment before, erupted into frenzied cheers. Ashmadu's heart leaped in his chest before he realized why they were cheering. He turned to look over his shoulder and watched as the En of Eridu emerged from the E-Abzu and descended the steps to the archway two paces above where he sat. The En was taller than the average Sag-gig-ga, a citizen of Kur-gal, with a full beard manicured and tightly braided over tanned skin complimenting shoulder-length gray hair—also braided, brown eyes, and a hawkish nose—he was very handsome for a man in his eighties. In the tradition of their people, he wore a long kilt held at the waist by a large pin crowned with lapis lazuli stones in gold settings. Ordinarily bare-chested when the weather was warm, the En tonight wore his ceremonial soft flax robes fringed with purple-dyed wool and accented with gold and silver jewelry, most of it set with precious gems dominated by more lapis lazuli. Upon his head, he wore an ornately decorated cylindrical Sañdul, a headdress that served as a symbol of his high office—Ruler of Eridu and High Priest of Enki.

Ashmadu couldn't help but smile as the En took in the cheers and adulation of the people for a long moment before raising his arms, staff held high in his left hand, to quiet the mass of his followers below. Ashmadu knew that this was what En Ipqu-aya lived for. Not that he was vain or arrogant; he just loved the attention. With incredible discipline, the crowd hushed rapidly.

Ashmadu had aged over the past three decades that En Ipqu-aya ruled Eridu. Yet as old as he was, the En was many years older, and Ashmadu marveled at how energetic the old priest was still. Most of the adults in the city had grown up under his rule and admired him as their ruler their entire lives. His benevolence and just government had endeared him to the freeborn peoples in the city, regardless of social stratum. The slaves were indifferent and hardly cared who ruled as long as they were treated well. Ashmadu knew this to be true from his own experience.

Yet even the slaves must honor the En, Ashmadu conceded to himself. To all worshippers of Enki, free or slave, the En was the direct representative of the deity, and his words were taken as if spoken by the god himself. Ashmadu knew this particular En was a wise ruler who owed much to the pragmatic counsel of the Anunnaki, who had brought prosperity to the Sag-gig-ga. Ashmadu revered the Anunnaki as well and at the same time found them unnatural, even if they were believed to be the direct descendants of Enki.

The Anunnaki had been a part of every citizen's life for more generations than the oldest elder could remember. As far as Ashmadu knew, this was the way of it in every city-state in Kur-gal. While he heard that there were only a handful of Anunnaki in the other cities, they had a subtle influence in everyday life where agriculture, education, trade, politics, social policy, and diplomatic relations were concerned. The En once told him that the Anunnaki never attempted to compel political leaders in any matter. Rather, they merely advised and guided as much as local leaders would allow. They were much admired and respected by all free people and a welcome part of Kur-gal society. Of course, as the En explained, the Anunnaki did have some measure of significant leverage over the city-states, since they controlled, protected, and maintained the Orichalcum Crystals that generated the power for magic housed within the Ziggurats. Ashmadu had met a number of them over the years and heard the stories they told the En during their consultations. Whether the stories were true or not, the Anunnaki always provided sound and wise advice to the En in Ashmadu's humble opinion.

En Ipqu-aya was a powerful priest-king with influence as far as the city-states of Unug and Bad-tibira to the north, the Sa-ti-um Mountains to the east, and the Pishon and Gihon Rivers to the south. As Ashmadu gazed down at the attentive multitude below, he knew that the residents of Eridu represented no more than a quarter of those before him. The rest were citizens from every part of Kur-gal, including many wealthy landowners and aristocrats. They had come to worship one of the primary gods of their religion and knew that they would be welcomed and treated well within the walls of Eridu.

Ashmadu waited eagerly like everyone else. The Creation of Man ritual would be celebrated for twelve days, as were most rituals in Kur-gal, and tonight it was the job of Enki's En to commence the festivities in resounding fashion. The En was about to speak. Ashmadu watched and listened attentively.

"Followers of Enki! Welcome!" En Ipqu-aya announced to the enthusiastic cheers of the crowd.

His voice was amplified for all to hear by a simple spell he had cast for the occasion. Ashmadu knew every nuance and every word of what the En was going to say and how he would say it. They had practiced it together every night for the past two weeks. En Ipqu-aya was a stickler for dramatic assertion that would enthrall the crowd and stir the people's imagination, and so far he never failed in his delivery.

"Tonight I will remind you of the Creation of Man story and our purpose to serve the gods!"

Shafts of lightning simultaneously struck above the towers on the walls surrounding the city, punctuating the En's last words with the crack of electricity that echoed across the city. Initially startled, the people responded with cheers and screams of exaltation. At the locations where the lightning had struck near the towers, tall pillars of light formed, stretching toward the heavens and fading from sight. To everyone's amazement, each light pillar began to unfurl horizontally like a scroll along the top of the wall and to connect with the ones on either side of it until the entire city was surrounded by a solid band of light twice again as high as the wall itself.

Those who had never seen one of En Ipqu-aya's dramatic rituals would be amazed, and those who *had* would be amazed all over again. Even though Ashmadu knew everything that was going to happen, actually watching it unfold in front of him left him as mesmerized as everyone else.

Right on cue, the priests lining the Ziggurat began their low, rhythmic chanting again, and the crowd quieted once more.

"So we begin," En Ipqu-aya announced softly. "When the heavens and earth were new, and the gods toiled the lands . . ."

Images appeared on the band of light, showing the gods working the land, planting, and harvesting with their own hands. The transfixed masses responded with gasps of surprise and awe. Ashmadu knew the words but had not seen the images the En was going to conjure, and they were astonishing.

"They began to become distressed by the hard work and gathered to complain, but Enki was sleeping and did not hear their words."

The images changed to show the suffering gods crying and Enki sleeping without hearing them.

"Then his mother, Nammu, the Primal Sea, came to Enki and woke him and implored him to fashion servants for the gods so that they need not toil so."

The images changed again to show Nammu and Enki with the gods crying at their feet and suffering from their work in the fields, in the mines, and on the river.

"After some thought, the wise Enki brought forth his best crafters and artists." Images reflected a host of craftsmen and artisans gathered with Enki.

"Enki told his mother that they would fashion the servants in the image of the gods. They would use thick clay from the earth molded by his craftsmen."

Clay figures began to take shape in the images around the city.

"Nammu, who gave birth to heaven and earth, then created the limbs of man as the craftsmen and artisans completed their work."

The clay figures were fully formed now, remarkably accurate. Ashmadu found his mouth agape and closed it without embarrassment.

"Then the Mother Goddess, Ninmah, breathed life into the clay forms."

Ninmah appeared and animated the clay figures, transforming them into flesh and blood and giving them the breath of life.

"The gods rejoiced—and celebrated with a great feast. No longer would they toil in the fields, plant, harvest, or grind grain for bread!"

Images showed a great feast, with the gods laughing, dancing, and giving thanks to Enki.

"Man has taken the burden from the gods! It's our cause in this world to toil for their benefit!"

More images showed man performing daily tasks, from farming, crafting, building, and trading to governing, worshipping, and serving as priests. The crowd, still silent, took in the images with solemn acceptance. Ashmadu was sure people from another culture might have been horrified by the idea of being created as slaves to their gods, but not the Sag-gig-ga of Kur-gal. This was what they knew, what they had always known. They fully accepted their identity and purpose.

"We serve the gods. But that does not mean we cannot serve ourselves as well!"

The images now changed to display beautiful young serving girls holding bowls, plates, and platters of the finest delicacies. The girls were easily ten times the size of an average person and stood shoulder to shoulder with their bounty. Hundreds of them stretched along the walls of the city. The crowd cheered at the obvious symbolism, and even Ashmadu found himself cheering and clapping, as well.

After a few moments, the servers appeared to move forward from the walls and toward the city center, where the people were gathered. The girls continued onward, through buildings and along the streets, with no effect on anything they touched. The people gathered in the plaza nervously packed closer toward the center. And just as the serving girls converged on the outside edge of the wide plaza, they suddenly shrank to the size of ordinary people and solidified into reality.

The worshippers were surprised and astounded at the transformation and began to cheer wildly. The now-real serving girls, wearing short, soft flax dresses, walked through the crowds and offered their delicacies and cups of Kas and Kas-du beers that never seemed to empty. At the same time, music echoed throughout the grand plaza from an unknown source. It began with a single haunting voice, clear and pure, backed by the plucking of a single lyre. The voice and lyre were soon joined by a chorus of voices and many lyres, lutes, and reed pipes in a fast-paced song of celebration. The Ziggurat itself was illuminated by some magical means, revealing dozens of gala priests singing and playing musical instruments on the broad terraces between the stairways. While the devout freeborn followers of Enki celebrated their enslavement to the gods, Ashmadu looked over the crowd and admired the irony.

"Rejoice in the bounty of our Lord!" En Ipqu-aya announced before retreating up the stairs and into the E-Abzu at the top of the Ziggurat. For a man in his eighties, Ashmadu marveled at his physical strength and constitution.

Feeling energized and inspired by the En's opening of the ritual, Ashmadu barely noticed how the cold had stiffened his joints from sitting so long. He carefully made his way up the steep steps of the long stairway, following the En into the E-Abzu. He was proud of his master's performance this evening, especially considering how hard the En had worked to create a unique and memorable experience that pleased his people and simultaneously glorified Enki. Tomorrow would be an even bigger night that would test the limits of the En's abilities. If he got it right, the people would write songs and legends about it.

Chapter 3

The Nam-en

𒐏𒌋𒐏 𒌋𒐕𒌋

Inside the E-Abzu, Ashmadu served En Ipqu-aya beer bread and a refreshing temple-brewed sweet beer called Kas-du. Aside from Ashmadu and the En, only one other man occupied the room. He was Terrikan of House Elbian, the Anunnaki High Priest to Eridu. More properly known by the title of Nam-en, the high priest was an older gentleman of typical Anunnaki physique—elongated skull set with wide almond eyes, blue-tinted skin, narrow waist, broad chest, and thin limbs. His jet-black hair was shorter than most other Anunnaki's, reaching only to his shoulders, and framed his sharp features. Ashmadu thought he looked exhausted this evening, as if he'd had trouble sleeping, which was probably the case, considering the sad circumstance that he endured. Still, it was odd to see one of his kind in such distress, and despite his disquiet, the Anunnaki greeted the En with a broad smile.

Ashmadu sat down in a wooden chair near the refreshments. Although he was a confidant to the En and the Anunnaki knew it, he kept quiet and inconspicuous in the dimly lit room. Later that night, when he and the En were in the privacy of the official residence of the En, known as the Gi-par, the En would want to talk about everything, and Ashmadu would counsel as best he could.

"You performed your duties admirably," Nam-en Terrikan told the En warmly.

"Thank you, I pray that every night is joyous for my people."

Ashmadu could tell that the En felt immensely satisfied that the people enjoyed his performance, primarily because his illusions worked flawlessly—something he worried over incessantly in practice.

"May it always be so." The Anunnaki distractedly smoothed the layers of his long green robes.

"How is your wife today, my friend?"

Ashmadu recognized the concern in the En's voice. In public, they

26

used their official titles of En and Nam-en, but his master and the Anunnaki had known each other for decades and always spoke informally when they were alone.

Ashmadu was aware that Terrikan had held the position of Nam-en since En Ipqu-aya was a child and had been a friend to the En's father. The Anunnaki must age very slowly, he thought, since Terrikan had barely changed in the decades Ashmadu had been in service to his master.

"Your High Priest of the Healers, the First Ashipu Bikku-lum, tells me the sickness has spread throughout her body," Terrikan responded sadly while looking into his untouched cup of Kas-du. "She has only a few weeks left."

En Ipqu-aya paused a moment before speaking further. He had confided to Ashmadu that Terrikan had been looking for a miracle when he brought his wife back to Eridu from their homeland. Bikku-lum, the First Ashipu, was a very talented healer, but miracles were beyond even his considerable skills. It was unlikely that the En's healing priests would find a way to help when her recovery was even beyond the skills of the fabled Anunnaki healers. Most citizens thought the Anunnaki to be immortal. How surprised they would be to learn that the strange beings died as easily as any one of them.

"I am so sorry, my friend." The En leaned forward and placed his hand over that of the Nam-en's. To Ashmadu's eyes, it looked like a child's hand on top of the strangely long and lean fingers of the Anunnaki. "I wish there were something more we could do."

"Bikku-lum is a good man and has done everything that can be done. Sometimes there is nothing left but to wait and provide comfort."

"That is the truth of life," En Ipqu-aya agreed. Leaning back in his chair, he pulled at the wool on his long kilt. "But I prefer not to believe it absolutely."

Ashmadu spoke to the First Ashipu Bikku-lum many times on the En's behalf while keeping tabs on the progress of Terrikan's wife. Her name was Secria, and Ashmadu knew her image well. She was one of the most beautiful Anunnaki women he had ever seen. He was told that she had been sick for the better part of a year, and although every effort was made through medical and magical means in the Anunnaki homeland and then in Eridu to find a cure, her disease spread relentlessly through her body. Ashmadu learned that her condition was not conventional, nor was it unknown to the Ashipu priests and physicians who attended Secria. It was called the creeping disease by the Anunnaki, for it would begin in one organ of the body and spread to others over a period of time. Sadly, there was no known ostensible cause for the sickness that could be avoided. It appeared randomly in people from every class and culture and often occurred in family lines. Worst of all, few had ever survived its ravages.

"We will be leaving Eridu tomorrow for a period of time, Ipqu-aya. As much as she loves this land, Secria would like to spend her final days at our estate outside the City of Atlantis. My second, Nin-Digir Shonaturi of House Restander—your people will know her as a high priestess—will speak for me while I am away."

Ashmadu briefly wondered if the En would have the same informal relationship with the Nin-Digir as he had with the Nam-en and if it would be different because she was a woman. He reflected on how the Atlanteans walked a fine line in Kur-gal and kept their interactions with the citizens to a minimum. The Anunnaki were considered the demigod offspring of the gods of Kur-gal, equal to any En and presumed to be devoted primarily to Enki, Lord of the Primeval Sea. Many wore gold medallions engraved with the likeness of the ocean, which was interpreted by the people of Kur-gal as the Primeval Sea. Ashmadu recognized that the interpretation was incorrect and deliberately left uncorrected. The medallions were really symbols for their own primeval god they called Pontus.

"Perfectly understandable," the En responded, "but how will you return to your island in time?" The distance from Eridu to the Emerald Isle was immense and well beyond where anyone from Kur-gal had traveled. Ashmadu once glimpsed a world map left unattended by the Nam-en on one of his visits and was dumbfounded by the expanse of it. He knew of a few kingdoms to the west and others to the north and always believed that was the true extent of the world. As it turned out, it was only the extent of *his* world.

The Anunnaki paused a moment to take a long draft from his cup. "The queen has been gracious enough to send an airship to aid in our expeditious return. Secria is her older sister, after all, and the queen is anxious to see her before she passes. But don't worry—the airship will arrive tomorrow night, well above the city at the Tower of Tongues, so as not to alarm the populace."

Ashmadu's master chuckled nervously but appeared relieved that the conversation had returned to a lighter topic. "Where the Anunnaki are concerned, nothing surprises the people."

High Priest Terrikan laughed and clapped his hands together. "Not since our first dramatic arrival so many generations ago, just outside this very city!"

"That is true, old friend. Our people thought you were gods descending to Earth in your great airships. And when the first of you emerged from them! What strange beings you must have seemed. I have read the original accounts from that day. We have the tablets stored right here in the temple library, and they speak of the fulfillment of prophecy."

"The people of Kur-gal were one of the first foreign peoples outside of the Emerald Isle that we approached. We feared that your ancestors might run away or attack us, but we never expected to be worshipped."

Terrikan was drinking now, his mind outwardly no longer consumed with the state of his ailing wife. *It was good to see him this way again,* Ashmadu thought to himself with a smile. While Ashmadu was almost never a part of their conversations, he was present for nearly all of them and felt a particular closeness to Nam-en Terrikan. The En had been suffering memory lapses for the past few years and required Ashmadu to attend him when he was not at the temple, where temple scribes recorded everything for him. Ashmadu refilled their cups and offered more Bappir, beer bread.

"If it weren't for your people's arrival, we would still be scratching in the mud and living in stick huts." The En wiped crumbs from his robes. "The records speak of a few minor incidents with the more ignorant Sag-gig-ga who didn't want to accept your help, but you came in peace. You shared the knowledge of advanced agriculture and irrigation that helped us settle in one place. We were no longer forced to migrate with the herds as our only food source."

"I'm not sure if I ever shared this with you, Ipqu-aya, but there is still some debate among the scholars in Atlantis about whether or not we should have accepted your belief in us as the Anunnaki. Our ancestors debated it as well, and at the time they thought it best to accept the belief rather than disrupt the mythology. What we learned set a precedent with many other civilizations that we made first contact with for centuries afterward."

En Ipqu-aya sat back down in the chair next to his friend. "The Sag-gig-ga's belief in the Anunnaki is so ingrained into our theology and religion that to take it away from us would have created a rift in our faith beyond mending. Your people made the right choice."

"Yet it was also decided that only one among you, the En of Eridu, would be enlightened by the truth." The Anunnaki glanced at Ashmadu, acknowledging his awesome responsibility to keep his master's secrets safe. "You call the citizens of Kur-gal 'Sag-gig-ga,' but even as the En you are still one of them. Until you became the En and I told you the truth of us, you knew only as much as any other Sag-gig-ga. Has the knowledge not shaken the theological foundation of your beliefs?"

"Not at all. In fact, your people have fulfilled the prophecy of the coming of the Anunnaki. What Sag-gig-ga could say that the Anunnaki cannot be something else to another people as well? You have taught me, and every En before me, that the world is filled with many varied people, cultures, and civilizations. Because those people were not written in the prophecies, does that mean the people of Kur-gal can't believe in the prophecies? I don't think so."

The Anunnaki fingered the gold medallion hanging from a thick glass-like chain around his neck. "Do you remember the map of the world I showed you once so long ago?"

Without a doubt, Ashmadu remembered, it was one of the most jarring moments of his life. En Ipqu-aya was also excited by the memory, "It is impossible to forget! I was so astonished and wanted nothing more than to deny what I was seeing! The world is far vaster than I could have ever dreamed. You pointed out some of the major civilizations and described their cultures and traditions. There were so many, and they were all so different. I could never remember them all, but a few were unforgettable. Lyonesse, whose warriors clothe themselves in metal from head to toe and believe in conducting their lives in accordance with rules of conduct called chivalry. The Dvergr Dwarfs, shorter even than our people and twice as wide, who live within a massive active volcano, which they mine for precious metals. The Elves of Avalon, magical humanoids who are almost one with nature and live in seclusion within the Sylvan Forest north of Atlantis. The Olmec people, who built temples much like our Ziggurats and live in a forest jungle even farther west than the Emerald Isle. The Huaxia Kingdoms and their mystical Yellow Emperor on the other side of the world. Mu, where the feared Mus-Lu Kingdoms reign. And, of course, the Emerald Island of Atlantis itself. I have always hoped that one day you would tell me more about them all."

The Emerald Isle was where the Anunnaki—or Atlanteans, as Ashmadu sometimes heard the Nam-en refer to the Anunnaki in private—originated. And on that isle was an incredible city surrounded by alternating rings of land and water with walls of silver, gold, and liquid-coated Orichalcum. It was a place of magic and wonder, prosperity and abundance, the impossible and the improbable. Ashmadu heard stories of ships and chariots that could fly and mysterious creatures that lived among them and protected them in the water and on land. He learned about the isle from his master a few years before, and at first he had assumed it existed in the Primeval Sea he knew as the Abzu, but since the revelation of the map, he knew it was a real place.

Terrikan smiled mischievously. "I broke a few rules showing those maps to you in the first place. Our rulers have always feared that giving other cultures too much knowledge might encourage their species' natural desire for conquest. But for you, I will make an exception. I know your heart, and it has no desire to dominate other peoples through conquest. When I return, I will bring my maps."

The En offered a humble smile. "With or without the maps, you will be welcomed back."

"Thank you, Ipqu-aya. As usual, I enjoyed our talk, but I must leave you for a while and return when it is appropriate." The Anunnaki stood from his chair and set his cup on the table, nodding to Ashmadu.

"Farewell, my friend." Nam-en Terrikan embraced the En firmly before departing.

"Be well, Nam-en Terrikan of House Elbian. I will continue to speak with Enki about comforting your family." The En's words followed the Anunnaki down a back passageway that led to the exit of the Ziggurat below.

Ashmadu felt sympathy for his master, who would surely miss his Atlantean friend. So many nights they stayed up late to discuss theology, politics, the world outside of Kur-gal, and life in general. They were of a similar mind in many respects. Although Terrikan had assured the En that he would return to Eridu, Ashmadu wondered if he ever would. Surely it would be emotionally painful to come back to a place where he lived so long with his wife. Perhaps the En would find a way to visit his friend one day in Atlantis. In his mideighties now, En Ipqu-aya was unlikely to take on a journey of such magnitude. *Well,* Ashmadu mused, *perhaps he could visit in his dreams.*

~~~

Ashmadu allowed the En to sleep late the next morning. Nevertheless, his master was taciturn while he sat at the long wooden table, waiting for Ashmadu to prepare his breakfast. It certainly didn't help that the Sanga, the En's second and High Priest of Temple Economics, was tapping his foot impatiently on the white mosaic tile in the shadow of the En's bedroom door.

The Sanga, Irra by name, was a portly man shorter than most other men in Kur-gal and nearly as old as the En. He exhibited a shaved head and a narrow, long, well-groomed gray beard smartly tied in a braid. He wore clothing of precious material—a white flax kilt trimmed with gold and a matching cover over his shoulders accompanied by several pieces of gold and silver jewelry studded with lapis lazuli. Ashmadu noted that the only time the Sanga wasn't in a rush was when he was reading or explaining something he thought was of great consequence to the En.

"En Ipqu-aya, the sun is already high toward the noon hour, and there is so much to do. Please review these tablets while you break the morning fast." The Sanga placed the stack of clay tablets beside the En.

"Irra, sit down and quit hovering." The En squinted his eyes in annoyance. "Break bread with me, and let's discuss the day. Whatever is not done today will be waiting for us tomorrow—if we live that long."

"I cannot. There is so much to do, perhaps another time. I will send one of my scribes to retrieve the tablets after your breakfast." Irra bowed quickly and exited the room.

From the corner of his eye, Ashmadu could see the En watching the Sanga leave and was sure the man already regretted how he had spoken to his second. Everyone knew the Sanga was a dedicated, competent priest whose loyalty and devotion to the En were beyond question. But the En often complained that the Sanga's relentless nature was overwhelming, even if the Sanga second was his most beloved friend.

Ashmadu placed a tray before the En. Breakfast would consist of a fish-and-red-lentil pottage, a loaf of barley bread drizzled with honey, and a cup of Kas-du.

Noticeably reluctant, the En began to look over the endless columns of the cuneiform script on the tablets while he ate. After a few moments, he put down the tablet he'd been reading and turned to Ashmadu with a heavy sigh. "Sit with me, Ashmadu. In my chambers, you don't have to pretend to be only my servant. You can be my friend."

Ashmadu sat down at the table near the En and broke off a piece of bread.

"Why are you so formal all the time"—the En threw his hands up dramatically—"even when we are alone, and you don't have to be?"

Ashmadu wanted to roll his eyes. This was not the first time they'd had this conversation. "If I am informal with you here, then I might slip when others are around," he explained patiently, "and you would be forced to reprimand me. If it happened more than once, some might question your credibility. You are the En, and our great Lord Enki speaks through you. What Sag-gig-ga could take seriously an En who relies on the confidence of his house servant?"

His master grumbled that he didn't care, but Ashmadu knew that he did.

The En hardly ate. Distinctly preoccupied, he made swirls in his pottage until, after a few awkward moments, he spoke up. "I owe him everything."

Ashmadu stayed quiet. The En would speak more if he chose to.

"Have I ever told you the truth about how Irra and I came to positions of power in Eridu, the greatest city of Kur-gal?"

This was interesting, Ashmadu thought. The En never spoke of this before. Why was he bringing it up now? "No, Master. I assumed you were both elected by the council." He knew little of the council, except that they were the group of elders that approved significant decisions and budgets, providing a system of checks and balances to the En and the Sanga. They were known as the Zi-ik-ru-um. Truth be told, though, he never heard of them going against the En or the Sanga on any issue, and they basically sat as more of an advisory council. The En and the Sanga had been in office longer than any of the elders had been on the council, and the council seemed to trust their leaders' abilities to run the temple and Eridu as they felt necessary.

En Ipqu-aya laughed. "Not even close. Fortunately, so many years have passed now that few remember the circumstances and would have no reason to question the outcome. There are only three of us on this earth that know the truth, and if I tell you, then your life will be tied to mine forever, maybe even in the underworld, Kurnugia."

"My life is already tied to yours, En, and you know it to be so. We share many secrets. What is one more?"

"Of course you are right. I have wanted to unburden myself of this for some time now, and Irra refuses to speak of it anymore."

Ashmadu removed the wooden breakfast tray, refilled the En's decorated clay cup with Kas-du, and poured one for himself.

The En waited for him to sit again before he spoke. "Irra and I came to the E-Abzu as novices, but what most didn't know was that we were friends from childhood. We were a good match. Irra was the academic intellectual who seemed to know everything about anything, and I was considered blessed by Enki in the magical arts and to have 'a charming disposition,' according to my mother." The En smiled at the recollection. "Over the years, as we progressed in the hierarchy of the temple, we developed something of a rivalry, yet we quietly remained fast friends. We used the apparent antagonism to our advantage and gained prominence and position because of our little deceit. By the time we were both Firsts in the temple, the current En was old, and his health was failing. That was when Irra came to me with an idea." The En paused to coat his throat with Kas-du.

"Sounds like the usual temple politics so far," Ashmadu said.

"This is where temple politics took a turn for the extreme. The Sanga had died the year before, and the En had not chosen another to replace him. We knew that when the En died, there would be several strong contenders for his office and that of the Sanga's. If we joined together, we would never have enough support from the various factions in the temple to succeed, and even if we did, it was still far less likely that we would capture both offices." The En paused to take a long draft from his cup of Kas-du. "Instead, we colluded to be in extreme opposition, with each of us bringing together the factions most in line with our stated ideals. That was an ugly time, a time I am not

33

proud of. Nor was Irra, because we committed unconscionable sins to consolidate our positions in power. By the time the En finally died, two camps emerged—one supporting Irra and the other me. The temple was essentially split in half, with no clear advantage to either, and the Zi-ik-ru-um was unable to come to a consensus on a decision."

Ashmadu had to ask, "Were you not afraid that a conflict might erupt between your supporters and Irra's that could spread to the city and even the military?"

"There was that danger," the En agreed, "if we allowed the situation to go on, but this is where the brilliance of Irra's plan came into play. He publicly announced that he had a solution. Since there was no En for Enki to speak his wishes, they would pose the question to the people of Eridu with the hope that Enki would declare his will through them. I, of course, agreed.

"The freeborn of the city gathered in front of the Ziggurat to listen to each of us state our case for ascension as the next En. Irra volunteered to speak first and laid out a very logical and rational argument for the people to choose him as their future En. Irra's supporters were very pleased and confident that the people would see with clarity that Irra was the best choice.

"Then it was time for me to speak. I remember speaking at length not of myself but of Enki, the other gods, and Enki's relationship with the Sag-gig-ga. It was the first time in my life that I truly felt touched by divinity—as if Enki was speaking through me. The words I spoke were regarded as beautiful, painting a portrait of our god so vivid and real that the people were moved by them. When I finished speaking, some wept, others were silent and reflective, but most looked at me with expressions of wide-eyed rapture. Even the priests of the opposing faction were caught up in the moment. I remember almost nothing of the words I spoke and never would have known them had the scribes not written them down."

"There was no doubt who the people wanted for their next En, and Irra conceded without even asking the freeborn for a decision. It was later promulgated among the people that it was Enki's words they heard with my voice that night, making it clear who would be the next En. To this day I believe it to be true."

"So how did Irra become the next Sanga?" Ashmadu asked. "Didn't your supporters expect it would be one of them?"

"They certainly did. As soon as I was anointed as the En of Eridu, my first act was to appoint Irra as my Sanga. You can imagine the shock and anger from my supporters. There were still serious divisions in the priesthood, but with Irra as Sanga, we quickly began to unite the priests again to focus on their duties in service to Enki without political distractions. It took a few years and more than a few dark actions, but the result was that the temple today is of one mind and direction. Irra has always said that had we not done what we did, the temple would never have been united and Eridu would never have become the great city it is today.

"I have my reservations, but Irra is probably right. He usually is." The En chuckled. "Sometimes I wonder which of us is truly in charge of the E-Abzu."

Ashmadu agreed that the Sanga was a powerful force in the temple, but he also knew what happened to those who underestimated the En. There were more secrets—much uglier ones, he was sure—and he prayed to Enki that his master never felt compelled to share those with him.

Chapter 4
Hall of Kurnugia
𒂍𒆠𒉡𒈤𒆠

Irra had much to do today. Just because the city was celebrating the Creation of Man ritual for eleven more days and half the priests and priestesses were busy with the ceremonies didn't mean that the everyday requirements of running the temple government had come to a halt. Sometimes he wondered what would happen if he weren't so diligent about the temple business. *Surely Eridu would descend into chaos.* He laughed at himself. That was just his hubris talking.

It had recently started raining, and he vaguely registered the heavy raindrops beating down on the kiln-fired mud brick and sandstone structure as he walked briskly through the dark halls of the temple complex. The passages were dimly lit by oil lamps and light globes casting ominous shadows around corners that shifted with distance and perspective. Irra only vaguely registered his surroundings, so busy was his mind with the endless tasks of the day. He was issuing orders to the crowd of scribes and initiates that followed in his wake, sending one here or there with a cuneiform tablet for various officials, ordering another to gather information for a report and yet another to perform a vital task elsewhere. All the while, he made notes on a soft clay tablet as he walked.

Abruptly Irra realized that he was alone. He had sent all of his attendants away. He stopped and considered where he was going. There was a pain in his joints that always came with the rain and humidity, reminding him of his age. Irra never let it bother him—he had far too much to do—and right now he was going somewhere with purpose, if he could only remember what that purpose was.

"Ah, yes," he said aloud, "the Hall of Kurnugia."

Irra never liked going there. It always smelled of death and was often crowded with distraught families that could afford to send their deceased relatives to the Hall of Kurnugia to be appropriately purified, oiled, and wrapped in a shroud for burial by the Abrig, purification priests. The priests would then perform a ceremony of blessing over the body before allowing the family to make their private observances. Finally, the Isib, burial priests, would take the body from the Abrig and conduct the burial rites in the graveyards outside the city. Irra mused that the ancient builders of the hall had either possessed a sense of humor or been very morose to construct it beneath the Ziggurat. Kurnugia, after all, was the name of the underworld and literally meant "earth of no return."

Irra was going to the Hall of Kurnugia to inspect the body of a man who had apparently become deranged and murdered several patrons of the inn that he owned near the market. The victims had been killed in their sleep with a sharp object like an ax or butcher's knife, and their blood had been used to write strange symbols on the walls of the room where they had been slain. An Anunnaki Abgal from the Tower of Tongues was invited to view the writing and recognized the symbols as Demonic in origin. How anyone in Eridu would know about such symbols was of grave concern, according to First Usgadi Namzu's report sent to him earlier.

Only after nine people had lost their lives at the inn was its proprietor found to be the culprit. He was clubbed to death by the guards when they attempted to detain him; he had fought them with the very knives he likely used to kill his victims.

Irra was asked to inspect the remains for signs of disease that might have caused the innkeeper's apparent insanity. Was there a health risk to the community? That worried him more than the idea of a serial murderer. Nothing could shut down a city and destroy the economy more swiftly that the threat of an epidemic. Thus far there were no other infections that he knew of, so he expected the danger was likely very low, but he was pleased that Namzu informed him of the possibility and asked for his inspection of the remains. Although he did not know the First Usgadi very well, he knew him by reputation as a very diligent and pragmatic man.

He turned down a descending passage that lead to the hall. There, only his own footfalls echoed ahead of him. This section of the temple was always silent, with few Sag-gig-ga trespassing the corridors so frequently traveled by only the dead. The dim silence accompanied by the knowledge of where he was set his teeth on edge and gave him the eerie impression that he was not alone, even though there was no one else in sight.

It is always so dry down here, he thought to himself. The humidity he felt above was no longer present, to the relief of his old joints, and not a single drop of moisture seeped through the cracks of the stone floor and walls, even with the heavy rain. He always wondered if it was a natural phenomenon of the subterranean structure or Abrig magic that kept the dankness at bay. Ahead, Irra could see the entrance to the Hall of Kurnugia, and already the pungent stench of human decay was noticeable in the stagnant air. When he was close, he could see the angled characters of the cuneiform script of a prayer inscribed on the floor below the wide arched entrance:

O Ereshkigal, Queen of the Great Earth, pass this soul freely through your seven gates to kneel at your throne in Kurnugia.

Pausing before the archway, Irra repeated the prayer, then cast a quick spell to negate the rising stench and entered the vast hall.

Inside, the room was broad and long, with high ceilings displaying images of Kurnugia from the most popular stories. Ereshkigal, queen of the underworld, on her throne in Kurnugia; representations of each of the seven gates and their gatekeeper Neti; and several dark images of Anzu and Utukku, Demons, which represented warnings to the dead. Along each side of the hall were unadorned stone blocks, waist high and long enough for a man to lie upon. Several were in use at the moment and in various stages of preparation. Small hearths were built into stone foundations down the middle of the hall to keep the great room almost comfortable, but it was not a natural chill that made him shudder.

At least a dozen Abrig priests moved silently through the room, respecting the eternal slumber of their charges and carefully attending to their transition into the afterlife. They all looked up for a moment when he entered and then continued about their business as if the Sanga walking in were nothing more than a curiosity. Only one acknowledged his arrival and smiled warmly.

The attentive priest was Iblinum, the First Abrig, the principal priest who oversaw the Abrig sect. He approached purposefully and bowed. "Silim sum, Sanga."

"Silim sum," Irra replied.

"I apologize for my colleagues," the First Abrig vaguely motioned toward the open room. "Sometimes they are unsure if what they see is real or the Gidim of one of their remains. Are you here to inspect the innkeeper?"

Irra had heard that the Abrig developed the ability to sense spirits of the dead, known as Gidim, from the bodies they prepared for burial, sometimes visually. Were it his duty to work in the hall, he imagined that he might be a little touched in the head as well. "The innkeeper, yes, if you would guide me to his place," Irra replied while pointedly ignoring the proceedings around him.

"Of course, Sanga. Be warned, however, that the innkeeper was brought in during the night and we have not yet begun our work on him."

Impatient to put this part of his morning behind him, the Sanga nearly rolled his eyes at the First Abrig. "That's fine. I will see him now."

As with all the Firsts, Iblinum sent Irra regular reports pertaining to the day-to-day activities that occurred in the Hall of Kurnugia. Rarely did

Irra get beyond the first two columns of the cuneiform script before the reports inevitably degraded into lists of organ weights and fluid volumes. He didn't expect that the First Abrig's conversation in social situations was any better. Irra appreciated how passionate Iblinum was for his work, but he could barely stand more than a few minutes in his presence.

"This way, Sanga." Iblinum slowly escorted Irra to the far side of the long room where a stone table held the remains.

The innkeeper's body was bare-chested but still clothed in a long kilt and sandals. His hair and face were matted with blood, with dark, crusty-red splatters across his shoulders and chest. He was beaten so severely that the bruises and welts covering his arms, torso, and face were swollen and made him look less than human.

"Would you like to examine the organs?"

"Yes, that is my purpose here today," Irra replied with undisguised exasperation in his voice. Why did the man have to be so costive?

"I will gather the tools." The First Abrig bowed again, then slowly walked away to collect the instruments.

Irra lifted the arm of the corpse. It was cool to the touch but not cold. The body had not yet begun to stiffen. It was not his business to be around the dead often so he presumed everything was as it should be, but the few corpses he inspected in the past were quite a bit more stiff and cold to the touch.

Finally, the First Abrig returned with a clay tray holding a variety of small knives, handsaws, and a bucket of water. He set them on a stone table next to Irra and then moved to the opposite side of the table.

"When was he brought here, exactly?" Irra asked while inspecting the body.

The First Abrig wiped dried blood from the areas of the body where the Sanga would cut into the cadaver. "Last night, Sanga. We have just been too busy to attend to him yet."

Irra began to cut into the man's chest. "Last night, you say? That's impossible. He's not even cold yet." His words got stuck in his throat when his blade drew blood from the deep cut he made. "You fool!" Irra looked up at Iblinum angrily. "He's still alive."

The innkeeper's swollen eyes popped open and stared straight into his own. Irra was stunned. Before he could step back, the corpse reached up and grabbed him tightly by his robes, pulling him closer. Terrified, Irra was unable to pull away from the man's powerful grip. He was face-to-face with the man's bloody gaze, their noses nearly touching.

The bloodstained innkeeper, intent on nothing but Irra, seemed to search the Sanga's soul through the blood-red pulp that was his eyes. Frothy red bubbles appeared between his lips as he struggled to speak, and then he opened his mouth, expelling a violent cough that spewed blood across Irra's face and priestly robes.

Still fighting to break the innkeeper's grip, the Sanga kicked at the stone table, desperately seeking leverage. The First Abrig was no help, dumbstruck by what was occurring in front of him and rooted in his place from fear.

The innkeeper hissed, *"Geh ozien,"* as he released a long, final breath.

His grip on the Sanga's robes relaxed, and Irra jerked back so violently that he fell on the floor. His head was spinning. Something was wrong.

The First Abrig knelt beside him, while several other Abrig rushed over to help. "Sanga, are you okay?"

"I need a moment," Irra wheezed and tried to slow his breathing. Unable to see straight or regain his footing, he sat back against the stone table. Somehow his mind had translated the disquieting last words of the innkeeper as *You are mine.*

He jerked his eyes back to where the innkeeper lay, but the body on the slab above him was still.

"I will fetch you some water and a cloth." The First Abrig moved somewhat faster than he had earlier, all the while looking over his shoulder as if to reassure himself that the innkeeper was no longer animated.

By the time the First Abrig returned, Irra was on his feet again. He drank the water and cleaned himself as well as he could with the cloth. Then, with an unsteady hand, he took one of the knives from the clay tray and rammed it through the innkeeper's heart. The man did not move this time. Not even a twitch.

"Do you suppose he is dead now?" the First Abrig asked sarcastically.

Irra glared at the First Abrig and then addressed all who were present. "Speak of this to no one." Without another word, he stormed out of the Hall of Kurnugia.

~~~

Namzu was alone in his office, staring at the array of cuneiform tablets spread out on the desk before him. It was raining, and the rhythmic pitter-patter of the rain on the mud-brick wall and ceiling was making him feel drowsy.

No matter how hard he stared at the tablets, the drawings on them made no more sense to him than they did when he drew them. They were copies of the mysterious symbols scrawled in blood on the walls where each of the crimes had occurred. There were seven tablets in front of him, one for each crime scene, with a total of nine victims.

The Anunnaki Abgal's brief visit to the inn the day before provided some insight into the symbols' meaning but not the reason why they were drawn in the first place. The Abgal's given translation had been cryptic and especially chilling.

Namzu picked up the tablet from the most recent murders and slowly traced his finger over the first symbol. "This land bleeds unto me," he whispered to himself and then traced the second symbol. "These people, let them become my servants."

He moved on to the third, "The servants are mine to rule."

Then lastly to the fourth, "I am here."

He stopped before completing his finger's movement over the symbol. "I am here," he repeated to himself.

Who is here? Namzu wondered. Had the innkeeper been taunting them, hinting that *he* was the killer and "here" at the inn?

It was too simple. How would an innkeeper know symbols such as these anyway? There had to be something more to the designs. Namzu felt it in his gut. Even the Anunnaki Abgal appeared shaken by the presence of the symbols, and his warning about the innkeeper's body struck him as unusual. Namzu wished for the hundredth time that he would have asked for translations of all of the symbols he had written down, but the Abgal left in such a rush. A few of the symbols from the last crime scene were repeated from earlier murders, and then there were others that did not repeat at all. But the one symbol that was only present at the last crime scene was the one that meant, "I am here."

Namzu realized he might have to go to the Tower of Tongues to ask for the Abgal to help him translate the rest of the symbols, but before he did that, he would check with the temple librarians, the Lukur priestesses. There might be tablets with some ancient or obscure reference to these symbols that would give him the answers he sought. He would go to the library that afternoon once the rain stopped. In the meantime, he still had lots of evidence to sort through. Maybe there were other connections between the murders he had not yet found.

There was a knock at the door.

"Enter!" Namzu shouted.

The door opened and in walked Sabum, wet from the rain, with droplets of water still running down his face.

A Subur, temple slave, entered behind him and handed the Usgadi a towel before addressing the First Usgadi. "Would you care for refreshments?"

"Yes, Yaqarum," Namzu replied, "and bring Kas, not Kas-du."

The Subur left the room, and Namzu motioned Sabum to a chair next to his desk. "Is the deluge finally upon us?"

"The gods are practicing yet." Sabum dried his shaved head with the towel as he sat. "I came to give you an update on the sightings of the Mus-Lu."

Namzu looked up from his tablets alarmed. "Are they massing again?"

"I don't think so. From the reports we have gathered from the patrols, tree cutters, farmers, and hunters, they appear to be a small population that has settled in the hill country near the base of the Sa-ti-um Mountains."

"If they are not a threat now, how long until they will become one?"

Sabum scratched the side of his large, angular nose. "Not now, but if they were to gain a foothold on this side of the Sa-ti-um, they could provide supplies and support for a far larger force."

The Subur, Yaqarum, returned with the Kas and then quietly left the room, bowing on his way out.

"So what do you recommend?"

"Well, the Sanga has already instructed Ninkum Shubure to put aside a large reserve without any cause or justification, and no doubt the little whore will be running to the En any day now to find out why. So it looks like the En is taking their presence very seriously."

Namzu raised a dark eyebrow. "Whore? Haven't you tasted her nectar on more than one occasion?" Shubure was the priestess in charge of the temple treasury, or Ninkum, and her ability to get her way utilizing her impressive feminine attributes was well-known.

Sabum shrugged but didn't respond to the obvious bait. "You should just stick to playing your games of politics, and in the meantime, I'll have Shatamurrim and his Ursagmuda ready when you want them. That is my recommendation."

Namzu laughed. "Sabum, my favorite Usgadi, you are so sensitive!" He stood and kissed the man on top of his shaved head.

Sabum's cheeks reddened, and Namzu sat back down, still chuckling.

"I see you are still obsessing over those symbols."

"I need to find out what they mean," Namzu replied, his mood souring. "Perhaps the library will have something on them. Would you like to come?"

"Absolutely not—unless you order me to," Sabum responded with a smile. "Why do you care, anyway? The innkeeper is dead, and there's no doubt in anyone's mind that he killed all nine of the victims."

"There's something more, Sabum, and I think finding out what these symbols mean will help me determine the answer. I don't think this is over yet."

"I hope you're wrong, but Enki as my witness, you are right more often than not. Let me know if you need my help—as long as it's not in the library."

Namzu watched Sabum leave, then drank his Kas alone. Now he had something else to worry about, the damned Mus-Lu. He picked up a small clay figurine that sat at the corner of his desk. It was a likeness of a Mus-Lu that he received as a gift from . . . he couldn't remember. They were traditionally placed in homes to ward off evil, but mostly they were playthings for children. In his lifetime he had seen only one up close. The creature was a captive from an attempted invasion by the Mus-Lu a few years ago when Shatamurrim and his Ursagmuda, his Warrior Dogs, almost single-handedly routed a far superior force.

The creatures were terrifying in real life, not like the obscure features of the little doll he held in his hand. He recalled how reptilian they appeared: green leathery skin over a lithe, powerful physique; long snakelike head filled with sharp teeth; and large slanted eyes with slits for pupils. Worst of all was their purported taste for human flesh.

Namzu shuddered. He hoped they weren't back in force, although he couldn't conceive of any other reason why they would be on this side of the Sa-ti-um unless they were being pushed by some force farther east. Whatever the case, they wouldn't be allowed to stay in the vicinity of Kur-gal. Sooner or later they would have to be compelled to return back across the mountains from whence they came.

Liquid dripped from his clenched fist. He looked down and was surprised to see that he had crushed the clay figure of the Mus-Lu and cut his hand in the process. Blood was pooling on the wood surface of his desk. It was almost prophetic. If the Mus-Lu came, there would be a lot of spilled blood . . . on both sides.

Chapter 5

The Ninkum

𒀭𒊩𒌆𒆳

Ashmadu walked a step behind the En on their way through the city to the temple with a number of initiates and scribes in tow. Usually, the En was animated and talkative with his entourage when the weather was pleasant enough to walk to the temple in the morning.

Well, midmorning, Ashmadu thought. The city would have to be burning down around our ears before the En got out of bed earlier. He must be preoccupied with the presentation he was planning for the ritual that evening.

The people they passed were in good spirits, and it was for this reason that Ashmadu loved the celebrations. Everyone appeared happy and productive, with little misery in their lives, and they greeted the En respectfully on the street. Ashmadu knew they wanted to ask—but would never dare—about what was in store for the second evening of the ritual. It was ironic, considering that the current celebrations were in honor of Enki's Creation of Mankind, which had sentenced man to a life of slavery in service to the gods.

Ashmadu knew better. The En had confided once, on a night when too much Kas had flowed, that Enki himself had said that the gods cared little for the daily struggles of the Sag-gig-ga and that the real necessity of the priests was to keep the masses civilized. The En had explained that Enki would speak to him in dreams sometimes and even send visions from time to time. He had been so sincere that Ashmadu knew he must be speaking the truth.

The En's mood lightened a bit when they entered the Old City, and he began to chat idly with Ashmadu. "I love this city—every mud-brick house and paver."

While the Ziggurat was painted and bore carvings of the gods and various rituals, the district itself was simple and unadorned. The residential area of the Old City was made up of clusters of single-story, windowless houses connected by common walls and separated from other groups of homes by narrow alleys. Each contained a central courtyard open to the sky and with a number of rooms that entered into it. Some houses were more extensive than others, depending on what the family could afford, and each entryway opened onto the main pedestrian street through a single wooden door.

The En had grown up in just such a neighborhood—or so he said. "Ah," he mused, "the aroma of cooking and the sounds of conversation and laughter bring me back to my childhood."

Ashmadu couldn't imagine the En as a child. When he tried, all he could visualize was a small version of what the man looked like now. It was so vivid in his mind's eye that he almost laughed out loud. *Maybe the En was born a powerful old man,* he mused. *Yes, that fits better.*

The next section of the city they passed through was for trade and markets. The economy of Eridu was strong, and vendors of every sort conducted a brisk business. The buildings here were similar to the residential section, but there were also many two-story structures and large warehouses for goods, pens for livestock, and stalls with fruits and vegetables. Canals spidered down the back alleys, running from the harbor on the Buranuna River to facilitate the transportation of goods. Although it was nearly dark, the markets would stay open until an hour before the rituals began that evening, and some, especially the inns and taverns, would open again afterward.

Keeping to the main road, the entourage left the trade district and entered the sprawling orchards of date palms east of the E-Abzu and temple buildings, including the Ziggurat. The groves, laid out beautifully in perfect rows, were cared for by the priests themselves and produced the most plump and succulent dates in Kur-gal.

It was no mistake that the En had chosen this route to the temple complex. Ashmadu knew the En needed to relax before the ritual this evening, and the orchards always made him feel calm and content.

Once they entered the temple grounds, the En released his followers to go about their business—except for Ashmadu. Ashmadu usually didn't accompany the En to the temple, but today was different. The En was very tired and needed an additional buffer against his closest Nig-aga, and if he needed anything, Ashmadu would be there to see to his comfort as well as serve as his second set of ears.

The temple complex was surrounded by a high wall that formed a wide U shape connecting to the east side of the main wall that surrounded the entire city. Ashmadu could see the temple Aga-us, guards, patrolling the walls, and he admired their diligence—they kept watch despite long hours of boredom and frequently extreme weather. The Sanga often sent the En reports when something notable occurred involving the Aga-us on temple grounds, and the En would share the more interesting and humorous tidbits with him.

The most exciting event in recent memory had involved a dispute between a priest and a merchant whose onager had defecated on the holy man's sandaled foot. He couldn't remember how the whole ordeal was settled, but even the En surmised that the pompous priest probably had it coming and afterward couldn't resist sending a note to him saying that it was almost certainly Enki's will. En Ipqu-aya was known to have a crooked sense of humor that nearly every high priest had been the subject of at one time or another. And they loved him for it.

Ashmadu followed the En toward his office, greeting priests and merchants along the way. There seemed to be more merchants than priests within the temple complex most days. The merchants moved Kas, Se-nis-e-a, Se-lum-lum, and Zid-bar-si grains and flour, among others, from temple storerooms onto canal boats and wagons. The goods would eventually be sold in the markets or exported to other city-states. This was the real treasury of Eridu, Ashmadu knew, for the city was rich in agriculture and bountiful harvests.

"By Enki, may it always be so," he murmured to himself as he avoided a cart of Se-lum-lum sprouts headed toward the temple brewery.

They passed several mud-brick buildings, mostly single story and used for trade and worship. The grander and more essential structures were fewer in number and coated with a mud-based plaster to give them a smooth appearance much like that of the Ziggurat itself. As they neared the temple bakeries, Ashmadu could smell the delicious fragrance of Bappir, which would be twice baked and later used in the production of Kas and Kas-du beers in the temple breweries on the other side of the complex. The priestesses who oversaw the baking and brewing were among the most respected in the temple and, due to their youth and beauty, a constant distraction to many of the male priests and tradesmen.

They passed through the grand plaza, which was overshadowed by the imposing Ziggurat, where the En would be speaking later. The En, clearly anxious, didn't even look up at the E-Abzu at its apex. In a few hours, the mostly empty plaza would be crowded with thousands of Sag-gig-ga from every part of Kur-gal, just like the night before. Already the city was bursting at the seams with the followers of Enki, and thousands more were still on their way. Ashmadu had observed several camps erected outside the walls of Eridu in anticipation of their arrival. The next eleven days would see the population triple in size, bringing an economic boom to the local merchants, tradesmen, and temple revenues that he was sure would please the Ninkum.

The En's office was located across from the Ziggurat. It was usually at this point that the En complained that he wished he had traveled by chariot. But the walk was good for him, and although Ashmadu would have preferred the convenience of a chariot himself, he encouraged the exercise.

Ahead of them, finally, was the door to their destination. A young Nig-aga stood outside, waiting for the En's arrival. From this distance, Ashmadu thought it might be Pirhum, a quiet boy who was very attentive and hardworking for his age. The En often referred to him as a young version of Ashmadu. Whenever the En was away, a Nig-aga would wait diligently outside his office to greet him no matter what time it was or how long he had to wait, rotating every four hours. Upon seeing the En approach at a distance, the Nig-aga opened the door and spoke a word to someone inside. Then he offered a deep bow and waited for them to enter. Through the main entry, another Nig-aga was waiting with a large cup of Kas-du next to a table with a bowl of water and towels. Breaking all protocol, the En took the cup and drained it before washing his face, hands, and feet.

"Our little secret," he said and smiled at the Nig-aga before walking through another door that led to the back entrance of his spacious office.

Such actions were the little things that endeared him to the Sag-gig-ga, and these Nig-aga were future temple initiates that were very impressionable. The En always believed in treating even the lowest with respect and often looked to them as practical choices for promotion due to their connection with the ordinary people.

The air was scented with spice and comfortable inside, despite the lack of windows for ventilation. Several stone and wood tables provided plenty of workspaces for the scribes, and the walls were carved to hold thousands of tablets. A large hearth was set into a stone frame on the east wall for warmth, and several chairs had been arranged opposite where the En's chair sat.

En Ipqu-aya sat down in a large ebony chair carved with the cuneiform script on one side and hieroglyphic symbols on the other. The chair had been a gift from the Praa of TaShemau some years ago to mark their friendship. TaShemau was a reliable trade partner, along with its sister kingdom TaMehu. Both realms were situated many leagues to the west, along the Aur river that emptied via a vast natural delta into the Great Sea. Ashmadu admired their strange symbolic writing and always wished he had the opportunity when he was younger to learn how to read it.

"Silim sum, En Ipqu-aya," Ugazum the Umbisag, master of scribes, greeted with a bow.

Ashmadu sat on an unremarkable chair just behind and to the right of the En and quietly observed, as was his usual duty.

"Silim sum, Umbisag Ugazum. Anything urgent?" The En stifled a yawn as he spoke. "Excuse me, I am very tired and need to rest a while so I can be fresh for this evening."

The Umbisag shrugged. "Nothing on a tablet that cannot wait, but the Ninkum is in the sitting room and has been waiting for you to return for some time now."

The En pressed his fingers into the flesh between his dark eyebrows and massaged the area vigorously.

"Is everything okay, En?" Ashmadu asked with concern. "Should I call for an Ashipu?"

The En looked up. "No, no, I will be fine, Ashmadu. Ugazum, send her in, but no one else today unless it is Enki himself come to pay me a visit!"

The Umbisag bowed again and smiled. "Yes, En Ipqu-aya." He turned and strode to the main door of the office.

Ashmadu always felt awkward and insignificant when he came to the temple with the En. Here he watched and listened in case the En missed anything and asked about it later. Ashmadu smiled to himself. At the Gi-par, *he* was in charge.

Moments later, the Umbisag announced Ninkum Shubure, temple treasurer, as she entered and bowed the En. "Silim sum, En Ipqu-aya."

Shubure was a pretty woman not long past her prime. She had an angular nose, dark eyes circled with pigment, and hair styled in traditional braiding to just below her shoulders. The Ninkum was known to wear on her neck, ears, and wrists jewelry made of silver and set with lapis lazuli. A multitude of bracelets on her arms and ankles clinked together like chimes when she moved through the room. From where he sat, Ashmadu could smell her fragrance, an intoxicating mix of cypress and myrrh that he heard often distracted the men around her. The oils that carried the aroma glistened on her long neck almost seductively.

Ashmadu was aware that she had never married and was popular with rich and powerful men. She was also known to use her charms to get what she wanted, or so it was said. Nevertheless, she was a shrewd and intelligent priestess, almost fanatically devoted to Enki, and, most importantly, she protected the temple treasury with frugal alacrity. The En had spoken highly of her on many occasions.

"Silim sum, Ninkum Shubure," the En replied with a conservative smile. "How may I be of service to you?" He waited for her to strut closer without offering her a seat, perhaps hoping their meeting would be a short one.

"I come with some concerns that I thought would be prudent to discuss with you." She ran a hand down her long, snug wool skirt, which was decorated with beads and shells and accentuated her shapely body. "I hope to gain some . . . clarity."

Ashmadu knew she would never attempt her sexual wiles on the En, who had made it clear when he appointed her as the Ninkum that such tactics would not be tolerated by him or the Sanga. Despite that, he openly admired how she amassed wealth for the temple without imposing onerous taxes on his people. Indeed, the citizens of Eridu rarely paid any taxes at all due to the temple's economic prosperity.

The En, taking her cue, emptied the room of staff and servants, except for Ashmadu. "Why haven't you brought your concerns to the Sanga, Shubure?" he asked once the others had left. "Wouldn't he be a better guide in these matters than I?"

The Ninkum raised an eyebrow at Ashmadu.

"Ashmadu is my personal house servant." The En waved away her concern. "He is bound to me."

She visibly relaxed and spoke more familiarly with the En. "Ipqu-aya, it's because of the Sanga's recent request that I am here."

The En directed her to a chair close to his and motioned for Ashmadu to pour them both Kas. "I can't imagine a situation in which the Sanga could be implicated in anything perverse in his personal life or temple business. He is beyond reproach!"

"This is not about his character or loyalty to the temple," Shubure replied with a smooth, calming tone. "He asked me to prepare a substantial reserve in the treasury for a 'special project,' as he called it, and would speak no more of it. I can only assume that you are aware of the nature of this project and can offer further understanding of how the reserve will be used."

"I'm sure it's for a building project," he said dismissively. "The roads could use some work, and there are places on the wall that need reinforcement."

Shubure snorted and looked at him askance. "You did not appoint me Ninkum because I am an idiot, Ipqu-aya."

The En looked up at her sharply.

"There have been no budgets or plans drawn up," she continued. "Nor has there been a special committee assigned to the task. You and I both know these things must happen before a reserve can be appropriated—except under one circumstance. Are we about to go to war?"

The En appeared taken aback. Had he underestimated her brilliance, or was he just playing her game? He sighed deeply. "We don't know yet. The

Eastern Tribes have reported sightings of the Mus-Lu, and we need to be better prepared this time. If it wasn't for Shatamurrim and his brave Ursagmuda, who knows what might have become of us only two years ago."

Ninkum Shubure smiled sweetly and batted her eyes at him. "See," she said, touching his hand softly, "that wasn't so difficult. It's always so much better when we can share the truth between us rather than leaving it up to my own active imagination!"

Ashmadu smiled on the inside. The En always allowed her to get away with some innocent flirtation. What old man didn't want to feel young again?

"I need not remind you to keep this to yourself," he said. "We don't need wild rumors disrupting our economy or stirring panic in the population. The Creation of Man ritual will continue as normal. I will not have my work impeded in this way, Shubure!"

She rose from her chair and bowed. "You have nothing to fear from me, Ipqu-aya. I am nothing if not Enki's servant at the pleasure of his En."

The En gave a brief nod in reply and watched her leave through the main door.

Beautiful and smart with coin, Ashmadu mused. She could be the perfect woman.

"Help me up, Ashmadu," the En said wearily as his Umbisag and Nig-aga reentered.

Ashmadu helped the En from the large chair and escorted him through the back hallway from his office to his private room. His master looked exhausted after the long walk and then the discussion with the Ninkum Shubure. He needed a nap to regain his strength before being summoned for the night's rituals.

In addition to their private residences outside of the temple, the En, the Sanga, and all of the Firsts had private chambers attached to their offices. Serving Enki often went late into the night—and sometimes began early in the morning. There were many weeks that went by in a year when Ashmadu barely saw the En because he chose to stay here rather than take a late night chariot ride back to the Gi-par. Chariots were rough on an old man's bones, Ashmadu knew from experience.

Ashmadu sat with the En until he fell asleep and then gathered a few blankets and made a comfortable space on the floor next to him. He was tired as well from looking after the En all day, and tonight would not be any shorter than the last. He drifted off to sleep knowing that the ritual in the evening would be the most exciting one yet, and from hints dropped by the En, perhaps legendary.

Chapter 6

Arwi-a

Irra's mind raced. Something was wrong, and it wasn't just the ugly day outside. He just didn't feel right. Whatever had happened in the Hall of Kurnugia had affected him deeply. Even the urgency of his duties had not dissuaded him from seeking solace in his bedroom at his residence in the city. He had tried to sleep to no avail, and so he paced, feeling as if something was tugging at his mind.

Arwi-a, Irra's wife, nervously offered suggestions to improve his condition. "Please, dear one, go see an Ashipu or let me bring one. You are not well." She followed him constantly, her long, blue wool dress swishing as she moved. "Drink some water," she said, extending a cup in her hand.

"No." He turned away. He was happy that she had not yet put on her jewelry. The clinking of all those bracelets and trinkets would have caused him even more distress.

"How about Kas? I'll get you a cup of Kas."

"I'm not thirsty," he said irritably.

"Would you like a sweet date?" Arwi-a asked. "That would make you feel better! Have one."

"No! I don't want any food or drink now. I just need to think."

His response only caused his wife to press further and try whatever she could to relieve his suffering. He knew she did it out of love, but he didn't care at the moment: misery ruled his mood.

"Would you like to lie down?"

"I can't sleep. Why do you think I'm up now?"

"Walk around then, husband," she said in a soothing tone. "I will keep you company."

"I don't need any company. I need peace!" Irra felt frantic, as if he were losing himself, who he was, his identity.

"What is it that will make you feel a little better?"

Arwi-a was very sympathetic, and any man would have appreciated the mothering, but Irra could not stand it for another minute. His mind was spinning. "Why can't you just leave me be?" he snapped at her harshly.

He had never spoken to her this way before. Nor had he felt so much anger toward her in the past. It was undeniable that she was upset at his behavior and worried, terribly worried, but that didn't matter when he was losing control of his sanity—he could feel it. He just wanted to be alone, and she was smothering him. He couldn't breathe.

"Dear one, I am only trying to help . . ." There was concern in her eyes, and hurt, from the things he had said to her, and how he had said them. He could see it clearly, but it didn't matter.

She continued to speak, but her voice was becoming gibberish, and even though she stood close to him, he couldn't understand her.

He felt like he was watching everything happen to someone else, as in a dream, but he could recognize the person as himself. He was saying bad things to his wife, and she followed him from place to place, crying now and desperate to see her husband right again. Then he was back in himself once more, and he could feel the rage, confusion, and uncertainty coursing through his body.

He didn't know what to do or what to think. How could he stop this? He felt the fury mounting again, far stronger this time. He turned away, and this time Arwi-a tried to take his hand sympathetically, but he jerked it away.

How dare she touch him!

The rage and fear consumed him, then words unbidden came from him that, at first, he did not comprehend: "Teloch i zonrensg vomsarg!" And without thought or will he grabbed Arwi-a by the head and snapped her neck in one smooth motion.

Dead.

Her braided brown hair fell to her shoulders from where she'd had it tied atop her head, and her body twitched with the spasms of nerves before going limp in Irra's steady arms. The bitch was dead and would never aggravate him again. He dropped her body to the floor, and feelings of relief flooded through him.

He was grateful for the quiet in the room again. But it was too quiet—so quiet it was deafening.

Then the shock and horror of the sudden act of violence sent his mind reeling. "What have I done?" he screamed to the empty bedchamber. "Enki! Is this really happening? Arwi-a!"

Tears blurred his vision, and he sank to the floor, holding her body close to him as he wept. Cruel laughter echoed in his head, and the strange words that he had spoken gained clarity, *Death is delivered unto every one of you.*

Irra did not feel lucid. Everything that had just happened seemed like a terrifying nightmare. It could not be real, could it? His wife lay dead in his arms with a broken neck. Her eyes remained open, staring into eternity with a look of disbelief that seemed to slowly morph into the unblinking gaze of accusation. In her last second of life, she knew his crime.

There was a loud knock at the door to his bedchamber.

"Master! Is everything okay? Do you need help?" It was one of their house servants.

What would he do now? He would be humiliated, stripped of his office, and likely thrown into the river by his own son. His son! How could he have done this to the mother of his son? He loved her so much!

Then there was heat rising inside him again. Anger.

Why had she been so persistent with him? Why had she pushed him so? She had brought her own death upon herself! He wailed with sadness, regret, and anger. He was losing his mind.

The banging at the door became more insistent.

"Master! I will break down the door!"

There were others outside the door now. Irra had forgotten about the servants. He would not be undone by them. They would have to die, as well.

He dropped his wife to the floor, with no more care than a bag of harvested grain, then rose and walked calmly to the pounding door.

~~~

Ashmadu sat in his usual place at the top of the Ziggurat. He knew little of what the En was planning this night and expected that the events of the evening would be as much a surprise to him as they would be for the devotees in the plaza below. Since the En had spent most of his preparation time with his priests at the temple and had not planned an extensive preamble, Ashmadu had been left in the unusual position of having no idea what his master was going to do next.

Earlier, the En seemed nervous about the proceedings. All his energy had gone into the formation of his design, and it showed in the tension on his face. Soon enough he would have time to rest. After tonight, he would not be expected to preside over the nightly rituals until the last evening of the celebrations. The lesser priests would handle them and most of the other requirements during the day.

Tonight was expected to be uniquely special.

Having worked with his Suba, stone priests, for weeks in advance and using advice from the Anunnaki, the En was going to perform a spectacular feat that everyone would remember for the rest of their lives. That was all Ashmadu knew. The En was apprehensive about actually succeeding, but the Anunnaki had assured him that it was a matter of faith, something that his master always seem to have in abundance.

En Ipqu-aya stood at the entrance of the E-Abzu for the second night quietly looking over the hushed masses before descending the stairway to the altar under the arches. Just as the previous night, he was in his full regalia, and he held his staff high when he began to speak.

"Enki has bestowed a great gift upon his people tonight!" he announced to the crowd. "A reprieve from the struggles bestowed upon mankind by the gods? No! Tonight you will live as the gods and know their pleasure!"

The throngs roared their approval. For what, they did not know, and neither did Ashmadu, but it sounded extraordinary. The En enjoyed the cheers for a moment before he motioned for them all to quiet once more. Then he raised his staff high again and began to chant.

The dozens of Suba priests standing on the east and west terraces bolstered his chant, and a mild tremor reverberated from beneath the plaza, causing the thousands on hand to stir nervously. The En's chanting became more persistent and echoed off the surrounding buildings, and the ground shook again. This time, the people in the crowd hastily separated as thousands of shoulder-width clay mounds pushed through the hard-packed soil at their feet. Hundreds of priests, deliberately stationed among the masses in the plaza, urged the crowd to remain calm.

En Ipqu-aya's chanting had become frantic as he continued to hold his staff aloft, thrusting it forward vigorously in time with his incantation. Ashmadu had never seen his master in this state, and he began to worry. Then, when the earth shook once more, the En shouted, "Zi, Zi, Zi!" and the mounds on the ground grew.

Ashmadu was surprised to see the En falter for just a moment while he conjured. His master was always so careful and prepared that it was highly unusual for him to stumble when he spoke, especially during an invocation. Whatever had happened passed quickly, and the En's voice became strong and confident again, determined.

No one else seemed to notice, and Ashmadu relaxed but continued to keep a close eye on the En. *Perhaps it was nothing*, he thought, *He's just exhausted.*

When he glanced down at the plaza, Ashmadu was shocked to see that the dirt mounds had grown to man-sized columns and had begun to sprout limbs. Moments later, standing among the throngs in the massive courtyard were thousands of earthen forms in the shape of thick-bodied humans.

Tearing his gaze away from the clay statues, Ashmadu looked back up to the En. He was standing with his arms far apart and with his face looking up into the dark heavens.

"Ninmah! Grant me your breath of life!" he shouted, and then flung his arms forward violently.

From the north, there was the peal of thunder. It was far out beyond the walls of the city, above the irrigated crops, but so loud that it felt right on top of them. There were frightened screams from the crowd below and then a nervous silence. Something was coming.

The first sign was the muffled boom when it hit the north wall, and then there was a flurry of leaves, branches, and linens that had not been brought in for the night. It was all pitched high into the air and flung about wildly between the north wall and the plaza as the wind raced forward. Then abruptly, everything was still, and the leaves, dust, and linens casually floated back toward the ground. It was like an inhalation.

The concussion of wind that came down from the sky was so sudden and violent that it cast every living soul to the ground where they stood. It lasted but a second, and even though Ashmadu had not been directly under it he felt the surge from the updraft and nearly tumbled down the high stairway.

Recovering quickly, Ashmadu looked down again at the plaza and stared in disbelief; the earthen statues were *moving*. Others in the plaza had noticed as well, and there were gasps of surprise and screams of shock.

"Do not be afraid!" En Ipqu-aya shouted to the people below. "These are gifts from your god, Enki. The Sahar-nitah! Until dawn they are yours to command! They will serve you in whatever fashion you desire—except violence. Once the light of morning appears above the horizon, they will crumble to dust and be no more. Enjoy the gift of our god. Have them fetch your Kas or attend to your labors. They will serve you as we serve our gods!"

The previously fearful masses erupted in ecstatic cheers. Everyone in the plaza had their own Sahar-nitah to serve them until dawn. Ashmadu watched as some exited the plaza with their golems in tow, no doubt bound for their workshops, but the majority compelled their helpers to bring food and drink from servers around the plaza. The people appeared to enjoy the ability to control another creature in service to their own needs.

Ashmadu tore his eyes from the incredible scene just in time to see the En slouched in the archway, propped up only by the strength of his staff and the stone altar.

He rushed over to help his master. "Are you unwell, En?" he asked with concern.

En Ipqu-aya wearily looked up at Ashmadu and smiled. "Just very tired. That took more out of me than I expected. Especially that last part."

Ashmadu helped him slowly climb the stairs back into the E-Abzu and set him in the elevated stone chair of his station so he could see the revelers below. Then he brought him a cup of Kas and a blanket.

The En gratefully sipped the Kas while he watched the people in the plaza with their Sahar-nitah. "I miss Terrikan," he confided to Ashmadu. "He would have been impressed with what we accomplished here tonight, even being an Anunnaki!"

Ashmadu sat down in a small chair against the wall. "I'm sure he will enjoy hearing about it when he returns," he said and then thought about the Nam-en's sick wife. The En quietly nodded his agreement.

Master and servant sat quietly together for some time listening to the revelry below. It was Ashmadu who finally broke the silence. "May I ask a question, En Ipqu-aya? If you're not too tired. It's about the Anunnaki."

"Of course, Ashmadu," the En replied graciously. "I always welcome your curiosity."

Ashmadu thought a moment. He wanted to be sure to form his words correctly to avoid being misunderstood. His question could be viewed as controversial, although he doubted that the En would take it that way, regardless of how it came out. "I know the stories of the Anunnaki that have been taught to me since I was a child, but as your humble house servant, I have heard things that have challenged my beliefs. So I must ask, what is the true nature of the Anunnaki? Are they truly the offspring of our Lord Enki? The Nam-en speaks of himself as an Atlantean and accepts the role of Anunnaki, but he also speaks of his home as the Emerald Isle and a city called Atlantis in *this* world—not the Abzu where our gods dwell."

The En stared at Ashmadu for a long moment before smiling warmly. "The Anunnaki must be considered as they are to the Sag-gig-ga, which is the teaching I have endeavored to pass along to all of Enki's followers as his earthly representative. But I will tell you this, my old friend—the Anunnaki are interpreted by many different people in many different ways. This world is far larger and more full of wonder than you could ever dream. It makes me feel small, in truth, and the knowledge they have given me sometimes burns at my soul."

The En paused a moment to scratch his long white beard thoughtfully. "Nam-en Terrikan told me once to look at the stars and tell him what I saw. I told him that the stars were made of Lil and for the pleasure of the gods. He laughed and asked me to imagine a world where every star was a sun like our own with worlds like ours that circled many of them. At the time, I was sure what he said was a farce, and we both laughed, but looking back, I wonder if he was trying to carefully pass along some wisdom about our true insignificance in the incomprehensible vastness of the Primeval Sea."

Ashmadu was stunned. What he thought had been a simple question with a simple answer would forever change the way he viewed the world around him, especially the stars.

The En must have seen the conflict in his expression. "Fear not, Ashmadu, there is much we will never understand, and we accept the life of a Sag-gig-ga. We have joy, love, laughter, and no shortage of Kas!" He laughed, and Ashmadu couldn't help but laugh with him.

Let all the Abgals, Ens, and Zi-ik-ru-um worry about wisdom and the hereafter, Ashmadu thought. He would console himself with the simple pleasures of life.

The En was old, and so was Ashmadu. There would not be too many more years to enjoy moments like this. His master already showed signs of aging, lately with his absentmindedness, which came and went. Ashmadu thought he had done a pretty good job of concealing those moments so far. And, fortunately, they mostly occurred in the mornings and evenings, when the En was at home.

Ashmadu would protect the En for as long as he could from anything that threatened his well-being. He owed the man that and more. His life would have been much different had the En never brought him into his household and treated him with respect. They had known each other from his years as a Subur, slave, at the temple when the En had been just a priest.

His master had noticed his strong work ethic and taken a liking to him long before he became the En. And he had made sure Ashmadu had a place in his household when he ascended as the ruler of Eridu. After Ashmadu was released from his slave service, he decided to stay with En Ipqu-aya as a paid servant. The En was a kind master to him and never allowed him to be mistreated. Ashmadu was content and beneficially provided everything he needed.

What more could he ask?

Moreover, the En had been a father figure to him in many ways while Ashmadu was younger and a friend as he grew older. They shared a friendship through their experiences together that would last until their last day. That unbreakable bond, based on trust, kindness, and affection, had been built on decades of unashamed reliance on each other.

Still seated in the elevated chair, the En could be seen by the people in the plaza below. Spontaneously, the celebrating crowd began to chant, "En-Ki, En-Ki, En-Ki!" The chant grew louder as more people joined in.

The En appeared to bask in the adulations for a little while before waving and stepping down from the chair. He was undoubtedly happy that he could give this gift to his people. Several dozen Suba priests and priestesses had helped him prepare the Miracle of the Sahar-nitah, as it would become known, and Ashmadu could see he was proud of all their hard work. Removing the cylindrical Sañdul from his master's weary head, he pretended not to notice the tears that glistened in his master's eyes. It was a moving moment that he would remember for the rest of his life.

Chapter 7

Sahar-nitah

𒈗𒃶𒊏𒉿𒈗

En Ipqu-aya was sleeping in later than usual given the extraordinary efforts of his performance the night before when he conjured the Sahar-nitah. Always anticipating his masters every need, Ashmadu had already set the small table in the En's bedchamber with his favorite breakfast—a bowl of pottage with a drizzle of honey and chunks of fresh dates from the orchard. He hoped the En felt good today after his success. Sometimes the stack of tablets the Sanga left on his table each morning took away much of his enthusiasm.

After setting the En's sandals at his bedside, Ashmadu prepared a large bowl of fresh water for him to bathe his face and a split reed to clean his teeth when he finally awoke. Lastly, he poured a cup of sweet Kas-du and placed it on the En's breakfast table. As he left the bedchamber, Ashmadu absently wondered why the Sanga was so late with his tablets this morning.

Less than an hour later, he heard the En calling out to him. "Ashmadu! Ashmadu, come in here please!"

Ashmadu was nearby and hurried into the bedchamber without knocking. This was not unusual, considering that he oversaw all of En Ipqu-aya's household affairs and managed the small staff of Subur. Ashmadu had once been a Subur himself, a slave in service to the temple. His parents had sold him to the temple at a young age to pay their debts, and then they had moved away to another city. He had not seen or heard from his parents since, but now was not the time to contemplate the past.

"How can I be of service, En?" he respectfully asked with a bow.

The En was circling the sizeable wooden breakfast table. "I don't see the Sanga's tablets here this morning. Please bring them."

Ashmadu was surprised at the request. "I apologize, En, but the Sanga has not yet arrived."

The En stopped and stared for a moment in surprise. "The Sanga has been leaving tablets for me every morning without fail for the better part of two decades, usually prior to me getting out of bed—to the Sanga's eternal irritation." He began to pace. "Irra has never been absent without sending a message first. This is highly unusual, don't you think, Ashmadu? Send a Nig-aga to see that he is well. He did not attend the ritual last night either, and I'm becoming concerned."

"I will do so immediately," Ashmadu replied and hurried from the room.

Upon finding the young Nig-aga Pirhum in the kitchen, Ashmadu sent him running to the Sanga's home with all haste. The Sanga did not live far away, and Ashmadu expected the boy would not take long running there and back. In the meantime, Ashmadu returned to the En's chambers to keep him calm until Pirhum returned with any news.

Ashmadu found the En eating his breakfast alone and in silence. He could tell his master was deeply worried about the Sanga. In their old age the two of them often bickered and snapped about insignificant things, but he knew they loved and respected each other no matter their petty differences.

The En looked up from his breakfast. "If he had fallen ill, surely his wife would have sent word, and if something violent had occurred to him, the Aga-us would have notified me immediately."

The En was known to levy strict punishments against those who committed a violent crime in Eridu, so it was a rare thing indeed if someone was assaulted, let alone murdered in his city. Although the recent string of bloodshed at an inn near the trade district had everyone in the temple on edge.

Ashmadu feared that his master would work himself into a frenzy, so he attempted to minimize the En's fears. "The Sanga probably just drank too much during the celebrations and slept in this morning."

In truth, Ashmadu knew this was absurd because he had rarely seen the Sanga drink in the many years he had known him. Better to just wait and hear what the Nig-aga had to say when he returned. Continued speculation would only heighten the En's anxiety further, and there was certainly no need for that, particularly since there was probably an innocent explanation for the Sanga's absence.

In the meantime, Ashmadu helped Ipqu-aya wash and dress. Since there were no windows for ventilation in the mud-brick home, they climbed to the top of the third story and onto the roof so the En could breathe the crisp morning air. The En's Gi-par was the only residence on the temple grounds not attached to an office. From the high vantage point, they could see most of the buildings beyond the temple complex all the way to the city walls to the west.

Most notable in their line of vision was the central street market that serpentined through the trade district. The market was busy as always, and the streets around it were already congested with merchants, tradesmen, and patrons. At this distance, the shapes were not clear, and the men certainly couldn't recognize anyone they knew, but many of the forms moving about were unusually familiar.

"Do you see those dark shapes moving in the streets?" the En asked Ashmadu.

As he studied them, Ashmadu realized that the strange shapes were more substantial than the people around them. They looked almost identical to each other and moved with the same slow mannerisms.

Before he could answer, the En whispered, "It can't be . . ." and made a quick gesture followed by an incomprehensible utterance to cast a spell.

Ashmadu was becoming concerned by the way the En was reacting to the dark shapes. "What is it, Master?"

The En had completed his spell and was looking through the circle formed by his hands and fingers. "Enki, how is this possible? Look for yourself, Ashmadu." He held his hands out to the side without breaking the circle so that Ashmadu could peer through them.

The image in the circle was magnified, so Ashmadu could see the market as clearly as if he were standing at the edge of it. Then he saw the dark shapes close-up.

"Master, are those not the Sahar-nitah that you summoned last night?" he asked while slowly moving the En's hands so he could see other parts of the city.

"They are," the En confirmed, "and they should no longer be animated. I expected every one of them to have crumbled to dust by dawn."

Ashmadu stepped back, and the En retracted his hands to look through them again himself.

"Why are they still here?" Ashmadu asked.

En Ipqu-aya seemed at a loss for what to say. "Perhaps the spell lasted longer than I calculated, or maybe Enki intervened to extend the gift to his followers. The truth is, I don't know."

The En had told Ashmadu many times that Enki cared little for his worshippers and it was unlikely that the god had extended his hand for their comfort. Whatever the reason, it felt very wrong.

"I will summon the Suba priests when I return to my office," the En said. "In the meantime, let's observe the constructs and their interaction with their masters and the people around them." He turned to Ashmadu. "Make a circle with your hands like I did."

Ashmadu did as he was instructed, and with a few short words, the En cast a spell to magnify the space between the hands. Now both men could see the city close-up.

For a while, they watched the Sahar-nitah in silence.

Then Ashmadu made an observation. "It seems that many of them have been sent on tasks that do not require direct supervision—to the market to buy dates and bread, or to the fields outside the city to deliver tools, or even navigating the small boats in the canals to transport goods."

The En nodded in agreement. "These are tasks that require higher-level thinking. Astounding! The spell that I cast last night was intended to summon the elementals for a short period of time and do only the most elementary tasks, like retrieving Kas or carrying a drunken master home to bed."

The reed mat that covered the opening to the roof stairs suddenly flipped open, and Ashmadu turned to see Pirhum poking his head through the opening. Ashmadu quickly waved for the slave to join him and the En on the rooftop.

Out of breath, the Nig-aga bowed to the En. He had apparently run the whole way back from the Sanga's house. "En, the Sanga did not answer his door. I stayed for a while in case he or his wife might return soon, but no one arrived, and the servants were away."

The concern deepened in Ipqu-aya's eyes. "Find Irra's son—you know him, he has been to this house many times—and summon him here. Oh, and Pirhum, find him no matter what and don't take no for an answer. Tell him I demand it, if you must, and he will come."

"Of course, En. I will not return without him." Pirhum bowed again before departing the rooftop at nearly a sprint.

Ashmadu knew that Shatamurrim would come just because the En had asked him to, no matter the reason. Together, they watched the market for a while longer before returning to the En's private chambers downstairs.

After a few moments of pacing, the En announced, "I must summon my Suba now. Ashmadu, please send Shatamurrim to my office when the Nig-aga returns with him. I can't just stay here and pace."

"I will bring him myself, En Ipqu-aya," Ashmadu assured his master.

The En placed a hand lightly on Ashmadu's cheek and looked at him as a father might look at his son. "I am so grateful that I have you. Never forget that." Without waiting for a reply, the En quickly departed the Gi-par.

As Ashmadu stood quietly where the En had left him, he felt like a young child again and smiled in gratitude.

~~~

The room smelled musty, like an ancient tomb just opened, and it reminded Namzu of when he had been an initiate plying the dim corridors between the stone shelves in search of knowledge. That was the last time he could remember setting foot inside the temple library.

He stroked his long, graying beard and wondered where he should start. His eyes followed the floor-to-ceiling shelves up three levels of balconies that formed the interior perimeter of the long room. There must have been tens—no, *hundreds*—of thousands of tablets in the massive chamber. This was a task that would require the help of a Lukur. Lukurs were chaste priestesses that were considered "clean" and "pure," their purpose being the accumulation of knowledge without the distractions of earthly desires. They were the teachers in charge of new initiates to the temple. And even after so many years, Namzu remembered well the sting of their tongues and, worse, the crack of their canes when he neglected his studies.

As he walked the corridor that led through the center of the library, Namzu searched the aisles formed by shelving on either side for a Lukur that might be close at hand. About halfway down the hall, he found one—a young woman in a long white Gada-bar-tug that covered her form loosely from neck to ankles.

The scuff of his boots on the stone floor caught her attention, and she turned to greet him. "Silim sum, First Usgadi, how may I help you?"

She was pretty and doe-eyed, with dark hair cropped in the appropriate style of a lady of the temple. For a moment Namzu felt sad for her. She was a Lukur and would never feel the touch of a man. Perhaps he was really just feeling sorry for himself. There was no end to the things he could imagine doing with such a beauty . . .

Namzu pulled himself from his lurid thoughts. "Silim sum, Lukur. I am surprised you know who I am."

She offered an alluring smile. "Of course, First Usgadi. You wear the chain of your office around your neck. How could I miss it?"

Embarrassed—and hoping it didn't show—he fumbled for one of the tablets in his side pack and showed her the symbols he had drawn upon it. "I'm looking for any reference to these symbols. I need to translate them, and based on what an Anunnaki told me, I believe the most ancient sources you have here might be the best place to start."

Her eyes lit up at the mention of the Anunnaki, and she smiled again, revealing a pair of dimples. "You know the Anunnaki?" she asked excitedly.

"Just Abgal Ferulianreg. He is helping me with an investigation."

He knew it was an exaggeration, but he couldn't disappoint her. He wanted to see her smile again.

Her eyes widened in surprise. "An Abgal! You have met an Anunnaki Abgal? You must tell me everything about him! Please sit here with me and tell me of this Abgal."

She took his free hand and led him to a stone bench at the end of the row of shelves. Namzu didn't resist and forgot about the clay tablet in his hand as he described the Abgal in every detail he could remember. She sat close, and he lost himself in the excitement in her eyes and the smile that lit up her face. He hadn't been so happy to please a woman in years, and by the time he heard the approach of heavy footsteps, it was too late.

Thwack!

Something impacted with the wall above his head, and he jumped just as the young Lukur stifled a startled scream. They looked up in unison to see the stern visage of the First Lukur standing over them.

"I am encouraged to see that you still have the initiate's flinch, Namzu." She turned her gaze toward the pretty Lukur. "Go about your business, Amare. I will speak to you later."

Her name was Amare. He would remember that.

The Lukur priestess rose from the bench with a dejected look on her pretty face and hurried away, stealing a quick glance back at him before disappearing around the corner of the bookcase at the end of the aisle.

"So, Namzu, shall I sit with you now so that you may complete your tale?" Her bland tone only deepened his chagrin. "It sounded quite riveting."

The First Lukur was the oldest woman he had ever seen. He knew her well enough, though. She had been one of his strictest teachers, and he often saw her when the Zi-ik-ru-um convened each month. Sabum had been a student of hers as well, and if Namzu had allowed it, his Second would have ripped her stinging tongue from her head years ago.

"I am here on an urgent matter," Namzu began.

"Yes, I could see that," she interrupted sharply, her arms crossed over her white Gada-bar-tug with gold trim.

Namzu did his best to control his tone. He knew she was probably the only one at the temple library with the knowledge to help him find what he needed. He had just been . . . distracted. "First Lukur Ninedinni," he said with as much respect as he could muster, "this is important." He held up the tablet still in his hand.

Ignoring the tablet, she tapped the cane on her palm. "And where is your sidekick, Sabum? He must be sniffing around here somewhere."

Namzu sighed. "It is just me here today, Ninedinni."

"Well, make sure you tell him I still have my tongue!" She slapped the rod on her palm for effect. "Yes, I remember his insolence after all these years."

"Please, Ninedinni. I need to know if you can help me with this." He held the tablet up again.

She took it dismissively with a dramatic *harrumph* and reluctantly studied it. A moment later, her stern face turned as hard as a stone. "Where did this come from?" she whispered, never letting her eyes leave the tablet.

"I can't tell you exactly, but it is part of an investigation. The man who wrote them is dead, so it may be irrelevant. They were scrawled like graffiti on a wall. I am just trying to tie up some loose ends." That was not exactly the truth, but she didn't need to know more than what it would take to help him.

"You say a dead man wrote these symbols? No *man* should be writing them. Namzu, you should not have even *copied* them."

"Can you translate them? Do you know what they mean?"

"No, I cannot translate the symbols, but I do know what they are. Come with me."

Namzu followed the First Lukur down the corridor and wondered if he would ever see the pretty smile of Amare again.

Chapter 8

Fallen

𒀭𒁁𒌋𒈤𒇲

Irra was disposing of his wife's body, piece by bloody piece, in the smoldering hearth that Arwi-a once used for cooking when someone banged on the front door.

"Sanga! Arwi-a! I am the Nig-aga Pirhum sent by the En. Please answer if you are home!"

Irra ignored the call and continued with the task at hand. There was no way he could answer the door covered in blood. He had already hidden the servants, and if there was time later, he would feed them to the hearth as well. Irra's guilt and sorrow were gone now, replaced by a need for self-preservation, and he took to the task at hand with no remorse.

The stench of burning flesh was intoxicating, but he knew that he would have to do something about that before the neighbors, passersby in the street, or the Nig-aga at the door noticed and raised the alarm. He cast a quick spell to clear the air and then placed more linen on the floor to soak up the blood.

After a long while, the knocking finally ceased, and there was silence throughout the house again. Irra would have to come up with a story to explain his absence from the ritual the night before and again this morning when he should have dropped off tablets at the En's home. He could feign illness or, better, the death of a friend of the family. It didn't matter. Once he was finished disposing of the woman, he would go to the temple and ferment a story that the En would believe. It shouldn't be too hard, considering the En trusted him completely.

Disposing of a human body was no easy task. First, Irra defleshed the corpse of Arwi-a, removed all of her organs, and pounded most of the bones into smaller shards and fragments. As he worked, Irra consumed as much of the choicest parts as he could during the night and even regurgitated twice to eat more, but the rest had to be burned. The blood and gristle that had fallen on the floor he cleaned with linens, creating thick crimson swirls on the mud-brick pavers before soaking the fabric through. He had no time to clean up all the blood. Much of it had dried already anyway, making it more difficult to remove. He would do a more thorough job later when he returned in the evening. The desecrated linens he threw in an empty basket inside the kitchen storeroom, where earlier he stuffed the disfigured servants' bodies into grain baskets.

His bloody work done, for now, Irra washed and donned his most traditional kilt and tunic of neutral color before departing for the temple. He left the house in good order except for the kitchen. What a shame it would be to just burn it down, but perhaps that would be the best way to cover his activity. It would merely be regarded as a tragic kitchen accident that had taken the lives of the Sanga's wife and her servants if he arranged it properly. If he decided not to burn it, he would have to remove the symbols written in blood on the kitchen wall. They already served their purpose anyway. Irra would deal with that when he returned later.

Although the rain stopped the day before, the streets were still damp. Small puddles occupied shallow depressions where the pavers were broken or worn. The stagnant air, still thick with humidity, was interrupted only occasionally by the cool summer breeze that furled his tunic, making him wish he had worn a long coat. The temple wasn't very far, and had he cared about such things, he might have considered it a pleasant day for a walk.

It was not yet noon, but the thoroughfare was busy with Sag-gig-ga going about their business, and any that he passed called out a blessing. He wanted to tear them all to pieces for their pious loyalty to the thick chain of office around his neck. *It could be worn by anyone,* he thought, *and they would still scrape and bow.* Irra restrained himself from his impulses and smiled and nodded in return. For the first time in a very long time, he had a more significant role to play, and he had to be careful not to squander the opportunity. He noted with some satisfaction that many Sahar-nitah were wandering the streets and wondered if the En might be pulling his beard out trying to figure out why. In all likelihood, the En was confused about why his creations had not already crumbled to dust and frantic that he was unable to contact his Sanga. Such a fool, Irra thought—so willing to trust blindly in his beliefs and those who served him.

After passing through the open gates of the temple grounds, he was pleased that no state of alarm had been called and everything seemed routine. The guards flanking the entryway stood at attention in their thick leather skirts and caps, bowing sharply when he went through while others kept watch more informally atop the decorated walls. Priests from every discipline talked casually as they strode around the complex and several approached him to speak, but he waved them away while trying to avoid eye contact that might be misconstrued as an invitation for conversation.

The Ziggurat was a structure he held in particular contempt. The idiots built them in every city-state, some larger than others, as a way of elevating a platform that would bring them closer to the gods. Maybe they thought the gods would be more likely to notice their leader standing atop a pile of mud bricks. The truth was the gods didn't care much what the Sag-gig-ga did as long as they continued with their blind adulation. It made him want to spit in disgust, but that would likely have garnered the type of attention he needed to avoid right now.

Irra entered the main temple complex and was immediately flanked by a dozen scribes and initiates who were apparently waiting for him, and they immediately began asking questions. Annoyed, Irra sent them away with a sharp command and a curt wave of his hand. They looked surprised and unsure of what to do next when he left them behind. Why he would tolerate these fools around him all day was beyond him.

When he arrived at the En's private office, where only a Nig-aga was present, Irra sat in one of the comfortable chairs without invitation and sent the servant away. He would wait for the En to eventually return to his office and then try to create an opportunity to speak with him alone.

Irra had been here many times, but he never paid much attention to the austere interior. The office was large and sparse, with little more than a few tables, chairs, and floor rugs scattered around the room. It hardly appeared to be an office worthy of the most influential man in Kur-gal. Even the mud bricks that formed the walls of the room were unadorned with any sort of decoration. The only item worth noting was the ornately carved wooden guzza that the En sat upon when he received official visitors. It was a gift from the Praa of TeShemau, another stone-stacking culture. At least they had an appreciation for proper embellishment. Why hadn't the En decorated his office more appropriately? It was the very room where he conducted state business. Knowing how Ipqu-aya was, he was probably trying to serve as a frugal example, Irra scoffed.

Too bad Ipqu-aya was so dedicated to his god and devoted to his people. There was so much potential in the man, and he squandered his power on light shows, serving girls, and clay men. With followers in the thousands spread out all over Kur-gal, he could have easily dominated the northern cities and brought the entire country under his rule. Power of that kind could have helped him conquer the Ugarit kingdoms to the west and the kingdoms on the edges of the Glass Sea to the east. *It doesn't matter,* Irra thought. He would never attain those heights of glory either, and he didn't care.

Without announcement, the En rushed into the room. "Irra! I've been so worried about you! Where have you been? Why weren't you at the ritual last night? Are you okay?"

Irra stood and offered a smile. He was pleased the En was by himself. "Everything is fine, Ipqu-aya. I was distracted by the death of a family friend and felt compelled to comfort the relatives. I should have sent word. I am so sorry to distress you, my old friend."

The En lowered himself into a wooden chair cushioned with stuffed pillows and breathed a sigh of relief. "Please do not put me through that again, Irra. I was so concerned that I sent a Nig-aga to your home, and when he couldn't find you there, I sent him for your son."

"My son?" Irra replied thoughtfully as he took a seat near the En. "Oh yes, Shatamurrim. He will be alarmed, of course, but once I explain the circumstance, he will probably find humor in the whole misunderstanding."

"Yes, yes. I am sure you are right, Irra." The En placed his hand over Irra's and squeezed tightly. "As much as I sometimes despise the carts of tablets you leave me with every morning, I know you're just doing your job, and the truth is I rely heavily on my exceedingly diligent Sanga to administer this massive beast of a temple complex. And more importantly, I worry about the well-being of my friend."

"Never will you worry again, Ipqu-aya, as I will be sure to keep you advised of my situation from this moment forward. Now about those tablets—"

The En had become very pale and was no longer looking at him.

"Ipqu-aya? En? Are you not well?"

He watched while the En began to sway in his seat. He reached out to Irra, and as he attempted to stand, his eyes crossed and he crumpled to the floor, releasing a low groan before falling unconscious.

Irra sat motionless throughout the whole ordeal, never once making any effort to assist the En. Finally, he stood and stepped over the unconscious body of his friend. "Fool," he uttered in disgust.

Just then, Ashmadu entered the office with Irra's son, Shatamurrim, and stopped dead in the doorway. "What happened?" Ashmadu exclaimed when he saw the En on the floor with the Sanga standing over him.

"He collapsed just before you arrived. There was nothing I could do to help him, so I was going to find an Ashipu. Stay with him, Ashmadu. I will return swiftly with help." He tried to make his voice sound panicked and desperate. He thought he did a pretty good job. While they hurried over to check on the En, unmoving on the floor, Irra made his way around them and toward the door.

He left the room at a trot to find a healer, then slowed to a walk as soon as he was a few steps down the corridor. There was a Nig-aga in the hall, and Irra grabbed him roughly. "Get an Ashipu and bring him here quickly! The En has fallen ill and needs immediate help!" He let go of the frightened servant, who ran off as fast as his legs would carry him.

Irra returned to the room to see Ashmadu and Shatamurrim kneeling over Ipqu-aya. "The Ashipu are on their way," he announced between heavy breaths. "Is he alive?"

Ashmadu was gently shaking the fallen En and encouraging him with soothing words. "Wake up, En. Please wake up. I am here with you now, and help is coming."

There was no response from En Ipqu-aya, although there was a definitive twitch on the right side of his face that had not been present before. With tears in his eyes, Ashmadu asked Shatamurrim to retrieve a pillow and blanket to make the En more comfortable.

Shatamurrim grabbed a pillow from a chair and a blanket from a nearby table and helped Ashmadu reposition the En while they awaited the Ashipu. After what seemed like hours, but was in reality only minutes, the Nig-aga returned with two Ashipu priests. They rushed to the En and began chanting over his quiet body.

Shatamurrim, still anxious about his father's well-being, whispered, "Are you okay, Father? Ashmadu said the En was distressed about your health. Perhaps his fears were misplaced."

Irra's son was a lean, muscular young man with long, well-oiled black hair and attractive masculine features that garnered frequent attention from the young ladies. He was always in his black uniform—leather tunic, boots, vambraces, and a thick leather skirt reinforced with metal plates—a striking figure. And when he smiled, it was warm and inviting, inspiring trust. The boy was almost perfect.

Irra embraced his son. "All is well with me. It was just a simple misunderstanding. Our worries are now with the En."

After some time, Ipqu-aya's eyes opened—to the relief of nearly everyone in the room. He tried to speak but managed only a blubbering sound unintelligible to any of them. The Ashipu, concerned with the En's condition, recommended that they take him to the temple infirmary for further evaluation. Irra agreed, and the priests carried the En through the office door on a hastily made litter. Ashmadu followed.

"Thank you for coming," Irra told his son, "but as you can see, I am fine, and I must manage the affairs of the temple until the En recovers. I will send word to you on his situation later."

"Very well, Father. Give my love to my mother, and if you need anything, send for me."

The two embraced again before Shatamurrim left to follow Ashmadu to the infirmary.

He watched his son leave and considered how formidable the boy might be if he made himself a nuisance. Shatamurrim had grown to be a talented and robust warrior without any direct influence from Irra or the En and gained the high rank of Sar within the military of Eridu at a young age. Shatamurrim was not only physically gifted but intellectually without peer when it came to military strategy and the deployment his Ursagmuda to effectively defend the city. Twice in the past several years, he proved his brilliance as a military leader by protecting the city from invaders and driving them away. He even earned the distinguished Honor of Enki, the highest award bestowed for valor. Shatamurrim was the pride of his mother, his Ursagmuda, and the whole of Eridu.

Irra could spare no time for idle thoughts now. When the word got out about the En's sudden collapse, there would be fear and confusion. Everyone would be looking for him to take command of the temple and rule the city until the En recovered. At least they would assume he would improve. But eighty-year-old men died every day of living too long. Why should the En be any different? It was time for a few changes in this city anyway, and Irra had a few ideas. He unveiled a wolfish grin to the empty room.

Chapter 9

The Library

Why don't I know about this place?" Namzu asked as he followed Ninedinni through the dark, winding corridor beneath the temple library.

"The last time you were in the library, you were an initiate. Do you think we would allow an initiate to know where we kept our most sacred and protected writings? Only the Zi-ik-ru-um, the Firsts, the Sanga, the En, and, of course, the Anunnaki are allowed to know of this place."

Their voices echoed eerily in the narrow subterranean passage, and the light globes they carried cast the only light in the darkness. Ninedinni's lanky figure moved faster than Namzu would have expected, considering her advanced age, and at times he had to hurry to keep up.

"That still doesn't answer my question. I have been a First for many years, yet I don't know about any of this."

They passed several side passages and descended rough-hewn stairways during their gradual descent to wherever they were going. Until now, Namzu did not realize the library was been built upon a rock foundation. He could only speculate on how many generations it had taken to carve out the smooth tunnels. So far they kept to the main corridor. Otherwise, it would have been easy to get lost in the dark maze, he thought.

"If you had ever come to the library since becoming a First, I wouldn't have hesitated to inform you of the underground and its purpose." She shook her head, causing the beads in her close-cropped gray hair to click together. "You don't really expect that I would seek you out, do you?"

There was an edge of a smile on her face. She was enjoying this. Namzu felt like her student again, and he was sure that was exactly what she wanted. He reminded himself to play nice. He would probably still need her help, even if it was just to get out of here later.

They took a sharp turn, and the passage abruptly ended at a reinforced wooden door. Ninedinni pushed through the unbarred door and into a circular room dominated by what appeared to be a bottomless pit. Namzu stopped beside the First Lukur at the edge and stared down into blackness. He could not see the bottom, but the sides of it were smooth, and its opening was at least twice as wide as he was tall.

"Why are we here?" he asked.

Without looking at him, she assumed a somber tone. "There is a door at the bottom of this shaft that leads to a room. You will find your answers there."

"I don't see a way to go down. How deep is it?"

"Let's find out."

Namzu felt the pressure of her hand on his back, and his feet slipped over the edge. He flailed his arms to stop from falling forward, but it wasn't enough. Over the side he plunged, screaming into the blackness.

He realized with a start that his "fall" was more like sliding through water, and he stopped screaming only to want to start again in response to the hysterical, high-pitched cackle that assaulted his ears from above.

Struggling to right himself, he found that he could maneuver his body into a standing position so he might float downward with a little more dignity. Looking back up to the rim of the pit, he watched the First Lukur casually step into the air and slowly descend at the same rate above him. Namzu decided right then that he hated this woman and might let Sabum have her tongue after all. At least then no one would have to suffer that laugh again. Despite managing to hold on to his light globe, he still couldn't see the ground, but he could make out the pit's smooth black walls around him and realized that he would never be able to climb back up if he had to.

Namzu checked his anger as best he could. "How far below is the ground?" he yelled. He wanted to add *witch*.

"Not enjoying the ride?" she called back with a trace of humor in her voice. "You were always so impatient."

Namzu resolved to be quiet and wait. Only a few moments later, he could see the glossy black tiled floor enter his field of light, and he saw what appeared to be skeletal remains, shattered and scattered on the floor, of several people. Upon landing gently, he avoided the bones as best he could and waited for Ninedinni.

"What happened to them?" he asked when she landed next to him.

"They didn't float, obviously."

"Why did we float safely?"

"The magic is triggered by your chain of office." She shook the one around her own neck. "Don't forget that."

Namzu gestured to the bones scattered on the floor. "Who were these people?"

"Thieves, mostly. Maybe an overly curious initiate. People who shouldn't have been here."

"And how do we get back up?"

Ninedinni pointed to the door leading from the pit. A small bell hung next to it. "Ring the bell, and the flow will reverse."

She led him through the door and into a small sitting room, where tables and chairs were set. Everything was dusty, even the floor. They left footprints wherever they stepped. On the opposite wall, another wooden door opened into a more substantial room filled with shelves stacked high with cuneiform tablets. Some of the tablets emitted an eerie green glow.

"It's been a while," Ninedinni said as she shuffled through the stacks of tablets. She wiped away the dust that covered the wedge-shaped markings on them.

Namzu studied the tablets nearest to him, curious as to their contents. "Most of these seem to be the same stories about the gods and heroes of Kurgal that can be found in the library above us. What makes these special?"

"They're the originals," she responded absently, "and all that would likely survive if something happened to our civilization."

"And the glowing ones?"

Ninedinni raised her eyebrow. "They are tablets written by an Anunnaki Abgal many centuries ago. Most of them relate to his observations about the Sag-gig-ga, and others are songs and legends he heard firsthand from the priests of that time. Why he made them glow green, no one knows for sure. Perhaps it is written somewhere among the tens of thousands of tablets stored down here. It would take many lifetimes to go through them all."

The First Lukur straightened and held out three tablets in her hands. "I believe these are what you are looking for."

Namzu's heart leaped as he took hold of the brittle tablets. They felt like they were a thousand years old and might fall apart in his hands at any moment. He followed Ninedinni back into the sitting room, where they carefully laid the tablets out side by side on one of the tables, next to the ones he had brought with the symbols drawn upon them. Then he sat and began reading. "They tell a tale from the city of Yarikh, far to the west, almost to the Great Sea, but it's hard to tell how old the story is. Do you know anything about this place?"

"Some," Ninedinni nodded. "What do you want to know?"

"Anything would be helpful, as I am only vaguely familiar with it."

"Yarikh is a small agricultural city on the eastern shore of the Sea of Salt," Ninedinni began, "inhabited by the Natufian people."

"The Natufians?" Namzu was surprised. "I thought they were tribal nomads who followed the herds across the grasslands."

"They are." Ninedinni agreed, "It was only a few generations ago that they established Yarikh as their first city and developed agriculture with the help of the Ugarit. They named the city after their moon god of the same name. It means, 'He who illumes the Heavens' in their language."

"Last I heard, the Ugarit and Natufians were at war with each other. It's odd that they would have helped their rivals build a city and taught them farming," Namzu commented.

"Initially the Ugarit Kingdom governed the city." Ninedinni explained. "It was intended to be a stopover in what would become a vital trade route extending south to Aylat and other cities on the Narrow Sea."

"It appears it didn't work out too well for them."

The First Lukur sighed. "Just the opposite, it worked out so well that the Natufians decided they wanted a cut of the profits and overthrew the Ugarit governor. They have been in conflict ever since."

"Thank you for that lesson Ninedinni," Namzu said sincerely, "it has been quite a few years since the last one. Now, to get back to these tablets . . ."

The First Lukur nodded and then sat in a nearby chair waiting for him to begin the reading.

Namzu scanned the tablet alternately reading it and summarizing, "There were murders in that city, as well. Terrible murders, violent and hideous, that shook the foundations of the community. At the site of each murder, symbols were written on walls with the victim's blood or carved into their skin. No one understood what they meant."

Namzu peered up at Ninedinni in the dim light and noticed how the shadows softened her hard features. She remained quiet and waited.

"Some of the words are damaged," he continued, "but it looks like as weeks passed and the murders continued, many people began to leave the city. They were frightened for themselves and their families. The priests were in a panic, unsure of what to do, and then came word of a holy man who lived in a cave outside of the city who was touched by the moon god and had visions. It was thought that he might be able to help. They went to the cave and told the old hermit the story of the tragedies in the city and showed him images of the symbols they had found. The old man agreed to conduct a ritual that would allow him to contact the spirit world in a transcendental state so that the spirits could speak through him the higher knowledge no earthbound creature could know."

Namzu studied the second tablet, which detailed the preparations and sacrifices conducted before the ritual. Ninedinni waited silently for him to go on.

"The ritual began in a small cavern inside the holy man's cave," he explained. "A priestess generated smoke by splashing unblemished spring water onto embers burning in a depression carved into the cavern's floor. Another priestess sat next to her and tapped rhythmically on a hollow drum, its sound amplified by and echoing off the walls of the open chamber. There was tea, blessed earlier by the priestess, that contained a plant extract with an unfamiliar name, and it was given to the holy man to consume. When this was done, he began to sway with the rhythm of the drum and the priestesses' quiet, soothing chant.

"The pace increased, and so did the holy man's untamed movements until they became quite violent. He tossed his head back and forth, sending his long gray hair in wide arcs around his shabby robes. Then it all stopped abruptly, and he stared straight ahead, his eyes glazed over as if he were seeing into another place and time."

"That's when a third priestess brought out her tablet and asked questions about the symbols she had written," Ninedinni added in a soft monotone as if she were reliving the moment.

"Yes," Namzu glanced over nervously before he went on, "The priestess presented the first symbol on her tablet, and he spoke, 'Inoas moooah cnila.' The voice that came to his lips was high-pitched, strained, and unsettling in a language they had never heard, yet the holy man was still in control, and the answers came. She followed with the second symbol, 'Odfaorgt gahalana siaion baltoha!' and then the third, 'Babalon doalim.'" Namzu was reading faster and faster, caught up in the narrative. "The holy man—or what spoke through him—became increasingly agitated by the questions, but the priestess continued to press until he answered. His body contorted as if a struggle were taking place with an unseen adversary. The priestess screamed the final questions, trying to hasten the answers and be done with the ritual, but the replies were reluctant and difficult to understand in the holy man's agitation. Finally, she showed him the last one, with one priestess holding his head still and another his eyelids open to force him to see, and it brought on a particular turbulence that was almost transformative. 'Maoffas!' he screamed, 'Maoffas!'"

"The terrible words are free." Ninedinni sobbed.

Namzu was breathless and paused for a moment, "Finally, his body calmed. The holy man was still in an altered state, but his eyes were different now. He stared at the priestess with the blackest eyes filled with what could only be described as hatred, and he spoke words—more words that were unintelligible—in a voice that was harshly guttural and inspired fear: '*Tox sabaooaona dorphal odipvran gmicalzoma, trian crp ors gahalana!*'"

Ninedinni once again joined the narration, adding, "It was at that moment that everything changed."

Namzu found it disconcerting that she spoke so assuredly from where she sat in the shadows. She apparently knew this story intimately. Did she somehow understand the strange words as well?

"With a throaty scream that came from him and not what he had channeled," Namzu continued, "the holy man reached up and furiously removed his own eyes and placed them in his mouth. Blood poured through his broken teeth and over his chin onto the cavern floor. No one moved. It had all happened with shocking swiftness. The holy man smiled defiantly as he swallowed his eyes and then began to slam his head against the rough stone floor."

"He was no longer in control," Ninedinni once again interjected.

Namzu didn't even look up this time afraid, of what he might see in the shadows. "They tried to stop him, but his injuries were fatal, and he died a short time later."

Namzu picked up the third tablet and saw that a dark stain covered much of its surface. *Was it the holy man's own blood that had left its mark as a warning?* A shiver went through Namzu as he involuntarily glanced over at the First Lukur, who was watching him patiently.

The third tablet—actually just the top half of the tablet—contained the symbols, the strange words and the translations written by the priestess. Namzu noticed the first three symbols the Anunnaki had identified. The fourth, "I am here," was not present. Four others matched one or more of those on his other tablets.

"How did the priestesses translate the words?" he asked.

Ninedinni shrugged. "If it was written, then it might have been on the lower half of the tablet that is missing or a fourth tablet we have not found."

He hurriedly read the inscriptions. The first and fourth crime scenes had the same sentence in common: *(They) will be purified with blood.* The first differed in that it included the following: *This (place) will be the temple of (my) sanctity.* The second, fourth, and sixth had one word in common: *sloth.* Finally, the third and fifth crime scene displayed the same two words: *unholy transgression.* At the end, just above where the break had occurred, was the translation of the last words spoken by the holy man: *He whose eyes look about and shall not see with the power (of) understanding shall only in darkness exist.*

Namzu placed the tablet back on the table and leaned back in his chair. He felt mentally and physically exhausted.

"I read this tale long ago and always thought it was just a story." Ninedinni's voice shattered the silence, startling Namzu. Yet you have found these symbols somehow. What are you involved in, Namzu?" She sounded sincerely concerned—and frightened.

"I can't say. I'm sorry. When this is over—and maybe it already is—I will tell you all about it. I promise."

She gave him a sharp glare. "You wouldn't be here if you truly believed whatever it is was over. In any case, I will pray to Enki for you."

Namzu believed she meant it.

Chapter 10
The Infirmary

𒀭𒉿𒌷𒌋𒐀𒈨

"Will he live, First Ashipu?" Ashmadu was sitting beside his master, who had been placed on thick layers of soft linen atop a waist-high solid stone table.

Many such exam tables in the large room also served as beds in the temple infirmary. Most were not occupied, although a few held patients tended by other Ashipu. The lighting was deliberately dim except for spotlights composed of light globes in cone-shaped shades that projected bright white columns of light onto the patients beneath them. Only a few were in use at the moment, leaving the rest of the room flooded with a warm amber glow that suggested a tranquil, calming effect on those within.

"He will live." The First Ashipu moved his hands slowly over the top of the En's head. "But the natural state of his mind may never return."

Ashmadu watched silently while the First Ashipu rolled up the sleeves of his gray Si-tug, a long-woven garment that covered him like a thin robe, and with the help of another Ashipu began washing the En's body. The unusual mixture of warm water and scented oil was part of a purification and healing rite that left the En's skin soft to the touch and pleasantly fragrant. The En surely would have complained if he were conscious; he never let anyone wash him, not even Ashmadu. But he had not regained consciousness since the brief moment he was awake when they carried him from his office. Even then he was unable to speak and apparently disoriented.

Ashmadu leaned away from the bright column of light that illuminated his master's body. Its brightness hurt his tired eyes. "Is there any way to know how he came to this state?" He felt a little nauseated from the spicy-sweet scent of purification incense. It was thought to keep away illness and infection, but to him, it smelled of death.

The First Ashipu sighed. "We see this sickness from time to time. It's an affliction of the mind and body not caused by a forceful blow or falling. The best we have been able to determine is that pressure builds within the head that damages parts of the brain controlling speech, mental functions, and physical control. I am not aware of a cure. He will likely never

79

be lú-silim again."

Lú-silim—a perfect or healthy man. The En would never return to his former self, according to the diagnosis of the First Ashipu.

As the thought began to sink in for Ashmadu, his eyes welled with tears. "Will he ever be able to speak again? Or write on the tablets?"

"With some aid, he may regain some limited speech and movement. His condition is severe, and whatever gains he makes may take years. If he ever wakes, he will never write on the tablets again. Nor rule, I'm sorry to say."

The First Ashipu finished washing En Ipqu-aya while Ashmadu wept and prayed quietly by his master's side. The infuriating healer delivered the distressing news in a clinical, matter-of-fact tone that made Ashmadu want to strike him. Even if he was right, and the best they could hope for was the En eventually regaining his speech and movement, then he would pray for it. Ashmadu would be by the En's side no matter his state and help him live the best life he could for as many years as he had left. His only worry was how his master would deal with not being the En any longer. Ashmadu knew his master well enough that it wouldn't be the power and control that he would miss, or even the affections of the crowds when he addressed them. *Well, maybe a little*, he corrected himself. But the office was so much a part of who he was, and had been for decades, that removing him from it would be like taking his identity, maybe worse.

This was the upside of his condition according to the First Ashipu, but the healer forgot one thing. En Ipqu-aya was the anointed, earthly representative of Enki, Light of Lights and first among his people. Surely Enki would intercede in this matter, especially if he had intervened in the circumstance of the Sahar-nitah. Ashmadu would keep hope and faith that the En would wake in a day or so and recover well enough that he could return to his duties. What other outcome could Enki want?

The First Ashipu rose from his stool and placed a hand on Ashmadu's shoulder. "Everyone knows of your love and dedication to the En," he said in a soft, consoling tone. "He could be in no better care than yours. I have sent for the Anunnaki to confirm my diagnosis of the En's condition. Perhaps they can give us a better insight into his recovery."

Ashmadu felt ashamed for allowing himself to become angry. He nodded silently as the First Ashipu walked away. What—if anything—could he do now?

Before losing consciousness, the En tried to tell him something important, something about what happened to him. He knew it. *What could it have been?* He was alone with the Sanga, a trusted friend, at the time. Could the Sanga have somehow caused the En's affliction? No one would believe that. *Ashmadu* could not believe that. The Sanga was an honorable man with a righteous reputation. But the En had stared intently into Ashmadu's eyes as if desperate to impart something important. A few unintelligible sounds escaped his lips, and his eyes shifted in Irra's direction several times.

Ashmadu understood that something happened that involved, or was witnessed, by the Sanga that put the En in this circumstance. But without a word from the En, how could Ashmadu make an accusation? And what charge could he make?

The Sanga had been a close friend to the En since childhood. They had ascended side by side through the ranks of the temple together, and they shared secrets. Ashmadu could think of only one thing that could have driven the Sanga to strike out at the En. But there was no way the Sanga could have ever discovered that thing.

It was unthinkable.

It had to be something else. There was nothing left but to hope for the En to recover his speech well enough to dispel the mystery. And that might not be for some time, if ever, according to the First Ashipu.

Ashmadu, already tired from the exertions and stress of the day, felt drowsy under the soothing amber lighting. He laid his head on a small table next to his master and soon fell asleep.

~~~

"Which one is he?" a man asked gruffly.

There was a long pause before a woman replied in a wavering voice, "The little one in the corner with the blocks."

Heavy footfalls stopped behind the young child facing the wall. He was cheerfully playing with blocks the size of his little hands. Scratched roughly onto the cubes were numbers in cuneiform or pictures vaguely resembling common farm animals. The man reached down with a thick hand and roughly lifted the small boy to his feet. The boy stood on his own and turned on unsteady legs. He had not been walking on his own very long.

Fearfully, the child looked up at the big man, and then he began to whimper and back away into the corner. The face of the man was scary, with lines and pockmarks that blemished his skin and a scowl that made it all the worse.

"Don't hurt him!" the woman begged. "I will take him to the temple today."

"Fine with me. Are you sure they're going to forgive our debt for him?" The man pointed back over his shoulder at the child.

"Yes, all of it," she confirmed before adding quickly, "but he must be unmarked."

"Very well. Take the boy!" The man turned and left the dark, dingy room.

Once the angry man had departed, the small child smiled and ran to the woman. She sat on the floor and hugged him for a long time. She pressed his soft hair and skin against her own so tightly and desperately, as if to impress the feeling into her memory. Somehow the tiny boy was also memorizing those feelings, even if he didn't know it yet. The moment would leave a strong impression on his subconscious mind forever.

"I'm going to take you to a safe place where no one can hurt you," she told him in a soothing voice. Tears ran down her cheeks as she spoke. "You will be under the watchful eye of Enki now, so always do your best to be good and do the right thing. Above all, never, ever forget that I love you, my little Ashmadu."

~~~

"Ashmadu, wake up. Wake up. The Anunnaki is here." The First Ashipu, who had tended the En earlier, gently shook Ashmadu's shoulder.

The healer had changed into a new gray Si-tug with the thick chain and medallion that marked him as the First Ashipu. His kind face radiated a warm smile from beneath his cleanly shaven head. Ashmadu felt as though he had just fallen asleep, but the stiffness in his bones suggested hours had passed. He was fully awake now.

The First Ashipu helped him to his feet before handing him a cup of water. "Drink."

"Is the En okay?" Ashmadu, still a bit unsteady, drained the cup.

"As well as he was before," the First Ashipu replied. "The Anunnaki is here to see to him. I will bring her in if you are ready."

"Of course, First Ashipu. Please don't delay." Ashmadu tidied his clothing and quickly splashed his face with water from a nearby bowl.

The healer departed through a side passage and returned a few moments later followed by a tall, slender, middle-aged Anunnaki woman. She wore long, layered robes in shades of sea green and blue with a heavy gold medallion engraved with the image of the Primeval Sea that hung below her rigid neck collars. Her hair was long and brown, flowing from her elongated skull in waves below her shoulders. She was beautiful, as it seemed all Anunnaki were blessed to be, even with the odd blue tint of their pale skin and large, almond-shaped brown eyes. He had been taught from childhood that they were the children of Enki, god of sea water, crafts, and creation, so Ashmadu supposed their almost aquatic appearance made sense.

"Ashmadu," the First Ashipu said, "this is Nin-Digir Shonaturi of House Restander."

Ashmadu bowed deeply. "Thank you for coming to see my master, Nin-Digir Shonaturi. I am grateful for anything you can do for him."

The Anunnaki looked Ashmadu over carefully. "Are you a slave or servant to En Ipqu-aya, Ashmadu?"

"I came to the priesthood as a slave many years ago. After earning my freedom, the En invited me to serve in the Gi-par as his personal attendant. He has given me everything and treated me with respect and kindness. I owe him my life."

"How unusual, or is that a typical sentiment between master and slave in Kur-gal?" There was no sense of judgment or expectation in her question. It was almost as if she were researching an academic subject.

Ashmadu shrugged. "Not so typical, I am sure. But here in Eridu, we believe in kindness and empathy even unto the slaves. 'A well-kept slave is a productive one,' so the ancient adage goes. In this city, many slaves stay with their masters for life even after they have worked off their debt or crime."

"Nin-Digir Shonaturi is a recent arrival in Eridu," the First Ashipu explained, "so she's not familiar with our culture and customs yet."

Ashmadu wondered if the First Ashipu knew from where the Anunnaki was a recent arrival.

"May I examine the En now?" she asked, already inspecting the En with her eyes.

"Yes, please Nin-Digir." Ashmadu stepped aside.

The Anunnaki stood over En Ipqu-aya with her hands hovering just above his still body. His breathing, slow and even, did not betray any stress or discomfort. She began at the En's feet, moving her hands slowly up his body but never touching him. Ashmadu noticed an almost electric feeling in the air as the hair on his brown arms stood on end. She chanted softly in a strange tongue, producing what at times sounded like an ancient, forgotten, forlorn song. Her hands hovered the longest over his chest and head. Then she went back again over his legs and arms. After what seemed like an eternity, she stopped.

The Nin-Digir turned to Ashmadu and the First Ashipu. "He has sustained a clot in his brain that temporarily disrupted blood flow long enough to cause significant damage. Then for some reason, the clot largely dissolved. Clots of this nature usually develop in the chest or legs and then get trapped in the smaller arteries of the brain. I see no evidence to suggest that this happened. It's as if the clot formed and then dissolved of its own accord inside his brain. Otherwise, he is in excellent health for his age."

"Can anything be done?" Ashmadu asked quietly.

The Nin-Digir smiled warmly, defying his initial impression of her as cold and dispassionate. "You love this man as a father, don't you? I will do what I can to restore some of his functions, but understand the damage to his brain is permanent and cannot be undone. Our best hope will be to construct pathways around the affected areas that will help his brain function recover to some extent."

"Will it take very long?" Ashmadu was feeling hopeful now.

"A few weeks, maybe more. I will start now and return every day until I have done everything I can. You have my word."

Ashmadu thought he was all out of tears, but the tears he shed now were hopeful ones, and he was glad to have them. "Thank you, Nin-Digir. I will be forever in your debt."

The Nin-Digir laughed. "You were a slave long enough. I do not accept your debt, only your gratitude." Without another word, she returned her attention to the En and the work she had ahead of her.

Ashmadu got comfortable once again in his chair. Determined to be there if the En regained consciousness, he vowed not to leave his master's side. The Anunnaki had given Ashmadu a glimmer of optimism, something he could hold on to for now. He wasn't ready to discount the possibility that the En would wake up at any moment and resume his life normally again.

Ashmadu had never been much for prayer, but he began to pray now. If Enki had any compassion, Ashmadu thought, he would hear the prayers of the servant to his most devoted and righteous En.

Chapter 11
Hearth and Home

𒈗𒌋𒁲𒂷𒌋𒊏𒋫

Shatamurrim walked through the neighborhood where his family home was located. It had rained earlier in the day, leaving the grooves between the sun-dried brick pavers glistening with the excess runoff. Trails of moisture ran from the rooftops in jagged rivulets, barely penetrating the homes' mud stucco. The street teemed with slaves and freeborn, the Dumugir, running their errands, and since the season was still cool, they wore longer kilts and thicker wool tunics to keep the chilly wind off their skin.

Nearly every house stood with its front door open, letting in the fresh air and creating a cross breeze from the courtyard into the inner rooms of the structure. Shatamurrim had grown up on a similar street and wondered if his mother was airing out the house and sending servants to the market today as well.

As much as Shatamurrim enjoyed the distractions, his thoughts were filled with worry for the En. Shatamurrim recently left the temple infirmary and stayed only a short time before deciding he was getting in the way of the Ashipu doing their good work. He would go back after his duties, and by then, the En would have been thoroughly examined. Perhaps the Ashipu would also know the cause of his malady.

En Ipqu-aya had been like an uncle, even a second father to him, his entire life. The man had attended every important celebration and special occasion from the time Shatamurrim was a small child. Shatamurrim was astonished to realize that he had more memories of growing up in the En's house than in his own. How odd, he thought, that he would think of the En, his mother, and Ashmadu more than his own father when he thought of family.

His father, the Sanga, had not been around very much during his childhood, instead, attending to temple business by day and staying at his office residence most nights. That was the life his father had chosen. He knew his father loved him, but he also knew the temple would always be his first love and priority. Shatamurrim never resented the Sanga because of it; he accepted it. His was not the only father who worked long hours and rarely spent time with his family. Shatamurrim was more fortunate than most that between his mother and Ashmadu there was hardly a moment when he was not distracted by one activity or another, and when he did see his father, it was a treat. For now, his heart felt heavy as his silent prayers went out to his other father, the En.

Somewhat deliberately, he found himself near the neighborhood where his parents lived and decided to stop to see his mother. It pained him to bring sadness to her, but she deserved to know. She would be the only one he would speak to about the En, since anyone else might tell others and cause panic in the city. Besides, the people were so happy today. The En said that the Sahar-nitah would crumble at dawn, but they were still present. Maybe they would persist for the remaining few days of the celebration. Only the Sahar-nitah that left with the foreign adherents after the second night had crumbled to dust a league outside the city, and no one seemed to know why.

He certainly enjoyed having his own earthman. Even now the thing was cleaning and sharpening his sickle swords, axes, and numerous spears. Although the Sahar-nitah could not speak or communicate beyond offering the occasional nod, they appeared to understand everything and learn very quickly. Not for the first time that day, he considered how they might be used in a military application. Of course, the En would never allow it.

Upon arriving at his parents' house, he opened the unlocked door and entered. Unlocked doors were not unusual, since crime in Eridu was almost unheard of. If anything, he was surprised that the door was not open to let in the fresh air.

"Mother!" he called out once he reached the courtyard. "It is I, your son, Shata!" Silence followed. Only the trickle of water from the large fountain in the center of the courtyard broke the silence. And the silence was deafening. It was on the edge of this fountain that Ashmadu or his mother had read to him when he was a small boy, sharing stories about the gods and legendary heroes of the Sag-gig-ga. At its center were the four stone fish jumping from a plume of sculpted sea spray—the sculpture had seemed so much higher back then. He remembered looking up from the base of the fountain and marveling at the streams of water projected from the mouth of each fish and splashing into the reservoir. As he studied it further, he mused that it must have shrunk with time, since it was no higher than his own height now.

He glanced around expectantly. Perhaps his mother was enjoying the comfortable weather on the rooftop. The breeze would suit her, and she liked to watch the passersby on the street below and wave to those she knew. He climbed the stairs to the roof but found it vacant aside from a few idle birds. *Where is she?* He asked himself. *Where are the servants?*

Back in the courtyard again, Shatamurrim began checking each room in the house. Many of the chambers opened to the courtyard, but it was a large house with a second floor and a kitchen in the back with multiple storerooms. Why was there no one to receive him? If his mother had gone to the market, she wouldn't have taken all of her servants. Surely one should have been present and heard him calling.

He made his way to the kitchen and found it still hot from the hearth, just recently cooling from earlier in the day. His mother must have been cooking that morning, he thought. Perhaps she'd left some of her tasty Nindagu bread in one of the baskets in the corner. To his delight, he found a few loaves there, but they were hard and not recently baked. It didn't make sense; she only baked bread in the morning. As he walked through the kitchen, he noticed his boots sticking to the floor with each step. Someone probably spilled something and hadn't cleaned it up properly. The room was illuminated only by the waning glow of the hearth, and all he could see was the shadow of a stain that spread away from it. Such oversight would have earned him a scolding as a child, and no servant would be foolish enough not to clean it up thoroughly.

There was something else. A faint odor in the kitchen that seemed out of place. It reminded Shatamurrim of the stench of burned fat from the tail of a sheep—a resource his soldiers used in the field to fuel their campfires. The source of the scent was probably what they had been cooking, so he walked over to examine the hearth closer.

As he knelt down next to it, the hearth gave off the unmistakable stench of death, as if a servant had thrown a rat into it for disposal. He noticed darker stains on the floor around it. His mother would not be happy about the mess. Perhaps the servant had spilled the noon meal chasing a rat and failed to clean up suitably before running out to gather more ingredients to start again prior his mother's return. That might explain why no one was in the house, although he realized how much of a stretch his speculation was. His mother was stern but fair and treated the servants well. However, they were held accountable for their actions. The servant who had done this would probably have to clean out the entire hearth and might even get the rough end of a cane, Shatamurrim mused.

As he enjoyed a quiet laugh at the thought of the servant's punishment, he noticed something odd about the hearth's contents. There were unusual remnants of bones mixed with the ashes. The bone fragments were much larger than any rat he might imagine. What had they been cooking? Upon closer inspection, the floor appeared stained with dried blood, as if they butchered the animal where he stood. In the dim light of the windowless room it was hard to see, so he pulled a light globe from his pouch to illuminate the area better.

It was definitely blood. He cast his gaze quickly around the room and noticed that the stain was enormous, covering the entire kitchen floor. Parts of it had a pattern resembling a swirl, as if it were partially wiped up. He spotted a metal rod behind the bread basket that he could use to remove one of the bones to take a closer look. But he froze in place even as his hand touched the cold handle, his mind unable to register what he was seeing.

A severed hand lay palm up on the floor behind the basket. On the wrist of the hand, just above the clean cut from the rest of the appendage, was tied a bracelet of small shells.

An icy chill ran up his spine. It was the bracelet he had given his mother when he was only six. She never took it off, yet there it was on this severed hand that he could not tear his eyes away from.

As the unbelievable truth sank in, the room began to spin. Shatamurrim stumbled backward and fell roughly to the floor, the metal rod clattering noisily across the kiln-fired glazed tiles where he dropped it. His eyes traveled up the wall and stopped dead when he saw three strange symbols written in blood just above the hearth.

He couldn't believe what he was *seeing*.

He couldn't believe what he was *thinking*.

He, like everyone in Eridu, heard rumors of the murders at an inn in the city. He'd heard about the carnage, about the symbols from his father. And now he was sitting in the sticky pool of his own mother's dried blood, staring at those symbols.

Suddenly overwhelmed by grief, he cried without shame or humiliation. Someone murdered his mother, dismembered her, and disposed of her like an animal in her own hearth. What monster could have done this? Rage and sadness coursed through his body like a mad river of fire. He hugged himself tightly, trying to hold himself together, but it was useless. His emotions erupted in carnal screams that echoed through the house that was once his home.

When he composed himself enough to stand, Shatamurrim walked out the front door in a daze and blew the shepherd's horn that all soldiers and Aga-us carried to sound an alarm. People in the street and nearby houses stopped and looked his way in surprise. They were familiar with the sound of the alarm from regular exercises, but this was no drill. They ran for help. They ran in fear. And those who knew him ran to comfort the man who had grown up among them. Shatamurrim sank to the ground in the doorway of the home that he had until today considered safe and full of only beautiful memories.

By the time the patrol arrived, Shatamurrim was in control of his emotions again, but he refused to reenter his parents' house. Instead, he explained to the Aga-us who he was and what they would find inside. It was hard for him to get through the details—he felt numb inside, and he wanted nothing more than to be away from this place.

The patrol leader and two of the guards went inside the house and emerged a short while later horrified and ashen faced. One emptied his stomach around the corner. The patrol leader sent another of his men to notify his Sar and then waited abjectly with Shatamurrim, without a word, for his arrival.

A short time later, a four-wheeled chariot sped up the road, followed by several more chariots of the same type carrying at least a dozen Aga-us. The lead chariot was driven by a lone man. He was a short, stocky man with close-cropped black hair, and he wore a simple kilt with metal plates and an ivory tunic that flowed dramatically from where it was tied around his neck. Shatamurrim did not know this man personally, but he knew that he was the Sar of this district of Eridu by the way he conducted himself. Shatamurrim occasionally heard rumors that this particular Sar was arrogant and full of his own self-importance, but also that he was relentless when it came to tracking down criminals who committed crimes in his district, no matter how petty the offense.

The Sar jumped off his chariot before it came to a full stop and approached the patrol leader almost at a run. "Give me the details. The stories from the man you sent are unbelievable."

The patrol leader motioned to Shatamurrim, standing beside him. "This is the Sanga's son. He came to his parents' house and found what he believes to be his mother's remains burned in the kitchen hearth." He glanced at Shatamurrim in apology for having to verbalize the gruesome scene.

The Sar bowed to Shatamurrim. "Silim sum, Sar Shatamurrim, I am Sar Unzi. Your heroic deeds are known well to the men of the Aga-us and myself. I'm distressed to meet you under these circumstances."

Shatamurrim nodded to the Sar but had no words.

The Sar turned back to the patrol leader. "Show me what you found."

The patrol leader took the Sar inside, and just as before, the men appeared shaken and sickened when they exited the house a little while later.

"Send a man to bring the Sanga and another to inform the First Usgadi. He will want to investigate." The Sar turned to address Shatamurrim. "I'm sorry for what has happened. I'll do everything in my power to find the person who did this and bring him for judgment."

Shatamurrim nodded appreciatively. "I know you will, Sar. I know you by reputation, and I know you won't rest until you're done with this."

The Sar sent men to block off the surrounding streets and question some of the people who lived nearby. While they waited, Shatamurrim considered how he would tell his father about his mother and begin the long road of sorrow they would share for the rest of their lives. Even though his father was absent much of his childhood, he knew that his father loved his mother dearly and would be devastated by the loss and haunted by the way her life ended. If there were a way to keep the worst details from him, Shatamurrim would. But his father was a very deliberate man and would demand to know every fact no matter how much he would suffer from the knowledge.

It took some time, but Shatamurrim's father and the First Usgadi, whom he knew to be Namzu, finally arrived on chariots of their own. Shatamurrim couldn't remember seeing so many chariots together at one time other than on the battlefield.

His father hurried to him without stopping to speak with anyone else. "I have heard terrible words from other men. Is it true, my son?"

"It is, Father. My mother is dead." Shatamurrim felt tears well again in his eyes. He never expected to utter those words to anyone, much less his father.

Irra held him in a tight embrace while the First Usgadi, accompanied by Sar Unzi, went inside without disturbing their sad reunion. Shatamurrim sat on the low mud-brick wall that surrounded their house, and his father sat with him, stretching his arm around Shatamurrim's shoulders in a show of comfort. He couldn't remember his father acting in this way before, comforting, sensitive. "Shatamurrim, you're not a child anymore. You must be strong. You're a seasoned Sar of thirty-six hundred elite warriors of Eridu. You have seen the worst that men can do to each other. I have seen you weep with your men over the loss of one or many of your brothers in battle."

Shatamurrim wondered for a moment what his father was talking about. Perhaps he didn't know how to deal with his own grief. It was true that Shatamurrim had seen terrible things in battle and lost men to war, but this was his *mother*. Having never taken a wife, he often returned to her for comfort during difficult times. She embodied the goodness in humanity, proving that unconditional love was not just a convenient myth invented by others to assure themselves of their relevance in this hard world.

"I am worried about you, Father. What will you do now? Where will you find comfort?"

His father always had a smile for him, even in the worst of times, but not today. "I will stay in the temple for a while and do what I have always done. Enki will provide comfort and strength through prayer and sacrifice. But I will not rest until we find the treacherous person who has committed this evil in our house."

Shatamurrim dried his face on his father's robes, and for a brief moment, he was a young child comforted by his father again. It was unfortunate that they had not been closer over the years, but the time they *had* spent together was precious to Shatamurrim, and he knew only good memories.

"My men and I will spend every moment searching the city until we find the murderer, Father," he vowed. "They are my brothers and will feel the pain of loss nearly as much as I do."

His father's face darkened, and he moved to hold Shatamurrim sternly at arm's length. "This is not the duty of your warriors. They are not fit for this work. It's likely they will cause more harm than good. No, this must be handled by the Usgadi and the Aga-us. It's within their expertise, and they will be diligent and thorough in their investigations. I will make sure of it." His expression softened. "A pack of dogs is useful for hunting a lion, not a snake, my son."

Shatamurrim had to agree. His warriors were trained for covert warfare—concealment in the environs, eluding the enemy, ambush, and night tactics. They were disciplined and, when they fought, vicious. The Ursagmuda, or Warrior Dogs, were feared by their enemies, who knew them by reputation if not by the sharp end of their blades.

"You are right, Father, and I will heed your counsel. If you don't mind, I would like to stay here for a time. I need to feel Mother's spirit around me, and I will make our home clean again for you to return to soon." Shatamurrim couldn't explain why he felt the need to stay in the house where his mother was murdered. He just knew that he must.

His father held Shatamurrim close again. "That is appropriate, my son. I will return only when the murderer has been captured and your mother's spirit is at rest. We will give her remains a proper burial tomorrow, and I will pray for Ereshkigal to have pity on her and take her through the Seven Gates to Kurnugia without delay."

The Sanga looked beyond Shatamurrim toward the house, "Ah, here comes the First Usgadi. Perhaps he can tell us more about what happened here today."

Chapter 12

Symbols

Namzu inspected the kitchen and noted the effort to dispose of a body and clean up the mess afterward. This scene was unlike the others, and he might have considered it unrelated except for one thing: the three symbols written in blood on the wall above the hearth.

"Sar Unzi, send a man to inform Sabum that I need him here and to bring his team. Oh, and get everyone else out of the house, including your men."

"Yes, First Usgadi. I will see to it and send our fastest chariot."

The Sar turned and marched out. In his long skirt reinforced with immaculately polished bronze plates and his black leather cloak thrown precisely across his broad shoulders, he looked like he was on parade. Several Sars served in the command structure of Eridu's military and city guard, and this one was as rigid as they came. Nevertheless, Unzi was diligent when it came to his duties, so Namzu found it difficult to begrudge the man's arrogance.

He turned his attention back to the symbols on the wall. When he was summoned by the Aga-us, he hadn't expected to be investigating a murder at the home of the Sanga, let alone staring at these damned symbols again. He wished he hadn't left his tablets at the office. It didn't matter. He would draw these and compare them to the others when he returned to the temple later.

Strange, he thought, that the killer had made an effort clean up the scene and burn the body in an effort to either hide its identity or the crime altogether. If that were the case, why would he have written the symbols and done such a clumsy job of covering the crime? He crouched and passed his light globe over the floor, taking note of the footprints that crisscrossed nearly the entire surface of the kitchen. One pair of prints would be the killer's, but which one? There were so many who had been through the kitchen, including Shatamurrim, several Aga-us, the Sar, and now Namzu himself added to the mix. It would be a waste of time trying to sort through them all.

Then there was the hand. Namzu moved the basket aside so he could use his light globe to get a better look. It was the only recognizable part of the remains, small and delicate as a woman's, with an identifiable piece of jewelry still on it, and there was one other thing—blood on her fingertips.

Namzu picked up the hand to examine it further. It was cut cleanly from the body, and only the first three fingers had blood on them. Those fingers were straight and pressed together, whereas the thumb and small finger were curled in toward the palm.

He held the hand in the fashion he suspected, reached toward the symbols with it, and began to trace the dried blood.

"Well, this is awkward. Do you need a moment?" Sabum and his dark humor.

Namzu turned, still holding the hand. "He drew the symbols with the victim's severed hand."

"That's a new twist. I thought we were done with this after the innkeeper was killed." Sabum eyed the rest of the kitchen, taking in the details.

Namzu quickly brought Sabum up to speed on everything he knew so far. "Have your team look through the rest of the house. There may be more victims. I haven't seen a single slave since I arrived."

Sabum nodded and left the kitchen to retrieve the three Usgadi who had come with him. He sent them off to various parts of the house and then went to work surveying the kitchen.

He motioned to the symbols. "Do you know what any of those mean?"

"Just the last one," Namzu replied. "It means *I am here*. The other two I'm not sure about."

"How was your visit to the temple library?"

"It was . . . painful on many levels. Ninedinni has changed very little since we were initiates."

"Did she ask after me? You know what a special relationship we've always had." Sabum modeled a wicked smile on his face.

"Yes, in fact, she did. I can't remember her exact words, though."

"I'm sure she misses me." Sabum entered the storage room and came back almost immediately. "I found the slaves."

Namzu followed him back into the storeroom. At first glance, the various baskets and bags containing cereals, fruits, and other provisions looked undisturbed. But as they probed further, the illumination from the light globes showed dried blood trails on the floor and oversized storage baskets hidden in the back with blood soaked through their tight weaves. Sabum removed their lids, and there they found three slaves stuffed inside, bent like reeds. Another basket was filled with blood-soaked linens.

"He must be very powerful, physically, to have doubled the bodies over to fit them inside the baskets." Sabum sounded impressed as they inspected the baskets and their gory contents.

"Shatamurrim was the one who found the remains in the kitchen, but there was no mention of this. I think he is probably credible."

Sabum shrugged. "The Hero of Eridu? I would hope so. Otherwise, we would have to ask him to return his medal."

Namzu laughed at Sabum's crude joke. "We could start with that. I think I'll go talk with the Sanga and his son. Let me know if you find anything else."

Sar Unzi joined the First Usgadi after he exited the house. "Is there anything that my men or I can help with?"

"You can come with me now, then have your men bring anyone with even the smallest bit of information here for my Usgadi to question."

Sar Unzi nodded, and they walked together to where the Sanga and Shatamurrim were waiting.

"Sanga, Sar." The First Usgadi bowed respectfully to each of them. "I am First Usgadi Namzu. We found remains of a woman in the kitchen and three servants stuffed into baskets in the adjoining storage room. It appears that the murders were willful and not the unfortunate result of a random robbery. Your wife kept a very clean and orderly house. The only disturbance was in the kitchen, where all four must have been when the intruder found them."

"Any indication as to who committed this atrocity in my home?" the Sanga demanded angrily.

The First Usgadi took a deep breath. "So far, no; however, we are just beginning the inquiry. I assure you, Sanga, that no effort will be spared during our investigation. May we have the house for the day to fully examine every detail?"

"Of course, Namzu. Also, I would like my wife's remains sent to the Hall of Kurnugia before sunset so that she may be properly prepared for burial. Please inform me immediately if you find anything."

It sounded like a request, but Namzu knew that it was meant as a command. He was subordinate to the Sanga, although the majority of their interaction was through messengers and the weekly report Namzu sent to his office.

Namzu bowed and turned to go back inside just as Sabum exited the house. Namzu dismissed Unzi, then walked only a few steps before waiting for Sabum to join him. He was still within earshot of Shatamurrim and the Sanga and strained to pick up their conversation.

"Go back to the temple, Father. I know it pains you to be here. I will stay for a while and meet you in the Hall of Kurnugia this evening to pray for Mother's passage through the Seven Gates." Shatamurrim sounded hopeful.

"My poor Shata, you know that Ereshkigal may not hear our prayers, and if she doesn't . . ."

Sabum arrived, and Namzu brought a finger to his lips. They pretended to intently study a tablet he was holding.

Shatamurrim apparently wasn't ready to consider the worst. "I know, Father. Her soul will stay in this world, but we must try."

Namzu had been taught, like all Sag-gig-ga, that the bodies of the deceased must remain intact in order to successfully traverse the Seven Gates into the Underworld. Those that were dismembered, burned, or mutilated required the intervention of a deity. And that was nearly impossible.

"Bring some of your mother's favorite possessions for the burial tomorrow." The Sanga placed his hand on his son's shoulder. "They will give her comfort once she reaches her destination."

"I will, Father. Now get some rest. You are the Sanga of the greatest temple in the world. You will need all of your strength if Enki or Ereshkigal is to hear you tonight."

Out of the corner of his eye, Namzu watched as father and son embraced before the Sanga climbed onto his chariot and slowly trotted off in the direction of the temple.

~~~

The body—or what was left of it—was arranged in roughly human form upon a silk sheet, imported from TaShemau, laid over one of the stone block tables in the Hall of Kurnugia. It was shocking how much fire could reduce a body. All that remained were small bones, fragments of bones, and ash. The priests had done a remarkable job placing the remains in their proper places, but even had they erred, who would have known the difference with the body in such a state?

Shatamurrim stared down at Mother's remains. He had just finished placing her jewelry among them. These were her favorite possessions—a lapis lazuli necklace from his father that she had worn since the day of their wedding, a thick silver ring from her late sister, the clay figurine of Enki given by the En that she never prayed without, and the bracelet of seashells.

Her hand was the only body part with flesh intact. It never made it into the hearth and now lay cleaned and oiled beside the bones and ashes. Shatamurrim was disgusted and comforted by that hand. It was the only part of his mother that was left that he could touch with familiarity.

Shatamurrim recalled one of the proudest moments of his life. He had been six years old, and Ashmadu had taken him to the banks of the Buranuna to collect shells. He found several handfuls of different shapes and sizes that he thought were beautiful and saved them in a large pouch that he brought with him. They'd spent hours at the beach that day finding shells and cooking mussels, after which Ashmadu took a copper pin, heated it in their small fire, and used it to poke holes through the shells Shatamurrim collected. Then they took a leather thong and threaded it through all the shells. There must have been over a hundred of them. When they were done, they had a beautiful bracelet that Shatamurrim would proudly present to his mother when they returned home.

His father had not yet arrived at the hall. Shatamurrim knew he would come, but how would he react to his wife in this state? It was worrisome. He could already detect his father's detachment. He was changing. Perhaps it was his way of dealing with the horror of what happened, and he wondered if his father thought the same of him. He knew that his heart had hardened and that his anger was palpable. Would he ever be the same? It was a terrible dilemma for them both.

"Shata, you are here." It was his father next to him. Shatamurrim had been so engrossed in his own thoughts that he had not heard his father's approach.

Without looking up, he placed his hand over his father's. "Yes, Father. I'm sorry you have to see Mother like this."

His father was silent a moment before responding. "It saddens me. And it hardens me. If I ever find joy again in my life, it will only be with you and the gods." They stood together in silence for a long while before his father said, "Let's begin."

For the next hour, his father performed rites of purification and prayers over her remains. Shatamurrim imagined the complete body of his mother lying there rather than the few grisly remains, and when it was done, he was overcome with emotion and simply wept on his father's shoulder.

After they left the Hall of Kurnugia, Shatamurrim accompanied his father back to his private chambers next to his office. He was surprised to be greeted by two young, lovely priestesses. They took his father in hand and bade Shatamurrim goodnight. Shatamurrim always pondered the thought that maybe his father kept a mistress in the temple. It wasn't unheard of, and no one would have cared except for his family. His father never seemed the type, though—always so virtuous, taking pleasure from his work. Shatamurrim could not think about it. If his father chose to be with other women, then that was between him and his wife. He supposed it didn't matter anymore anyway.

~~~

The unassuming green field surrounded by a low mud-brick wall was crowded with thousands of mourners gathered to honor the passing of the Sanga's wife, Arwi-a. Rows of small clay bricks stretched into the distance and marked each grave with the name of the deceased Many of the plots were supplied with bowls of food and pitchers of Kas as offerings to sustain the dead in the afterlife. These offerings were believed to give relief to those residing in Kurnugia and the dreary shadow of the life they had led while alive.

The crowd went silent while the Isib, burial priests, brought Arwi-a's remains into the cemetery. They were followed by Shatamurrim, his father, and a group of gala priests chanting in a low, sorrowful rhythm. The pitiful remains were carried by the lead Isib in a small basket, which only deepened the melancholy of the sad occasion.

Shatamurrim was surprised that so many people were in attendance, including many from the temple, his entire company of Ursagmuda, and his beloved tutor, Ashmadu. His eyes watered when he noticed that they all brought offerings for his mother's comfort. He imagined the feast she would enjoy to the envy of even Ereshkigal in Kurnugia.

The unhappy procession threaded its way through the clusters of mourners until they came to the place where a small hole had been dug in a section reserved for priests and their families. The Isib raised the basket in the air and intoned a prayer to Ereshkigal before placing Arwi-a's remains in the ground. Then Irra and Shatamurrim buried her with their own hands while the gala priests sang Er-šem-ma and the bereaved looked on silently.

After the Ritual of Burial was complete, Ashmadu approached Shatamurrim and his father, who were standing together. "I share your sorrow for her loss. May Ereshkigal hear the love in all the prayers sent on her behalf."

"Thank you for your words," the Sanga replied before receiving condolences from several of the Firsts, including Bikku-lum from the infirmary, Ninedinni of the library, and Namzu the Usgadi, among others.

Shatamurrim took the En's servant aside. "Ashmadu, I know my mother was special to you as well. She always spoke very highly of you and the care that you showed me when I was growing up. I have no doubt that we share the same pain and sense of loss. Thank you for giving her good memories."

Ashmadu's eyes were red from the tears he had shed, no doubt a reflection of his own, and his lips trembled as if to speak, but he couldn't allow the words to come without releasing his sorrow at the same time. In a gesture reminiscent of Shatamurrim's childhood, Ashmadu took the Sar's head in both hands and gently brought him close to kiss his forehead. It was a sweet expression that spoke volumes about their relationship and the reverence a poor, unknown servant had for his mother. There was an unashamed beauty in that moment—hero and servant, for just a blink of time, sharing a depth of emotion that defied the stigma of class and culture. Then the two men embraced before Ashmadu, still unable to speak, departed.

Shatamurrim scratched his clean-shaven chin and wondered at the unexpected grief his old friend displayed over the loss of his mother. He would visit Ashmadu more often from now on. He knew his mother would like that, just as he would. Maybe he could learn more about the relationship the En's servant had with his mother during his early years.

His father approached him as the crowd began to depart. "Your mother is at peace now. It's time for me to return to the temple, and I'm sure you have your own duties to attend to. She would not be happy with either of us if we neglected our responsibilities." His father looked tired, as if he hadn't slept at all the previous night.

"Yes, Father. I will stay here awhile before I go. There are things I must say to her before she is too far away." He lowered himself with legs folded to the ground next to the grave.

"Very well, son. I will see you in a few days." Irra leaned down and kissed the top of Shatamurrim's head before walking back toward the city alone.

As soon as his father was out of earshot, Shatamurrim whispered, "Mother, if you can, please help Father find his happiness again soon. He will miss you, as I will until we join you one day in Kurnugia. And while you wait, I pray we make you proud."

He sat next to his mother's grave for a long time, thinking about his life, the happy times he had spent with her, and the sound of her voice. He feared to lose those memories and did his best to solidify the details in his mind.

The light breeze was brisk, and the sun was bright. He felt happier sitting there than he had at any other time since his mother's death. Maybe it was his imagination, but for just a moment, he could feel his mother's fingers run through his long, dark hair.

98

Chapter 13

The Abgal

𒉌𒅖𒁉 𒌋𒂠𒊑𒀭

The Anunnaki's sharp eyebrows were creased with uncertainty. She was standing over the En, who was still unconscious and unresponsive. Her hands were clenching the folds of her delicate robes as if she were frustrated with the results of her tireless efforts

"I don't understand why I'm having so little effect on his recovery," she told Ashmadu. "Without fully understanding the cause, I'm unable to treat the condition."

Except for attending Arwi-a's burial, Ashmadu had been by the En's side day and night since the day the En had collapsed in his office. He was physically stable but had not responded to the First Ashipu and Nin-Digir's considerable efforts to bring him from his coma.

"Is there nothing left we can do for him?" Ashmadu asked hesitantly.

The Nin-Digir frowned soberly from the other side of the bed. "There is one thing, but it's dangerous, considering we don't know the cause of the damage to his brain." She sighed deeply, as if she might regret the words she had started to speak. "We have a . . . Abgal . . . that can connect his mind to another's and 'see' into the En's memories, thoughts, desires, and secrets. In this case, we need his memories. Our Abgal can link with the En, relive his last moments of consciousness, and communicate what was happening and how he was feeling. It could give us a clue to the answers we seek, kill the En, obliterate his mind completely, or accomplish nothing at all."

"If that's all that's left, then you must do it." Ashmadu was adamant. "The En would rather die than to live the rest of his days like an overripe date hanging from a tree." The En had spoken to Ashmadu many times in recent years about not wanting to be a burden to others if he were ever in the condition of not being able to care for himself. Ashmadu had never thought much of it at the time considering he never believed it could happen, yet here they were.

The Anunnaki Nin-Digir nodded. "I will summon him to us, then."

She cupped her hands together gently and blew through a small opening between her thumbs. A blue radiance appeared, becoming brighter and brighter from something forming inside them. Slowly, she opened her hands, and a small blue bird stood in her palm, radiating a bright blue glow while twitching its head back and forth. The priestess leaned in and whispered something to the bird. It cocked its head toward her lips and then, after she had finished, hopped onto her finger and flew out of the room at an impossible speed, appearing more like a bright blue streak than a bird when it departed.

She turned to Ashmadu. "He will be here soon." Then she sat down in a chair close to the En's side to wait.

Astounded, Ashmadu stood for a moment before silently taking another chair nearby. He was continually amazed by these people called the Anunnaki. Surely if anyone could cure his master, it would be them.

Time passed slowly in the silence between them while the Nin-Digir continued to weave her magic into the En, who lay unconscious and motionless. The room was not silent, however, since many Ashipu attended to others requiring medical attention. He could see a sobbing boy who had broken his arm doing something foolish and a moaning man who had been bitten by a venomous snake, and he heard the periodic screams of a pregnant woman who was suffering active labor.

Ashmadu had been sitting a long time and was dozing off when he felt a cool breeze and heard sheets flap in the wind rushing through the opening door at the far end of the room. He looked up and could just make out the tall silhouette of another Anunnaki in the doorway.

"He is here," Nin-Digir Shonaturi remarked without turning.

The Anunnaki Abgal entered the room and slowly made his way toward them. His pale blue skin was luminescent in the dim light, and his long blond hair matched the layers of yellow robes he wore. As he walked, he stopped at the stone tables that were occupied, touching each patient gently on the forehead, leaving them calm and without pain or discomfort when he moved on. At the table where the woman was giving birth, he touched both the woman's forehead and her abdomen at the same time and then lingered for a moment, whispering to the Ashipu that attended her. The woman calmed, and then the Ashipu priestess pulled from her womb the pale form of a newborn trailing the cord of life back into its mother. After a quick clearing of its mouth and throat, a sharp cry echoed through the room, and the woman began to cry with tears of joy.

The Anunnaki continued on. No Ashipu objected to his intrusion or attempted to stop him, and each respectfully bowed before returning to their work at hand. He stopped at several more tables before finally reaching them, leaving the patients he contacted calm and at ease. The Anunnaki acknowledged each other with a nod in silence, and the Nin-Digir rotated her palm in the direction of the En.

Before approaching Ipqu-aya, the man turned to Ashmadu and lightly laid a hand on his forehead. For some reason, Ashmadu had expected the touch of the Anunnaki to be cold, but it was warm like any other's.

"I am Ferulianreg of the Yellow Hall. I am what the Sag-gig-ga call an Abgal. This is your master that I have been summoned to inspect?"

Ashmadu nodded, all the while wondering why the man's lips did not move as he spoke. "I am the En's personal houseman, not a slave."

"The Nin-Digir has warned you of the dangers and possible outcomes of my interference?" The Anunnaki's voice seemed to echo inside Ashmadu's head.

Ashmadu nodded again. "She has, and I can attest that the En would not wish it otherwise."

"I will do what I can to find the source of his ailment." The Abgal released him and turned back to the En.

Ashmadu felt a presence leave his mind that he had not previously detected and realized with a chill that neither of them had spoken aloud.

"This may take some time," the Abgal told Ashmadu and the Nin-Digir. "Please be at ease."

Ashmadu was startled at the man's voice, only now hearing it for the first time. It held a deep resonance and was calming at the same time.

The Abgal put his hands on the En's head and then pressed his fingers to his temples and forehead. And there he froze as he delved deep into the other's mind.

Ashmadu had moved closer to the Nin-Digir to give the Abgal space to do his work. He leaned over and whispered to her, "Did he heal all of those people when he came in?"

The priestess's lips curled up into a slight smile. "No, dear one, he simply calmed their minds and gave them comfort, although often that, in itself, is all that is required to heal."

Time passed slowly. The Abgal barely moved but whispered arcane words from time to time. Ashmadu felt drowsy again and began to drift in and out of sleep while the Nin-Digir continued to monitor the En for any sign of movement or stress.

~~~

"Ashmadu, pour the Kas from the pitcher to the cup as I've shown you," the Lukur lectured. "Remember that you will fill it just more than halfway, not all the way. Careful! Don't spill a drop or overfill. If you do, the En will be very cross with you for staining his clean white robes."

The little boy was careful, but his small hands were not practiced enough to be steady yet, and he spilled a few drops outside the cup. He cringed, expecting a blow from her cane, but it never came.

As she looked down at him sternly, he thought he saw an expression of sympathy flash across her face. "Is that what you are used to from the other Lukur, child? Do you see a cane in my hand? There has never been one, and there will never be one. Your punishment for not doing a thing correctly will be to repeat it over and over until you do. Wipe that up and try again."

At only five, he was learning many of the advanced table service duties that were usually reserved for children seven or eight years old. He learned quickly and displayed a calm demeanor for a child his age. The Lukur who oversaw his training now was new to him and, though stern, seemed more compassionate than the others. She told him to call her Sipa, his shepherd, but others called her by a different name that he could not remember.

He wiped the liquid from the table and slowly attempted to fill the cup again. The pitcher was heavy when full, and he struggled to hold it steady above the rim with his small hands. Once more, he spilled outside the vessel.

"Again," she said.

It took several more tries until he worked out how to properly balance the pitcher over the cup without spilling.

"Very good." She smiled and handed him a sweet date. She was beautiful when she smiled and reminded him of his mother, whom he had not seen since she'd left him with the temple.

He had never asked about her—he was always too afraid—but with Sipa, he felt comfortable, and it just came out. "Sipa, will my mother ever come back for me?"

The priestess's smile faded. "No, child, the temple is your mother now, and I am your shepherd. Think no more of it if you can."

Ashmadu was not upset. He did not cry. His place here seemed natural, and he was beginning to like Sipa with the sweet dates. Maybe there would be more if he tried hard to please her.

That was the last time he spoke of his mother. He had a vague memory of being hugged tightly by her, the smell of her hair and her voice. She had told him that she loved him and always would, but never anything about coming back or visiting him. It seemed so final the way he remembered it, and the reality appeared to be no different. He put her memory away that day and decided to only look forward from then on. If Enki willed it, he would be happy. This much, at least, he had learned from the temple.

~~~

Ashmadu was startled awake by sudden movement. It was Ferulianreg falling into the chair next to him. The Annunaki looked exhausted. His face was flush with sweat, and his hands shook a little while resting on his knees. The hour was late, and the infirmary was quiet, with only a few Ashipu watching over their charges. Ashmadu must have slept for at least two hours.

He could barely constrain himself from asking questions while the Nin-Digir stood, took the Abgal's hands in hers, and said a few incomprehensible words. When she released him, he was no longer shaking and appeared less tired.

"That will temporarily relieve your exhaustion, but you must get some rest soon." Her fingers brushed the Abgal's cheek as she retreated back to her seat.

An Ashipu, seemingly unbidden, brought a cup of water for the Abgal and then returned to his work.

After drinking every bit of water he could drain from the cup, Ferulianreg looked at Ashmadu. "You were the most important person in this man's life," he said and gestured toward the En.

Ashmadu was speechless. The En was not married and had no children or siblings, yet Ashmadu had never expected that he played such an essential role in his master's life.

"In fact," the Abgal continued, "he has left everything he owns to you when he dies or is unable to care for himself. Everywhere I probed in his mind, and nearly every memory, held a piece of you in it. My impression was that he thought of you like a younger brother or son, someone he cared for deeply and also respected."

Tears ran down Ashmadu's face. He could hardly believe the gratitude of this great man, who had humbled himself so to a servant. But Ashmadu would have traded everything, even his own life, for the health and recovery of his master. "Will he return to us?" he asked. It was all he wanted to know.

The Abgal adjusted his yellow robes and glanced at the Nin-Digir before answering quietly, "Not likely."

Ashmadu's heart sank, and the feeling of loss began to pervade his being like he had been thrown into the icy water. When he looked away from the En, both Anunnaki were watching him with expressions of genuine sympathy.

He had to know. "Did you discover how this happened?" he asked in a hoarse whisper.

The Abgal shook his head. "Not definitively. What I did learn is that his condition was not the result of physical degradation. He was in very good health. Something unnatural, perhaps magical, caused the blood to cease in parts of his brain. Whether it was deliberate or incidental, I cannot say. After searching his memories, I found nothing recent that caused him distress except for his most immediate concern for the Sanga. In fact, given his position, he led a very mundane, simple lifestyle."

Ashmadu smiled. "It's true. He is a pious man who believes the luxuries of life come from the heart. Some believe that his devotion is so pure that Enki himself takes the time to speak with him."

"Do you share in that belief?" the Nin-Digir asked.

"I know it to be true," Ashmadu responded without hesitation.

Abgal Ferulianreg narrowed his large almond eyes and appeared to regard Ashmadu curiously. "The last conversation he had—in fact, it was during this conversation that the episode began—was with the Sanga."

Ashmadu nodded. "Yes, when I brought Shatamurrim to the En's office, we found him collapsed on the floor, and the only other person in the room was the Sanga." He went on to explain the events of that morning that had brought him to the En's office with Shatamurrim.

"So that is why the En was so relieved when he arrived and the Sanga was waiting for him," Abgal Ferulianreg said. "That's the point I started experiencing his memories."

Ashmadu became alarmed. "Were they arguing, or was the Sanga pressuring the En in any way that might have upset him?"

"Not at all. It was a very casual conversation. No anger, no disagreement. Just small talk, really. And friendly at that."

"Could you tell how the En was feeling at the time?" Ashmadu asked.

"He was relieved and happy. He did not become stressed until his episode began."

Ashmadu leaned back in his chair, feeling defeated. "We will probably never know why he had the attack. Maybe the First Ashipu was right when he suggested that it might have just been a natural effect."

"There was one thing . . . at the end." The Abgal seemed hesitant.

"But it might have been just a distorted perception brought on by his distress. The last image the En registered before losing consciousness was the face of the Sanga looking down at him, smiling almost triumphantly. Was there any reason that the Sanga would wish the En ill? Did he covet the En's position?"

Ashmadu shook his head. "They love each other as brothers. The two of them have known each other well since they were young, and it has been whispered that they conspired together to put themselves in the positions they hold now. The Sanga never had an interest in being the En. His strength and joy is in the work he does as the Sanga. For that matter, the Sanga mostly had his way when a rare disagreement between the two occurred. They always discussed their differences and never got angry with each other. They would drink, one or the other would relent, and they would move on. The Sanga is a brilliant organizer and administrator, and the En has always been likable and charismatic, a man that the Sag-gig-ga could relate to."

The Nin-Digir, who had been listening silently, spoke up. "Ferulianreg, could one with your abilities cause the same physiological effects in another body?"

The Abgal cocked an eyebrow. "That would require an enormous level of talent. I'm honestly unsure if I could duplicate such a feat. Perhaps after years of practice and countless wasted lives. It would be a significant challenge. Besides, if the Sanga had such enormous power and skill, it's doubtful I would have missed that."

"The possibility should be considered," she responded, "even if it is unlikely, given that there is no other explanation."

Ferulianreg stood and stretched. "I wish there were more I could know from him, and I'm very sorry the news was not better." He laid a comforting hand on Ashmadu's shoulder. Then he turned to the Nin-Digir. "If I can be of any further service, please call upon me."

She nodded, and their eyes met for a moment. Ashmadu was sure that they spoke more—but not in a way that anyone but they could hear.

The Abgal walked back through the quiet infirmary, speaking briefly to the Ashipu he met along the way, and out the front door into the chilly night.

"What shall I do now?" Ashmadu asked the Nin-Digir after the Abgal departed.

Shonaturi looked down at the En sadly. "You look after this man for as long as you are willing. You can take him back to his home if you wish as early as tomorrow. I will speak to the First Ashipu and make sure he has a staff to attend him day and night."

"But I—"

"You will need their help to care for him," the priestess interjected. "You cannot do it alone. If you try, soon *you* will be sick and unable to care for him or yourself. Don't worry. You will be in charge, and they will follow your direction."

Ashmadu was unable to resign himself or the En to the state that everyone seemed to be sure would never change. "Will you return again and evaluate his condition from time to time?" he asked.

Shonaturi smiled and kissed the forehead of the former slave as she stood. "You will see me every week for as long as he lives, and I will never give up hope for him. And now you, good man, need to rest awhile. The next time we meet will be in the comfort of your home."

She touched his left temple with her index finger, and he felt his eyelids drooping as he began to fall asleep in his chair. Then she unfolded a blanket from a nearby table and covered him up to his neck to keep him warm. After one last glance at the En, she followed the same path the Abgal had taken out of the infirmary and disappeared into the darkness. Ashmadu watched her depart between the cracks of his drooping eyelids before he, too, disappeared into the darkness.

Chapter 14

Suspects

𒄑𒀭𒌷𒊩𒍣𒀭

Namzu reviewed his notes from the murder scene and the others that preceded it. From everything he had seen so far, he did not believe the crime to be a random one. In fact, he was confident that the murderer was well acquainted with the family and not considered a threat by them—so much so that Arwi-a was caught completely by surprise. There had been no struggle, no cry for help heard by neighbors, and no defensive wounds on the hands, arms, or faces of any of the victims. Considering that nearly every home in Eridu left its door open to the fresh early-summer breeze—and the number of people in the streets during the day going about their business—somebody should have heard something if there were a scream, cry of pain, or desperate scuffle.

In any other case, this would have led him to suspect the husband or the son, but both individuals were beyond reproach and held high-level, respected positions within the temple government of Eridu. And neither of them had a motive that he could determine.

Shatamurrim was a distinguished Sar who led the famed Ursagmuda and had quickly ascended the ranks in the Eridu military. He was by all accounts devoted to his family, especially his mother, and according to the neighbors, none ever witnessed disputes within the household during his visits. Additionally, everyone agreed that his parents supported his choice to join the military, where he proved his strategic intellect on more than one occasion. Everyone the Usgadi spoke to considered him a hero, and his parents were known to be proud of his success.

The only disagreement that Namzu could uncover between Shatamurrim and his mother involved when he might find a wife and father children. She wished for grandchildren sooner rather than later, but Shatamurrim was in no hurry to marry. The disagreement was a playful one and had never caused a true rift between them.

A little less was known about the Sanga, considering most of his time was spent at the temple. However, the neighbors likewise reported that he and his wife, Arwi-a, seemed happy together, with no apparent conflicts between them. In fact, the Sanga was rarely at home to begin with. That in itself could have been a source of conflict, but no one ever heard Arwi-a criticize her husband for it. In Namzu's experience, sometimes a situation where the husband was always away and the wife was alone at home led to infidelity and jealous lovers. But this did not seem to be the case. Arwi-a was not known to have inappropriate visitors while her husband was away, nor did she complain about her husband's activities when he was not at home. The consensus was that she was a devoted mother to her son and respectful to her husband. Likewise, the priests that worked closely with the Sanga knew him to be a hardworking, no-nonsense, pious man wholly devoted to his work with no interest in moving beyond his current station. Further, he and the En got along well, and their friendship went back decades even before they joined the temple.

Namzu wasn't surprised at the findings. If one of them committed the murders, then he went to great pains over an extended period of time to plan it perfectly or it was entirely spontaneous. The questions were endless.

In Namzu's mind, the answers would come from better understanding the symbols that were found not only at the Sanga's residence but at the seven previous murder scenes at the inn. There must be a connection that would reveal . . . something. The Anunnaki Abgal translated four of the symbols from the last murder at the inn, and then Namzu found translations to four more in the writings deep in the bowels of the temple library. A total of twenty-seven symbols were found at the murder scenes, although many of them had been repeated in different orders from one murder to the next. That left five symbols that still lacked meaning.

Something didn't fit. The innkeeper, for one thing. Either he was not the murderer, or there was more than one. But why would he have attacked the Aga-us if he wasn't guilty? Could he have been hiding something else, or was the most straightforward explanation that he was just deranged and happened to be the innkeeper of the inn where the murders occurred? There was also the possibility that the murderer knew the innkeeper was on the edge of sanity and used that as an advantage to misdirect the blame. Maybe that's why he tried to cover up the murders at the Sanga's house before being interrupted in some way. There were far too many maybes for Namzu. He couldn't put his finger on what was troubling his thoughts about the whole thing, but he was determined to find out. Even if everything he learned was true, something had changed.

He wasn't ready to completely rule out members of the immediate family yet, despite their apparent incorruptibility. The family that appeared the closest often harbored the darkest secrets and hidden troubles. He would uncover those secrets if they existed.

Namzu's next step was to widen the investigative circle. He would send his Usgadi to interview the casual friends and associates of the family. He was disappointed that the En had fallen ill; he might have provided a much more in-depth layer of understanding about the Sanga's family since he had known them all for so long. Namzu hoped that a suspect might emerge just outside their inner circle, someone no one would have considered. Sometimes it happened that way—a disgruntled work associate, a jealous cousin, a vindictive house servant, and so on.

Namzu was determined to uncover the truth. He always did. No secret could be kept forever, and often the person who committed the crime couldn't help but tell another—especially if they thought they had gotten away with it. That would be their undoing.

He planned to visit the infirmary this morning. It was two days since the En had taken ill, and perhaps he was well enough to speak again. Besides, Namzu had to get out and do something. He was not the type to sit in his office and wait for the answers to come to him.

With that expectation, he left his office in the section of the temple complex dedicated to the judiciary and law enforcement. This was his domain. All the Usgadi and Sars that protected the citizens and enforced the laws had been his responsibility for the past twenty years. His predecessor died holding this office after a long and respected career. He hoped to be as lucky. It was his job to keep the laws fairly administered within the city and surrounding territory controlled by Eridu. No man or woman, from En to slave, was beyond the law.

Fortunately, he succeeded a man who all but eradicated corruption and violent crime, which, for the most part, made his job relatively straightforward and uncontroversial. Not that he was resting on the man's laurels—quite the contrary. Namzu would do everything humanly possible to make sure Eridu didn't slide back into the old days of lawless chaos. That was just another reason he must catch the murderer and show that he was in control.

As Namzu walked through the temple grounds toward the infirmary, he observed many Sahar-nitah going about tasks that the young initiates would have customarily performed. Sometimes their priests were with them, and sometimes not. He did not have one of the earth-men himself, and he hoped the En would be rid of them soon. Too many of the priests from every sect, not to mention the Sag-gig-ga in Eridu, were becoming dependent on them to do their work.

The Sahar-nitah had been among them for several days longer than they should have been, and already the productivity of the city slowed to a lazy crawl. *At least they cannot be compelled to do violence,* Namzu thought with relief. The En said they would crumble to dust the morning after their creation, but they persisted. It was rumored that Enki strengthened their fortitude and that they would fall to pieces at the end of the Creation of Man celebration. That would remain to be seen. The only earth-men that had not survived were those that were taken more than a league from the city. In each of those cases, they inexplicably became frozen like an earthen statue or disintegrated where they stood. Even those carted back to Eridu remained inanimate.

The Zi-ik-ru-um summoned Namzu recently, asking him to investigate their nature further. They were concerned that the Sahar-nitah might remain for a longer time. If that were the case, specific restrictions would have to be put upon their use. Otherwise, the city might suffer economically, which translated into a loss of influence and power in Kur-gal, which, in turn, might leave them vulnerable to both foreign and domestic adversaries. Without the En to consult on the matter, not much was known about the earth-men. Even the Suba priests who helped the En create them were at a loss.

When Namzu arrived at the infirmary, an Ashipu directed him to where the En lay unconscious on a stone table. Another man, a little younger than the En, was asleep in a chair next to him—probably a house servant, by the look of him. Namzu motioned to a nearby Ashipu and inquired after the En's condition.

"He is in a deep coma, from my understanding," the Ashipu said, "and may not wake for some time. I do not know the specifics, but I believe this afternoon he will be taken home, where his care will continue."

Namzu frowned thoughtfully. "Whose care is he under? I would like to speak to the Ashipu who has the details of his condition."

"The First Ashipu and the Anunnaki Nin-Digir Shonaturi are the most informed about the En's condition. At present, the First is meeting with the Zi-ik-ru-um and will probably not return until late this evening, and the Nin-Digir has been here every day since the En's arrival and only departed early this morning after another of their kind spent the night examining him." The Ashipu seemed unsure about the second Anunnaki.

"I see," Namzu replied without any outward show of surprise. "Thank you for your help."

The Ashipu bowed and continued about his rounds.

Namzu was only a little surprised that the Anunnaki had taken an interest in the En's care. After all, he was the most powerful En in all of Kur-gal, although Namzu doubted that mattered to the Anunnaki as much as the unusual nature of the En's sudden illness. Namzu would have to return the following day to speak with the First Ashipu—unless he was bold enough to seek out the Nin-Digir. If he did, Namzu might also gain more insight into the mysterious symbols.

He glanced at the En and then his house servant still sleeping in the chair next to him. The man, either exhausted or in a deep sleep, had not been awakened by Namzu's conversation with the Ashipu.

His mind made up, Namzu left them and the infirmary to find the Nin-Digir Shonaturi. Standing again in the daylight, he let his eyes adjust to the light while he considered where to find the Nin-Digir. He knew that the Anunnaki spent almost all their time at one of two places within the city— either deep inside the Ziggurat, where the Orichalcum Crystals were held, or at their residence in the Tower of Tongues. The latter was where the Nin-Digir would likely be at this hour.

Fortunately, the Tower of Tongues was located within the temple complex and not far away. Namzu could see it from where he stood—and likely from every part of Eridu due to its extraordinary height. An impressive structure, it was constructed with a white marble stone unknown to the Sag-gig-ga and built in a style unfamiliar to his people. A Suber priest told him once that the stone from which it was built was a material similar to alabaster from TaShemau, but it was magically altered to withstand weathering.

The tower was the highest structure in all of Kur-gal with the exception of the Ziggurat. If the old stories were factual, while far more expansive, the Ziggurat was built to the exact height of the tower but not a feather's width more for fear of angering the gods that commanded it to be erected, or so the legend went. And while every city-state in Kur-gal was constructed around a Ziggurat dedicated to one god or another, none of them approached the size of the one in Eridu.

According to the Zi-ik-ru-um, the tower was constructed by the Anunnaki a few years before the first city arose in Kur-gal and shortly after they initially arrived on the plains where they first appeared to the Sag-gig-ga. They said the purpose of the tower was to provide all the people of the world the ability to understand each other in a common language, regardless of their native tongue. It is said that without the tower, civilizations would have a much harder time communicating with each other, trade would suffer, and conflicts would arise.

Namzu paused to admire the tower and those who dwelled inside it. It was correct that there was no language barrier with any foreigner he ever met. It was also true that there were many different languages and regional dialects, yet still, he understood them all when they were spoken to him. Maybe that was the key. When spoken to directly or when the person speaking intended for others to hear their words, then the language was understood clearly. When not spoken to directly, as when he passed through the markets, he could hear the native language of the person speaking, maybe even know where they were from, but he did not understand the words. Namzu did not pretend to know how it worked or the power that it must have required to achieve such a feat. It was just another aspect of the Anunnaki's capability that contributed to their awe-inspiring and intimidating standing in Kur-gal culture.

Wide at the base, the tower tapered as it rose skyward, each section separated by a terrace, with the spaces in between quilted with numerous broad balconies adorned with hanging gardens and lush foliage. It reminded Namzu more of a step pyramid, which he remembered from a visit to TeShemau a few years before, rather than a traditional tower. Except that the Tower of Tongues was far taller. And instead of a sharp point at its zenith, it featured a flat landing, upon which figures could be seen moving about from time to time.

Although Namzu never witnessed any in his lifetime, there were stories of great ships under massive sails that could fly through the air as well as ply the seas. Purportedly, these ships would dock at the top of the tower, where the Anunnaki could disembark. Less than a week ago, a farmer swore to one of his Usgadi that he saw one of these ships in the early morning hours sailing on the winds from the direction of Eridu and toward the west. Everyone the poor farmer told laughed and suggested that he not drink so much Kas.

Namzu wondered how many Anunnaki lived in the tower. A hundred or more could comfortably call it home, he guessed, but he never saw more than a handful out of the temple complex at a time, making their rare appearance almost a spectacle. Once in a while, he would see a few of them emerge from the tower and travel toward the Ziggurat or see them in the city shopping at the markets. There were men and women of every adult age, although they seemed to get older far slower than the Sag-gig-ga. Every one of them dressed in the fashion of a priest or priestess, with a preference for lighter blues and greens. Although some, like the Abgal he met, wore far more bold colors. Not once had he seen one that he would have described as a warrior, but why should he? From everything he knew about them, they were magical beings who needed no mere mortal weapon or armor to protect themselves. Of course, most Sag-gig-ga, including himself, considered them higher-level creations and the offspring of Enki.

The Anunnaki were known to befriend many in the city, especially within the priesthood, but other than perhaps the En and the Sanga, no one had ever been in the tower. If anyone else had, they never shared their stories publicly. For Namzu's part, he recognized their stabilizing presence in Kur-gal and appreciated the fact that the Anunnaki never violated any laws. For that matter, they were a strong influence in the laws' creation, according to the history tablets.

He arrived at the massive double doors of the Tower, which were fashioned from a shiny metallic material like polished silver. No one was around. He would just have to knock. How, he wondered, would he manage to see the Nin-Digir? Would they let him in or send him away? *Perhaps she will answer the door herself*, he mused with a chuckle.

Just when he was about to bang on the massive doors, they began to slowly open toward him. He backed up and waited, and when the breach widened enough, he could see the form of a tall man wearing flowing yellow robes standing on the other side. *These Anunnaki are so damn tall*, Namzu thought. And so intimidating, considering how short the average Sag-gig-ga was. As he looked up at the man's face, he saw that he was smiling. A good sign.

"Silim sum, First Usgadi Namzu. It is good to see you again. The Nin-Digir Shonaturi has been expecting you. Please come in."

Namzu's heart nearly leaped from his chest. He was not sure if it was because the Abgal remembered his name and was expecting him or because he had just been invited inside the Tower of Tongues.

"Thank you, Abgal Ferulianreg," he replied, maintaining his composure while, at the same time, wondering if he'd said the man's name correctly. "I remain grateful for your help at the inn last week, and I do have important business with the Nin-Digir regarding our En, who has been stricken with a terrible illness." Why was he speaking so much?

The Abgal smiled again, as if he'd known everything already, and merely said, "Please follow me."

If the outside of the tower was impressive, the inside was spectacular. The interior was hollow, with the exception of several wide walkways around the perimeter and beautiful, arcing bridges crisscrossing from one end to the other. Namzu looked straight up and could see the clouds in the sky high above through a wide hole at the very top of the tower. Directly below it at floor level was the most beautiful exotic garden he had ever seen, and in the center of that was a massive statue so detailed and lifelike that he would not have been surprised had it blinked.

The statue resembled a creature of legend, part man, and part fish. Instead of legs, he had the scaly tail of a fish that supported his human figure above the waist. He was muscular, with long, curly blond locks that fell from his extended skull to his shoulders. His full beard complemented large, brown, almond-shaped eyes and a straight nose similar to the Anunnaki's. In his right hand, he held a spear with three barbed spikes at the end that he thrust forward toward the sky in a commanding gesture. In his left hand, he held what appeared to be a very unusual abacus. And hanging from a long, thick chain around his neck was a medallion engraved with the symbol of the Primal Sea. It was just like the ones worn by many of the Anunnaki. At the base of the statue, which was elevated just above the top of the gardens, was a plaque bearing a title in a strange, flowing script that seemed to waver like ripples on the water's surface.

Namzu, feeling bold enough to ask, pointed at the plaque. "Abgal, what is the meaning of those words?"

The Abgal stopped for a moment, and his perpetual smile widened. "'Pontus, Lord of the Primal Sea.' A prayer is written below it."

"Is this a god or hero that is unknown to the Sag-gig-ga?" Namzu asked.

The Abgal looked thoughtful. "The best interpretation for the Sag-gig-ga is that Pontus is a form we regard like that of Enki."

Namzu wasn't sure what the Abgal meant exactly, but he refrained from pressing further. Perhaps Enki had many forms and this was the one favored by the Anunnaki. It unquestionably would not be unusual considering that many of the gods of the Sag-gig-ga could transform into animals and humans at will.

Namzu's attention constantly shifted as they walked, trying to take in every detail of the wondrous tower. Dozens of Anunnaki walked the passageways above him and the ramps that spiraled up the interior wall. Some even floated on disks of light that hovered a hand's width above the floor. Children ran here and there, laughing and playing. He couldn't remember ever seeing an Anunnaki child before. It never occurred to him that they could procreate at all.

A narrow shaft of sunlight descended from the opening above, and natural light somehow emanated from the interior walls appearing to project a diffused glow, chasing away the shadows. At every level of the tower, Namzu could observe broad doors that presumably corresponded with the balconies on the outside of the tower and likely led into each residence. And everywhere, high and low, were colorful statues of marble and alabaster that represented different peoples and animals from around the world. Some were ordinary and typical from lands he was familiar with, while others were so strange that they stretched the boundaries of his imagination. Taking it all in, Namzu had the impression that the Anunnaki lived within the walls of their tower, not unlike the ants that he witnessed living in man-sized cones on the southern planes.

"It's not far," the Abgal said suddenly in a deep and steady voice.

Namzu, so in awe of his surroundings, was startled when the Anunnaki spoke, nearly tripping over his own sandals. He was definitely feeling out of his element here. To his great relief, the Abgal appeared not to notice. "Shonaturi will meet us in the garden."

The gardens in the center of the tower looked healthy and lush. Some of the trees and bushes appeared to bear fruits and nuts that Namzu had never seen before but assumed were edible. At the far edge of the garden, crops were arranged in rows of leafy, linear stalks as tall as the Anunnaki themselves. On each, there were half a dozen or more long pods the length of Namzu's forearm with bunches of fine yellow hair extending from the top of each one. Was this how they reproduced?

An Anunnaki man wearing brown robes and tending the garden broke off one and removed the tight, leafy layers enrobing the pod to reveal an oblong yellow fruit or vegetable with neat rows of pulpy lumps covering its sides. He threw it in a pouch hanging from his shoulder and moved down the row to the next stalk.

Namzu felt foolish for wondering if this was how they engendered their children. His imagination could run wild standing in this place with so many unbelievable sights. He would have to regain his composure before he met the Nin-Digir Shonaturi.

Chapter 15

Tower of Tongues

The Abgal led Namzu in the garden down a winding path that was intersected by narrow trails that wound away in many other directions. They arrived at a shaded clearing and there, on a stone bench at the edge of a still pond, sat a beautiful Anunnaki female of perhaps middle age. She stood as they approached and smoothed the wrinkles from her layers of green and sea-blue silk robes.

The Abgal bowed to her. "Nin-Digir Shonaturi, I present the First Usgadi Namzu, here to see you about the En."

Namzu bowed as well.

"Silim sum, Usgadi Namzu. I am very pleased to meet you." She smiled what had to be the most beautiful smile he had ever seen, then gestured to a nearby stone bench. "Please sit."

The Abgal sat down next to the Nin-Digir, and Namzu sat across from them where she had indicated. Before anyone could speak, a young Anunnaki priest emerged from a side path with a tray holding three cups and handed one to each of them.

Namzu ignored the cup in his hand and focused his gaze on Nin-Digir Shonaturi. "How did you know to expect my visit?"

The Nin-Digir tried to hide a smile behind her cup, but Namzu noticed. "Are we not Anunnaki?" She said it as if that explained everything.

"Well, yes, but—"

The Abgal cut Namzu off. "We believe that we have reached the same conclusions that you have regarding the En, and given your reputation for being thorough in your investigations, we anticipated that you would come to us sooner rather than later. If not, we would have brought our determination to your attention soon enough."

"I see." Namzu's investigative brain was fully engaged now. "And what conclusions have you come to that you believe we share?"

The Nin-Digir leaned forward and whispered for dramatic effect, "That the Sanga and his son, Shatamurrim, were the only ones that could have killed the Sanga's wife and servants."

Namzu's mouth nearly fell open with surprise. How could they know this?

"And you are uncertain as to which it could have been," the Abgal continued in a normal voice after rolling his eyes at the Nin-Digir, "considering their respective positions and stellar reputations. But there is also something that you don't know."

Namzu couldn't understand how they had somehow come to the same conclusion that he had. "And what is it that I don't know?"

"The Sanga appears to have disabled the En as well," the Nin-Digir stated succinctly.

This indeed was a revelation to him. "Can you be more specific?" he asked calmly. Inside, his heart was thumping wildly, and he prayed that they couldn't hear it.

The Abgal took up the conversation. "The En suffered a catastrophic restriction of blood in his brain that stopped the flow long enough to cause permanent damage. It resulted in the coma he is in now, which could last another day or the rest of his life." He paused and glanced again at Nin-Digir Shonaturi. She nodded for him to continue. "Four factors indicate the Sanga was behind the En's impairment. One, there is no physical cause for the interruption of blood flow to the brain, implying that it must have been caused by unnatural means. Two, the disruption occurred while in private conversation with the Sanga, and no one else was with them at the time. Three, the Sanga made no effort to help the En when he began to fail. And four, the Sanga had an expression of satisfaction, even a smile, when the En fell to the floor."

Namzu stood abruptly and nearly shouted, "How do you know this?" What they were implying could not be known with any certainty without the En being able to tell them so himself.

The Abgal's smile disappeared, replaced by a slight frown. "I am an Abgal of the Yellow Hall. My specialty is in understanding the ways of the mind, and I have seen his last memories through his own eyes."

"Be calm," the Nin-Digir cautioned Namzu. "We are here to help you. Do not presume that we will tolerate an interrogation."

Namzu lowered himself to his chair and tried to relax. "I deeply apologize, Nin-Digir. I have allowed my passion for the truth to overtake my good sense."

It was true. Namzu had forgotten himself and nearly gone into full interrogation mode. The Anunnaki were known to be a benevolent people who highly valued respect, and he was teetering on the edge of pushing them too far. He preferred not to imagine the grim results of angering a demigod.

"Rest assured, First Usgadi, you will leave here with all the information you require," the Abgal said. "As I was saying, my particular talent is that of a mentalist of sorts. Without resistance, I can delve into the mind of another, read their thoughts, and access their memories. That is how I was able to gain the information from the En."

Namzu regarded the Abgal sharply. "Are you reading my thoughts now?"

"No," the Abgal said with a laugh. "It would be inappropriate for me to enter your mind unwelcomed unless it was a matter of life and death or you were an adversary intent on harm."

Namzu felt stressed, and his throat was dry. For the first time, he looked into the cup he had been given and was taken aback by the blood-red liquid that floated therein. Did they give him blood to drink? Reluctantly he took a sip and was surprised to experience a velvety wine with flavors of spice and vanilla that was far superior to the kurun wine that the temple imported from the north. "What is this wine?" Namzu asked. "It is the finest I have ever known."

The Abgal smiled. "It is a vintage from an outstanding vineyard on the Emerald Isle. It is called Mekali Red. It would be my honor to send a Gur-gur to your office to enjoy."

A Gur-gur, large vessel, of this amazing wine! Namzu's friends would be impressed. Quickly draining his cup, Namzu retook his feet and addressed them both, feeling somewhat embarrassed. "Thank you for the information. I am sure it will prove invaluable, and I again ask your forgiveness for my momentary disrespect."

The Nin-Digir nodded, and the Abgal tilted his head to the side. "Wouldn't you like to see the En's last memories for yourself before you leave?"

Namzu was stunned. "Is that possible?"

"Of course," the Abgal replied. "With your permission, I will transfer the memory to you so you can judge the events for yourself."

Namzu hesitated. He wasn't excited about the idea of allowing the Anunnaki to access his mind. There were far too many secrets there that only he and dead men shared. After some thought he agreed. The need to know what only the Abgal could show him overrode his reservations, and he allowed Abgal Ferulianreg to place his hands on his forehead and temples. The Abgal pressed firmly, and Namzu received a flood of images. At first, it was overwhelming to the point that he felt nauseous. Then the Abgal said something, Namzu didn't know what, and his stomach calmed, and the swirl of images began to resolve into something he could comprehend. He recognized the En's office. He could hear the mundane conversation with the Sanga and feel the contentment within the En. Then there was a sudden pain—pain in his head that became excruciating—and his eyes started to cross as a loud buzzing intensified in his ears. Namzu felt the pain and fear as if they were his own, and he fell to his knees, holding his head in agony just as the En fell to the floor in the mental images.

"One moment," the Abgal spoke softly. "I will reduce those effects."

The pain, fear, and buzzing diminished to a tolerable level, and Namzu could see the Sanga clearly. His expression was oddly lacking emotion—no surprise, no shock, no concern. He just sat there while the En crumbled to the floor. Before the En lost consciousness, Namzu detected what could only be a smile on the Sanga's face, and then darkness followed.

"Now those memories are yours just as if they were your own," the Abgal told him when he released Namzu's head.

"It was exactly as you described," Namzu whispered, slowly regaining his feet. "That must have been terrible for the En."

"This information will help you to pursue justice," the Nin-Digir's voice held a hint of anger. "The difficult part will be proving it—or at least convincing your Zi-ik-ru-um that it's enough to have him removed from his office."

"I don't have much time," Namzu replied. "As soon as the First Ashipu declares the En unfit to carry out his responsibilities, the Sanga will elevate to the position twelve days later. It will be much harder to remove an En than a Sanga, especially one with decades of influence and few enemies."

"Are you still in pain?" the Nin-Digir asked.

"It is still very present in my mind. Will it go away soon?"

Nin-Digir Shonaturi stood and approached Namzu after he returned to his seat. She placed a single long-nailed finger on his forehead, and the pain evaporated instantly.

Namzu felt tremendous relief. "Thank you, Nin-Digir. Thank you."

She smiled in a motherly fashion and sat down again.

Namzu thought through what he learned. "Although the images you have given me suggest the Sanga may have been pleased with the En's sudden episode, it does not mean that he had anything to do with it. The images you showed me imply that perhaps he had hidden ambition and realized that he had an unexpected opportunity to assume his office."

The Abgal nodded in agreement.

"And how do you suppose the Sanga brought about the illness to the En?" Namzu asked. "A poison perhaps?"

"We don't believe poison could have caused the illness and left no trace of its presence," replied the Abgal. "There are other means."

Namzu tugged at his beard. "Magic? Did the Sanga cast a spell that caused it?"

The Abgal frowned and shook his head. "Not exactly. We believe he may have access to an ability similar to my own—either through his own power or an ally willing to do it for him."

Namzu puzzled over such a scenario. "What do you call this ability that is like magic?"

"We in Atla—" The Abgal cut himself short. "Anunnaki call it psionics."

Namzu noted the slip and wondered what it meant. He decided to catalog the thought for contemplation later. "Have you ever known of a Sag-gig-ga to possess this ability?"

"No," the Abgal admitted. "That's why I suspect there is someone or something helping him."

"I think that somehow what we are discussing today is related to the symbols we have found now at eight murder scenes," Namzu said. "I was hoping you would help me understand them, particularly the last five, which I have not been able to translate."

"Eight? There has been another since the innkeeper died?" The Abgal leaned forward in alarm and exchanged glances with the Nin-Digir.

What might alarm an Anunnaki? Namzu wondered. "Ah, yes," he replied. "I thought you might have known. The last three symbols were found in the Sanga's home."

The Abgal leaned back in his chair. "Shonaturi, it is as bad as we feared."

"Let's hear the rest, Ferulianreg, before we make hasty judgments," the Nin-Digir replied in an unsteady voice.

Was that fear?

"Show me the symbols," the Abgal spoke in a voice barely more than a whisper.

Namzu had brought his pack with all the tablets in case he needed them. He sorted through them quickly, retrieved the one with the symbols drawn at the Sanga's residence, and handed it to Ferulianreg.

The Abgal took it with a steady hand and studied it silently.

After a long wait, Namzu turned to the Nin-Digir and raised his eyebrows in question.

The Nin-Digir must have agreed that it had been an excessively long time and gently shook the Abgal. "Are you okay, Ferulianreg?" Her hand lingered on his arm.

The Abgal looked up. His eyes seemed to stare past her. "Yes, dear one, I am." He laid his hand atop hers, giving it a small squeeze.

Namzu felt as if he were viewing a private moment between the two.

The Abgal turned back to him. His smile was gone, and so was his sense of humor. "I can tell you what they mean."

The hair on Namzu's arms stood as if a lightning storm were imminent. The silence was excruciating, but he waited without speaking.

Ferulianreg held up the tablet and pointed to the first symbol. "This one means, *(The) land becomes sick from their bodies.*" He pointed to the next. "And this one says, *There will be sacrifice for (my) hunger.* The third says, *(I will) cover mankind like a garment.* The fourth reads, *Pervade their parts.*" He pointed to the last one. "Finally, this one says, *Evil calamity.*"

"You've done it," Namzu said. "You've completed the translations. Thank you, but . . . what do they mean?"

The Abgal and Nin-Digir stared at each other. Something was happening between them. The Nin-Digir clenched her green and sea-blue outer robes, white-knuckled even though her face was calm and expressionless. In contrast, the Abgal was the personification of intensity as he stared unblinkingly back at her.

"Tell him," the Nin-Digir finally whispered, breaking the spell between them.

The Abgal turned his gaze back on Namzu with a look in his eyes filled with pity at the knowledge he was about to transfer. "What this means is something terrible for Eridu, Kur-gal, and even the world as a whole. The last time words such as these were written was well over a millennium ago. Until a few days ago, I might have believed it impossible that these symbols could ever exist again in this world."

Namzu felt a cold pit forming in his stomach as he watched the Abgal use a stylus to arrange the symbols on a new tablet.

When he was done, the Abgal held it up for Namzu to inspect. "What you have found, poor Namzu, is the Anagoge of the Unholy Scripture, from the Colloquy of the Utug, found only in Ki-hul, as you know it."

Namzu's blood ran chill in his veins. Ki-hul was a place of evil, where the dead who committed evil acts in life dwelled. He read the passage, and as he did, that chill spread to the pit in his stomach and crept up his spine, spidering along every nerve in his body.

The Sag-gig-ga (become) my servants
The servants are mine to command
This (place) will be the temple of (my) sanctity
There will be sacrifice for (my) hunger
(They) will be purified with blood
Unholy transgression
(I will) cover mankind like a garment
Evil calamity
I (will) pervade their parts
Sloth
(The) land becomes sick from their bodies
This land bleeds for me
I am here

Namzu read the passage again and again. His mind didn't want to accept what he was reading—or what it meant for Eridu.

"If this scripture could only be known by someone or something from Ki-hul," he said finally, "that means the murders have been committed by an Utug—one that was summoned, perhaps by the Sanga or another, to commit murders toward some malevolent end."

The Abgal stood and paced. "Not just any Utug, First Usgadi. This one is the Demon of Sloth, one of only seven named Greater Demons from what we call the Infernal Planes, or Ki-hul as it is known to the Sag-gig-ga. His sacred name is Maoffas, but that is of no consequence unless you meet him."

Namzu was perplexed. "Then how is it the Anunnaki know this language and recognize the symbols so well? Could an Anunnaki somehow be involved with summoning this Utug?"

The Nin-Digir Shonaturi spoke. "We know because we must. The language is the celestial language, the language of gods and Demons and spoken on this earth by those known as the Tuatha De. It was they who trapped this Demon with others within a pithos long ago."

"Others?" Namzu prompted. Did that mean there were more?

"As the Abgal said, there are seven named Greater Demons, and they were all trapped together. If one is loose, then they all are." Fear, as distinct as it was unmistakable, appeared in her eyes as she spoke.

"Are you saying I have *seven* Utug to deal with?" Namzu exclaimed.

"No, no," Ferulianreg replied quickly. "They would never stay together. However they escaped, they likely scattered to the winds. The other six are no doubt planning their particular brand of chaos in other parts of the world."

"How come they are loose in the first place, and how could they have escaped whatever constraints you had on them?"

"That's a very long story, First Usgadi," the Nin-Digir replied, "and only the En may know the answer to that question. We are forbidden to discuss that with any other Sag-gig-ga. I'm sorry."

"Can you at least tell me how it can be defeated?" Namzu implored them, feeling helpless against the powerful being.

The Abgal cleared his throat. "This we can do. It will not be easy, and many may die trying."

"What choice do we have? We can't leave the Utug free to do as he pleases."

"True enough. The only way to defeat a named Demon is to either subdue him and exorcise him back to Ki-hul or banish him using his True Name, which would do the same. And before you ask, I don't know if there are any Anunnaki who would know where to find his True Name."

"I will leave that part up to you," Namzu said, standing up again. "In the meantime, I'm going to see how much I can find out about the Sanga and form a plan to confront the Utug, wherever it may be. I will let you know when I discover something."

Nin-Digir Shonaturi stood as well. "Be well, First Usgadi Namzu. We will keep watch and aid as best we can until we have what we need to banish the Demon."

The Abgal escorted Namzu back to the entrance. Absorbed in his thoughts, Namzu neglected to take in the wonder of the tower's interior before his departure. Once outside, he thanked Abgal Ferulianreg for all his help.

"I have something for you before you leave." The Abgal retrieved from a pocket in his robe a small Orichalcum Crystal set into a plain copper frame that hung from a leather thong. "This will provide protection against intrusion into your mind. Use it as you see fit."

"Thank you," Namzu responded. "I'm sure it will come in handy."

As the door closed behind him, he thought he heard the Abgal mutter to himself, "Let's hope not."

Namzu would have to return to the infirmary and talk with the En's house servant. Had he realized the nature of the En's illness earlier, he would have woken the servant to answer a few questions when he was there. Namzu left the shadow of the Tower of Tongues knowing far more than when he arrived. Knowing far more than perhaps he wanted to, and it brought fear that he had not felt since the days before Ipqu-aya was En.

Chapter 16

Mus-Lu

𒀀𒈜𒋾

Shatamurrim felt oddly comfortable in his old room, despite both the horrific events that occurred on the other side of the door and the fact that he left his parents' home several years ago. Only three days had passed since his mother was murdered here. The servants had been replaced, and all signs of the bloodshed had been removed. But aside from his room, the rest of the house gave him the chills, defiled by evil.

Sometimes when it was quiet, he could almost feel his mother's presence. On more than one occasion, he was sure he heard her humming, the sound echoing softly through the hallway from the room his parents once shared. He would rush toward the sound, only to find no one there. It was strange that nothing changed since his mother had died. Her room was exactly as she left it, almost as if she might return to it at any moment. Often he could smell the cedar and myrtle incense she loved, although none was lit in the house. Were the humming and the fragrance a creation of his imagination? He missed his mother and longed for her comfort. The night before, he dreamed that she was singing to him as she had when he was a child, and he awoke in tears, a grown man feeling alone and sad. Shatamurrim was relieved that he and his father's prayers had been answered and that his mother was granted access to Kurnugia by the gods. He took great solace in the knowledge that he would be with her again one day and that gave him a small measure of peace.

It was still morning, and Shatamurrim had eaten his breakfast and seen the servants off to the market. Alone in the house now, he noticed he felt closer to his mother when no one else was there. It was so quiet when the house was empty—silent like a tomb. How fitting, he thought, considering the solemn reverence he held for the spaces where his mother once lived. Now so different than the home he had grown up in, it felt like the home of a stranger.

He wondered if his father would ever come back to the house. It would not be an easy thing for him, Shatamurrim was sure. In the days following the murders, he had seen his father only a couple of times and never in his own home. He stayed at the temple and slept in his private chambers there. Shatamurrim feared that his father would never be the same again. He seemed unlikely to ever return to the family home even after the poignant memories began to fade.

Shatamurrim planned to travel to his mother's burial site that afternoon to leave offerings of Ninda and Ebla, baked bread and beer. There would undoubtedly be many other offerings from family friends and admirers so he wouldn't know if his father had been there. His father would need time. Until then, Shatamurrim would provide for his mother, even if that meant doing so for the rest of his life alone. The offering was the only way to ensure her comfort across the Seven Gates and final portal to the Underworld, Kurnugia. He was glad to do it. It also gave him the excuse to sit at his mother's burial and talk to her about whatever was on his mind. He was no fool—he knew his mother couldn't hear him—but it made him feel better, and it was what he needed right now.

There was something else on his mind as of late. Something he didn't think he would ever have to face again. The Mus-Lu reemerged along the foothills of the Sa-ti-um Mountains east of Eridu. Just the thought of them turned his stomach. They were a grotesque, reptilian people that looked as if a snake had somehow mated with a human. There were sightings of them to the southeast foraging for food near the Gihon River and trapping fish from the shores. This was a good indication that they were supplying a more substantial force or settlement hidden in the caverns and ravines within the mountain range. So far there were no reports from the local tribes in the area of contact or confrontation, but with the Mus-Lu there usually never were any warnings until they advanced en masse. Shatamurrim had no doubt that patrols would be sent out and that sentries would be posted to monitor any changes in their behavior.

The Mus-Lu were dangerous adversaries, and as far as Shatamurrim knew, there was only one reason for them to be anywhere near human habitations: to feed upon them. It was not just part of their strategy of provoking fear. They genuinely enjoyed human flesh, and aside from seizing resources, it seemed to be their primary motivation. In times of conflict, the Sag-gig-ga knew that if they surrendered or were captured, they would be carried away to a gruesome fate.

Shatamurrim doubted that there was a man, woman, or child in Kur-gal who didn't hate the Mus-Lu. They were a terrifying force that had a uniting effect on the city-states, unlike any other enemy. Even the Anunnaki, who customarily arbitrated disputes between the city-states and foreign powers, dealt harshly with the Mus-Lu. There was no negotiating or compromise with them, only death, and that was something he and his Ursagmuda were skilled at delivering.

Shatamurrim stared at the gold medallion that hung on the wall in his room. The engraved image of Enki gleamed brightly on its polished surface, and the leather band that held it was well-oiled. It had hung in that spot for more than two years without collecting dust. After he received the Honor of Enki, he dedicated it to his mother, who had been the one to hang it in his old room and keep it maintained all this time. He wished he could go back to that time again—almost. There was terrible loss and death in those days as well.

It was because of the Mus-Lu that he was awarded the medallion. Shatamurrim recalled the day he learned some twenty-thousand of their kind rushed out of the Sa-ti-um Mountains, overwhelming the tribes that lived between them and the Idigna River. They came so fast and unexpectedly that the villages never had a chance. Only a few escaped while thousands died, but it wasn't enough for the Mus-Lu. They began to swarm west toward Eridu, intent upon overrunning the city and destroying everything in their path like rabid locusts.

En Ipqu-aya sent the military out of the city to meet them before they could cross the Buranuna River and destroy their crops and irrigation. The Eridu troops were to be joined by forces sent by the Unug and Bad-tibira, city-states to the north, which would easily swell their numbers to match that of the approaching Mus-Lu. But they were still several days from Eridu, and at their current pace, the Mus-Lu would overrun them before the reinforcements could arrive.

They needed more time. Shatamurrim recalled the fear and panic that fell upon Eridu when word got out about the approaching Mus-Lu. The En ordered the evacuation of every man, woman, and child who could not hold a spear and began to prepare Eridu for assault. When the Mus-Lu reached the walls, there would be no siege. The Saggina, military generals, made it clear that the only way to fight the undisciplined reptilian horde was in the open field where they could skillfully maneuver with phalanxes and chariots. The walls were no barrier anyway. The Mus-Lu could merely dig their clawed hands and feet into the clay and scale them without the need of grapples and ladders. If they got past the phalanx and entered the city, the En was going to make sure they found it abandoned.

It seemed like only yesterday that the En called Shatamurrim into his office and asked him to take his Ursagmuda across the river and do what they could to delay the advance of the Mus-Lu. Many thought it was suicide, and his mother begged him not to go. She even pleaded with her husband to send another in his place, but it wasn't their choice to make, and Shatamurrim would not let his brothers down. It hurt him profoundly to tell his mother of his decision, but she surprised him by accepting his judgment stoically once he made it. That was his mother. She would fight for what she wanted but would tolerate the outcome and support him as well as she could in the end.

Shatamurrim remembered the fear he had felt inside but kept hidden from his men. The Mus-Lu were vicious and hard to kill. They were also disorganized, which was to the advantage of the Sag-gig-ga, who fought in formations of disciplined units and utilized strategic planning. Shatamurrim and his men would never see that kind of fighting. Instead, they would strike, run, hide, and harass to slow them to a crawl or even stop them for a while if they could.

He had fought the Mus-Lu before, ambushing their skirmish parties and capturing a few. Yet nothing compared to the scale of the force that approached Eridu at that time. He heard that one of the captured Mus-Lu was sent to the Praa of TaShemau as a gift and that the others were taken away by the Anunnaki, never to be seen again. Sometimes he wondered about their fate, even today.

Shatamurrim thought about the men who had followed him in those terrible days. He knew all thirty-six hundred of them by face and name, many of their mothers' names as well. They followed him to face certain death with the grim knowledge that if they fell to the Mus-Lu and their bodies were vulgarly consumed, they would never be allowed to enter Kurnugia.

Still, they followed him. He was so proud of them, every one, and could to this day name each of the brave souls who had fallen. He could never forget their names.

Vivid memories of their first contact with the Mus-Lu flooded through his mind. It was on a moonless night fifty leagues east of the Buranuna, and the enemy was caught utterly by surprise. His Ursagmuda almost effortlessly cut through their inattentive sentries and sleeping ranks before melting back into the darkness. *Not a single man was lost that night,* Shatamurrim thought proudly. He would never know the extent of the damage they inflicted in that first assault, but he knew it was significant and lifted the morale of his men.

The next night, they set up a decoy camp with stuffed blankets and campfires a league south and beyond a line of hills that were sure to be spotted by the Mus-Lu patrols. As expected, a large force of the reptilians was sent to the camp in the early morning hours, only to find themselves surrounded and cut to pieces while they struck at blankets filled with grass and reeds. No Mus-Lu survived the ambush, but the Ursagmuda felt the agony of their first casualties as well.

Over the next several days, they continued to harass the Mus-Lu, always at night and from a different direction. By then the reptilians were expecting an attack and were far more prepared to defend their flanks, which took a greater toll on the Ursagmuda in each assault. Each night there were men who died in the fighting whose bodies could not be retrieved from the battlefield, their fate sealed. The Mus-Lu suffered severe losses as well, and most importantly, they barely moved during the day, so exhausted were they from the nightly onslaught.

Shatamurrim fingered the gold medallion but found no honor in it. It all seemed heroic at the time—until the end. There was no glory in the end.

By the fifth night, he was down to less than a thousand warriors. Many hundreds had been buried all over the plains, and hundreds more were left for dead and dragged away by the Mus-Lu. He dispatched a message the day before to Eridu advising the En of their progress and their current condition. Shatamurrim prayed to Enki that the Ursagmuda had given their people the time they needed to consolidate their forces on the other side of the Buranuna. His men were tired, and each was wounded to some degree, yet their spirits remained fierce, and they encouraged each other with quiet songs of inspiration.

To his men's credit, the reptilians had not moved at all the previous day. Instead, the Mus-Lu took the time to rest and prepare their defenses for what they knew would come that night. Shatamurrim's diminished Ursagmuda engaged the Mus-Lu camp for the last time during the predawn hours, slashing and burning as they waded deeper and deeper among them. Perhaps it was because his mind was exhausted or because of the loss of his Second the previous night, upon whom he depended so profoundly, that Shatamurrim made a fateful mistake. Whatever the reason, he pushed too far and found his small force surrounded. He should have disengaged earlier. He should have realized the resistance was too light, drawing him deeper into their encampment.

Shatamurrim recalled the last hours bitterly. They faced a desperate situation, but his men never faltered and never forgot their training. They fought their way up to the top of a ridge near the edge of the Mus-Lu camp. The path they followed was narrow, allowing them to defend against the surrounding enemy with fewer men while maintaining a strategically superior position. Wave after wave advanced up the crowded narrows, only to be repelled each time, and finally, after a few hours, the enemy pulled back to regroup, leaving the Ursagmuda to rest and tend to their wounded.

Shatamurrim knew that none of them would leave the ridge alive and consigned himself to his fate. There were less than seven-hundred capable of fighting, and soon it would be dawn, at which time they would lose a significant advantage and become vulnerable to spear, sling, and arrow.

He prayed and sang loudly with his men to keep their spirits up and to keep his own from faltering. Surely the Mus-Lu, so close to their position, could hear them. Would they find it odd that they were singing? He proposed to his battered company that with the dawn they should break from the ridge and attack the enemy straight on. They agreed to a man that it was better to go out fighting shoulder to shoulder with their brothers than to be picked off like goats on the ridge, and they swore to exact a mighty toll upon the Mus-Lu before they were done.

Shatamurrim remembered every detail of the sunrise as the golden light first crested the peaks to the east. It wasn't so different from the light reflecting off the medallion he still held in his hand. He expected that it was going to be the last sunrise he would ever view, and perhaps as a result, it was the most beautiful he ever experienced. He remembered thinking about his family, especially his mother. His father would be proud and make sure that he and his men were properly eulogized with a monument, maybe even a day of celebration in their honor. And his poor mother, she would be sad and broken, tending his sepulture and bringing offerings. That was the future he faced, at best, if they managed to give Eridu and the other cities the time needed to consolidate their forces. At worst, everyone he knew would be dead, and none of this would matter. He had no doubt that all the brave men sitting with him on that ridge were having the same thoughts as his in those dark hours. Still, they were Ursagmuda, and the darkest thoughts were the fuel that inspired them to go on. They knew that for every Mus-Lu they killed it would be one fewer facing their brothers mustering outside of Eridu, and they were determined to thin that number considerably before they breathed their last breath.

Then, by the dim light of the rising sun, he began to make out the thousands of reptilian forms arranged in dark, writhing mobs around the ridge where they crouched. Such monstrous creatures! He wondered why the gods ever allowed them to exist. In contrast to their singing, the Mus-Lu had begun to hiss. So many thousands of them hissing was almost maddening and would have sent many good soldiers running in a terrified panic, except that his men were Ursagmuda, and they never ran in fear of anything.

It was almost time. When Shatamurrim turned to his men gathered on the ridge behind him, he saw only faces etched with determination. That was the proudest moment of his life. It was an image so powerful that even now he could close his eyes and relive every detail. Not a single man showed any fear or regret, and it gave him the confidence to lead them with the strength and determination they expected of him. They were all doomed to walk this place where they died for eternity, and they knew it. There was no hope for burial; their fate was to sacrifice. And in an odd way, he somehow knew they all accepted, maybe even welcomed it.

Shatamurrim signaled his men to prepare for their final charge. He had no doubt now that every last one of them would follow him without hesitation or blame. He wanted to weep for them, to weep for himself, but his rage burned away every tear while they waited for the sun to illuminate the way down from the ridge. It would be just moments before the last of the Ursagmuda would sacrifice their lives for their people.

Shatamurrim raised his spear to signal the final assault when he heard an impossible sound. He was sure he imagined it. He cast his gaze behind him, and his men murmured in disbelief. They heard it as well. Then the wind brought the sound again, louder this time.

"Za, Za, Za!"

It came from the west, distant but not far, from the voices of thousands appearing over the low hills and flowing down the other side toward them like the head of a massive flood of salvation. A beautiful flood in which Shatamurrim would gladly drown. He could not believe what he was seeing, and the tears finally came. Facing certain death only seconds before, he now had hope for the lives of his men. Some of them, many of them, might live to see their families after all, and those who fell would not be Gidim.

The surprised Mus-Lu turned to see the Sag-gig-ga charging with formations of chariots along their flanks. The reptilian captains ordered hasty defensive positions, causing the Mus-Lu to become even more disorganized and panicked in their chaotic movement. With their attention now refocused on the advancing army, Shatamurrim did not hesitate and ordered his men to charge. No longer leading doomed men, Shatamurrim and his Ursagmuda were energized and enthusiastic about life for themselves and life for their people. Never was there a more motivated brotherhood of men.

Two years had passed since the Mus-Lu had been crushed, but the emotion of that time was still fresh as if it occurred just yesterday. The battle raged less than an hour before the reptilians were either dead or in full flight. Few escaped. Shatamurrim ended the day with only four-hundred warriors, including the wounded. It was an astounding loss of life for the Ursagmuda that he would never allow himself to forget.

He held the gold medallion tightly in his hand, wishing he could crush it. The image of Enki stared back at him through the cracks between his fingers, mocking his inability to do so. His rage was tempered only by the memory of what his men accomplished in those nine days of bloodshed and the results of their sacrifice. A few days after the final battle with the Mus-Lu, when the dead were collected and committed to the earth, his father shared a report with him that had been sent to the En. The tablet was prepared by the Saggina of Eridu, and it estimated that Shatamurrim and his Ursagmuda had succeeded in diminishing the Mus-Lu forces by more than half—around twelve-thousand of the creatures—over the course of their campaign of harassment. It was even postulated that the Mus-Lu would never have been able to advance on Eridu, given their losses. It was unanimously recommended that Shatamurrim and the surviving Ursagmuda be awarded the Honor of Enki for their impossible achievement.

All four-hundred of those survivors were still with him today, but not a one wore their medallions. They didn't have to. The Ursagmuda would be legends forever, and the city revered them. Another legacy grew around the place where they fought the Mus-Lu, a legacy born out of tragedy and loss even beyond the grave. That place where men died and became nutriment for the Mus-Lu became known as the Plains of the Gidim. It was something of a holy place to the Ursagmuda, and even though the Gidim could never enter Kurnugia, every year the people brought offerings anyway.

Shatamurrim gently replaced the medallion on the wall. Soon he would have to leave the house and go about his duties. Today he and his men would be training in the marshlands that abutted the temple. He needed the distraction of disciplined military exercises to keep his spirits up and the exhaustion it provided to help him sleep at night—that and a healthy serving of strong Eridu Kas.

After gathering his gear, he stepped out into the crisp, late-morning air. His four-wheeled chariot, already equipped with javelins in the quiver and hitched to four onagers munching on grass, was ready for his departure. He took the reins and snapped them sharply, sending the beasts into a quick trot. The memories of those days were distinct, and even as he rode, he found himself muttering prayers that his Ursagmuda would not be sent against the Mus-Lu as they had been once before. He decided not to think about the reptilians for the remainder of his journey. The weather was beautiful, and he felt strong. This would be a good day.

Chapter 17
Gi-par

𒂍𒎯𒉺𒅕

Namzu waited respectfully just outside the open doorway to the En's private chamber at the Gi-par. Inside, the room was brightly lit by light globes and a warm hearth in one corner that kept the evening chill at bay. The En Ipqu-aya lay on a thick mat that was his bed, wearing his night robes and covered to midchest with sheets of silk and warm wool blankets. The layers of the coverings were perfectly smooth and unwrinkled, reminding Namzu of the prepared corpses ready for burial in the Hall of Kurnugia. The En was either sleeping very soundly or still unconscious, Namzu thought with trepidation. Next to him sat his house servant, Ashmadu, who was looking over a clay tablet and issuing instructions to a young Ashipu priest.

Earlier Namzu returned to the temple infirmary only to be told that the En had been transported to his home, where his long-term care would be more comfortable. The First Ashipu, Bikku-lum, was there at the time and confirmed what Namzu already knew: that the En was unlikely to fully recover, and even if he did, it could take years. Bikku-lum was also quite sure that Ipqu-aya would never be able to resume his duties of the office of the En. Namzu was saddened by the somber news.

There was a time when he knew Ipqu-aya before he was the En. In fact, the man played a significant role, along with Irra, in helping Namzu ascend to the exalted post. Those were dark and dangerous days when Namzu was a young initiate in a temple rife with ambitious priests greedy for power and influence. He was handpicked by Irra from the office of the Usgadi because of his shadowy talents and relative obscurity. Somehow the three of them managed the impossible and brought the temple back to the proper service of Enki and the people of Eridu. But it was not without sacrifice and nefarious deeds of their own that they accomplished their well-meaning design. Namzu was not proud of the things he had done, yet because of it, there was stability and prosperity in the temple and Eridu today. His reward was the position of First when the time came, endorsed by the En and the Sanga above far more experienced Usgadi and the grumblings of the Zi-ik-ru-um. By that time he barely knew them anymore, their personal association lost, not unexpectedly, to the passage of time. None of them ever spoke of the earlier days, although there was always respect between them and the shared responsibility of what they had done together so many decades before.

"Silim sum," the house servant finished with the Ashipu, then turned to greet Namzu. "How may I help you?"

"I am Namzu, First Usgadi of the E-Abzu." He kept his voice even and respectful, even though he addressed a servant. A servant who might hold the key to what happened to the En and perhaps others. "I am personally leading the investigation into the tragic murders of the Sanga's wife and servants."

Ashmadu stood and bowed to the First Usgadi. "Please have a seat and be comfortable." He turned to an adolescent boy whom Namzu had not noticed before. The boy was sitting quietly against the wall on the other side of the room. "Pirhum, please go to the kitchen and bring refreshments for the First Usgadi."

Without a word, the boy jumped to his feet, brushed crumbs from his simple gray robe, and hurried from the room.

"I see that there are a number of Ashipu in the house," Namzu said as he took his seat. "May I assume the En is well cared for?"

"Yes, First Usgadi, the First Ashipu has assigned several of them to keep watch over the En day and night indefinitely. Most are young initiates and have little medical experience, magical or practical. They keep him clean, and his skin oiled, exercise his limbs, and feed him as best they can. His condition will be monitored twice daily by more experienced Ashipu and often by the First Ashipu himself, so I am told."

Namzu sighed. "The En is loved by his people. I have no doubt that his needs will be seen to for as long as he takes a breath."

"I was sad to hear of the Sanga's wife and servants. So many tragedies at once. The Sanga must be in a terrible state. Have you been able to hunt down the culprit yet?" Anger simmered in Ashmadu's eyes that belied the casual way that he asked the question.

The First Usgadi adjusted his seat so that he could face Ashmadu and still see the En. "No, but I am turning over every rock in that effort. I have sworn to the Sanga that we will."

The young boy, Pirhum, returned with a tray holding barley flatbread, a bowl of sweet dates, and two mugs of Kas. He set it on the small table beside Ashmadu and Namzu, bowed, and then returned to the place against the wall where he was sitting previously.

As they enjoyed the refreshments, Namzu casually inquired about Ashmadu's long relationship with the En, the events on the day the En was stricken with his affliction, and the details of the days afterward in the infirmary.

"I met with the Nin-Digir and the Abgal this morning," Namzu confided. "They related the astounding details of the Abgal's search of the En's last memories. You must know the Sanga well, considering the close relationship between the two of them."

Ashmadu shrugged. "I knew him as a frequent caller to the Gi-par, but I never conversed with him in a social manner. That would have been inappropriate. I may be a free man, but I am also still a servant in service to the En."

"Understood," Namzu said with a nod. "But knowing him from your perspective, does what the Anunnaki say surprise you?"

"Just as I told the Anunnaki, the En and the Sanga are like brothers after a fashion, and they both love and excel in the positions they hold. It would be astounding to me if the Sanga had designs on wearing the mantle of the En considering his aversion to the position all these decades." Ashmadu shifted uncomfortably as if very troubled by the idea.

Namzu pressed further. "But given the circumstances of the last interaction between the En and the Sanga, does that leave you with any doubt?"

"I have been considering that very question during the night and quiet moments of the day, and it does, I must admit."

"And were there other times over the years when you might have had a brief moment of doubt about the Sanga?" Namzu was trying to keep the conversation casual. He didn't want their discussion to come off like an interrogation.

"That's the odd thing," Ashmadu answered. "What the Anunnaki has told me—something I didn't see with my own eyes—is the only time that I've ever considered the Sanga to have ill motives concerning the En."

The Abgal had not shared the memory with Ashmadu, Namzu realized. He merely told Ashmadu of his observation about the Sanga.

The two men sat in silence for a moment before Ashmadu asked, "What is going to happen next?"

Namzu took a deep breath. "Within a few days, the First Ashipu will likely declare the En unfit to continue his service, giving the Sanga the option to step into the position himself or confer with the Zi-ik-ru-um Council to elect an En from the high priests and Firsts of the temple. Either way, twelve days after the First Ashipu makes his declaration, there will be a new En."

Ashmadu's face flushed with anger, but he kept his voice calm. "So soon? And what if En Ipqu-aya awakens and is healthy enough to resume his work?"

"En Ipqu-aya will never resume his position once relieved of it. If he were to someday recover well enough to continue his work at the temple, he would likely return as a Zi-ik-ru-um. To remove a sitting En just because Ipqu-aya had a change in fortunes could be very destabilizing for Eridu."

Namzu was beginning to appreciate the relationship that Ashmadu shared with the En. It was not the usual relationship between master and servant. They seemed more like. . . Friends.

Ashmadu stood and began to pace. "Could you ask the First Ashipu to delay for a while making such a declaration? Just a few more weeks, perhaps?"

Namzu adopted a somber tone. "The First Ashipu has already been dragging his feet, and no one is pressuring him. He is a friend to the En and hopes as much as anyone that he does recover. But he cannot delay much longer. The governing of the city has been at a standstill far too long as it is. For the sake of Eridu and the people, he must make a declaration very soon if the En does not recover. As for me, I cannot influence the First Ashipu in this regard. You know that."

Ashmadu lowered himself back into his chair and heaved a long sigh. "Of course, you are correct. Please forgive my inappropriate suggestion."

Namzu stood and clasped Ashmadu on the shoulder. "Send for me if anything else comes to mind about what we spoke of today. I will make an offering at the E-Abzu tonight on behalf of the En. May Enki hear our prayers."

Ashmadu thanked the First Usgadi and sent Pirhum to show him the way out.

Once outside the En's house, Namzu considered what, if any, new information had been gained from the meeting. He mulled every detail while he walked back to the temple. By the time he reached his office, it was nearly dark, so he retired to his private chambers after making a few notes on clay tablets. He would stay near his office tonight so he could get an early start in the morning. Tomorrow he would meet with his Usgadi who were scouring the streets and their contacts for information about the murders. Perhaps they would have something useful for his consideration, although he doubted it after what he learned from the Abgal. The best he could hope for was a hint of someone new and unknown that might have been seen with the Sanga lately, a new relationship like a lover or confidant, who could be described or even identified. He needed something that would point to the Utug in whatever form it might take.

He decided to give the assignment to Sabum. If anyone could cast a net around the Sanga that would capture the answers, it would be him. *But how much should I tell my second?* Namzu thought. It wasn't a question of trust as much as it was a question of liability. He didn't know the extent of the Utug's power, the Abgal wasn't clear about that, but what he did know was that it could enter a man's mind. Better to give Sabum just the information he needed, Namzu decided, at least for the time being.

~~~

Ashmadu sat quietly next to the En. He was exhausted, having slept little the night before in a constant state of worry for his master. And now he had even more to worry about. The First Usgadi asked a lot of questions regarding the relationship between the En and the Sanga, and he was evidently asking others the same questions and more. Ashmadu hoped the First Usgadi was done asking him questions. If the First Usgadi somehow came across the truth . . .

Ashmadu leaned over and whispered in the En's ear, "I will never reveal our secret."

The room was quiet and warm. The Ashipu had gone about their business, and Pirhum was curled up asleep on the floor. Ashmadu was not even sure how late it was, but he let himself drift off to sleep where he sat in the wide, well-cushioned chair.

~~~

"Sipa, are you proud of me?" the young man asked. He was crouching next to his gravely ill Lukur, who lay on her mats and appeared so much older now.

"Exceedingly," the Sipa replied. "You have excelled beyond my every expectation, my lovely Ashmadu."

"What will happen next?" he asked. "What future shall I expect?"

"That is up to the new En. He has requested that you become his new house servant. You will be a Subur for only three more years, and then you will be paid for your service if you elect to stay." Her voice exuded pride.

"Is he a good man? Or shall I fear him?"

"En Ipqu-aya is the best of men," Sipa assured him. "He will treat you well."

"Will you come with me, Sipa? Will you still be my teacher?" Ashmadu felt he was losing her and held her hand tightly.

"I am old now, Ashmadu, and my health is failing. You no longer need a teacher, for I have given you all the knowledge that I can. But I will always be here for you while I live." She smiled warmly.

"You have been a mother to me, Sipa, when my own did not want me. You are the one who has given me hope and love in the years that should have only been despair. I can't imagine a world where you are no longer a part of my life."

"You are stronger than you believe, child, and when you think of me, you will always be reminded of that. Think of how much you have accomplished, the honor you have received by being selected by the En, and how much you have overcome already in your young life. My time grows short here, and soon I will pass to Kurnugia. But have no fear, my little Ashmadu. I will always pray for you."

Ashmadu awoke in tears. His Sipa passed to the Underworld that night, so many years ago, having fulfilled her obligation and so much more to Ashmadu. He tried to go back to sleep, but all he could do was toss and turn. The dream left him feeling as if he lost his mother all over again.

~~~

Shatamurrim was exhausted after a long day of training with his Ursagmuda in the marshes outside the city. He was glad to be back at his parents' home and looked forward to sleep. He even looked forward to his dreams, since that was when his mother would usually come to speak with him. The experiences were becoming more real, leaving him wondering if they were dreams at all. But he knew they had to be dreams since they were always about his childhood and never the terrible events that occurred not long ago under this very roof. Shatamurrim was glad because it gave him comfort to rest and grieve her loss. He also knew that his mother was in Kurnugia. Not even the most potent magic—not even a god—could reach out from there, according to the temple.

The servants had already prepared a light meal for him and a bowl of warm water with which to wash. Then he was off to sleep. Tomorrow would bring more of the same with his Ursagmuda, as would the day after that and the day after that one, with many to follow.

While he settled into the plump cushions, pillows, and blankets that had belonged to him since childhood, he thought about his men and the fellowship they shared. They never complained. That was not the kind of men they were. The Ursagmuda viewed everything as a challenge to be overcome, one that would make them stronger, and they knew their Sar needed the distraction.

With the hard training came laughter and comradery. Shatamurrim thought about the humiliating names they called each other to encourage determination to work harder and inspire anger, names they laughed about together later. *Surely there were new ones I could invent before I fall asleep,* he thought with a smile. He realized with a start that they were the closest thing he had to family now, besides his father and Ashmadu. His mother was gone, and the En had one foot in Kurnugia. Even still, Shatamurrim was luckier than most. He had thirty-six hundred men who loved him like a brother and would follow him into Ki-hul with a song on their tongues if he bid them to. That made him think of the Mus-Lu again, but he was too tired to dwell on those monsters. If they needed killing, then he would go kill them. His mind wandered until the darkness took over and he was peacefully at rest.

Chapter 18

A True Name

𒀭 𒈹𒊭𒁉 𒉿𒊩

Irra slept fitfully, yet his consciousness required no sleep at all, and he was endlessly irritated by the fragility of his body, which required so much rest. Why did he have to be so old? He had to concede that being younger would only constitute a slight improvement to his physical requirements, so he used the unproductive time to contemplate the details of his short-term goals.

Sometime during the night, while his thoughts were consumed with his planning, a quiet disturbance began to cause mild distress to his body. Without waking, his mind reached out to his physical sensations to determine the annoyance.

It was cold, unnaturally cold. The chamber where Irra slept never felt this cold before, and the weather was only mildly bitter lately, even at night. Slowly, he allowed his eyes to open and found the room was in complete darkness. The hearth had been allowed to go out. *That will get one of the girls a beating in the morning,* he thought. Lifting his right hand, he snapped his fingers and muttered a word, and a small light globe brightened the room dimly from a short pedestal nearby.

He jumped with a start. The illumination revealed the form of a woman standing at his feet. More shocking than her presence was her physical condition. Blood trailed from her mouth, and much of her body appeared severely burned. Her hair that would by custom have been braided was in extreme disarray, as was her tattered and torn dress, which hung in pieces from her disfigured extremities.

Irra recognized the wretched creature as his own wife, Arwi-a.

"Do you see me, Demon?" she asked. "Do you see what I am?"

Irra was not afraid—intrigued, but not afraid. Still, he replied through dry lips, "I see you, Gidim. You look better than last I left you." He smiled. "Why have you come here?"

"Pure evil, you are!" she shouted with anger. For a second, Irra though she might strike out at him, but her anger turned suddenly mournful.

"You have left me between worlds. I cannot return and have been denied entry through the gates to Kurnugia."

Irra was unsympathetic. "That is the foolish commandment of your primitive gods. What do you want of me?"

Arwi-a grew enraged again. "Vengeance! I seek vengeance, Demon, and I will never give you peace until I have delivered retribution upon you!"

It was colder now. Irra could see his breath, visible in the dim light. It didn't bother him; he knew she could cause him no harm.

A laugh erupted from his chest almost involuntarily. "Vengeance, you say? What vengeance can you take upon me? Perhaps you are terrifying to these frail hearts you haunt, but you have no power over me."

It was the spirit's turn to laugh. "Inanna gave me a gift for your treachery. A great gift indeed: I know your True Name."

Irra laughed again, although this time it was forced and he felt uncertain. "You cannot know. None of your kind could know, except perhaps a few of the Anunnaki, as you call them."

The ghost of Irra's wife rose above the floor and floated over her possessed husband, who now sat atop his thick mats and pillows. "Deceive yourself if you will, Edimmu, Utug, or whatever you wish to be called, for I know you have many names. But it's your True Name that gives me power over you, Alu-Abad."

Irra was taken aback by the realization that somehow this dead spirit really did know his True Name. Fear, an emotion he almost never experienced, coursed through the body he commanded. If she were flesh, she would have possessed the power to send him back to the Underworld. What power did she have as a spirit?

As if she saw the question in his eyes, she continued. "I will commune with you nightly until my husband is at rest without you. There is nothing you can do to stop my intrusion, and you will be tormented by my anguish while he sleeps. You will suffer, Alu-Abad. I will make you suffer, and I will ensure your destruction."

And then she was gone.

Had Irra been himself, he would have thought it a dream and laughed it off. But the Demon inside him was not laughing now. Even knowing his True Name, the spirit was not strong enough to force him from her husband's body, although he did not doubt that she would cause him endless aggravation. Worse, she might be able to communicate his True Name to another among the living, and that would almost certainly spell his departure. Even though she could only appear and be heard by someone she was close to in life, he knew he would have to deal with this spirit quickly.

Alu-Abad allowed Irra's physical form to return to rest. He would need its energy for the next day, and now he had even more to contemplate. He considered what he had and what he would soon have. This level of earthly power was unfamiliar to the Demon. Until now, he had at best been fortunate enough to possess a wealthy merchant or minor noble. Unfortunately, those possessions rarely lasted long before his host died or was killed and he was compelled to find another.

Although there were only a few ways a Demon of his power could be forced from a host once he was able to take control of its mind, it was an endless cycle of jumping from one body to another. Alu-Abad despised the process. If the host died or, on rare occasion, had the exceptional mental strength to resist, then he would be thrust out of his host and in search again. The problem was, no matter when he was compelled to leave his host, he only had until dawn to find another. Otherwise, he would be flung into the nearest living creature or banished back to the Infernal Planes if he resisted. Sometimes that resulted in very awkward experiences. Alu-Abad found himself driven to possess rats, cats, and even a horse once. Continually moving from host to host was the sad life of a Demon outside what these Sag-gig-ga called Ki-hul. He knew it as the Infernal Planes, and he would do anything avoid returning to that purgatory. No matter the difficulties in this world, he thought with a sardonic laugh, it was better than the one he came from. Had he stayed there, he would have been the slave of an Arch Demon that would have happily tormented him for eternity. Fortunately, he was one of only seven Named Demons that was able to escape captivity several millennia ago and enter this world, where he had the power to do the tormenting rather than being the subject of it. That is until those damned Atlanteans arrived and with the help of the Tuatha De rounded up all the Demons lose in the world and sealed them together in a pithos for eternity. If it weren't for the curiosity of Anesidora and a foolish old priest, he would still be in there . . .

He searched Irra's memories to catalog anyone that the Gidim Arwi-a might find a sympathetic ear. Only one name was an apparent hazard: Shatamurrim. Alu-Abad contemplated the child of Irra and weighed the threat before he came to a decision. He would have to dispose of the Sanga's son. With luck, he could make it look like a tragic accident that would not fall under suspicion, but whatever the method, he knew the boy must die before his damned mother could deliver to the True Name—if she hadn't already. Alu-Abad would have to be cautious. Knowing his True Name would give any mortal the power to send him back to the Infernal Planes with little effort. Tonight he would have to murder the boy in the same house where he killed the mother.

He woke the body of Irra and dressed to go out. He would be tired the next day after sleeping so little tonight, but that was a small sacrifice in exchange for removing a grave threat.

Tomorrow he had much to do. His first meeting would be with the First Ashipu, Bikku-lum, who oversaw the temple infirmary, to get a report on the En's condition. By the end of that meeting, the priest would be "convinced" to declare the current En unable to carry out his duties sooner rather than later, leaving the path open for Irra to take the office. In the span of two weeks, he would be the En, and Alu-Abad would have the power to do as he pleased in Eridu.

None of that would happen if he didn't act fast with the Gidim. Pulling a hooded cloak over his shoulders, he stepped out into the chilly night, careful to avoid any slave or servant who might be about. Then he disappeared into the darkness intent on murder.

~~~

"Shata, Shata, wake, my son. It's your mother. I have something important to speak to you about, Shatamurrim!"

Slowly Shatamurrim opened his eyes to see his mother standing over him.

"Yes, Mother. I am awake. What shall we talk about tonight? The time I brought frogs from the reeds to live in your storage bins? Or the times we went sailing on the Buranuna?"

"No, my son." Her smile faded. "There's something I must tell you. And you must be strong to hear it."

"Of course, Mother." This was not like his other dreams at all. His mother appeared the way she always had when she came to his dreams. She wore a long, light blue gown that hung to her ankles, a gold necklace, bracelets, and rings—almost all of which had at least one lapis lazuli stone set into them—and her long braided hair was wrapped tightly around her head. There was khol around her eyes and color on her face—not too much, just enough to accentuate her features. What was different was her expression and manner, and he began to feel a little fear rising within him.

As if reading his mind, she said, "Shata, dear one. This is not a dream."

A chill ran up his spine. This must be a dream, he thought. It has to be a dream. If not, then . . .

Sadness distorted her features momentarily. "Yes, Shata. I can see in your eyes the only conclusion you can come to. I am not in Kurnugia, and I will likely never be."

"But, Mother, Father swore to me you had made it! You cannot be here now. I must be dreaming or losing my mind." He felt frantic that his reality was coming apart. Who should he believe? Why would his father lie? To save his feelings? He wasn't a child anymore.

His mother's voice became firm. "Shatamurrim! Listen to me. That is not important now. I must tell you about your father. Take hold of yourself!"

Shatamurrim knew his mother meant business when she spoke in this tone. Dream or not, he had to calm and listen to what she had to say and decide later if it was all real.

He got up from his bed and stood before his mother. "What is wrong with Father? Is he ill or injured?"

"No, Shata. He's alive but not well. His mind has been taken and corrupted by something evil. I do not know how, but it controls him. He is no longer himself." She reached out to him, but to his astonishment, her hands passed through his body.

Shatamurrim couldn't believe what he was hearing. What evil could have corrupted his father? "Mother, you must be mistaken. I was with Father after your murder, and he was devastated by your loss. Together, we sanctified your remains and performed the rites. He was himself, Mother."

His mother's eyes widened in desperation. "No, Shata. It was the evil inside him playing the role of your father. Don't you see, my poor little one? It was your father who murdered the servants and me!"

Shatamurrim was beside himself. "No, Mother! That cannot be true! Why can't I end this dream? I want to wake up. I want to wake up!"

"Shata, you must listen to me," his mother pleaded. "There is more that you must know."

"Don't listen to her," a voice behind him boomed, nearly sending him through the roof he was so startled.

Shatamurrim spun around and was stunned to see his father. "Father! What are you doing here? Are you now part of my nightmare? Did I dream you here as well?"

"This is not your mother, Shata. It's a shade of her, treating you cruelly. An evil Gidim! Send it away and tell it never to return!"

Shatamurrim turned back to his mother. "Is this true? Are you a Gidim speaking evil words for the pleasure of watching my suffering?"

"How did you know to come here, Demon?" his mother screamed at his father.

Shatamurrim had never seen her so angry, especially at his father.

His mother calmed and spoke softly to him. "I am a Gidim but not evil, Shata. Everything I told you is true. There is a Demon inside your father. It has destroyed his mind and taken his body. The rites that you and your father performed over my remains were real, and I was found by Inanna, but she could not take me through the gates to Kurnugia without becoming trapped herself. Yet she took pity on me and told me something important about the evil that has taken possession of your father."

"What is it, Mother? What did she tell you?" Shatamurrim didn't know who to believe. His father was alive and contradicting his mother's Gidim, who was dead. Yet there was something about his mother's words that rang true, and he felt more and more convinced by her words.

"Don't listen to her!" his father yelled from behind him.

His mother stared at Shatamurrim intently. "He is a powerful Demon, and his True Name is Alu-Abad."

Shatamurrim was stunned by his mother's words, unsure of what to say next, when he felt a shock to his body, and his mouth involuntarily opened wide. He tried to speak, but only a raw croak erupted from his mouth. Then he coughed, and blood sprayed across the floor in front of him. There was something heavy on his back, and the room felt like it was crowding in on him and going dark. Why was he falling?

"Shata." His mother barely got the word out before he fell forward and right through her. His last sensation was the rough floor slamming into his face without pain or discomfort. Then the darkness overtook him.

~~~

Alu-Abad smiled at the irony of the metal rod protruding from between Shatamurrim's shoulder blades. It was the same one he used to shift the bones in the kitchen hearth when he had disposed of the body of the boy's mother. He watched the Gidim's expression of shock turn to horror at the realization of what just happened. Her face was wide-eyed and her mouth stretched wide open as if she were trying to inhale the entire room. She stared in disbelief at her dead son, unmoving, with blood running in thin streams down his sides to pool on the floor beneath him. The Demon found the unexpected silence fascinating while he waited for her reaction.

When it came, it shook the room like a crack of thunder, shattering the silence with emotional intensity. Arwi-a's Gidim wailed with sounds the likes of which no temporal body had ever heard, and it rose to such a high pitch that it must have awoken every soul in the city. When it fell in tone, it bore a depth of mournful loss and sorrow that many would surely be brought to tears with the heartfelt pity in it.

When it finally ended, Shatamurrim's mother was gone.

Even the Demon was shocked by the pure sadness of the sound she made and was unable to bring himself to revel in his triumph. Instead, he hoisted the body and took Shatamurrim's right hand to make symbols on the nearest wall. He was compelled to make the symbols every time he took a life. He did not know why. He just accepted it as part of being the cursed creature that he was.

Finally, he rolled the body into the blankets the boy was sleeping on earlier and hurriedly left the house with it slung over his shoulder. After climbing aboard his chariot, he cracked the backside of one of the onagers with a stick, and they carried him swiftly down the road and into the darkness.

An hour later, he arrived at a secluded area along the bank of the Buranuna and threw the body into the rapidly moving waters. It quickly bobbed out of sight. He knew that eventually it would be found, but he hoped that he would be the En before that happened.

The sky was still black in the predawn darkness when he arrived back at his office at the temple. He was confident that anyone who might have seen him couldn't have known who he was, except for the Aga-us at the temple gates. Those he compelled to sleep, and if any of them had the misfortune of recognizing him before he put them out, then he would deal with them later. If he became a suspect in Shatamurrim's murder, it would be another reason to dispense with the First Usgadi, who was still tenaciously pursuing the murderer of Arwi-a and asking too many questions about the En. Alu-Abad didn't need any more scrutiny than he already had from the man and his Usgadi.

That night when Alu-Abad attempted to put Irra's body to rest, the Demon struggled with the unexpected and powerful emotions emanating from the lost consciousness of Irra. They were powerful enough that he feared losing control of his host and decided to force his physical form to rest. By morning, the mind and body that belonged to Irra—husband and father—would be manageable again.

~~~

A mournful wail, coming from somewhere in the city, roused Ashmadu from his sleep. At first, he was petrified with fear. Then it filled him with so much sorrow that he couldn't hold back the tears that flowed down his cheeks unbidden. His thoughts were filled with the sadness of what had become of the En and the misery that lay ahead for his master even if he *did* wake up. He also felt sadness for himself and the stark reality he faced, for his lot now was to care for a dead man the remainder of his life.

By the time the sorrowful wail ended in a low moan, he felt a chill colder than death pervade the room. He looked around. The En was still in

146

the same position he was always, and Ashmadu could see by the clouds of humidity that his master exhaled that his breathing was steady and gentle. Pirhum was gone, no doubt back to the comfort of his own room and the hearth was still glowing with heat from its embers. But it was so cold, deathly cold. And then something stirred in the still night air . . .

Chapter 19

Disappearance

〈𒀭𒈬𒍝𒊏𒀀𒈾〉

Namzu stayed awake for hours after hearing the terrifying wail echo across the city that night. It wasn't just the sadness it left in his soul afterward but the memories that he thought long buried that were resurrected as a result. He lay on his warm mats, alone with his memories.

In the darkness, unable to sleep, his mind wandered back in time to when he was a different person, with a different destiny that the gods would deny him. Once, long ago, he was happily married to the daughter of a wealthy merchant. His future was bright with dreams of prosperity and family. He was on track to become a merchant priest for the temple. He was good at it and was well-liked by those who would guide his ascent. After only two years of marriage, his wife became pregnant with their first child, and Namzu couldn't be more pleased. Everything he prayed for in life, Enki was providing. He was starting a family and had worked himself into a good position in the temple to provide well for them. Nothing was standing in his way, and it seemed nothing could dampen his spirit of hope and optimism for a life of comfort and contentment.

And then tragedy struck.

His beautiful wife died in childbirth, losing both her life and what would have been his firstborn child. It was a boy. Namzu was utterly devastated by the loss and cursed Enki for it. Why would his god allow such a thing to happen? He was a young man and passionate about his family. Now they were gone, and he was alone. His rage and heartbreak nearly caused him to leave the priesthood and abandon his god. His pain and sorrow were unbearable, and he lost his faith. Namzu was at a breaking point, and if it hadn't been for what at the time seemed like a random meeting with an Anunnaki, he would have probably ended up a poor merchant or farmer.

He couldn't remember the circumstance of the meeting, but he would never forget the wise words the Anunnaki imparted to him that day. "Look not to any god for guardianship. You will be left wanting. Instead, look to the gods only for redemption. But beware. You may still be left wanting."

It was the first time he had ever been spoken to by an Anunnaki, and he had been inspired by the pragmatic sincerity of what he said. Because of those words, he eventually recovered enough to love Enki again. But that forlorn wail in the darkest hours of the night left him feeling loss and sadness as if he were reliving the pain once more. He had not thought about that time in many years.

He left the comfort of his sleepless bed and sent Usgadi and patrols of Aga-us out to discover the source of the sound, but by dawn, they still had no answers. Something significant had happened—he could feel it in his bones—but he would have to wait for it to come to light. It was early morning when Namzu finally dozed off and entered a dreamless, quiet slumber.

Seemingly moments after he had fallen asleep, one of his young Subur, Yaqarum, woke him. "First Usgadi, I'm sorry to wake you, but Usgadi Sabum is here. He says it's urgent."

Namzu sat up feeling disoriented. He hadn't felt so exhausted in years. "Tell Sabum that I will meet him in my office momentarily."

He always welcomed Sabum, no matter the time. One of Namzu's most aggressive and successful investigators, Sabum was instrumental in solving a number of inquiries, probes, and inquests over the years. Most outside of the temple didn't know him as an Usgadi priest because he preferred to do his work quietly and with as little attention as possible.

Physically, Sabum was an imposing man, with a muscular build and shaved skull. Those who trained with him greatly respected his mastery of hand-to-hand combat. But his quick and cunning intellect especially stood out to his associates, and it was whispered throughout the temple that Sabum was being groomed as the next First Usgadi. Namzu knew all of this and even agreed that Sabum would likely succeed him, with his blessing. Namzu liked the man and appreciated his ferocious loyalty.

After washing his face and arms, Namzu gathered his robes about him to ward off the chill. He was surprised that it was already midafternoon. He slept much longer than he had expected, and there was still so much to do. It would be another late night.

Sabum entered the room, and the two greeted each other warmly before sitting together at a table set with afternoon refreshments.

"I understand you have urgent news, Sabum," Namzu remarked wearily. "There is so much going on in this city lately, I can't even guess at the subject of your report."

Sabum leaned in toward the First Usgadi. "The Aga-us were called to the home of the Sanga again this afternoon. When they arrived, they came across an unusual scene and an unusual story told by the servants of the house. They immediately sent for the Usgadi, and I was the first to arrive."

Namzu remained quiet as Sabum took a long draft of Kas.

He continued with his report. "The servants were awakened in the night by men speaking loudly in another part of the house. They are sure that one of the voices belonged to Shatamurrim. The other they did not recognize. Then they heard a loud thump and that stunning wail that seems to have terrified the whole of Eridu. The servants believe the wail came from within the Sanga's home. It was so loud and so close, it made the house tremble. Not long after that, they heard the hooves of onager and the creaking wheels of a chariot departing from the front of the home in a hurry."

"Did the servants see anything?" Namzu asked. His mind raced as he tried to make connections between recent events.

"They were too terrified to leave their rooms until late morning," Sabum replied. "When they went to find Shatamurrim, they discovered his room empty. However, they also noticed a pool of blood on the floor and a bloodied metal rod nearby, and his blankets were missing from his bedding."

"Was there anything else?"

Sabum nodded reluctantly. "There were symbols. Three of them. I have a tablet with their likeness." Sabum handed the tablet to Namzu.

"Did you check with the residents along all the routes leading from the house in case they saw who was leaving in the chariot?" Namzu questioned further.

Sabum rolled his eyes. "Of course I did. My men and I spoke to every resident. Everyone was too frightened to come out of their houses in the darkness after hearing that wail. However, there were a few north of the Sanga's home that also heard the chariot pass while moving fast."

"Interesting." Namzu considered what it all meant. "North is toward the river."

Sabum agreed. "Yes. I already have several crews scouring the banks downriver as far as the Pishon. If there is a body to be found, we should find it."

"Has anyone informed the Sanga of what has occurred in his home?" Namzu asked.

"The Sar Unzi of the Aga-us was adamant about informing the Sanga himself," Sabum replied sourly. "The fool thinks his career will somehow be improved. By now the Sanga is aware, I'm sure. You should allow me to gut that idiot and be done with him."

Namzu calmed his friend. "Leave the Sar to me. What I need you to do is drop everything you're doing and keep an eye on the Sanga. This is important. I need to know everything he does, everywhere he goes, and everyone he speaks with and about what. Put your best people on it, and don't get noticed."

"Yes, First Usgadi. I'll be sure not to leave out a single detail." Sabum smiled in a way that suggested he understood the situation.

"And one last thing," Namzu said. "The Sanga is not behaving like the person he was before. Do not underestimate him based on what you think you know about him."

The smile disappeared from Sabum's face. "I will take every precaution," he assured Namzu.

The men drank their Kas in silence for a moment before Sabum hesitantly brought up the symbols again. "I think I found something more regarding the symbols."

Namzu was intrigued. Not much bothered Sabum when it came to blood and violence, but whatever he had on his mind had him a little . . . shaken. "Go on," Namzu prodded quietly.

"I was thinking about the murder of Arwi-a and how her own hand was apparently used to write the symbols above the hearth. So I reviewed my tablets for each of the previous murders at the inn, and I think I may have discovered something curious."

Namzu remained quiet and listened. He felt the tension rising and waited for what was next.

"In every case, we found the victim's own blood on their fingers. Sometimes their whole hand, but always on their forefinger and index finger."

"So he used their own hands to draw the symbols on the walls as he did with Arwi-a," Namzu said. "Except that they had not been dismembered."

Sabum nodded. "It's more than that. Based on my notes regarding blood patterns on the floors and the positioning of the bodies, I believe that most of them were alive when the symbols were drawn."

A chill swept through Namzu. *The victims had been alive!*

"Somehow the killer was able to control them to such an extent that they willingly scrawled the symbols without struggling, even though they were injured and using their own blood. How is that possible, and for what purpose?" Sabum sat back in his chair, shaking his head.

"I think there is power in that for the killer," Namzu said, "and if the Anunnaki are correct, there may well be an Utug involved with the ability to possess and control another's mind."

It was Sabum's turn to remain quiet as Namzu worked through this latest revelation. He hadn't intended to tell Sabum this much, but the Usgadi was smart and had put many of the pieces together already. Not to reveal the remaining details now would have been like deceiving him, and Namzu respected Sabum too much to do that.

"I must think on this more, Sabum. What is the latest on the Mus-Lu?"

Sabum sat up again and scratched his beardless chin. "There are more of them in the mountains than we have ever seen. Their foraging parties are collecting far more fish and wild game than a small settlement would require. And worse, there have been reports that hunters from the local tribes are disappearing."

Namzu scowled. The taste of the Kas soured in his mouth, and he felt sick to his stomach. They were coming again. "Something is pushing them from beyond the Sa-ti-um. They must know we're aware of their presence and will be ready for them if they cross the Gihon. Make sure the Saggina is briefed, and send missives to the Sagginas of Unug and Bad-tibira. If they start to mass, we don't want it to be a surprise to anyone. Not like the last time." Namzu sighed heavily. "What a time to lose Shatamurrim. It looks like we will need the Hero of Eridu to lead his Ursagmuda again if he yet lives."

Sabum nodded his agreement. "There will be trying days ahead for all of us."

"Put it out of your mind for now," said Namzu. "I need your full attention on the Sanga for the time being."

"Very well, I will send word of anything unusual. By the way, you look terrible. Get some rest." Sabum stood to leave.

The two men embraced each other in friendship, and it was decided that Sabum would report again the next morning.

As he watched Sabum leave through his office door, Namzu couldn't help but say a prayer to Enki. He hoped he hadn't sent his friend into the lion's den.

He sat again and studied the tablet where Sabum had drawn the symbols. All three said the same thing—*I am here*—as if to make a point of it. Namzu shuddered. How could he stop this thing?

~~~

After a late lunch of sun-dried salted fish and Nindagu bread, Namzu was ready for his next visitor, Unzi, the Sar of the Aga-us. On two occasions now the Sar was called to the Sanga's residence, which happened to be in the district he commanded. He was a deliberate man who thought too much of himself, but despite his arrogance, he was dutiful and considered himself a protector of the people.

Yaqarum escorted the Sar into the First Usgadi's office at precisely the time expected. *He is punctual if nothing else,* thought Namzu watching them come in. Unzi was a short, stocky man, roughly handsome, with dark features and deep-set brown eyes. He wore a long skirt, which was reinforced with immaculately polished bronze plates and a black leather cloak draped across his broad shoulders. His sickle sword and spear had been left with a servant in the reception room, as was the custom upon entering the office of a temple official.

"Silim sum, Sar Unzi," Namzu said, greeting the officer.

Unzi bowed respectfully in return. "Silim sum, First Usgadi."

The two men sat together at the same table where Namzu met with Sabum earlier. On the table, Yaqarum had already placed two cups and a pitcher of Kas, which he poured for each of them before he left.

"We have had two tragedies at the same house in the span of what— a few days now?" Namzu said. "The Sanga must be terribly distraught. I understand you were the one to bring him the news about his son."

Unzi looked perplexed. He had never been one to hide his emotions. "Yes, I brought him the news. I wanted him to hear it directly from the Sar rather than from a regular of the Aga-us or via rumor."

Namzu studied him closely. "You seem to have some unrest about the meeting. Of course, giving a father news about his missing son would be difficult under any circumstance, but it's more than that, isn't it?"

Unzi frowned. "Yes, First Usgadi, I have had the displeasure of telling family members terrible news about their loved ones on too many occasions in my career, but this was the first time the response was so . . . unemotional."

"Tell me exactly what you told him and every detail of his response," Namzu pressed. "Hold nothing back, no matter how small." Unzi was clearly uncomfortable. Conflict raged across his face. The First Usgadi was his superior, but the Sanga was second only to the En himself. What choice did he really have? The Sar probably knew that he would never leave this room alive if he didn't tell Namzu everything.

The Sar, having apparently come to this conclusion, spoke very sincerely. "I told him we had found a terrible scene at his home—the blood on the floor of Shatamurrim's room, a bloody rod, and his son nowhere to be found. I expressed our concern that his son may have been murdered and taken from the home, and I asked him when he had last seen Shatamurrim." Unzi frowned. "He was reading tablets when I was brought to him, and he didn't even put them down. He didn't seem upset and didn't ask any questions. He did say that he hadn't spoken with his son in two days. To my shock, his overall manner was mainly disinterest. Finally, he told me, almost dismissively, to let him know if we found out anything further."

"And that was everything?" Namzu asked.

"Yes, that's the whole of it."

"What about the symbols? Didn't you tell him about the symbols?"

"No, I assumed he would be upset by that point in our conversation and thus hadn't prepared any remarks about the symbols. Did I err in not mentioning them to him?"

Namzu smiled warmly at the Sar. "I know that must have been difficult for you. You must remember that people grieve in different ways. Perhaps he simply cannot accept the idea of losing his son so soon after his wife was taken from him. Don't be hard on yourself. You handled yourself properly. And no, the symbols are related to more than one crime in the city and therefore should not be discussed or speculated upon outside of this office."

"Thank you, First Usgadi." Unzi seemed genuinely relieved. Perhaps he expected gratitude from the Sanga or for the Sanga to break down in his arms after being told the unfortunate news. Unzi's arrogant nature likely led him to believe such fantasies.

"The investigation is in our hands now," Namzu said. "We will find Shatamurrim sooner or later. However, I may need your assistance further before this is over. Please keep your men vigilant and ready."

Unzi stood and bowed smartly to Namzu. "We will be ever present and ready when you need us, First Usgadi."

"And Unzi, make damned sure that next time you feel it necessary to personally make a report to the Sanga or anyone of station above yours that you come to me first." Namzu smiled, but he didn't hide the edge in his voice.

Unzi stared at Namzu for a long moment as the implications sank in and then bowed again more deeply. "Yes, First Usgadi. I will not make that mistake again."

The First Usgadi was not to be crossed, and the arrogant Sar needed a jarring reminder. Namzu would not tolerate anyone undermining his authority by going over his head, and if he had to make an example of the Sar, he would. Fortunately, Unzi appeared to get the point. Otherwise, it would be a simple matter for Sabum to invent an "accident" that would require appointing a new Sar. He pulled his thoughts away from such dark contemplation. His obsession with the symbols and the Utug that created them had a subtle corrupting effect on his subconscious that he couldn't explain. The sooner he was done with that business, the better.

"First Usgadi?" Unzi asked, shifting uncomfortably.

Namzu realized he had been staring blankly at the Sar beyond the point that it had become awkward. "I apologize, Unzi, I have too much on my mind lately. You are dismissed."

"I am always at your service." The Sar turned to leave and practically marched out.

Namzu could barely hold back a chuckle. The Sar was a good, well-meaning man, he had to admit. He would prefer that Sabum not cut his throat for insolence.

The rest of the day and into the evening was spent issuing orders and receiving reports. There was no news of Shatamurrim, dead or alive. He had nearly every Usgadi and half the Aga-us out looking for him, mostly outside the city and along the river. Already the news of his disappearance spread through Eridu and rumors circulated that it had something to do with the awful wail everyone had heard that same night. The people were becoming fearful, and with an Utug on the loose, it would probably only get worse.

Sitting alone in his office that night, Namzu found the Sanga and the Utug dominating his deliberations, and he started to develop an idea about how to get closer to the Sanga without arousing too much attention. He needed someone to approach the Sanga whom the Sanga knew and trusted, someone who would not be received with suspicion, someone astute enough to pick up on anything unusual that might be seen or heard. More than anything, Namzu wanted a clue about the Utug that the Anunnaki were sure was involved. If he could track it down, confront it, maybe his Usgadi could subdue it long enough for the Isib to exorcise the Demon back to Ki-hul. It would be a complicated matter to organize and execute precisely, but he had few options unless the Anunnaki managed to identify the Demon's True Name. Namzu would pay another visit to Ashmadu the next day. He might be just the one he was looking for.

Chapter 20

Fishing

𒈗𒂍𒀭𒁉𒊑

The Buranuna River, swollen with the recent rains, flooded the flat grasslands it flowed through except where there were trenches for irrigation. Those trenches nourished the land, which in turn grew nourishment for the Sag-gig-ga. The territory around Eridu was especially blessed with fertile soil, and the crops always produced more than the city's demand, even in the years with less rainfall.

Barely noticing the chilly water, Sabum stood in the overflow up to his knees. His eyes were steady on the fast-moving current as it rushed by. He had been standing on the shore since dawn, just watching. His haggard features shone in the orange glow from the young sun just above the horizon. He had not slept well since the night he was awakened by the wail. He had too many haunting memories leftover that morning, which left an uneasy residue over his usually unwavering disposition.

It didn't help that the river and the small fishing village within sight to the south reminded him of his own childhood. He didn't like to think much about it. Indeed, he wished he could erase those memories from his mind forever. Undaunted, the memories relentlessly slipped through his determined concentration, and he thought about how he was born and raised in one of those small fishing villages. His father, curse his soul, had been a fisherman and an inebriant. When he wasn't fishing, his father was beating Sabum and his mother. Sometimes his uncle, also a fisherman, would intervene and take them away until his father was sober again, but sobriety didn't always mean things were better.

When Sabum was old enough, his father taught him the fishing trade. Once Sabum learned to pilot the sailboat and catch the fish, his father grew lazy and did nothing at all. It didn't surprise him. Not really. His father lived like a pauper lord, drinking his life away and demanding the daily income while his young son did the work of a man. If it hadn't been for his good mother filching away a portion of his catch every day, they would have starved.

Tears formed at the edges of his eyes. Only the memory of his mother could tug at his emotions in this way—and only when no one was around to observe him. *Those were the good times*, Sabum scoffed to himself.

Everything had suddenly changed on a summer day when he was twelve. Sabum arrived home after a long day of fishing only to find out from his uncle that his mother had died in a terrible accident. He was told that she had fallen from the roof of their single-story mud-brick hut and broken her neck. When Sabum found out that his father was with her at the time, drunk again, he knew it had been no accident.

Something foul took seed inside him that day. A cold, dispassionate darkness that would bubble to the surface when he was determined to do terrible things in his life. It served him well with his father and again in later years when the temple, or the First Usgadi, required particularly unclean tasks. Those who heard rumors of his vile deeds would come to refer to him as the Dark Hand of Enki—never within earshot, but he learned of it and enjoyed the unofficial appellation.

After his mother passed, he barely spoke to his father. Sabum would fish during the day and sleep in his boat or go out with his friends at night. They were all poor, and there was little to stimulate their young, energetic minds and few adults to serve as role models. The listless nights led them to do things that a better social standing and family life might otherwise have averted. At first, it was nothing more than petty theft—small things to entertain themselves—but soon it grew into daring robberies of homes and trade houses. Their small group of a few bored misfits evolved into a gang with members and connections across many villages along the Buranuna River.

A dark log floated by on the fast currents. Sabum noted the ridges on top of the trunk and watched when it abruptly changed direction and, impossibly, veered toward the opposite bank of the river. It was no log. The crocodiles were out again. Sabum had hoped the rain would keep them among the reeds a little longer.

He thought again of his father and the last time he saw the man. It had been just before dawn, and he was preparing to launch his boat with the first light. Somehow his father, drunk as usual, had managed to find his way to him in the darkness and demanded that Sabum pay him rent for the use of his boat.

Sabum snapped.

He knew his father had likely been responsible for the death of his mother or killed her outright. Sabum endured years of verbal and physical abuse and still brought home the earnings he made fishing. Now his father was demanding that he pay to use the boat that earned their only income.

Sabum had had enough and drove home the point by slamming his fist into his father's face. It was the first time he ever hit his father, although he had thought about it incessantly for years.

His father was stunned and then enraged, but Sabum, who had learned to fight on the streets, was not going to be the victim of the sickening wreck of a man before him again. He hit his father over and over. He recalled how it felt like beating a basket of grain. There was no hardness to him that one would expect from a man who worked his whole life. He remembered that it felt good.

His father tried to fight back, but all he could manage was to flail and stumble until Sabum connected solidly with his temple, sending him down in a heap, half in the river, unconscious. Sabum sat down on the edge of his boat, exhausted. He would have to carry his father back to their hut now if he didn't want to just leave him on the bank of the river for someone else to deal with. He felt a strange mixture of elation and fear, wondering what would happen when his father woke up.

Then suddenly it didn't matter.

There was a slap on the water, and something in the darkness jerked his father into the river. Sabum was stunned and didn't move. Not because he couldn't—he didn't want to. A sharp, gurgling scream split the stillness, followed by a brief, violent thrashing that sent sprays of blood-infused water onto him and his boat. Yet, Sabum remained seated. Then he laughed— harder and longer than he had ever laughed before in his life, the diluted crimson droplets falling from his face and into the hungry sand.

His father's body was never found, and Sabum never divulged what happened that dark morning. The disappearance became a mystery that no one cared about given his father's disfavor in the community. And for a while, Sabum led a life of careless freedom.

Eventually, the Aga-us caught up to Sabum's thievery, catching him and a few of his cohorts trying to sell stolen goods in a nearby village. He was brought before the local Usgadi—an imposing, well-respected man wearing expensive clothing—to be judged for his crimes. Sabum had trembled in the great man's presence. Everyone trembled. He was sure that he would be sent to the fields to work as a slave for the rest of his life.

Fortunately, his uncle was a friend of the Usgadi and vouched for him under the condition that Sabum agree to join the temple as an initiate. Now here he was, three decades later, staring across the same river he fished as a child and where his father died. He was thankful there were no rivers in the city to invoke these memories. More than that, he never forgot how much he admired and idolized the Usgadi from then on. They had power.

A chariot rattling down the muddy road behind him caught his attention. He knew the man guiding the four onagers that pulled it was Usgadi Nawirum-ili, from the nearby village.

Nawirum-ili pulled at the reigns, bringing the chariot to a sliding halt, and jumped off into the mud. "Sabum! I'm glad I found you! I have received word that a body has been pulled out of the water by some fishermen." He was nearly breathless in his excitement.

"Where?" Sabum asked in calm contrast.

"South of the village. Shall I take you?"

"Yes," Sabum replied, hopping over the mud and into the chariot.

Nawirum-ili tried to follow, but he had a less agile build and nearly fell into the mud, barely catching himself on the edge of the chariot. He flashed Sabum an embarrassed glance, took the reins, and turned the onagers back down the road the way he had come.

~~~

A group of Aga-us and fishermen gathered around a blanket-enshrouded form lying on the wet grass near the beached fishing boat that had brought it ashore. Nawirum-ili, leading the way, waded into the circle of men and ordered them to stand back so Sabum could approach unhindered.

Sabum noticed that the body had been wrapped in expensive blankets that only the most affluent Sag-gig-ga could afford, and the bundle was tied shut on either end by hemp rope. Whoever it was, the deceased was definitely not an Ungur or Subur that worked in the fields, nor was it a burial practice of the Sag-gig-ga to throw their dead in the river. The body was dumped in the river on purpose, and if it belonged to Shatamurrim, the news was going to rock Eridu to its core.

Nawirum-ili approached with an older man followed by two younger men behind him. "Usgadi Sabum, this is Ibi, a fisherman from the village, and his two sons, Atab and Kuda. Atab was the one who found the body."

"Did he get caught up in your nets?" Sabum asked.

"Yes, Usgadi," Ibi answered for his son. "How did you know?"

"I fished these waters in my youth. The nets seem to find everything except fish some days."

Ibi smiled. "You speak truly, Usgadi Sabum. My son cut one of the bindings to see what was inside. Once we realized it was a dead man, we let it be and sent for Usgadi Nawirum-ili."

"You are wise as always, Ibi," Nawirum-ili cut in. He turned to one of his Aga-us and motioned to the blanket roll. "Cut the bindings and open it up. Let's see who we have here."

The soldier carefully cut the remaining bindings and slowly unrolled the bundle. When he was done, the blankets revealed the bloated body of a man lying facedown and wearing only a long skirt made from fine flax. A bloody wound that stained the linens with crimson was clearly visible on his upper back.

Sabum stared down at the remains and quietly ordered, "Turn him over."

The soldier rolled the body over with his foot.

Nawirum-ili gasped. "I was afraid it would be him."

"May I ask who this unfortunate man is?" Ibi inquired.

"Of course, Ibi," the Usgadi replied. "He is Shatamurrim, son of the Sanga. He went missing two nights previous."

The fishermen stared at the bloated dead man as if they had never seen a body pulled from the river. Maybe they hadn't.

"It is very sad," Ibi said respectfully. "We will leave an offering for him this evening at the temple."

Sabum turned to Nawirum-ili. "I want you to quietly take the body to the Hall of Kurnugia in Eridu and then inform the First Usgadi."

Nawirum-ili appeared wide-eyed and apprehensive. Eridu was a few leagues north of his village, and he probably didn't go to the city often. It was also likely he had never met the First Usgadi. "Yes, Usgadi Sabum. I will leave at once."

Sabum was still staring at the dead young man who had been called the Hero of Eridu and the Honor of Enki. He thought of Namzu and the task he would have of bringing the news to the Sanga. It would be a horrible loss for him, especially after the recent murder of his wife. Then again, his reaction might prove illuminating if everything Namzu said were true. "And Nawirum-ili, make sure he is covered. I don't want anyone to see him like this."

The Usgadi bowed and hurriedly began barking orders to the Aga-us. Soon they had Shatamurrim's body wrapped tightly and loaded onto Nawirum-ili's chariot. As the Usgadi spurred the onagers forward slowly, the Aga-us assembled around the chariot in a kind of honor guard and departed on the road north.

Sabum watched the procession until it was out of sight. Then he walked over to where Ibi and his sons had begun cleaning their fish. The stench was striking yet also comforting to Sabum. Some of his most peaceful moments in life occurred while tired and alone after fishing all day. Only then, while cleaning his fish, had he been able to relax for a while and think of nothing but the task at hand.

"Fishing boats have changed a bit since I was sailing," Sabum commented to Ibi.

"They sure have. I remember my first fondly, though." Ibi glanced over at his sons. "I called her the *Ki-sikil*. Don't tell your mother, or she'll club me, even though it's been thirty years!" He smiled broadly at the look of shock on Kuda's face.

Sabum laughed.

Kuda, somewhat confused, asked, "Why would you name your boat that?"

"A man's vessel is like a woman," Ibi answered with a chuckle. "He must take care of her, protect her, and keep her happy—no matter the storms they endure together. I called mine *Ki-sikil* because she shook like a virgin every time I took her out on the water."

They all laughed.

Sabum felt a pull deep inside. Ibi and his sons seemed . . . happy. He had to know. "Fishing in your blood, Ibi?"

"Yes, Usgadi. My father and his father were both fishermen from this same village. Only my brother is not a fisherman. He tends herds of mouflons and aurochs in the countryside, although I think he'll do anything to be away from home." Ibi shook his head and chuckled again. "He has daughters that are close to marrying age, and his home is often chaotic with the drama of young women and their latest love interests. Most days he wants to be anywhere else just to be away from the frequent emotional shifts common to girls their age."

Sabum caught himself smiling. He liked Ibi and his sons. "And what about your sons? Are they following in their father's footsteps, as well?"

Ibi wrinkled his nose. "I wish them better, but my oldest there, Atab, is as good a fisherman as any I ever met. I already got him his own boat." He pointed toward his youngest son. "Kuda there—I'm not sure this is the life for him. It wouldn't surprise me if he decided to be a priest."

"That's not such a bad thing, you know."

Ibi bowed his head in respect. "Of course, Usgadi."

Sabum sat next to Ibi and began cleaning fish with him.

The old fisherman protested that Sabum would get the stench on him or soil his fine clothes.

Sabum waved away his concerns. "If your son wants to be a priest, send him to me, and I'll get him going in the right direction."

Ibi bowed again graciously. "You're an honorable man, Usgadi. May Enki always watch over you."

Chapter 21
Bearer of Bad News

Alu-Abad expected that Arwi-a, the Gidim, would materialize to rage at him during the night. After all, he had taken her husband as a host, murdered her and her son, and doomed her soul to wander the world as a spirit for eternity—not to mention that she promised to be a nuisance every night. For reasons unknown to him, she had yet to return. Perhaps the old hag was gone forever.

Or perhaps she was whispering to someone else.

That was the dangerous possibility he had been considering all night, but even after searching Irra's memories, he couldn't think of anyone who was close to her or the Sanga that he could point to as a potential threat. Irra remarkably had no close social ties beyond those with his family and the En. He was not antisocial; he mostly just kept to himself.

The Sanga's memories were populated by many people he liked and admired—a fish vendor at the market, various servants in his household, and associates in the temple—but none of them could be considered close friends. Alu-Abad would have to wait and see if anyone unknown to the Sanga appeared to avenge his family.

Either way, he would be prepared from now on.

His bedchamber was quiet except for the regular breathing of a young priestess who shared his bed. Alu-Abad reassigned almost all of the Sanga's staff to other tasks in the temple, and according to one of his scribes, it was assumed that he didn't want a host of spectators watching him grieve. Alu-Abad snorted at the idea, disturbing the priestess next to him momentarily. The truth was he didn't care to work hard enough to keep them all busy. In fact, he "temporarily" turned over most of his responsibilities to his high priests until he felt ready to resume them.

That was never going to happen.

He had no interest in doing the work of the temple, even to keep up with appearances. The tragedies that occurred in Irra's family would provide cover enough until he became the En. After that, he didn't care. He would have the power to do as he wished.

The Demon kept the two priestess initiates, who he quite easily mentally dominated, to serve the daily necessities of cleaning, doing laundry, and serving meals, as well as communicating his wishes to the rest of the temple hierarchy. They were lovely girls, including the one beside him now. She was new to the temple, with braided chestnut hair and innocent, wide brown eyes. Not so innocent anymore, he thought with a smile. The priestesses served his physical pleasures most nights as well.

He heard a light tap on the door to his bedchamber and knew before he answered that it was his other priestess, Gemeshega. With a flick of his wrist, the door opened, and she entered to stand before him.

"I do not desire you right now, Priestess," he told her dismissively. "I will summon you later."

Unaffected, the priestess uttered in a near monotone, "The First Usgadi is here with another Usgadi named Nawirum-ili. They claim to have urgent news regarding your son."

Irra sighed and looked around for his robes of office. "Very well, take them to the receiving room and give them refreshments. I'll be there shortly."

The priestess turned and left the room without a word, closing the door behind her. Alu-Abad was sure they were here to tell him they'd found the damn body of Shatamurrim in the river. Why else would they be here? He hoped they would not find it so quickly, but he noticed a few subtle changes since he'd disposed of the boy. New priests were always nearby—Usgadi watching him in the temple, following discreetly through the streets, and marking his movements. An Usgadi assassin called Sabum coordinated their activities. That one could be useful to him later.

He was alarmed by their intrusion at first and feared they somehow found out that he had carried out the murders of Irra's wife and son. Maybe they even suspected his true nature by some means unknown to him. Yet as he contemplated the situation further, he realized that they were more likely there to covertly protect the Sanga. Two family members were dead, after all, and he might be next. He also rationalized that they had not told him because they feared frightening Irra, especially now, considering his supposed emotional state after finding out his son was abducted or murdered. He sneered at the ignorance of these humans—unknowingly protecting the very creature that was killing them. Many more would die at his hands or command before long if they continued to interfere.

He pondered the temple hierarchy, including the Zi-ik-ru-um Council that seemed sympathetic to the Sanga, allowing him remarkable discretion, primarily due to the unusual circumstances surrounding the En. And until the

First Ashipu announced that Ipqu-aya was unfit to carry out his duties as En, the formality of elevating the Sanga to the office of En would have to wait. In reality, he was the de facto En and doing everything he could to manipulate the temple to quietly organize behind him.

The Zi-ik-ru-um would be a problem he would have to deal with eventually. They were a bunch of overopinionated, self-important old men who believed they were entitled to validate the En's decisions. With En Ipqu-aya that was never a problem, as they were well in line with his philosophical ideas. They wouldn't stop Alu-Abad. He would overcome any obstruction through manipulation and murder until he had the Zi-ik-ru-um under his control, or better yet, disassembled altogether.

Alu-Abad congratulated himself on his self-restraint; he had been careful not to shake the tree too hard with extreme orders. He largely let the temple run itself, and he planned to keep it that way. The changes he would make at first would be subtle and manipulative. Significant changes would occur—that was certain—and many of them, through his subversions, would be championed by respected high priests and Zi-ik-ru-um within the temple itself once he had the right people in place. His leadership style would be to advocate and popularize others' ideas, which he would quietly seed in their subconscious. And he had many seeds to plant. They would grow into a forest that needed cultivating in a few short years that would bring sweeping changes and serve his beastly pleasures.

Now, as the noon hour gave way to early afternoon, he would have to put on a performance of grief for these two idiotic Usgadi and his whole day would be consumed with rituals involving Irra's dead son. He wished he could have planned that one better. So far he had managed to leave too many hints of his involvement with two high-profile murders in his haste to be rid of them. Patience was not his strong suit, and he was compelled to kill by his nature. If he were going to stay in power long in Eridu, he would have to be far more cunning and utilize surrogates for his dirty work. He couldn't continue leaving symbols all over the city as he was cursed to do when he took life with his own hands.

With a sigh, he dressed in his robes and chains of office and strutted down the hall to the receiving room. If nothing else, perhaps he could carefully probe the First Usgadi's mind to reveal if he was a real danger or not. The last thing he needed was more surprises from these relentless people.

~~~

Namzu stood in the well-appointed room of comfortable chairs, divans, and finely crafted wooden tables that served as the receiving room for the Sanga. With him was the Usgadi who identified the body of Shatamurrim after it had been pulled out of the Buranuna. The room smelled odd, like the mix of sweat and blood that Namzu would generally associate with the wrestling pits—it was oddly out of place here. He had only been in this room a handful of times over the years and certainly would have remembered if it smelled like this before.

Irra strode into the room and appeared in a lively mood. "Welcome, Namzu," he said with a smile. "Welcome, Nawirum-ili. Please sit, sit. I understand you have news about my son. Good news, I hope. Is he alive and well?"

Oil lanterns cast long shadows on the wall, and the shadows reminded Namzu of the comedies with clay dolls that children loved. He was playing cat and mouse with the Sanga, who he now believed was involved—if not behind—the murders of at least his wife and son. Namzu couldn't believe the man was standing in front of him with a smile on his face as if what he was about to hear would surprise him.

Namzu was unable to return the Sanga's enthusiasm. "I'm so sorry, Sanga, but the news is not good. Your son has been found, but he no longer lives."

Irra's smile faded. "What has become of him?"

Namzu motioned to the other Usgadi with him. "Nawirum-ili is the Usgadi of a village a few leagues south of the city. He will explain the details of your son's recovery."

Nawirum-ili looked ill for a brief moment before composing himself. "I, too, am distressed at the loss of your son," he told the Sanga nervously. "He was found early this morning by fishermen on the Buranuna River. They brought him to shore and immediately notified my office. When his body was presented to me, I knew instantly who they had found, and taking every care with the remains, I transported him directly here under a guard of honor."

Irra studied the man carefully for a moment. "So you paraded my dead son through the city to where? Is he lying out front on the street even now?"

Namzu felt a slight twitch along his right eyebrow and noted that the forcefulness of Irra's reaction was designed to raise the tension in the room. It appeared to work on Nawirum-ili and only reinforced the strangeness of the interaction, almost as if it were contrived for the Sanga's own benefit.

Nawirum-ili stuttered as he groped for an appropriate answer. Nothing the Usgadi was going to say was going to come out right, so Namzu decided to take control of the conversation before it got worse for the poor man.

"Sanga," he said smoothly, "your son is under the care of the First Abrig in the Hall of Kurnugia. They're preparing his remains so that you may view him in a more favorable condition. I'm sure that Nawirum-ili was discreet while bringing your son's remains to us. He is very nervous meeting for the first time with the future En, especially under such difficult circumstances."

Namzu had taken the Anunnaki Abgal's advice and wore the Orichalcum charm. He wore it out of sight and was reminded of its presence by a slight warming sensation. Although he could not detect any magic being utilized in the room, he guessed that Irra or someone nearby was using what the Abgal called psionic power to affect him in some unknown way. The charm must have been working, since he did not feel any adverse effects.

Irra's stern visage relaxed. "I apologize, Nawirum-ili, for my rude behavior. I'm sure you understand the strain of loss I have been enduring over the past few days. Thank you for having the good judgment to bring this tragic news to me so swiftly and tactfully. I will not forget your kindness."

The near-panic on Nawirum-ili's face disappeared, and his voice steadied. "Thank you, Sanga. I am perpetually at your service."

"I will send word immediately once your son is prepared for you to administer the final rites," Namzu added.

"That will be all then, gentlemen," the Sanga replied, noticeably eager for them to leave.

Namzu and his Usgadi bowed respectfully and then followed Gemeshega out.

Once outside, Namzu bade farewell to Nawirum-ili and thanked him for his attention to duty and special care handling the transportation of Shatamurrim back to Eridu. The Usgadi was obviously relieved to be leaving the city as quickly as possible and return to his sedate life among the farmers. Without delay, he gathered his waiting Aga-us and turned his chariot toward the southern exit of the city.

Namzu hadn't needed to bring Nawirum-ili with him to inform the Sanga about Shatamurrim's body, but he wanted someone to absorb the Sanga's focus so that he could study the man's behavior unnoticed. It worked in his favor. The Sanga most definitely behaved in an unusual manner. Namzu met with the Sanga hundreds of times over the years, and never had a meeting been this bizarre. For that matter, they had all been close associates many years ago—he, the Sanga, and the En. Everyone else excused the Sanga's conduct as that of a grieving husband and father, but Namzu was convinced it was just a show.

He learned something else, as well. Priestess Gemeshega was more than what she seemed. Maybe she was the Utug in the guise of a temple initiate. Maybe she was pulling strings behind Irra. She did not have the usual humble demeanor demanded of every other temple initiate, and she glared boldly at him when first answering the door to the Sanga's office. Most illuminating was that not once had she bowed to anyone, not even the Sanga. And her stiff movements combined with the monotone way of speaking led him to believe that she was uncomfortable or not entirely in control of her own skin.

Namzu hoped it would go better with Ashmadu and wished he could go with him if he agreed to meet with Irra. He would have to instruct Sabum to position his team close to the Sanga's office in case Ashmadu got himself into trouble. Enki willing, the elder servant would find out something useful that would help him confirm the identity of the Utug—if there really was one. He was playing a dangerous game that could easily get the servant killed if he was not extremely cautious. Irra was never a stupid man and the histories written on tablets claimed the Utug to be highly intelligent as well. They played a covert battle of intrigue, and no one could know who had the advantage until it was over.

Just then, Namzu reached a decision he hoped never to arrive at again. If it came to Irra ascending to the office of the En in his current corrupted state, Namzu would have him killed to save Eridu. It wouldn't be the first En whose life he ended prematurely for a greater cause.

~~~

Alu-Abad was pleased with himself after the Usgadi departed. He handled them well, he thought. The one from the village might be useful one day. The fool would be quick to jump from now on when the Sanga spoke to him. Perhaps he would be a good candidate to fill the vacant role of First Usgadi that the Demon anticipated. No doubt he would have to deal with Namzu sooner or later. The man was too clever for his own good.

Normally, he could carefully reach out with his mind to sense another's intent without alerting them to an intrusion. Nawirum-ili was desperate to please him, but from Namzu he had sensed nothing. Not ambivalence, just nothing, as if he were somehow able to shield his mind from even the lightest probe. He knew very few who possessed such an ability. In a way, this was an unintended gift from the First Usgadi, because now Alu-Abad knew he must be especially wary of the priest. Of course, his first instinct was to kill them both right then and there, eliminating the problem. But doing so would have created more problems because he was sure others knew they had come to see him. It would also have been far more difficult to dispose of bodies from inside the temple complex. There were far too many eyes and ears about day and night watching him now. He would make every effort to be patient with the First Usgadi and find a way to deal with that one in a fashion that would leave no trail back to him.

Alu-Abad recognized another problem he would have to deal with soon. He received word earlier that the Sahar-nitah were beginning to break down. Some became damaged doing the work of the humans, and others fell victim to accidental causes, like falling from a roof or into the river. This was forcing many Sag-gig-ga to return to their labors and livelihoods. Perhaps he would inspire crafts and inventions that would do their work for them more reliably and return them to the corruption of sloth that he desired.

Then there was the Anunnaki. Alu-Abad knew them only as the Enlightened Ones. They were not human. They were something else—and powerful. He knew they did not interfere with the internal affairs of a government and culture. They offered advice, yes, but never interference. However, if they somehow discovered he was a Greater Demon controlling the Sanga, he had no doubt they would come against him, which would likely result in his permanent banishment back to the Infernal Planes. He found it strange that his kind knew so little about the Anunnaki. Even the mighty Archdemons feared them. It was said that they did not reside in this world as native occupants, rather that they came from the stars. *I doubt that,* he thought with a forced laugh. But whatever they were, he would do his best to avoid them.

Alu-Abad was in a good mood now and inspired after the meeting with the Usgadi. What he thought would be a waste of his valuable time turned out to be unexpectedly informative. Outwitting these thoughtless humans energized him. Perhaps he would summon Gemeshega after all, and she could wake the other one, as well.

Chapter 22

Plans

𒀸𒈾𒌉𒉡𒄴

Namzu was sitting in the same chair where he sat only two days before when he came to see the En's house servant. The En's condition had not changed and was not expected to. The Nig-aga, Pirhum, was filling cups with Kas and setting them on the table before resuming his place in a far corner of the room, where he would wait until he was needed. Everything was just as it was before except one thing—Ashmadu somehow appeared to be older. Maybe it was the poor lighting in the room or the servant's lack of sleep and constant stress that must have been taking its toll. For just a second Namzu almost decided not to burden him with his request, but the endeavor was too important, and there was no one else he could seek out to aid him in the matter.

"I've come again to speak with you about the Sanga," Namzu began. He could see a flicker of apprehension in the servant's eyes, and Namzu knew that he had every reason to be concerned. "It's actually more of a request or favor, if you be so willing to indulge me."

Ashmadu relaxed a little in his seat and leaned back. "If it is within my power to do so, First Usgadi."

Namzu cleared his throat before he continued, "This is no little thing that I ask, and it could be dangerous, more dangerous than you could possibly know."

"Look at what my life has become." Ashmadu gestured toward the En. "I spend my days and nights caring for, forgive me, a corpse. And I do so happily."

Namzu knew there was nothing derogatory in the remark. In fact, he could hear the utter sadness in the servant's voice. He looked so thin and tired, almost a reflection of the living corpse he tended.

"I need you to go to the Sanga under the pretense of offering your condolences regarding his deceased wife and son and to provide an update on the En's condition."

Ashmadu leaned forward. "For what purpose?"

"You have known the Sanga for decades through your service to the En," Namzu shrugged, "and I need someone familiar with his mannerisms to help me understand his odd behavior since the incident with the En."

Namzu had no doubt that Ashmadu was the perfect candidate, the only candidate. He was an unassuming house servant merely doing his duty by reporting on the Sanga's friend and current leader of the temple. Certainly, Irra would not expect any subterfuge by a mere servant.

"Most importantly," Namzu continued, "I need to know who he is close to, perhaps even deferring to or consulting with, while you are there. It might not even be that obvious. There may be someone quietly observing nearby, even a servant. The longer you can keep up the charade, the more we may learn from him."

The fatigue and despair that enshrouded Ashmadu before seemed to slip away and was replaced by barely constrained enthusiasm. "The task seems simple enough," he said. "I would be pleased to help you in this matter, First Usgadi."

Namzu was surprised. He thought he would have a harder time convincing Ashmadu to leave his master for a while to help him.

Earlier that day, when he and Nawirum-ili met with the Sanga, Namzu came away sensing something odd about him. It was as if the man had become unhinged in his grief. His behavior went beyond the unbalanced mania that Namzu usually associated with the loss of a loved one. The Sanga would be far less guarded and controlled around familiar people. He expected that, along with everything else, enough would emerge for him to bring his concerns to the Zi-ik-ru-um Council. He hoped he could prompt them to interview Irra and perhaps discover concerns of their own. It was a real stretch to imagine that they would declare him emotionally unfit and elevate someone else to the office of the En, but Namzu believed that there was something far more insidious going on with the Sanga. He just needed to prove as much and even better if he could unmask the Utug.

Namzu had once been closer to Irra, but Irra's decades-old conspiracy with the En caused them to distance themselves from him. He understood the reasons and begrudged them nothing. He had gotten out of it what he had wanted, regardless. He was in a position from which he could influence the fair and just governance of Eridu. The state of their relationship made him a weak candidate to have an unobtrusive conversation with the Sanga. Both of them would be on the defensive the entire time. That's why he needed Ashmadu.

Just before arriving at the Gi-par, he had been informed that the First Ashipu was expected to proclaim the En unfit to rule due to his health the next morning. That would kick off the twelve-day grace period before the

Sanga was confirmed as the new En—if he accepted, and Namzu had no doubt that he would.

Time was running short.

Sabum had not brought him any concrete revelations either. His agents had reported that the Sanga spent most hours in his private chambers in the company of the two young priestesses. The women would emerge from the private rooms once in a while to carry a message to this person or that, fetch food, clean laundry—nothing out of the ordinary. In addition, the Sanga saw few visitors, and those who came by without an appointment were generally turned away by one of the priestesses. Everything could be explained as a function of the Sanga's grief.

"There's something else you should know," Namzu said quietly, almost fearing the En would hear his words.

A look of concern appeared on Ashmadu's face. "Yes? What is it?"

Namzu kept his voice low, even though he knew he didn't need to. Ashmadu, taking the hint, sent Pirhum out on an errand, and there was no one else in the room. It just seemed appropriate with the En resting so close. "We recovered the body of Shatamurrim from the Buranuna River this morning."

The house servant stared at the floor before tears began to flow down his cheeks. He made no move to hide them until he abruptly released a sob. Then he covered his face with his hands and wept without shame in front of the First Usgadi.

Namzu was briefly taken aback by Ashmadu's sudden unexpected display of emotion. He did not realize that the En's servant had known the young Sar very well, considering he'd only perfunctory contact with his father, the Sanga. Namzu wondered if the old house servant was just overcome with emotion from all the stress he was under and began to worry that he might not be the right person to send in to see the Sanga after all.

Except that there *was* no one else.

"I'm sorry," Ashmadu said, recovering from his breakdown. "I knew he had to be dead, but just hearing it confirmed is somewhat overwhelming. I'm fine now."

Namzu nodded sympathetically. He was surprised that the house servant would be so confident. "Why were you so sure he was deceased?" he asked innocently.

"Because his mother told ..." Ashmadu checked himself. "His mother would have been presumed missing, as well, if her son had not found her remains in the kitchen, and so I can only assume the killer intended the same for her son."

An awkward pause followed between them. Every investigative sense in Namzu's body sounded an alarm that Ashmadu knew much more than he was letting on. He had to be careful not to press too hard. Otherwise, he might risk the trust of Ashmadu in the task ahead. Namzu would ask sharper, more probing questions later when Ashmadu returned from the meeting with the Sanga.

He steered the subject back to their collaboration. "I want you to wear this charm when you see the Sanga." He handed Ashmadu the Orichalcum necklace given to him by the Anunnaki Abgal. "It will provide some measure of protection in the unlikely case you need it." If the Sanga were colluding with an Utug with powers that allowed him to control or affect others with its mind, this would keep Ashmadu safe as it had Namzu. At least he hoped.

Ashmadu looked uncertain. "How will this protect me?"

"Just trust me, Ashmadu. I'm sure it won't be necessary, and there's nothing you need to do to make it work."

With a shrug, Ashmadu put the necklace around his neck. The red Orichalcum pendant twinkled with the light of the hearth before he tucked it under his tunic.

In truth, Namzu wasn't really sure how—or if—the charm worked. He had worn it earlier in the presence of the Sanga with no noticeable effects other than the slight warming. But that could have been his imagination, and it was possible nothing at all having to do with psionics had taken place. *Let it be so with Ashmadu*, he hoped. "When will you go to see him?"

"Tonight, if I may. Is there a reason to wait?" Ashmadu seemed unexpectedly eager to get his errand underway.

Namzu shook his head. "None whatsoever. And there is one more thing. Keep a wary eye on his initiate, Priestess Gemeshega. She is behaving suspiciously. Don't worry. I have Usgadi watching him, so if there is a problem, they are close by. Otherwise, I will be aware of when you leave and can meet you back here afterward."

Ashmadu merely nodded without looking at him. He was likely nervous about the meeting. *He should be*, Namzu thought. Although for all he knew, Ashmadu would be turned away like so many others when he arrived.

Namzu placed a reassuring hand on the man's shoulder to comfort him and then left the room. It occurred to him as he departed that he only looked at the En once the entire time during his visit, and that had been when he first entered the room. If the En could hear all that went on in his presence, Namzu wondered what he might think.

~~~

The evening was fast approaching, and Ashmadu stood looking down at the sleeping form of the En, wondering not for the first time, what his master would do in his situation. Probably the honorable thing—whatever that was. Ashmadu smiled to himself, and then tears began to run down his face with the reminder that the En would never return to his former self. He had been gone too long now.

Many Ashipu were on hand to see to his every need. They would care for him reverently until he died. The En no longer needed Asmadu, since there was nothing more that he could do for the man.

Except for one thing, and he would do it tonight.

Lately, he dreamed of Sipa, the Lukur that had overseen his development during his youth at the temple. She was much more than a teacher, of course. She was the closest thing to a mother he could remember. Sipa shaped so much of his character, instilled proper values, rewarded him with kindness, never once treated him cruelly, and never judged him for what he was—a poor indigent traded to the temple to forgive his abusive father's debt. If he owed the En everything, he owed Sipa everything else. They provided him with a good life.

Ashmadu was proud that he never judged the En on the decisions he had made over the past thirty years—not even the ones he strongly disagreed with and knew were wrong. He was an accessory to many of those decisions, many times, over many years. And truly, if he were going to reconcile what he had done, it was really one decision repeated again and again over many years.

Even though their subterfuge was wrong, it seemed like those were the best years of their lives. Ashmadu wouldn't have traded or changed them for anything in the world. It was all for the only woman the En ever loved, a woman who had touched both of their lives in a special way. A woman who was married to another. And a child that came later.

So many days—and even a few nights—Ashmadu received her at the Gi-par dressed as an ordinary servant. The En and his lover would steal off into the countryside or behind chamber doors. Ashmadu saw everything, and he saw nothing, but he remembered every moment. Two things allowed his conscience to collude with the charade. First, the En appeared genuinely happy. Second, although Ashmadu had almost no experience with romantic love, what he observed between the En and his lover seemed real.

He reminisced about the many days she would sit with Ashmadu and tell funny stories about the gods and heroes of ancient Kur-gal while waiting for the En. She knew so many that he was sure that she made them up, but he didn't care. They would laugh together, sometimes for hours, before the En would arrive. He could see why the En loved her, and over the years, Ashmadu came to love her as well—not in the same way as the En, of course, but for her intellect and humor.

He admired her.

One year she became pregnant, and they would never know if the father was the En or her husband. But the En told Ashmadu it didn't matter. His child or not, he loved her and would love the child even if he could only pretend it was his. For years afterward, she would bring the child with her to the En's home, and Ashmadu was delighted to care for him during her visits. He never imagined the joy of caring for a child before then. It was a life event he conceded early on that he would never be able to experience. How life had a funny way of altering one's expectations. He was fortunate to have many such alterations in his life.

As the boy grew, Ashmadu taught him practical things like reading and writing, understanding the world beyond Eridu, and playing games of intellect. The child's favorite activity was the Game of Twenty Squares, which utilized game pieces and tetrahedrons. The two players would race to reach the other's side of the board to win. Incredibly, the boy mastered the game's sophisticated strategy by the time he was five. Ashmadu still had the game stored in his room in case the opportunity arose that he would brush off the dust and put it in play once again. That would have been a happy day.

Caring for another's child was the closest Ashmadu would ever come to having a traditional family. And because of that child, the four of them became a family. An unusual family without a doubt, but a family nonetheless, sharing bonds between them that would last a lifetime. The early years were the best, Ashmadu recalled. The child was an innocent and never questioned why he was spending so much time at the En's house. His life was full of joy and wonder at all the new discoveries, things done for the first time and boundless energy. Ashmadu was there for it all and more.

As the child grew, his mother found it more and more difficult to find a plausible excuse to be with the En. She couldn't just sneak away while Ashmadu entertained the child anymore. So Ashmadu recommended that she bring him to a public location where the boy could join in activities with other children his age. Ashmadu relished the opportunity to watch him socialize and play with his peers.

At the age of seven, the boy enrolled at the Edubba, school, and Ashmadu became his tutor. He was almost always well behaved and rarely received the cane by his Um-mi-a, teacher. Ashmadu loved him too much to ever cane him, even though he might have deserved it once in a while. The boy was gifted in sports as well as academia and excelled in the wrestling pits. By the time he was grown and left the Edubba, he had several impressive belts to his credit and was considered one of the finest wrestlers in all of Eridu. Ashmadu couldn't have been more proud. He and the En often laughed about that time in their lives when the En was an unusually regular enthusiast of the wrestling pits.

When the boy became a man, he entered the military and began his adult life away from home. Away from the people who loved him. Ashmadu sometimes forgot how he wept like a child, and the boy wept with him, promising to visit every week. He kept that promise for the rest of his life, Ashmadu thought gratefully.

Sometimes Ashmadu considered it a blessing from Enki that the En had fallen comatose before his lover died. He would not have endured much longer anyway. Every moment of consciousness would have been spent in pain and suffering for her loss—and then all the more when the child he thought of as his own was murdered not long afterward. Ashmadu wasn't sure that he could live with the losses himself. If the En had died that morning he had been stricken ill, Ashmadu was sure he would not have been long to follow.

For the En's lover of more than two decades had been Arwi-a, wife of the Sanga, and her son was Shatamurrim.

With a kiss on the forehead of the man he knew as Ipqu-aya, the En of Eridu, Speaker of the Word of Enki, Holy of Holies, and the Light of Kurgal, he said goodbye to his old friend and master. Ashmadu was confident he had everything he needed, not the least of which was the pure hatred he felt in his heart. He had no real expectation that he would survive his meeting with the Sanga that night, and he was at peace with his fate.

~~~

Alu-Abad enjoyed a rigorous afternoon with his priestesses and hoped no one would bother him that evening, because it would take time for them to recover. For the women, the experience was mostly twisted and tortuous, while for him, it was all pleasure. Eventually, he would take their beauty from them and toss them away, replacing them with others. That was just part of the excitement for him. To consume a human was to take everything from them piece by piece until nothing was left. Some would fight, resisting every step of the way, while others would give up quickly and submit.

He liked the ones that fought better.

Either way, it all ended the same—broken beauty, broken bodies, broken dreams, and broken minds. He supposed it was terrible for those he used, but he didn't care. It was his own comfort and pleasure that was important. Compassion was plainly not something he possessed in any abundance.

If the desire struck him, as it had with Arwi-a, he might physically consume one as well. The taste of human flesh was never more satisfying than when it was from someone he knew intimately. It wasn't often that he felt compelled to feed on human flesh—to him it was no different than any other food required to nourish his host. He enjoyed it mostly because the thought of it was so horrifying to other humans.

Alu-Abad sent his mind out to see who was nearby. He'd enjoyed a wonderful epiphany during his play time with the priestesses and decided that he would act on it right away. He sensed a few initiates strolling the halls, a high priest, two of the Usgadi watching his doors, and their leader, Sabum, speaking with one of them. Sabum, yes—that was the one he wanted. He possessed exceptional talents that would make Alu-Abad's work easy for him.

The Demon put a thought into Sabum's head to call on him, and a short time later, there was a knock at his door.

"Please come inside, Usgadi." Irra smiled warmly. "It's good that you have come by."

"Thank you, Sanga. I suddenly had a concern that something might be wrong, so I decided to check in on you."

After Sabum closed the door behind him, Irra invited him to sit and share a cup or two of Kas in his office. They were going to become wonderful friends.

A little while later, Sabum left the Sanga's office, and Irra returned to his private chambers through a connecting hallway. The place was a wreck. It smelled of blood and sex.

He walked into the bedchamber where the priestesses were still sleeping and slapped them repeatedly. "Wake up, filthy whores! Wake up and clean up this mess! And bring me food and drink! Now!"

It gave him pleasure to watch the girls leap out of bed and immediately go about doing his bidding. They showed no emotion or fear, and they did as they were told without question or complaint. Their will was crushed, and their minds entirely subjugated by his domination.

Alu-Abad lay down on a divan and allowed Irra's body to rest. He was delighted with the results of the day. While chewing on a juicy, sweet date, he pondered what opportunities tomorrow would bring. Obstacles were falling faster than he expected, emboldening his confidence that he had succeeded in removing everyone who could threaten his progress. Of course, there would be others—many others—but for now, he felt safe. The only point of irritation that he couldn't dismiss was the absence of Arwi-a's Gidim. She still had not returned to torment him as promised, and he was concerned that she might have found another surrogate to try and destroy him. He would have to be wary of everyone around him, especially those he did not know. Meanwhile, he would stay in a constant state of readiness and wait. It would be exhausting to his host and a distraction to him, but his survival depended on it. Was it possible that this was her form of tormenting him? Making him think that there was a danger that was not there? He was giving her too much credit. She was in a rage before he killed her son and then in anguish afterward, but he didn't think he had broken her. He wished there was a way for him to know.

Although it was only the early evening, the Demon allowed his physical host to drift off to sleep for a while. He would need his strength for the following day when the Zi-ik-ru-um would ask him to accept the office of the En of Eridu. Of course he would, and then there would be endless ceremonies and rituals. Why did these Sag-gig-ga have to be so persistent with their ceremony to a god who didn't care for them? He supposed it was the same old story of controlling the population through religion. When he became the En, he would embrace the idea wholeheartedly.

An hour later, he heard a knock at the front door followed by voices as Gemeshega attempted to send away whoever had come calling.

Unexpectedly, she entered his bedchamber only a moment later. "A man is here insisting that he speak to you about the En."

Alu-Abad rolled over and growled, "Who is it?"

"He calls himself Ashmadu."

Chapter 23
Treachery

𒀭𒊩𒆠𒁺𒌋𒈗𒊭𒈨𒌍

Namzu was enjoying a walk back to his office after the late dinner he shared with friends at a local brewer's house just outside the temple complex. He was accompanied by two Usgadi priests who joined him that evening, Taribatum and Ahikibani, and they had all drunk way too much Kas, as evidenced by their unsteady gaits. Fortunately, the night held a crisp bite in the air and, combined with the brisk exercise, helped to sober them enough to consider drinking more Kas when they reached their destination.

Tonight, Namzu allowed himself to indulge in a much-needed release from all the stress of chasing symbols, murderers, and Demons. It wasn't often that he drank to excess—for that matter, it had probably been a dozen years or more—and he forgotten how good it felt to be numb and unburdened by serious thoughts. His companions, also not heavy drinkers under normal circumstances, had been kind enough to entertain his excess and happily joined him.

Taribatum and Ahikibani, talented middle-aged Usgadi, often joined Namzu on social occasions. Each held a judgeship within an Eridu district and was personally appointed by Namzu many years before. More than just work associates, they were friends and confidants. Unfortunately, he was forced to keep his current investigation to himself. Even in his inebriated state, he was cognizant enough of the consequences of allowing specific details to escape or be overheard—in particular, any reference to an Utug—could include hysteria in Eridu. Instead, he lamented about the sickness that had befallen the En and reveled in the night's celebrations of the seventh day of the Ritual of Man. When Namzu reached the front door to his office, he was still in a good mood and looked forward to enjoying more jovial conversation and Kas with his friends.

The first thing he noticed upon entry was Yaqarum entering through a door in the adjacent wall, carrying a tray with a single cup. Opposite him, Sabum sat rigidly in a chair staring at him. Namzu was surprised to see his old friend but not disappointed until he noticed the somber expression on his face. He smiled warmly at the sight of his Second. "Silim sum, Sabum. We were scheduled to meet in the morning, but you must have something important to discuss if you're here now. Give me a moment, and we can speak together privately."

Taribatum and Ahikibani, standing just behind Namzu, added their cheerful, Kas-fueled greetings.

Sabum stood from his chair when Namzu first began speaking and approached him. "I have a message from the Sanga."

"Sabum, can't—"

With no warning, Sabum rushed Namzu, taking him completely off guard. He heard Yaqarum's clay tray shatter on the floor just as the big man's hands wrapped tightly around the First's neck. It all happened so quickly, like a bad dream that he desperately wanted to wake from.

Taribatum and Ahikibani, initially startled at the sudden violence, quickly recovered and jumped to Namzu's aid. One tried to pry Sabum's fingers away from his neck while the other grabbed him around the waist.

Namzu was no warrior and knew well how lethal Sabum was with his hands, but he was no novice at hand-to-hand combat either and was capable of defending himself. With well-placed kicks and punches, he urgently flailed against Sabum's groin, chest, and face. To his dismay, the well-placed blows had no effect on the big man, and Sabum's legendary grasp hadn't faltered in the least.

Struggling for breath and feeling a crippling throb within his head, Namzu knew that he was close to losing consciousness and surely his life. But what frightened him the most was Sabum's black eyes, which stared unblinkingly into his own. Those were not the eyes of his friend. They were the eyes of something evil.

With his vision beginning to blur, Namzu fought to remove Sabum's hands from his neck, but they might as well have grown into his body like roots from a tree. All the while, the two Usgadi continued to punch and kick Sabum with no effect. He watched in horror while Ahikibani gouged Sabum's eyes until successfully blinding him, sending curtains of blood pouring down his face. Sabum didn't scream. He didn't let up on Namzu in the slightest. Nor did he attempt to stop them. How could he not feel the pain that was being inflicted upon his body? Didn't someone have a knife? Namzu could not believe what was happening and felt powerless to do anything.

From his bulging eyeballs, Namzu's distorted vision of Sabum's bloody, eyeless face constricted to a pinpoint with darkness closing in from every direction. He had little strength to continue the struggle, and if it hadn't been for Sabum holding him erect by his neck, he would have crumbled to the floor. There was no pain, no feeling at all, and if he could have spoken, he would have told Sabum that he forgave his Second.

He felt his body go limp, having lost all strength to resist, and the last sound he heard was the sickening crunch of his windpipe as it was crushed against the vertebrae in his neck. Then there was a vague sense of falling, and if his body ever reached the floor, he never knew it.

~~~

Ashmadu followed Gemeshega into a small sitting room next to the Sanga's bedchamber. She never spoke after instructing him to enter, so he remained standing after she left him. The young priestess had fresh bruises on her pretty face and delicate arms as if she had been beaten. He felt sorry for her and wondered if she had deeper wounds he couldn't see.

Before long, the Sanga entered the room from his bedchamber. Even though the evening was early, he was wearing light robes a man his age might typically wear to bed. He forced a smile but seemed irritated at being bothered.

"Silim sum, Ashmadu. Gemeshega tells me that you bring urgent news regarding the En."

"I do," Ashmadu replied with a bow.

"Then please sit and take a drink and tell me what is so important that you have come here in the night." The Sanga sat in a nearby chair and fixed Ashmadu with a blank stare. His eyes were blacker than Ashmadu remembered.

Not in any mood to sit and hoping to finish things one way or another, Ashmadu instead stood where he was. "The En will not recover from the state he is in currently." The scripted words poured out too quickly, and he tried to calm himself and slow down. "It's difficult to feed him, and with each week that passes, he wastes away further. Already he looks twenty years older, and his bones stretch his skin in an emaciated fashion. In a few weeks more, he will die, his body suffering from lack of nutrition. But you know this already."

The Sanga was nodding in a parody of sadness. Then he looked up suddenly at Ashmadu's last comment. "What do you mean?" he asked sharply.

Ashmadu could feel a slight tingling from the Orichalcum that hung from the leather thong under his robes. It warmed abruptly before cooling again. *It must be protecting me from something*, he thought gratefully, fearfully. "I recently received a gift from someone who I used to love like a sister and whose child I loved as if he were my own. Perhaps you, too, have spoken with her recently."

Ashmadu was mocking Irra now and only giving a hint of what he might know. Oddly, he enjoyed taunting this Demon that caused him so much pain and loss. If he could return even a fraction of the distress he caused him, it would be satisfying. His confidence to stand up to this monster was growing every second, especially now that he knew the charm Namzu had given him was working.

Irra jumped to his feet, shattering the wooden chair against the wall behind him. Unnatural light blazed with from within the dilated pupils of his eyes, and his face was contorted with rage. He pointed accusingly at Ashmadu with a finger crooked with age. "How could you have known them in that way? You are a mere house servant with no means of your own! Whatever you are presuming, you will burn for it. I will see to that personally."

Ashmadu was shocked at the Sanga's agility for a man of his advanced years. Then the door from the bedchamber opened with a bang, and the two priestesses who served him entered with purpose.

"Seize him!" the Sanga commanded, and they grabbed Ashmadu roughly by each arm.

Ashmadu felt the unnatural strength in the hold they had on him and wondered if he could break free of their grasp if he had to. Still, he courageously held Irra's stare before he made his move. "I know the truth now, Alu-Abad, and your name is your doom."

Irra's spine straightened, and he froze. Although there was no expression on his face, he exuded fear and hatred that Ashmadu could feel. Then, slowly, he relaxed and made no effort to hide who he was.

"This could be an excellent opportunity for you to become anything you want, Ashmadu. I can make you wealthy, give you beautiful women." He motioned to the two battered women holding him. "Power. Anything you want. Live in comfort and luxury the rest of your life anywhere, even your own palace. Imagine it! I can make it all happen for you. Rule by my side here in Eridu as my foremost adviser if you wish. We will reshape Eridu to our pleasure!"

"Can you restore the En?" Ashmadu countered aggressively.

He could see by the Sanga's expression that he was not expecting this response. The Demon surely would have predicted Ashmadu greedily snatching at the promises to elevate himself in wealth and influence. What more would a lowly house servant ever want? Ashmadu knew that even if he wanted those things, eventually the Demon would kill him just because he had the power to send the creature back where it belonged.

"You know I cannot. The old man was a fool!" the Demon screamed in Irra's voice. "The most powerful man in all of Kur-gal, and I was able to get to him so easily. He had no protection. Why would you want him back? He was nothing!"

Ashmadu glanced down at the floor to hide his tears and answered in a voice barely above a whisper, "He was everything to me." As his anger rose, he looked up at Irra just in time to see him move his hands in a strange pattern Ashmadu didn't understand. It didn't matter. Ashmadu had only one thing left to do before the women who held him ended his life. "Alu-Abad, I banish you." He heard the words in his head and felt his lips form them, but there was no sound. What was happening?

Irra smiled triumphantly. "Another old fool. You thought you could outwit a being of my intellect? I admit, you almost had me, but your ego got in the way. Now you will join my merry band of puppets."

The women holding Ashmadu suddenly jostled him as if he were on strings, and he realized he had little control over his own body. He expected the priestesses to show expressions of amusement or scorn, but as far as he could tell, they were devoid of any emotion whatsoever.

Irra spoke to his priestesses. "Tear off every stitch he's wearing until you find the charm or symbol that is preventing me from touching his mind," he ordered. "And if it's tattooed on his skin, cut it out."

The two priestesses ripped the clothing off his body with their bare hands like they might have stripped feathers from a wild bird. Ashmadu tried to struggle again, but they held him fast and caused him more pain the more he resisted. He could hear Irra laughing at him the whole time. The Demon was enjoying every moment of his torture while Ashmadu could only silently scream and curse the vile creature in vain.

"By now the First Usgadi is dead, killed by the one he trusted above all others. He's the one who sent you, I would guess. A clever move on his part. I didn't suspect you for a moment until you began taunting me. No servant would have the courage unless he knew he could get away with it." Irra smiled, and his face gave way to pure evil. "The En will be dead soon, you said? I agree, and I'm certain he will never recover. In fact, I made sure of it. There will be no one to oppose me."

Gemeshega found the Orichalcum Crystal pendant hanging around Ashmadu's neck. "Is this the charm you seek, Sanga?" With a sudden jerk that broke the sturdy leather cord on the back of Ashmadu's neck, the charm was in her hand.

Ashmadu screamed in pain but made no sound.

"It appears so, my little whore. Now throw it in the hearth." Irra smiled broadly at Ashmadu while she did as he commanded.

Ashmadu was terrified of what would happen next. He was vulnerable to the Demon's evil whims now and had no confidence that he could fight them off for long, if at all. Waiting impotent and unprotected, he was convinced about one thing, Alu-Abad was right, he was a fool.

Irra stepped closer, looming over him, dead eyes staring into his soul. "I must say, servant, that Arwi-a was a surprising adversary. I didn't expect her to be more than an annoyance. Nevertheless, twice now she almost had me cast back to Ki-hul, as you call it. I'm sure I haven't seen the end of her, but hopefully, she's run out of surrogates to carry out her deceptions. Now let's see what's going on inside that head of yours. I want to know everything you know about Namzu's plans for me."

Ashmadu felt the first hint of intrusion of another presence in his mind. Then it slowly began to probe his memories, and he was unable to resist regardless of his effort. Irra stood casually, still smiling, but there was no doubt they were both focused on what was happening inside Ashmadu's mind.

Ashmadu heard a voice inside his head. It was thick, hostile, and cruel—not like Irra's voice at all—but he knew who it belonged to.

"I can make you blind," Alu-Abad taunted.

To Ashmadu's terror, his sight dimmed to blackness.

"And I can make you deaf."

The world went silent.

"Now your full attention will be on the things I will do to you next." Alu-Abad laughed an icy, rumbling sound that made Ashmadu's skin crawl.

Without warning, there was agonizing pain. No, something beyond the agony that tortured every nerve in his body. Ashmadu's body went completely rigid, and his mouth jerked opened so wide in a silent scream that the flesh of his cheeks threatened to tear apart. The only movement he could manage was his rapid breathing and the fluttering of his sightless eyes. The priestesses' firm grip on his arms kept him from falling on to the floor, but he couldn't care less about whether he stood anyway. What little thought he could manage was the futile hope that his struggle would be over soon. Then it stopped as suddenly as it started, and he slumped like a flax doll between the women, gasping desperately for every breath. He was powerless to stop Alu-Abad from doing anything he wished inside his mind, and he prayed to Enki that the Demon would stop his breath next so that his shame and suffering would end.

"Just a taste . . ." the voice of Alu-Abad echoed in his skull.

Even as he prayed, he knew the Demon had no intention of letting him die so easily, if at all. Alu-Abad called him a puppet, and that was precisely what Ashmadu had become. The creature was going to make him suffer before destroying his mind, and he lamented that this was how it had ended for his master. Ashmadu wanted to weep at the sadness of it.

Driven by the overconfidence—no, arrogance—he indulged himself with the Demon, even after dire warnings from the Gidim of Arwi-a. Worse, he failed to avenge the En. He would suffer impressively because of it—and deservedly so. There was no absolution for his incompetence except by trial of suffering, which Alu-Abad would surely be happy to supply in abundance. Even then, his failure would not be reversed except by the intervention of the holy hand of Enki. But why should the god intercede? All Ashmadu had to do was say the words and banish the Utug when the Sanga first walked into the room, and it would have been over. No, he had to taunt and provoke the Demon, sounding the alarm that would warn his adversary and undo his scheme. Fool was a kind word for one such as him.

Ashmadu steeled himself for what was to come, and it wasn't long in coming.

He felt a stab of pain through his chest as if he had been impaled by a long needle. Alu-Abad laughed at his pain and intensified it. Ashmadu could do nothing but scream inside his own mind. No thought. No strength of will to resist, only the white-hot emotion of constant pain that seemed to go on for eternity.

Enki! he prayed. Let me die!

When it let up, he tried to focus on the memory of Arwi-a. She had come to him while he slept the night that Shatamurrim was murdered by his father. At first, he was terrified when he realized that he was not dreaming. She told him that the gatekeepers would not allow her passage into Kurnugia because of the manner of her death. She was cursed to forever roam the world of the living invisible, except to those who cared for her, and no others would ever be aware she was there. Ashmadu wept bitterly for her. In life she had a beautiful heart, she was a dear friend who loved him as a brother, and he loved her the same. They shared so much while she was the En's lover and even more once Shatamurrim was born. She was grateful for the love he showed her son and the care he provided so that she could be with the En. Because of her, he felt like family more than any servant should have a right to, and even the En came to see him the same way. Arwi-a did not deserve this fate, and there was nothing he could do to help her. He would have gladly died right then and there to give her life back; she deserved it so much more than he. She went on to explain that her death and that of her son Shatamurrim were caused by an Utug controlling her husband, the Sanga. It was an impossible possibility: the Utug were things of legend. What could one want with the Sanga?

Arwi-a claimed she had been given a gift by the goddess Inanna for her suffering while she cried bitterly at the first gate to Kurnugia. Inanna pleaded with her to stop her wailing because it was so sorrowful that it troubled those who were waiting their turn to pass. In return, the goddess proffered something Arwi-a would value, a tool that would help her exact revenge. Inanna's gift was the True Name of the Demon, which, if uttered by one among the living, would send it back to Ki-hul, the Underworld. Arwi-a said she was grateful for the gift and had returned to the realm of the living in the only form she could—as a Gidim.

Arwi-a tried to impart the gift to Shatamurrim, but the Demon killed him before he could understand the danger he was in. Even a Gidim could feel the pain of loss, especially that of a child, and her anguish was experienced by every living soul in Eridu. Ashmadu recalled it vividly.

His reflection was interrupted by pain again. This time it erupted in two places—his left leg and abdomen, and he could not have chosen which was the lesser. The pain was so excruciating that he lost control of his bowels and defecated on the floor. This sent the Demon into another fit of laughter, but Ashmadu didn't care. Inhibitions did not exist in such a desperate state. His mind clawed back to thoughts of Arwi-a when it finally relented.

The Gidim was in a rage when she first appeared to Ashmadu. Her son had just been killed by the foul Demon, and Ashmadu was her last hope to avenge their loss. He already made the decision to confront the Sanga, although he hadn't known until that night that Irra was the one possessed. Had she not told him, he would have gone to his death never knowing why. Instead, with this new information, he prepared to confront the Demon.

Again, fortune was with him, for the First Usgadi paid him a visit the next day and offered him the Orichalcum charm that would save his life.

And it would have, had he not been so foolish!

Only then did Ashmadu realize that the First Usgadi must have known somehow or suspected. Why hadn't he told him the reality of the danger he would face when he came to visit the Sanga? He felt anger at being deceived and used by him. Still, he had to admit that he could have told the First Usgadi about the visit from Arwi-a as well. Knowing that, the First Usgadi might have been more forthcoming, and they could have come up with a more precise plan. The Demon told him the First Usgadi was dead. If that was true, Ashmadu wondered by what hand he had died.

Realizing none of this at the time and armed with the charm and the Demon's True Name, he felt confident in his ability to exact vengeance for the harm that Alu-Abad inflicted upon so many of the people Ashmadu loved. Yet now he found himself undone by his own hubris. Idiotic!

Pain unlike anything he had ever felt coursed through his body, leaving him twitching and drooling in the iron grip of the uncaring priestesses still holding him erect. Ashmadu couldn't take any more. He willed himself to die. He prayed to die. He begged to die. But the Demon just continued to laugh inside his head, knowing his desire. Alu-Abad might be able to keep his mind from unconsciousness—but not from delirium.

Would he go insane now? He desperately hoped so. How could such torture leave a man with sanity?

Arwi-a told him one other thing that he hadn't divulged to anyone: Shatamurrim was the En's son, not Irra's. Somehow Ashmadu had always known that, or at least he hoped it was the case. The boy possessed particular features and displayed various mannerisms that reminded Ashmadu so much of the En, and he speculated about whether or not he was the only one who noticed. It turned out that Arwi-a had known all along. He couldn't help but wonder if the Sanga ever knew or suspected. Probably not. He wouldn't have been able to continue his relationship with the En in the same way. Unfortunately, the En would never know, since she never told him.

Ashmadu was falling. Was he sinking into the eternal depths of insanity now? Was this the end? He dared to hope before he felt the jarring impact of the floor and the pain from the back of his head thudding against the hard tiles without restraint. For a moment, he was gone, enjoying the sweet relief of numbing unconsciousness.

Then abruptly he was jolted back by pain radiating through the whole of his body. Except this was not pain caused by the Demon. This was the physical pain of the fall—or was it just a dream? He felt the heel of a sandaled foot back into him repeatedly as if someone were dancing next to where he lay. Still hearing and seeing nothing, he could smell sweat, blood, and his own excrement.

And now it seemed they were dancing over his body! In his irrational state of mind, he couldn't help but laugh hysterically at the scene he could only imagine—the two battered priestesses dancing and laughing with the bedeviled Irra in his nightclothes. Would Ashmadu be dancing with them soon?

Ashmadu suddenly became aware that something else was happening in the room, and he dared to hope. He could feel concussions likely caused by thunder or magic and the movement against his body as he was stepped on roughly—but not deliberately—over and over again. The heavy scent of smoke filled the air around him, and he feared he was near a fire. He wished he could see, hear, or at least move to protect himself.

Moments later, as if Enki himself heard his plea, the presence inside his mind was gone. Slowly he felt a tingling sensation throughout his body as he regained control of his stiff arms and legs. His vision began to clear, and his hearing gradually returned.

At first, all he could see were the blurred images of figures moving around the room chaotically, and he heard snippets of incomprehensible sounds. Men were shouting, a woman screamed in rage, there was thumping and bumping, furniture being toppled.

Ashmadu moved as best he could manage. Slowly and awkwardly he crawled toward the wall behind him. He closed his eyes tightly and tried to block out everything that was happening around him. *How ironic,* the thought came to him, and he practically laughed. The muffled sounds of the struggle for life became clear, and when he opened his eyes, his vision had returned entirely. What he saw, what his mind was nearly unable to grasp, was the nightmare that was unfolding in the chamber before him.

Chapter 24
Madness

𒐕𒈨𒌍𒃲𒌓𒌓

Namzu awoke to madness. He was lying on the floor, and there was Abgal Ferulianreg, the tall Anunnaki in yellow robes, alongside Bikku-lum, the First Ashipu, kneeling over him, moving their arms in unison. They were each surrounded by an aura of light, the Anunnaki's so much brighter that it made the First Ashipu's appear dim by comparison. They were combining their magic somehow, and he sensed that the Anunnaki was supplying vast amounts of power for the First Ashipu to weave his healing spells, which were exponentially stronger than any Ashipu would have been capable of producing. It was an astounding display.

He could see the magic they entwined.

Namzu vaguely felt the power moving through him, mostly concentrated around his neck. And there was pain—waves of it that caused him to scream like an animal. But somehow he was detached from it all. The chanting in the room came not only from the First Ashipu, and as he widened the scope of his view, Namzu could see two more Ashipu who he did not know and his two Usgadi, Taribatum and Ahikibani. They were all crowded in the small receiving chamber to his office, and there were wispy tendrils of light that connected to them where they stood. Laboring from the effort, each one had beads of sweat on his forehead, indicating the pure strain of concentration, and their limbs twitched from the tension.

Yaqarum, his Subur, crouched in a corner, eyes tight and lips moving, and produced a surprisingly strong tendril of light for one untrained. It was stronger than any of the others, maybe by two or three times as much, except for the Anunnaki's. All the ribbons of light flowed through the First Ashipu and into Namzu's body. Somehow the Abgal was linking their power and channeling it into the First Ashipu. It was astounding. He couldn't imagine how Ferulianreg was doing it, but he could see it happening before him.

In a jolt of consciousness, Namzu realized that he was floating above his body, watching everything that transpired. He placidly observed the tendrils of light and auras of magic that he should never have been able to see and had never known existed. It would have been exciting had he not realized with certainty that the people below him were in a desperate struggle to save his life.

He briefly became aware of another light source, above him and to the right, which was not connected to the magical illumination below. It had a calming effect that beckoned him to draw nearer, but he looked away quickly, somehow sensing that if his gaze lingered too long on that light, he would never be able to look away again. Instead, he concentrated on the activity beneath him, fully aware that the light above him was descending slowly closer and would consume him if he did not return to his body soon.

He tried to will himself back. That didn't work. He tried to move toward his body, but that didn't work either. So he watched and waited, hoping and praying to Enki that those who would save him did their work well and fast.

"Namzu . . ."

Was that the voice of his loving wife? She died so many years ago while pregnant with their first child. How could it be? No one could reach beyond Kurnugia.

"Namzu, my love, we are waiting for you . . ."

The voice came from the light above. It was closer now and drawing Namzu toward it. He wanted to go to it. So seductive was its calling, it felt like home or the dream of home, and it was so tempting.

He heard the cry of a newborn babe.

"Namzu, we have a son. Come be with him . . ."

A son! Namzu wanted to turn. He wanted to go to the light. Nothing else mattered. His gaze shifted upward toward the beckoning light. Then suddenly he was rushing back toward his own body.

His eyes shot open, and he let out a carnal scream full of rage and pain both emotional and physical. Why was he here? He wanted nothing more than to be with his wife and son. His unborn child was a son. How could he go back?

Then his vision slowly cleared, and the memories only seconds old began to fade and become less real. The Anunnaki and the First Ashipu were still leaning over him, their faces a study in concern. The room was dim. The auras and light tendrils were gone. It was all becoming fuzzy. The here and now was his reality. Wasn't there a light?

"Be calm, Namzu," the Anunnaki said in a deep, resonant voice.

Ferulianreg, was it? Yes, the Anunnaki Abgal and Bikku-lum, the First Ashipu. He remembered now.

His body felt like it had been on fire, each pore prickling as if exposed to intense heat, and then he began to itch everywhere. Most notably, his neck felt as if he had twisted it too far in one direction while sleeping, but far worse, and each breath stung mercilessly.

"You need to rest now, Namzu," the First Ashipu advised. "When you're ready, we'll take you to the infirmary."

He tried to speak, but it came out more like a croak, and it hurt as if he had swallowed metal blades. A man holding a cup appeared next to the Anunnaki. It was Taribatum, and the First Ashipu gingerly lifted Namzu's head enough so that he could sip the Kas. The pain was maddening, but his thirst overrode his discomfort. Even swallowing was torture.

Then he tried to speak again. "What happened?" The words came out weak, a raspy whisper, but the men understood.

Taribatum was the one to answer. "Yaqarum saved your life. He was quick to find these Ashipu." He gestured to the two men Namzu knew were there but couldn't see from his current position. "Then he brought the First Ashipu himself and the venerable Anunnaki Abgal, who, by Enki's exalted will, happened to be with him at the time. They performed a miracle this night and brought you back from the darkness."

Namzu was in no mood to discuss miracles. He was almost himself again, and his mind was churning. Last he remembered, he had been in a life-and-death struggle with a man with an ironlike grip around his neck. "Before that," Namzu managed to get out and then motioned for another sip of the Kas.

Taribatum turned and beckoned to someone behind him.

A moment later, he could see Ahikibani kneeling next to him. "Later, First Usgadi. You need to go to the infirmary before we talk more. There is still much work to be done to properly heal your injuries."

Namzu had never been a patient man, and he wanted answers, not platitudes. "Now," was all he said and took more of the Kas.

Ahikibani looked nervous, but the First Ashipu nodded, and he continued. "After Sabum dropped you . . ."

The Usgadi continued speaking, but Namzu heard none of it. Sabum? Not his friend Sabum! The memories flooded back, and he remembered the truth. Sabum must have been turned by the Utug and then sent to kill him. It was his fault. He should have been more careful. Sending Sabum to spy on the Sanga was foolish. The Utug would have found him easy prey, and Namzu should have known that. Using Sabum to kill him had almost succeeded, but why now? The Sanga had to have known he was onto him, and if that was the case . . . Ashmadu!

Namzu struggled to stand, but he merely flopped spasmodically.

The First Ashipu was alarmed. "Be still, Namzu! You may injure yourself further! Please! Calm yourself!"

The Anunnaki had not moved, and only in that moment did Namzu become aware that he was not alone in his thoughts. He never realized the Abgal was in his head the whole time, sharing his thoughts, listening.

Namzu calmed and spoke to the presence he knew was there. "Ashmadu is in danger. We must go to him now. You know what we're dealing with. Take my pain so I can function. I know you can."

The voice he heard inside his mind was soothing and calm and unmistakably the Abgal's. "There is a danger to you if I do. The healing we provided, as powerful as it was, is merely a bandage. You should have died. In the end, you wanted to. But we prevailed in bringing you back just in time. Do not jeopardize our hard work. Let us deal with this Utug and Irra ourselves."

Namzu felt desperation rising within him. "No! Ashmadu is my responsibility. I sent him to see the Sanga on a fool's errand. Listen to me, Abgal. I have reasoned it through! Something has changed. The Utug knows the will and memories of the Sanga intimately. How else could he have known about Sabum? And now that he has been in Sabum's head, he knows that I'm onto him. The Utug is *inside* the Sanga! We must go now, and I must be there to see it through. I don't care about the consequences. Take my pain so that I can do what I must!"

"Very well, Namzu. I will take your pain. But be warned: you will feel no pain at all, even if it is new, until I reverse the effect."

"So be it."

Namzu instantly felt as if he were a new man. There was no pain, no discomfort. His body felt numb, even his neck. He sat up slowly to the astonished looks of those around him. Then he stood, brushing off the efforts of his Usgadi and the First Ashipu to help him. He looked around and then back toward the darkest part of the room. There, in the shadows, he saw for the first time the body of his friend Sabum, who lay in a pool of his own blood. "How did he die?" Namzu quietly asked Ahikibani.

The Usgadi stared down at the floor, unable to meet his intense gaze. "After he released you, he stabbed himself in the chest until he was dead. I think if he wanted to, he could have killed us all."

Namzu crouched next to his Second, his friend, and touched his forehead gently. Sabum made the ultimate sacrifice and deserved a better end than this. The robes he wore, now red from the perfuse loss of blood, and the sightless sockets for eyes made him look like someone else. It was a sad representation of the man who was so important to the office and his life. The Usgadi after Sabum would never be the same.

Namzu addressed everyone in the room, his voice thick with emotion and eyes wet with unshed tears. "This was not of his own doing! Sabum is innocent and will be given every honor of burial. Do not forget. Yaqarum, put a blanket over him and see him safely to the Hall of Kurnugia. You, Ashipu, go alert the Aga-us to meet us at the Sanga's office and bring any Usgadi you find. The rest of you, come with me."

~~~

At first, Ashmadu was sure that he lost his sanity and that this was some bizarre scenario dreamed up from the darkest depths of his own mind. The door that led to the hallway and the exit to the street was blown to pieces. Small sections of wood still hung by its hinges. The hallway and front door beyond were scorched black as if torched, but there were no lingering flames. Smoke still hung thickly in the air. The furniture in the room was toppled and scorched, and a long, jagged mark on the wall splintered in a thousand directions along its length as if struck by lightning. And there was the pungent smell of burned flesh. It was an extraordinary scene that assaulted his senses, one that might have occurred in a story devised to strike fear and horror if read from a tablet.

Yet the worst display of savagery was left to the living and the dying. A man who looked like an Usgadi lay on the floor in a pool of his own blood. It was impossible to tell what finally killed him, he was so covered in crimson from grievous cuts and slashes. One of the priestesses who held Ashmadu earlier was likewise on the floor, unmoving. He wondered why he never learned her name. Her clothing was burned away, leaving extensive red and black burns all over her bare body. Ashmadu remembered how beautiful the young girl was, and now her distorted features, punctuated by exposed bone and muscle, contradicted his memory.

On the other side of the room, a battle still raged between another Usgadi and the priestess the Sanga called Gemeshega. The Usgadi's face had been smashed in, revealing a shattered cheekbone and a jaw that swung freely. Bloody foam escaped from where his mouth should have been positioned, but the spot was now indistinguishable from the rest of the mangled flesh under his eyes. Somehow the Usgadi had the strength to hold Gemeshega close to him by the front of her robes and pump waves of energy into her body that caused her to convulse and scream weakly with each surge. Her arms flailed, but they had no strength left in them, and her hands were covered in blood. In a grotesque twist of association, the sound they made together in death reminded him of two lovers in the last throes of exhausted passion.

The most intense contest was being waged at the center of the room in complete silence and devoid of any movement at all. The Sanga was frozen in place, with one hand pressed against the side of his head and the other extended toward Bikku-lum, the First Ashipu. Likewise, Bikku-lum was frozen in the act of trying to stab the Sanga with a long knife held high over his head.

The third man appeared oddest of them all, and not just because he was an Anunnaki. He stood a few feet directly in front of the Sanga in a state of complete calm, eyes closed as if he had fallen asleep standing up. His arms were folded in front of him against his yellow robes, and his stance was perfectly erect and still. The only sign of exertion was the sweat running down his face. Ashmadu recognized him as the Anunnaki Abgal who tried to help the En by viewing his memories to find the cause of his malady.

Ashmadu's attention was drawn back to the Usgadi and Gemeshega. She had crumpled to the floor, the front of her sheer white robes black and burned, as was the flesh of her exposed chest. The Usgadi stood over her a moment and briefly cast his singular undamaged eye in Ashmadu's direction before falling on top of her. That eye stared into eternity from the battered pulp of a face while his body convulsed with the final release of his life.

Just as Ashmadu returned his observation back to the three motionless men, the Abgal lost the strength in his legs and sank to his knees. The battle they waged with their minds was powerful indeed, and Ashmadu couldn't help but be impressed by the strength of the Anunnaki to stand up to the powerful Utug. Unfortunately, it looked like the Demon was gradually getting the better of the Abgal. Ashmadu knew he had to do something before the monster killed them all.

With tremendous effort, he tried to stand but faltered and fell again to the floor. He didn't have the strength and wanted to scream with fury for being so helpless. These men came to save him. Two of their number had already given their lives for him. *For him*—a house servant and former slave! Ashmadu gathered what strength and determination he had left and struggled to stand again. He just managed to steady himself on his knees with one hand on the wall.

"Enki, give me strength." He was appalled at the sound of his feeble voice. His voice! He had his voice! Ashmadu knew then what he would do, and hope sprang from his soul again. After taking a ragged breath, he spoke the words he knew would end the vicious struggle. "I banish you, Alu-Abad, back to the Underworld from whence you came!"

It was hardly a whisper. Ashmadu tried again and again—barely a sound emerged from his injured throat, damaged by his intense efforts to scream earlier. He glanced over at the Anunnaki, and a hot rage poured through him. The Abgal's sweat-drenched face showed the strain of his titanic struggle, and he breathed in rapid gasps. Ashmadu knew he was out of time.

Falling heavily on his knees, he pressed his face into a pool of blood—his or another's, he did not know—and sucked what moisture he could from it to coat his throat. Then suddenly, there was someone next to him, someone he knew but thought to be dead, and he smiled a grim, blood-soaked grin. There was still hope for salvation.

~~~

By the time Namzu entered the Sanga's office, everything was out of control. Despite his eagerness to lead, he was forced behind in the initial scramble. Not even his own Usgadi had allowed him to enter before they cleared the way. It was good they had not, for he would have died immediately. Although the Anunnaki had taken his pain, he was very weak and found breathing difficult under exertion. Worse, he was unable to tap into his considerable magical competence. In fact, he didn't have the strength to draw upon it at all.

Namzu was disappointed that none of Sabum's Usgadi that were supposed to be stationed nearby watching the Sanga were present. They must have been dismissed by Sabum after the Utug gained control of his mind. Having them here would have been helpful with their incursion.

The Anunnaki blasted through the outer doors of the Sanga's chambers and rushed in with the First Ashipu, followed by Taribatum and Ahikibani. It was as though time slowed to a crawl and he observed everything in slow motion. Then the violence and the struggle began, and time seemed to fast forward, leaving Namzu behind. He leaned heavily against the remainder of the broken doorframe and watched helplessly as both of his Usgadi friends died while making the vile priestesses pay dearly for their own lives. Meanwhile, a silent struggle ensued between the Anunnaki Abgal and Irra. Namzu noted with fascination the frozen charge of the First Ashipu, and then he saw Ashmadu.

The servant tried to speak and then collapsed in a pool of blood. Then, astonishingly, he began to drink from it. By the time Namzu arrived at his side, his face was a surrealistic mask of blood—and Enki knew what else.

The man smiled when he saw him. "Alu . . . Alu-Aba," he stammered with a voice dry and thick with the reeking, sticky liquid he consumed.

"Ashmadu, what are you trying to say?" Namzu whispered while he slowly pulled his dagger, intent upon thrusting it through the Sanga.

Ashmadu stopped him. "You . . . will . . . die," he said, shaking with fatigue as he pulled himself up on trembling arms.

Namzu lay next to Ashmadu in the blood and gore so he could hear the house servant clearly. "Then what can I do?"

"Speak ... its ... True ... Name." Ashmadu wore a look of desperation, of a man veritably damned if they did not prevail.

Namzu felt the same way. "What name shall I speak? Tell me! And the words to speak with it! You know them. Now speak them to me!"

Ashmadu appeared to have nothing left in him. His arms gave way, and his head fell back into the blood that had lubricated his voice enough to speak. His eyes were glazed from exhaustion.

"Speak to me!" Namzu demanded frantically. He pressed his ear close to Ashmadu's lips.

The En's servant whispered so quietly that Namzu nearly missed the words, but his hearing was sharp, and the name came through true. A thrill of excitement rushed through Namzu's body. He had the words that would put an end to this horror!

Namzu slowly rose to his knees, bloody and disheveled, with the blood-tarnished rank of his office prominent around his neck. The room was exactly as it was just moments before, as if it were frozen in time. The only movement came from Abgal Ferulianreg, whose entire body trembled from the mighty battle he waged with the Demon in his own mind. Namzu took a deep breath and spoke in a clear and commanding voice. "Alu-Abad! I banish you back to the Underworld from whence you came!"

If time had slowed before then, it seemed to stop the moment the words left his tongue. The flame inside the hearth froze, every chest rising with breath was suspended, and not even the drop of blood falling from Ashmadu's nose hit the floor. The room seemed to inhale, and then time rushed forward to reclaim its place as a black orb, blacker than the blackest night, formed behind the Sanga.

The orb froze Namzu's heart and filled him with paralyzing fear, leaving him fixed on his knees and gawking at the spectacle unfolding before him.

"Nooooo!" Alu-Abad screamed through Irra, whose physical form began to flail wildly as convulsions wracked his body. "Oi ipamis!"

The Abgal, released from his silent struggle, abruptly fell forward, panting on the floor, his large, oval eyes open and alert. He stared like all the others at the manifestation of pure evil that entered the room, and fear reflected from even his godly features.

The First Ashipu, also suddenly free of his paralysis, continued his attack as if he had never stopped and begun stabbing Irra repeatedly in the head, face, shoulders, and chest—wherever he could land a blow—until he noticed the black orb that was expanding before him. He froze for a moment before stumbling back, never taking his eyes off the pure form of evil taking shape.

Namzu, still frozen with fear, watched as Irra's body convulsed yet somehow continued to stand erect with more than a dozen bloody wounds that stained his robes and skin. The Sanga did not scream or wail at the pain he must have felt. There was no reaction at all, except from the Demon inside of him that snarled and growled like some beast trapped in a cage. And then his eyes rolled back in his head, and he slowly levitated above the floor. Smoky black tendrils extended from the dark orb behind him, encircling the body as it rose, causing the Demon to howl with renewed rage and fear, while Irra's arms flailed wildly and uncontrolled.

Namzu dared to pull his gaze away and glance around the room, relieved to see that the others were just as fixated on the terrible scene as he was. Fighting through the paralyzing fear caused by the orb, he scrambled over to the Anunnaki, who had just regained his feet and now stood just behind the First Ashipu. Whatever was to come, they would face it together, unashamed by their inferior strength, yet emboldened by the knowledge of the Demon's True Name.

Irra had nearly been consumed by the black void when the Demon inside him loosed a final, inhuman howl. *"Zir adrpan raasi ialpvrg donasdogamatatastos!"*

An invisible wave of force knocked them all to the floor, shoving furniture and bodies toward the back of the room. Then Irra's body collapsed in an unmoving heap on the floor. In the space where his body had hung in the air, the orb stayed suspended, its ultimate blackness absorbing the light from the room. The tendrils had receded back into it until only the edges of the void pushed outward, as if struggling to contain the essence of Alu-Abad that it had ripped from its human host.

Namzu's blood went cold, and he couldn't resist a shudder. Pure evil emanated from the blackness so dark that it was like looking at the reverse of the sun. The First Ashipu regained his feet and stood closest to the orb. He appeared enthralled by what he saw in its depths, and then he took a hesitant step toward it.

"Bikku-lum, come away from it!" the Abgal implored.

The First Ashipu seemed not to hear.

To Namzu's horror, Bikku-lum lifted his arm and brushed the edge of the inky blackness with his fingertips. Smoky black tendrils gently swirled around his fingers and hand and then slowly began to creep up his extended arm. Namzu's mind raced. He had banished the Demon. Was it somehow clinging to this world by its hold on the First Ashipu? He had to do something and rose to move forward. Beside him, the Anunnaki uttered several arcane words and then brought his hands together in a clap that boomed louder than thunder, sending through the room a shock wave that knocked everyone off their feet again. There was a flash of light, brighter than the sun, that blinded Namzu. It lasted only as long as a lightning strike, and when Namzu's vision returned, he could see that the black void was gone.

In its place was a black stain, shining like oily ash on the wall, and the First Ashipu lay on the floor next to what was left of the mangled remains of the Sanga.

Chapter 25
Recovery

The hour was late—only a few hours remained until dawn in Eridu—but the temple infirmary was a beehive of activity. Namzu, wearing a simple Si-tug, lay on a stone table thick with blankets. Earlier, the Abgal relaxed his body in order for it to heal more efficiently and also removed the pain inhibitor from his subconscious. Now he drank an unusual mixture of herbs to dull his pain. All things considered, he felt pretty good, mostly because he somehow survived.

Several notable patients had arrived with him at the infirmary in various states of distress, both physical and mental. On the table to his right lay Ashmadu, clean again, no longer covered in blood, stable and breathing comfortably. He slept with the aid of an herbal sedative administered by an Ashipu and probably would not wake for several hours. Namzu was relieved the En's servant survived the night. His conscience couldn't take another death of an innocent he sent into harm's way. Especially considering that the servant was integral to his plan to confront the Utug, selflessly putting himself in danger without entirely understanding what he was facing.

On the table to his left lay the Anunnaki Abgal Ferulianreg. He was complaining to another Anunnaki, the Nin-Digir Shonaturi, that he was fine and didn't need any healing. His resistance was purely rhetorical, however. She continued to examine him unhindered, one hand resting gingerly atop his.

Namzu was struck by the unusual display of affection between the two Anunnaki. It was not the first demonstration of intimacy that he witnessed between them, and he was surprised to realize that the two must be in love. *Even the Anunnaki . . .*

His mind drifted back to the events of the night and settled on thoughts of Sabum. He was angry at himself for not taking more caution and better preparing his Second for what he would face. And he was angry at the callous disregard for life that was the Utug's essence and pure nature. It was almost inconceivable. More than anything he would miss his friend, with his dour humor and pragmatic advice.

A little while later, the Nin-Digir turned her attention to him. "How do you feel, Hero of Eridu?"

"I feel alive, but I am no hero." When he spoke, he didn't recognize his own voice, the words sounded so severe and raspy. He gave her a solemn frown. "People died because of my failure to protect them."

The Nin-Digir returned his look with a sharp expression. "And people lived because you persevered."

"That may be true, but it does not make the losses any less intolerable."

Placing a hand on the side of his face with her forefinger pressing gently into his right temple, the Nin-Digir stayed silent. After a while, she released him and raised her eyebrow. "You are healing well. If you experience too much pain, let me know, and I will relieve it as much as possible."

"How is Ashmadu?" he asked.

"He will be well," she replied confidently. "Although it may take some time for him to fully recover."

"I am pleased that he will live, for his sake"—he was feeling encouraged—"and the sake of the En."

"Ah, yes," the Nin-Digir said. "The En will continue to be cared for by his faithful servant. And what about you? Eridu has lost its top leadership within the span of only a week. As the highest-ranking judge in the city, you'll be instrumental in sorting out the mess that the Demon left behind."

"Indeed. The Zi-ik-ru-um will no doubt want a full accounting of what has happened. It's all a little unbelievable—like a tragic tale from the Age of Legends."

The Nin-Digir's lips turned up in a near smile. "The Zi-ik-ru-um Council is already in a quandary. When the news reached them about the Sanga, they closed all ways into and out of the temple complex. I believe they're trying to contain information until they can control what will be reported to the rest of Eridu. In addition, they've already assumed control of the government so that they can at least demonstrate that Eridu is not devoid of authority. They are still trying to understand what happened themselves and will soon begin questioning everyone involved. The Abgal and I will volunteer as advisers to the council during this process, as I'm sure our advice will be invaluable."

It was said without arrogance or condescension, yet it was evident that she enjoyed "supervising" the elders, and Namzu couldn't help but wonder if all Anunnaki saw them as children. Indeed, he felt like a child next to them, and now that he had a relationship with two of their kind, he looked forward to learning more about their ways. Briefly, he allowed himself to hope they would invite him back to their wondrous tower before he felt foolish for considering the fantasy.

Namzu paused to assess his own injuries. "Can you tell me how badly broken my neck is? The Ashipu wouldn't give me a straight answer."

"I'm afraid he simply couldn't. The damage to your throat and neck is extensive." The Nin-Digir gently touched his neck. "Fortunately, the First Ashipu stabilized you fairly soon after the injury, and with our combined healing magic, we should have you good as a newborn babe within a few weeks."

"Did Ashmadu tell you anything about what happened to him before we arrived? He was unconscious by the time the Abgal closed the void, and I was unable to speak to him about it."

The Nin-Digir relayed everything to Namzu that Ashmadu told her about his encounter with the Sanga. He had not been awake long after arriving at the infirmary before the Azu's herbs put him back to sleep.

"He was very upset about his failure to banish the Utug when he first had the chance." The Nin-Digir shook her head sadly. "I will have to keep an eye on him. He feels responsible for the deaths of your Usgadi, and I am concerned he may suffer from severe depression because of it."

"There is enough blame to go around for many of us. It also explains why I found the charm in the hearth. What about the Demon?" Namzu asked. "How did Ashmadu know its True Name?"

The Nin-Digir furrowed her brow. "He was quite mysterious about that. All he would say was that it was a gift from someone special. He assured us that he would explain further when he was well enough."

Abgal Ferulianreg joined them and stood over the Nin-Digir's shoulder. She did not turn or act surprised by his sudden appearance; it was apparent that she knew he was there.

"How are you feeling?" he asked Namzu.

"Well enough to go home, although I can't move my neck very well." Namzu flinched a little as he shifted his neck into a more comfortable position so he could reach into a small leather pouch next to his right hip. "I retrieved this from the hearth in the Sanga's office. I'm sorry it's ruined. I gave it to Ashmadu to protect him when he went to visit the Sanga last night." He handed over the scorched Orichalcum Crystal, now lacking its copper setting and leather thong, which were burned away in the Sanga's hearth.

The Abgal took the small crystal and rubbed it with a cloth from the table. "The crystal will be fine. It would take much more heat than a hearth could produce to damage it." He held up the now-gleaming crystal for Namzu to see.

Namzu felt relieved. The potent charm had been placed in his care. To have returned it in a ruined state would have only compounded his shame over his failure to destroy the Demon before more people were killed or injured.

"How did you know it would be useful to me?" he asked the Abgal.

Ferulianreg smiled. "Remember, I have mental capabilities similar to magic. That is the specialty of my affiliation. I guessed something akin to my ability was being used by Irra or someone near him. If it were an Utug, as I expected, then that would explain how the Sanga was able to do the things that he did. When we spoke at the Tower of Tongues about your investigation into the murder of Arwi-a and the disabling of the En, it gave me near certainty that something significant changed with the Sanga himself. The Nin-Digir and I just weren't sure *what* changed and if the Utug possessed him or controlled him through another's body. In another few nights, I and others like me would have confronted the Sanga ourselves, which, without that knowledge, might have resulted in a very different outcome. Especially considering that we would not have had his True Name. Even armed with all that we knew tonight, we barely defeated him."

"What happened to the First Ashipu?" Namzu inquired. "I haven't seen him since we left the Sanga's office."

The Abgal lowered his voice to a whisper. "He was shaken very badly after his assault on the Sanga. He never would have believed he had it in him to do what he did. Even though he knew he was killing a Demon, it was the face of his friend, Irra, that he plunged his knife into. And he did his bloody work well. Bikku-lum will be haunted by that memory for the rest of his life. My greater fear is that he was touched by the darkness, and I do not know what lasting effect that may have on him. What I do know is that he is free of Demons. His mind is his own. For now, he rests in his chambers."

"Do you know what that black void was?"

"It was essentially a portal to the Infernal Planes, the Demon's home. The Sag-gig-ga refer to that place as Ki-hul. When you banished the Utug with his True Name, you called forth the portal that compelled him to return to his world. It would have receded to nothing after it took Alu-Abad had the First Ashipu not touched it."

Namzu was thoughtful, "What might have happened had you not closed it?"

The Abgal shook his head. "I'm not entirely sure, although I speculate that it might have taken the First Ashipu as well. I shudder to think of what horrors he would have experienced in that place."

"It would have been a terrible loss, especially after we had beaten the Demon," Namzu agreed. "What was it the Utug said in the end? Was it a curse?"

"If it was then he was cursing himself," replied the Abgal. "He said, 'I am cast down into the burning flames of hellfire!' at the very end."

Namzu didn't know how to respond. His neck and chest were hurting again, and he shifted to find a more comfortable resting position. The herbal drink the Azu provided helped take off the edge, but there was only so much he could drink of the unappealing concoction.

The Nin-Digir hovered over him again. "Be still a moment. I will relieve your pain. This will be different than what Abgal Ferulianreg did before and will wear off. Come back to the infirmary in a few days, and the Ashipu will relieve the pain again until you are fully healed."

"I'm grateful to you both," he replied sincerely.

The Nin-Digir chanted over him and massaged the back of his neck gingerly between her hands. Her touch was soft and warm on his skin, radiating heat into his neck and relieving the pain. Namzu relaxed immediately and almost fell asleep.

When she finished, he sat up and stretched. He felt pretty good again. He addressed the Abgal, "Something happened in my office when you and the First Ashipu were working to bring me back. I was not in my body. More like floating above it, and I could see everything that was happening in the room." He deliberately left out the part about his wife, calling to him from the light that appeared, and the baby. It was too personal, and he could only vaguely remember any details.

Abgal Ferulianreg was nodding without saying anything, and his eyes had a faraway look in them as if he was reliving the details of the experience. For all Namzu knew, the Abgal might have that ability as well.

"More than that," Namzu continued. "I could see trails, no, streams, of magic funneled into you from the First Ashipu, the Ashipu with him, and my Usgadi. Most notably was a very strong stream, much brighter than all the rest, that came from an unexpected source: Yaqarum."

The Abgal's large, almond-shaped eyes refocused on him then. "I cannot say why you were able to leave your body and observe what was happening from above, although I can tell you that for a few uncertain moments, the First Ashipu was sure he had lost you." The Abgal paused for a long moment, giving Namzu the impression that he was framing his next words carefully.

"There are those among our people who have a talent similar to what you described." He paused again before continuing in a very deliberate manner. "It is a rare ability that some from my particular order possess, and I am among them. I can only speculate that because I was the channel to manipulate the various streams that somehow you gained access to my ability while in the nether state."

"That's a very useful ability," Namzu responded. "It could be very beneficial to know the strength of your adversaries . . . and your friends."

The Abgal nodded. "The Subur you spoke of, Yaqarum, is very strong in his ability, although he is not yet aware of it. You should have him begin proper training as soon as possible. He is not Sag-gig-ga, is he? There is something different about him."

Namzu was surprised at the question. Even most Sag-gig-ga would not recognize Yaqarum as a foreigner. "He is a slave, a Suber, working for his freedom. We allow them to enter the service of the temple as initiates if they show a high enough aptitude. He is highly intelligent and diligent in his duties. I don't know how he came to us except that he was assigned to my office after the Lukur was done with him. He is from Ugarit, on the edge of the Great Sea, and likely taken as a slave by the Natufians before he was traded in Kur-gal."

"I advise keeping a close eye on that one," the Abgal said. "He will be worth watching."

"I agree," Namzu replied. "There is something about him."

"You look tired." The Nin-digir was sitting quietly, listening to their banter. "Now that you have the time to rest, you should take it."

"That is true," the Abgal agreed. "And since the Utug is gone, there should be no more symbols and no more brutal murders in Eridu. It is time for you to heal and recuperate. There will no doubt be many new challenges ahead."

"I'm glad it's over, although nothing will be the same again in Eridu for many of us."

"You have done your great city an invaluable service," the Nin-Digir Shonaturi said. "Had the Demon not been stopped, he would have changed Eridu and perhaps all of Kur-gal in ways you could never imagine."

Namzu silently agreed, although no matter how he calculated it, the cost had been high indeed.

Chapter 26
Loss

Ashmadu sat next to the En, monitoring his condition and holding out hope that somehow he would come back from the darkness. He watched with a numb detachment as Eridu began to slowly return to normal. Of course, he knew that he would never see the city, the temple, or the way of life he used to cherish in the same way unless the En had a miraculous recovery, and maybe not even then.

It had been many days since the night they had driven off the Utug Alu-Abad, and for anyone not at the center of that ordeal, it must have felt much like it did before the Creation of Man celebrations. Life would go on, for everyone else, anyway. Ashmadu felt like he was stuck with the unconscious En in a place he could never move on from. Or maybe he alone couldn't move on. It didn't matter. His will to be or do anything else but sit by the side of the En simply did not exist.

As promised, the Nin-Digir continued to visit every week and spend a few hours doing what she could, but there was never any progress. Sometimes the Abgal would join her, and they would sit and talk for a while about the latest news from the temple. It was the only reason that Ashmadu knew anything that was happening beyond the walls of the Gi-par. He was grateful for their visits, mostly for the sake of the En, even if he, himself, had little interest in what was going on in the world outside the Gi-par.

The Abgal told him that despite the Zi-ik-ru-um's best efforts to suppress the details of the events that devastated its leadership, hints of the truth had escaped into the general populace, creating unease across the city. Heroes emerged from the tragedies as well, although only a few in the temple were fully aware of the extent of their contribution and sacrifice.

Ashmadu also noted with some humor that the Sahar-nitah had by now succumbed to malfunction and failure, leaving Eridu and the surrounding countryside dotted with gigantic lumps of earth. Temple officials organized groups of workers to clean them up wherever they crumbled, but it would take many more weeks before they were removed entirely. Nearly everyone in the city hoped they would have lasted longer, except for the Zi-ik-ru-um, who expressed relief to the Anunnaki that they were finally finished with them.

Just a few days earlier, Ashmadu was summoned to meet with the Zi-ik-ru-um. Evidently, they already spent several days in closed-door meetings, speaking with everyone involved regarding the events surrounding the En, the Sanga, and the deaths of Arwi-a and Shatamurrim. He was reluctant to leave the En to answer the summons, but he was sure he had no choice in the matter and worried that if he tried to avoid them, they might not allow him to return to his master. To Ashmadu's relief, the Anunnaki Abgal and the Nin-Digir were in attendance to advise the council on the day he was sent for.

The Zi-ik-ru-um asked many questions and were particularly harsh regarding Ashmadu's failure to banish the Demon when he'd first had the chance. He withstood the admonishment stoically and accepted his responsibility in the events that led to the deaths of the two Usgadi. There were questions about how he knew the Demon's True Name, and he explained as best he could the visit from the Gidim Arwi-a. His explanations were met with skepticism by many on the council until the Abgal came to his defense confirming that he spoke the truth. Ashmadu left the council chambers unsure of whether or not he would be punished or forgiven for his negligence. Their deaths were an enormous weight on his shoulders, and any punishment they might consider would never compare to the sentence he already imposed on himself. The guilt of it all nearly drove him to ponder the unthinkable—ending his own life. It wasn't fear of death or even the method that dissuaded him from carrying it out. In the end, it was the living presence of the En. Ashmadu believed that if his master woke up and somehow recovered enough to speak to him, then he could make everything right again.

The results of the inquiry were never made public. However, on the day the First Usgadi returned home from the infirmary, it was announced that he would be the next En of Eridu. Ashmadu also heard that most Sag-gig-ga responded neutrally toward the news, having little exposure to the First Usgadi, but the general consensus was that the Zi-ik-ru-um made an appropriate choice. Ashmadu thought the First Usgadi was a good choice as well, but he was also saddened that this officially meant the end of En Ipqu-aya's rule, whether or not he eventually woke. He never did discover what the Zi-ik-ru-um decided about him, but he assumed they determined he was suffering enough without them adding any additional sanction for his foolishness. He was sure he had the Anunnaki to thank for that.

The previous morning, Ashmadu attended the burial of Shatamurrim, who was interred beside his mother in the cemetery outside the city. Nearly ten-thousand people, including the whole of the Ursagmuda, attended

Shatamurrim's final rites. The offerings were unprecedented and would undoubtedly continue for years in the belief that they would benefit Shata in Kurnugia. There was a hole in Ashmadu's heart at the loss of the young man he remembered so well as a child, which just compounded his misery even further.

Ashmadu spent a long time beside the grave after everyone departed. He spoke to Shatamurrim of his mother and promised to pray every day that she would somehow find her way to be with him and his father. The Sanga, too, was buried there with his wife and son—but with little fanfare and only a lone Abrig to administer his final rites. Irra had been loved by many in the temple and the Sag-gig-ga of Eridu, but he was the face of the Demon that nearly brought them all to destruction, and no one wanted to be reminded of that. Irra became the least appreciated victim of the Utug and in the end lost as much or more than anyone during his affliction.

Later that day, after Ashmadu returned to the En's home, a servant brought him news of the death of the First Ashipu. He was found dead that morning in his private chambers, having sunk a dagger through his right eye and into his brain with his own hands. Ashmadu heard that his sanity had been slipping day by day, beginning with night terrors and bouts of sleepwalking. His nocturnal screams and strange wanderings terrified everyone in his household, so much so that he was moved back to his private rooms near the infirmary, where the Ashipu could better care for him. Sadly, everything they tried had not helped. Even the Nin-Digir and the Abgal were at a loss for what was corrupting his mind, although they both agreed that his contact with the dark void somehow terribly altered him.

His death was a blow that affected Ashmadu profoundly. Because of his inaction, Ashmadu was responsible for three deaths now. He wondered how long he would be able to live with the remorse and shame that plagued his every waking moment and invaded his dreams. The stress was taking its toll on him, causing frequent pains in his chest and pounding headaches, no doubt exacerbated by little sleep. He reminded himself to ask one of the Ashipu attending the En to give him something to calm his nerves.

He sat numbly enduring the days and nights that blurred in the passage of one to the other. The Ashipu that attended the En on a daily basis constantly badgered him to eat and would leave only when he put something in his mouth. He had no appetite and was sure the Nin-Digir had put them up to it. The Anunnaki were a strangely wondrous people, and had circumstances turned out differently, he would have loved to come to know them better and learn about the Emerald Isle that they called home.

Late that night, Ashmadu was asleep on the floor next to his master, the former En. Before the banishment of the Utug, he would retire to his own room to sleep for a short while, but since then he preferred to stay with the

En throughout the night, sometimes reading tablets concerning the En's household expenses. Tonight was different. There was a disturbance that caused him to slowly rouse himself from a dreamless sleep, and he felt a pressure on his right hand closest to where the En lay on his mats. Without moving, he looked through heavy eyelids toward the source of the weight.

For a moment, he thought he was dreaming, for the left hand of the En covered his own. Then joy and hope surged through him, and he woke fully. The En was coming around! Without disturbing the En's hand, he placed his other hand over it and held it tightly.

Something was wrong.

The En's hand was rigid and cold. His beautiful elation turned to a cold streak of loss that shot through his body, leaving him feeling a jumble of emotions and desperate denial. Death found his master during the night, and somehow the En reached out to his servant for comfort. *Or maybe it was to comfort me,* Ashmadu thought—the En, in his last moments of life, comforting his servant.

It was too much for Ashmadu to bear.

His breathing became rapid as blood rushed to his head, and he felt a heavy pain in his chest, numbness in his extremities, and nausea. Darkness pervaded his vision, shrinking it to almost a pinpoint, and when he tried to stand, he only succeeded in lurching forward atop the En. There he lay without moving. He felt blood run from his nose and the edge of his mouth with the last breath of his life, and his eyes lost their focus as he descended into eternal darkness.

The next morning would find the master and servant in a cold embrace, together until the end.

~~~

Yaqarum, the Usgadi Subur, was waiting for his master to call him in. Namzu caught a glimpse of him sitting in the receiving room just outside his bedroom-turned-informal-office every time the door opened. It was important for him to speak to his initiate privately, but there never seemed to be an opportune moment. Namzu had been allowed to return home just that morning and was in nonstop meetings with various temple officials at his bedside ever since. Much business needed tending to, especially considering he was to be named the next En that very day. In twelve days, the city and much of Kur-gal would be bowing to him as the new representative of Enki. *If the god were going to speak to me, now would be a great time,* thought Namzu capriciously.

Namzu, more than anybody, never expected that the Zi-ik-ru-um would select him as the next leader of Eridu. He had not promoted himself for the position and never mentioned to anyone that he was remotely interested. He wasn't even sure that he wanted the job. He liked being the First Usgadi, and he would be leaving the Usgadi sect leaderless at a time when they needed rebuilding. Namzu had twelve days to appoint a new First, not to mention Usgadi for two city districts and another to head their intelligence gathering. They would be difficult positions to fill in such a short period of time. He would make sure he got that done before advancing to the office of the En, even if he had to work day and night to do so.

Then there was the task of selecting a Sanga. Ipqu-aya and Irra had held their respective positions for so long that there were probably precious few who had any idea of how to run the offices. Ashmadu and the scribes would be his best resource initially, and he was sure that the Ninkum Shubure would have some ideas. Although her views might not be restricted entirely to what he wanted to know. His thoughts turned to his old teacher, the First Lukur Ninedinni, momentarily, and he imagined that her head must be spinning at the news of his ascent. Even when he was the En, he was sure that she would find a way to make him feel like her student again. He would have to remember to ban her cane . . .

Yaqarum came in earlier in the day with a light lunch of duck broth, Nindagu, and Kas. But most of Namzu's lunch, by now cold, still sat nearby. There was little time to eat with the continuous stream of visitors throughout the day. The Kas had been welcome, though, and he was sure he would be drinking much more of it in the coming weeks.

The light began to dim as the day grew long, and with the irrevocable approach of evening, the last high priest finally departed. Exhaling a long sigh of relief, Namzu summoned his initiate. He wondered absently if the poor boy would have sat outside his room all night as he had done while Namzu was in the infirmary.

Yaqarum entered and stood respectfully at the front of Namzu's low bed of stacked mats.

Namzu looked up from a mountain of tablets piled all around him and greeted the young man. "Silim sum, Yaqarum. I wanted to thank you for making everything ready for my return home. It was also comforting to have you attend to my needs at the infirmary. Your performance far exceeded my expectations."

Yaqarum smiled proudly. "I would not think of doing anything less, First Usgadi. I'm glad that you're home again and recovering favorably."

"Have you been keeping up with the offerings at Sabum's resting place every day?"

"I have not missed a single day since the Abrig placed him in the ground a week ago, and I shall not until you tell me different."

Namzu smiled warmly at his initiate. "That is a great burden off my shoulders. He was a solitary man with few friends, and there are no others who would care for his comfort in Kurnugia. Once I am En, I will assign another initiate to take on the task, and I will try to go often as well. He was a good man, that Sabum, and I will miss him more than any other."

"I am happy to serve at your pleasure, First Usgadi."

"That's not all I wished to speak with you about." Namzu's delivery was casual, and even though he was tired, he felt a little mischievous as he deliberately set out to surprise the initiate. "Tomorrow you will go before the Zi-ik-ru-um Council and receive an award for your quick thinking and determination that saved the life of a First of Enki. Further, your actions enabled me to save Ashmadu from certain death at the hands of the Utug, which led to the creature's ultimate banishment. Sometimes a simple act can lead to extraordinary results one never expected."

"Thank you, First Usgadi," Yaqarum replied appreciatively. "Although I don't deserve an award for doing as I should. It will bring honor to my name."

"Yaqarum, this will be no token acknowledgment of your heroism. The council will be bestowing upon you the High Honor of Enki." Namzu smiled broadly as he waited for the anticipated reaction.

He got it. Yaqarum was stunned. Everyone knew that the High Honor of Enki was the highest distinction that could be bestowed upon a free Sag-gig-ga. Few in Namzu's lifetime received the honor. Shatamurrim and his surviving Ursagmuda had been among them, for their brilliant defeat of the Mus-Lu two years previous.

The Mus-Lu. Namzu was receiving disturbing reports about the dangerous snake people all day. It was becoming increasingly probable that Shatamurrim's successor would be tested sooner rather than later. Namzu would have a very full agenda when he assumed the role of En, and the Mus-Lu were not the least of his challenges.

Yaqarum slowly sank to his knees while tears flowed down his cheeks in rivers. He tried to speak, but his words were unintelligible.

Namzu was genuinely touched by the raw emotion. He sat forward in his bed, gently took Yaqarum's head between his hands, and kissed him on the forehead. "You not only saved a First of Enki, child, but you also saved my life. I will be forever grateful." He held the young man close to his chest.

Finally able to find words, Yaqarum stood and wiped the tears from his face. "I don't know what to say. There are no words to express the honor and pride I feel. If I died tonight, it would not matter, for there could be no higher achievement in my life. Thank you." He bowed deeply.

"No more talk of dying." Namzu waved as if shooing a fly. "We've had enough of that lately. And I foresee great things still ahead of you. Maybe you won't always be rewarded for them, but they'll be rewarding in and of themselves."

Yaqarum's face scrunched tighter as he asked, "How is it that the Zi-ik-ru-um agreed to bestow such an honor on a simple Subur?"

Namzu raised his eyebrows, he had forgotten that part. "They did not. You are now Nig-aga in service to the temple."

Yaqarum fell to his knees once more. "I am so grateful, First Usgadi. Since I was a child, I have felt like an unwanted outcast. You have given me purpose and responsibility. Thank you."

"There is one more thing. An honor to me if you would be willing." Namzu paused to take a sip of Lal-silim, a honey-and-herb drink the Ashipu provided. He was going hoarse again from so much talking after his injuries.

"Anything," Yaqarum said.

Namzu chuckled. "Don't be so eager to accept what you don't yet know. This is a sad honor that would mean a great deal to me since I won't be able to attend the ceremony tomorrow. You'll receive a gold medallion engraved with the likeness of Enki as a symbol to honor your bravery. The High Honor of Enki will also be awarded posthumously to my Usgadi, who died fighting the Demon's priestesses. You will present the medallions to their families at the ceremony."

For a moment, Namzu thought the initiate might weep again, but he recovered quickly. It had been an emotional evening for the young man.

"It would be my honor and privilege to present the medallions to the families of such brave men on your behalf."

"They said that they would be awarding me the honor along with the others," Namzu said with a shrug. "I told them that being selected as the next En was honor enough, but they insisted. So I would be pleased if you would accept the award on my behalf as well."

"You deserve the honor more than anyone, First Usgadi. Enki has truly smiled upon you." Yaqarum sounded so sincere. Before today, those words said together should have been the punch line of a joke.

Namzu took a deep breath to clear his mind of fatigue and then yawned. "I'm sorry, but I'm exhausted. There are a few more things we must discuss before I retire. I know you still have a few months remaining as an initiate. In twelve days I will become the En, and the first order I shall write will be to waive your remaining period before apprenticing to a sect."

For the second time that night, Yaqarum appeared shocked. "Why would you do that for me? I love serving your office, and you have already done more than I could have ever dreamed of in a lifetime."

"The Honor of Enki is from the Zi-ik-ru-um and your freedom bestowed by the temple. You earned them both. I commute your initiate probation as a personal gift from me to you. It's a small thing." He consumed more of the Lal-silim and cleared his throat again. "Have you put any thought into which sect you will serve?" Namzu watched an array of emotions cross Yaqarum's face and guessed that the initiate was reconsidering a tough decision he had made. The awkward pause prompted Namzu to interject, "Say what is in your heart, child—always. Never be ashamed of what it desires."

Yaqarum was hesitant in his response and couldn't even look Namzu in the eye when he finally spoke. "I don't want to disappoint you, especially tonight, after all you've done. But I had considered that maybe my proper place is among the Ashipu."

"Then that is where you shall be—an apprentice to the Ashipu in twelve days," Namzu commanded. "I would be disappointed in a choice from the heart only if you chose not to follow it. For myself, I would have been a gala priest if I had not followed my own heart rather than my mother's."

Namzu laughed at the thought, and after a moment, Yaqarum nervously joined him.

A fit of coughing put an end to Namzu's laughter, and Yaqarum hurried to refill his Lal-silim.

"Thank you, child," Namzu said and drained it.

Yaqarum refilled it once more and set the cup next to the bed.

"I must rest now if I am to be good for anything tomorrow." Namzu's eyelids already felt heavy, and he could barely keep them open.

A timid knock echoed in the hall outside the bedchamber. It came from the front door.

"Shall I send them away until morning, First Usgadi?"

Namzu wanted nothing more than to go to sleep but replied, "Find out who it is first, Yaqarum. I might as well get used to not sleeping."

Yaqarum bowed and then walked down the hallway to answer the door.

Namzu heard Yaqarum open the door and deliver a muffled greeting. A cool breeze rushed down the hallway and into Namzu's room, carrying with it the fresh scent of warm Nindagu baked with honey. He selfishly hoped that whoever it was would leave the bread after Yaqarum turned them away.

Yaqarum returned a moment later. "There's a young Lukur here to see you. She says her name is Amare."

For the first time in many days, Namzu smiled with genuine enthusiasm.

Epilogue

Nam-en Terrikan and his wife Secria sat in comfortable chairs on the elevated second-story balcony of their estate. The immediate property around the estate's foundation was finely manicured with interconnecting hedges, fruit trees, fountains, and a babbling brook forded by an intricately carved stone bridge. Beyond the gates, the terrain was dominated by lush grasslands and regular copses of deciduous trees that dotted the landscape here and there as far as the eye could see. One paved cart path led away from the estate for about a league to the main road that would take travelers toward the City of Atlantis another fifty leagues to the south.

From his vantage point on the balcony, Terrikan could see the passing of the hartebeest herds in the distance as they churned through the ground vegetation by the thousands. They never stopped their grazing during the day, a constant movement of bodies feeding on the land from west to east in the summer months and east to west in the winter. Once in a while a hungry Roc would track their progress and pluck one from the group. The herd in the immediate proximity would scatter briefly, causing ripples farther out, then return like a stone dropped in a pool of water. One of their number would be gone forever, but the collective never knew the difference. They accepted the natural order of life instinctually and did not mourn. Instead, they remained focused on their need to survive. Terrikan envied the hartebeest in many ways. Some because they were free and unburdened by responsibility and self-awareness, but mostly because they did not suffer loss or the anticipation of loss.

He always said that the best time to be home was in the spring. If he and Secria were lucky enough, they would see the next generation of hartebeest stumbling to keep up with their mothers and becoming part of the herd where they would live the rest of their lives. From the moment they were born, hartebeest had to walk and run. The herd never stopped except at night, and to be left behind meant no protection from their numerous predators.

This spring was different for Terrikan. He was not happy being home neither on this occasion nor at this time of year because he knew that every year hereafter would never be the same. But Terrikan knew that it didn't matter how he felt about it because he was not here for himself. He was here for his dying wife.

It was the time of year Secria delighted in most of all. In part because of the hartebeest, but more generally because nature was renewing itself, sometimes with tragic results and other times with joyful success. It was the way of life, and Secria reluctantly accepted it, although Terrikan knew she took it harder than she let on sometimes. They agreed long ago that they would never intentionally interfere with the circle of life on the grasslands and took comfort in the reality that even the predators were only killing the hartebeests and other prey for their own families' survival. Terrikan admitted to anyone wishing to debate that theirs was a simplistic view, but that's the way they liked it.

Laughing on the inside so as not to disturb his wife, he recalled how only a year or so after they were married they were sitting on this very balcony while the herd passed closer than usual to their estate. There was one young hartebeest that was having difficulty keeping up due to an injured hind leg. They watched as it was slowly passed by the rest of the herd then left behind altogether. Its mother, apparently realizing that her calf would not survive, abandoned it to its fate and continued on with the mass of animals moving east. The small hartebeest was exhausted and barely had the strength to stumble over to the high hedge that served as the estate's northern fence line to rest in the shade. It was late afternoon, and the predators were beginning to stir in the grasslands. There were half a dozen Rocs circling the herd high above, a pack of dire wolves could be heard howling in the distance, and the silent saber cats would never be seen until it was too late. There was no possibility, even as close to the estate as it was, that the lone hartebeest would survive the night without the protection of the herd. That's when the "controversy" began between him and his wife, although Terrikan was sure it was a full-fledged argument.

"I'm going to go down and bring that poor hartebeest in for the night. In the morning we can have our healer look it over," she announced.

Terrikan took her hand. "But dear one, we agreed to leave nature to its own devices and not hinder its legitimate course!"

"Legitimate?" She hated when he spoke to her like a diplomat. "There is nothing 'legitimate' about allowing a suffering animal to unfairly fall prey when it cannot defend itself." She had dug her feet into a rock on this one. Unfortunately, he was too stupid to realize it at the time.

Terrikan remembered foolishly pursuing the case and becoming angry with her. He was so young and witless concerning women at the time. "If we were not here to witness the injured animal what would nature do to defend it? Nothing! There is no concept of 'fair' where nature is concerned!"

It was the first time he was the target of the sharp look she gave him then. Forever afterward he would endeavor never to be on the receiving end of it again. "*You* are the only animal in this discussion!" she retorted angrily.

"I am going to let that poor hartebeest in and care for it until it's healthy enough to return to the herd!" She stormed off the balcony and down the stairs before he could respond.

That's when he made his third mistake. Yelling at his wife over the balcony, he took a stand. "I will not allow that beast on the property!"

Turning, she looked up at her husband from below, and in a voice dripping with acid, she responded just loud enough that he could hear, "Then I will stay outside with it!"

The whole affair would become one of Terrikan's few humiliations in life. He had to beg, plead, and promise everything under the stars before she agreed to come back onto the property . . . with him carrying the damn hartebeest. He was sure the infuriating thing would hobble away in fear of her, but somehow she had it following her around as if she raised it from birth. He learned a valuable lesson about women, marriage, and humility that day.

This time he couldn't contain his mirth and chuckled out loud. Secria looked at him and displayed her beautiful smile. "What's so funny, dear?"

"I was just thinking about that hartebeest you nursed back to health so many years ago," he replied, smiling back broadly.

To his astonishment, she thumped him on the head with her finger. "You were such an ass about that." She laughed.

Terrikan was man enough to admit when he was defeated. "So true, love. I think our marriage was better afterward for it, though."

Looking smug and victorious she agreed, "It was, for your sake."

Secria loved nature. It was Terrikan's entire motivation for accepting the assignment as Nam-en to Eridu in Kur-gal. She longed to explore the fabled country of rivers and witness firsthand the life that flowed with it. For years she and her retinue would range over the land discovering new species of animal life, their habits, and their way of life. She would talk endlessly about her encounters if he could stay awake long enough to listen. Still, he could see how it brought her joy as she cataloged everything in her journal, including multidimensional drawings in great detail that she would reproduce and colorize in larger formats later. It seemed like half the population of Atlantis received one of her paintings as a gift over the years.

Terrikan recalled how for many years Secria would host an annual ball at the estate for their friends and family. Each celebration had a different theme based on the region where they two lived or traveled to that year. At these events, she served various food dishes and beverages native to those lands, reproduced music on their instruments, and showed off her colorful paintings of the territory, its people, and mostly the animals. She made a point to identify animals by their native names. And at the end of the night, she would give all the paintings away, except for one or two that she prized above the others. Those filled their home now in every chamber, big and small.

It was all done in a festive and educational spirit, introducing exotic locales to those attending who may never have the opportunity to visit themselves. The balls grew so famous that her sister, the empress, and often the emperor with her, would attend every year along with a string of nobles, dignitaries, and ambassadors. Terrikan always considered himself a highly competent emissary of the empire, but he had to admit that it was his wife who really propelled his career through the years. He was proud of her for it and relieved that he didn't have to compete with her. She had a big heart and loved to share her experiences and inspire enthusiasm in others for her work. No one could ever confuse her passion for arrogance, and it was infectious.

Those days were behind them now, and Terrikan would miss them bitterly. He saw daily in her eyes that she knew her time was coming to an end in this world and that she cherished every moment she could spend with her family. He was surprised by how well she was dealing with her terminal struggle and was sure that even with the relief supplied by the healers, she was still in pain and continually exhausted from the contest.

Terrikan thought about their battle with Secria's disease. It was about a year ago when she first fell ill. Initially, the healers could not explain why she was feeling nauseous and bloated all the time, even when she had not eaten anything. Her symptoms progressed, and she soon felt the pressure and pain in her lower abdomen. That's when the severe swelling began. After several days of intense study, the healers finally determined that she was suffering from the creeping disease. There was no known cause of the disease, and it could originate almost anywhere in the body. In Secria's case, they believed it began in her lower abdomen or reproductive system and spread to the nearby organs. It was because of the way the disease slowly crept into other parts of the body, slowly damaging the infected areas, that it received its name.

Unfortunately, even the most talented of healers could not stop the spread of the malady through her body, and because it had infected so many vital organs before it was discovered, it could not be removed. Even with the Atlantean advancements in medicine and surgeries aided by magical means, the creeping disease was almost always fatal. At that point, the healers' only option was to manage her pain and discomfort and provide quality of life for the remaining few months she had to live.

Recently she and Terrikan returned from Eridu in Kur-gal. There she was examined by their best healers, the Ashipu. Sadly, they also had no answers, and Secria began the process of accepting her fate. Now that she was back on the Emerald Isle and her family was around her every day, she seemed to feel comforted and content. None of their children treated her as if she were about to die. They laughed around the dinner table and told stories about their lives in Atlantis, adventures where they traveled and amusing moments between them growing up. On the surface, it was like a long holiday full of music, laughter, and joy, but the truth that no one wanted to face was that, in reality, it was a death vigil. As the weeks passed, there was no way to hide the fact that she was losing weight and becoming. It wouldn't be long before she couldn't walk at all, finding herself confined to her bed or a chair.

Terrikan thought about his children as they gazed across the land. He and Secria had four grown children, two boys and two girls. Their oldest boy, Caagim, was a captain in the empress's guard. Given that Secria's younger sister was the empress, it might seem as if his appointment were a gift, but in fact, he earned the position, and in many ways it was harder because of the familial relationship. Neikrih, their youngest son, was the first mate on the trading vessel *Unedros*. It sailed mainly between ports like the City of Atlantis, Lyonesse, Eriu, and Andlang. He loved the sea since he was a child and one day hoped to own his own merchant ship.

Rwaxe was the eldest of their daughters, born between the two boys. She married a cousin of the emperor and now ran his estate east of the City of Atlantis. They had vast tracts of farmlands in the region where the majority of the mahiz and cereal crops were grown that fed much of the island's population. Rwaxe had recently given birth to a baby boy, their first grandchild. Their second daughter and the youngest child was Revane. She was a teacher of young children at a school in the City of Atlantis. She especially enjoyed teaching about world cultures, the places they lived, and the wildlife that lived around them. No doubt a love she inherited from her mother. Often she would bring one of Secria's paintings to class and read from one of her mother's journals.

All of them were here at the estate with her and would not leave until after her passing. Even the empress was here for the duration, although she could hardly be recognized as such in her simple gowns and familiar mannerisms around family. In their house, especially now, Secria never allowed the airs of aristocracy and rank to hold sway. All guests were equal and without a title. And for reasons he could never fathom, no one, not even the emperor himself, would defy her wishes. She had a particular charisma that made others want to please her, and although Terrikan thought he was immune to it, looking back, he was sure that he was not.

These days, their estate was bursting with family and guests coming and going. Everyone wanted to spend what time they could with his lovely Secria. Tears were strictly forbidden, and at least his wife never cast them except when they were alone together. Even those occasions were fewer now that the time was drawing closer. She was a strong person and often told him she didn't want to waste the few remaining days of her life crying and feeling sorry for herself. To his astonishment, many of their friends that came for a final visit in tears left with smiles and kisses as if they were on holiday and would reunite again soon. Secria had that way about her, often comforting those who came to comfort her. Terrikan was grateful that they allowed him the evenings alone with his wife on the balcony even though they all wanted to spend every second they could with her. He had a feeling that she had something to do with that.

"I am proud of all our children and thankful to have lived long enough to see them grow into adults," she said, breaking the silence. Terrikan was almost shocked: they were both thinking about their family.

"And our new grandson," he added.

Secria clasped her husband's hand. "Hopefully there will be many more to follow."

Terrikan stayed silent and returned his gaze to the grasslands. He didn't want to think about a future without his wife. They had been married for fifty-seven years and knew each other for a decade before that. He wasn't convinced that who he was now, with her, would be the same after she died.

"I worry about you, husband, and how you will deal with my passing," she said.

There she went again, reading his mind. Sometimes he wondered if she really could. They never spoke much about the time after she passed. He shuddered at the thought that they were going to have that conversation now.

"Perhaps you will return to Eridu?" she wondered. "You truly seem to enjoy the Sag-gig-ga, their traditions, and the lifestyle. And that friend of yours, En Ipqu-aya, I know you value the hours you and he would spend talking every day."

It was true. The two men, so different and from worlds so far apart, were remarkably similar in their ways and thinking, thought Terrikan. He also loved the culture and the people of Kur-gal as his wife expected.

"I feel sorry for the Sag-gig-ga," she continued. "Their gods do not care for them, and their afterlife sounds like a dismal version of the life they lead while living. It's comforting to know that Pontus cares about our people and that my next life will be among the stars."

The sun was setting on the grasslands and Secria's life. She smiled sadly and took her husband's hand into her own. "I will miss being an Anunnaki," she told him.

Without turning so that she could not see the tears glistening in his eyes, Terrikan replied, "You will be remembered as much or more as an Anunnaki as you will be remembered as Atlantean, my love, no matter whose sky your star graces."

Lament of the Gidim Arwi-a

𒆜𒈜𒉺𒀭 𒑱𒈨 𒈜𒅆𒊺 𒀀𒑱𒍑 𒉿𒶖𒑱𒁹𒁹

Love, the force of my life.

Now I am a shade of it, and it a shade of me.

Yet even if the gods proclaim that I am Gidim,

It will be a part of me.

For among the living or among the Gidim,

It will shelter in my heart and haunt a place in my soul.

So I must seek out those who share my affections.

Why will the gods not undo that of which I am?

Inanna blessed me to be so because she understood,

In the darkest depth of my sorrow a gift she gave me for it.

A gift that would bring vengeance for this curse upon me.

For my beloved husband, I will remember as long as I wander.

For my beloved son, I will mourn as long as I wander.

The gods who disapprove have only to allow my soul into Kurnugia.

Then my voice will be silent, for as much as my love will be with me there,

It does not matter the gods' approval or agreement with how I feel.

It's only how it is.

And in Kurnugia what is, is all that it will be, even in defiance of any god.

So it's with holy or unholy will that I wait, no matter the days or years or eternity.

I will wait until I am reunited with my love, my only love, the great and reverent.

O Holy of Holies, the representative of Enki himself on this land,

Ipqu-aya, love of my heart, light of my life and death, father of our lost son.

It's with him and them that I shall dwell for all of eternity,

If only the gods would will it.

Cast of Characters

Abgal Ferulianreg of the Yellow Hall: Anunnaki Wise-One and Atlantean Wizard of the Yellow Hall.

Alu-Abad: Ancient Demon of Sloth. One of only seven named Greater Demons of the Infernal Plans that once freely inhabited the earth until they were captured. Free once again, they sow chaos and evil where they can. The Sag-gig-ga know Alu-Abad as an Utug of Ki-hul.

Arwi-a: Wife of Irra the Sanga and mother of Shatamurrim.

Ashmadu: En Ipqu-aya's personal household servant and confidant.

En Ipqu-aya: The principal priest of Enki and ruler of Eridu in Kur-gal.

First Abrig Iblinum: Leader of the sect of purification priests.

First Ashipu Bikku-lum: Leader of the sect of healer priests.

First Lukur Ninedinni: Leader of the Knowledge and Teaching Sect of priestesses that are responsible for the temple library and schools. A former teacher of both Namzu and Sabum.

First Usgadi Namzu: Leader of the sect of judicial priests.

Gemeshega: Priestess initiate in service to the Sanga.

Ibi: Fisherman that lives in a village south of Eridu. He has two sons, Atab and Kuda.

Lukur Amare: Chaste priestess of knowledge and teaching that works in the temple library.

Nam-en Terrikan of House Elbian: Known to the Sag-gig-ga as the Lord of the Anunnaki, equivalent in rank to the En. He is also the Atlantean emissary to Eridu, husband of Secria. They have four children: Caagim, captain in the empress's guard; Neikrih, their youngest son and the first mate on the trading vessel *Unedros*; Rwaxe, the eldest of their daughters, born between the two boys, married to a cousin of the emperor, and recent new mother to the first grandbaby boy; and Revane, a schoolteacher in the City of Atlantis.

Nin-Digir Shonaturi of House Restander: Anunnaki High Priestess to Enki and Atlantean High Priestess to Pontus.

Ninkum Shubure: Treasurer of the temple.

Pirhum: Nig-aga in service to the Gi-par.

Sanga Irra: Second to the En, Responsible for the day-to-day running of the temple. Husband to Arwi-a and father of Shatamurrim.

Sar Shatamurrim: Sar of the Ursagmuda. Son of Irra, Sanga of Eridu, and Arwi-a.

Sar Unzi: Sar of the Aga-us within the district of Eridu where the Sanga's home is located.

Sipa: "Shepherd," Ashmadu's benevolent childhood teacher when he was a Suber in the temple.

Umbisag Ugazum: Head scribe to the En.

Usgadi Nawirum-ili: An Usgadi responsible for a village south of Eridu.

Usgadi Sabum: Second to First Usgadi Namzu, leader of the intelligence-gathering arm of the Usgadi, rumored assassin Finger of Enki, and a trusted friend of Namzu.

Usgadi Taribatum and Ahikibani: Usgadi of districts in Eridu and personal friends of First Usgadi Namzu.

Yaqarum: Usgadi Subur in service to the First Usgadi Namzu.

Glossary

Anunnaki: The Atlanteans. The Sag-gig-ga know them as the demigod offspring of the gods primarily devoted to Enki, Lord of the Primeval Sea.

A-zu: Physician, nonmagical, not usually a priest.

Abgal: Wise-One. The Anunnaki Abgal are Atlantean wizards, not necessarily of the same hall.

Abrig: Purification priest of the Hall of Kurnugia.

Abzu: The Primeval Sea in the Sag-gig-ga creation story.

Aga-us: Patrolman or city guardsman.

Anzu: Lion-headed eagle, Demon, although not necessarily evil.

Arad: Slave

Asag: An Udug, evil spirit.

Ashipu: Healing priest.

Bappir: Beer bread.

Dilmun in Edin: A place where the Anunnaki dwell.

Dubsar: Scribe.

Dumu-gir: Freeborn citizen, native.

E-Abzu: The building at the top of the Ziggurat where Enki is said to dwell.

Ebla: A watery type of beer.

Edimmu: An evil form of the Utukku (Demon).

Edubba: School.

Emegi: Language of Kur-gal.

En: High priest and ruler of a city-state.

Er-šem-ma: Compositions about the gods sung by the gala priests with the use of a tambourine.

Gada-bar-tug: Long linen coat.

Gada-dilmun-ù-lal: A dress of Dilmun linen.

Gala priest: Priest who is a ritual singer, lamentation.

Gi-par: Residence of the En.

Gidim: Spirit, possibly malevolent.

Gur-gur: Standard container for a volume of wine.

Guzza: Throne.

Isib: Burial priest.

Kas: Beer.

Kas-du: Sweet beer.

Ki-hul: Place of evil, something like hell or where the evil ones dwell.

Ki-sikil: An untouched virgin.

Kur-gal: "Great Mountain," a metaphor for temples and for the whole country as a place where earth and sky meet.

Kurnugia: The Underworld.

Kurun: Sweet red wine from the north.

Lal-silim: Honey-and-herb potion that soothes the throat.

Light globe: A perfectly smooth stone about the size of an apple that has been magically imbued with the power to produce light. The least costly last only a few months and must be carried in a pouch to obscure their light, while more expensive globes last years, produce various levels of light, and can be turned on and off with a verbal command.

Lil: The air that forms the dome above the earth, breath.

Lukur: A chaste priestess devoted to knowledge and teaching.

Lú-silim: Perfect man, completely healthy.

Mahiz: Corn, originated by the Atlanteans and shared with the Olmec.

Me's: Divine powers.

Mus-Lu: Reptilian people.

Nam-en: Lord of the Anunnaki, equivalent in rank to the En himself.

Nar: Minstrel.

Nig-aga: Temple servant, not a slave.

Ninda: Baked bread.

Nindagu bread: A type of bread.

Nin-Digir: Anunnaki high priestess.

Pithos: A traditional vessel for transporting wine, olive oil, and other liquids in Hella

Sag-gig-ga: The black-headed people, those native to Kur-gal.

Saggina: Military governors or generals, the highest-ranking military officers who report directly to the En. The Sar report to them.

Sahar-nitah: Earth elemental.

Sañdul: Simple hat or headdress.

Sanga: The second to the En and primarily responsible for the administration of the temple.

Sañtuš: Hat.

Sar: Commander of a force of men, usually three thousand six hundred.

Sa-ti-um: The Eastern Mountains.

Se-lum-lum: Barley sprouts.

Se nis-e-a: Harvested grain.

Silim sum: Greeting.

Sipa: Shepherd.

Si-tug: Long woven garment.

Suba: Stone priest.

Subur: Slave in service to the temple.

Túg-íb-dù: A woolen garment worn by women, close-fitting.

Túg-níñ-lám: A festive garment, dress.

Túg-šà-ga-dù: Cloth belt or belted woolen garment.

Túg-tar: Short robe.

Umbisag: Head scribe.

Um-mi-a: Schoolmaster, teacher

Ungur: Menial worker, not a slave.

Ursagmuda: "Warrior Dogs," trained for covert warfare—concealment in the environs, eluding the enemy, ambush, and night tactics. Led by Shatamurrim.

Ur-tud: Domestic servant.

Usgadi: Priests responsible for investigations, oversight, and enforcement of the law; priest judges.

Utug: Demonic beings.

Zid-bar-si: A type of emmer wheat flour.

Zi-ik-ru-um: Council of Elders.

About the Author

Born in Homestead, Florida, Ravek Hunter grew up in the United States and Belgium. He earned a bachelor's degree in marketing from Florida International University and went on to become a sporting goods executive. He currently serves as a consultant in the same industry and occasionally assists his wife of fifteen years at her floral design company. The proud father of two boys, Ravek counts reading, exercising, and family travel among his leisure hobbies.

Over the past thirty-five years, Ravek's passion has been researching ancient civilizations with a focus on the origin stories behind their mythology. His writing style attempts to immerse the reader into the story by bringing to life historically accurate and rich details of the culture and time period that frame the narrative.

Inspired by classic fantasy authors like Robert Jordan, Terry Goodkind, and R. A. Salvatore, Ravek writes to entertain and provoke his readers, who, he hopes, share his fondness for mythology.

<u>Connect with Ravek Hunter</u>

Thank you for choosing this work of blood, sweat and tears by *Ravek Hunter*! If you enjoyed reading this novel, please consider posting a review, telling me what you think on one of the social media platforms listed below or reach out via my direct email:

Friend me on Facebook:

https://www.facebook.com/Ravek-Hunter-Literary-LLC-238417183579740/

Follow me on Twitter:

https://twitter.com/RavekHunter

Subscribe to my blog:

https://www.goodreads.com/author/show/17885196.Ravek_Hunter

Visit my website:

https://www.WorldsofAtlantis.com

Email: Ravekhunter@gmail.com

.

www.ingramcontent.com/pod-product-compliance
Lightning Source LLC
Chambersburg PA
CBHW031948010726
47493CB00007B/2125